2 —

CROSSING
OVER

D1714597

A Novel

CROSSING OVER

AN ELLIOTT MURPHY ADVENTURE

By
Anthony Eddolls

DEDICATION

To my amazing wife, Chrissy, and my incredible kids,
Rob, Jackie, Hannah, Morgan, Nicole, Lesley, and Alexis.
Each of you inspires me.

Charleston, SC
www.PalmettoPublishing.com

Crossing Over
Copyright © 2023 by Anthony Eddolls

This is a work of fiction. All of the characters, names, incidents,
organizations, and dialogue in this novel are either the products of
the author's imagination or are used fictitiously.

Paperback ISBN: 979-8-8229-1071-3
eBook ISBN: 979-8-8229-1072-0

Printed in the United States of America

CHAPTER 1

The pulsing waves of the Caribbean lapped upon the quiet stretch of beach where its only occupant lay daydreaming, his exposed girth slowly frying despite a light coating of SPF 15. The vacationer had come upon this quiet stretch of solitude by accident, when earlier he had strolled along a path that led from the Sand Dollar Resort and Casino to destinations unknown. He heard the water breaching the shore, shoved his way through a thicket of tropical overgrowth to find his little slice of heaven, and reveled in the discovery with the glee of a child. He decided that *he* was in fact the first human being to have ever set foot on this silky, sun-baked ribbon of sand. He concluded this despite the fact that less than a third-of-a-mile away, albeit hidden from view, another beach was populated with most of the 1,500 guests of the resort. At thirty-six years of age, he could still discover virgin territory in his mind. In fact, that was always where most of his great accomplishments occurred.

Jack Horton had arrived on the island of St. Martens three days earlier with his wife and three young boys for their annual winter vacation. Now, for a few hours anyway, he had been given a reprieve from the tedium of his family. The problem he had with family vacations was having to bring his family along. But, the feeling was probably mutual as he often sensed they weren't thrilled with his company either, especially his wife and her incessant misery. The flight was too long, the resort too crowded, the boys were rotten and the room was too small. Poor, nagging Alice. Maybe he would go back to the hotel and find her to be nothing more than a figment of his imagination for the last thirteen years.

And then there were his boys. Of course they had their cute little moments, as do all six, eight, and ten year old; but the only one he could tolerate consistently was the youngest, Harry. The strange boy didn't have much to say, usually did what he was asked, and seemed to avoid interaction with the rest of the world. Jack could understand this mentality, although every once in a while he worried that the kid might suffer from some level of Post Traumatic Stress Syndrome living under the same roof with deranged brothers and a depressed, angry and borderline psychotic mother. Tim, the eight-year-old, had been diagnosed with Attention Deficit Hyperactive Disorder. He couldn't remain still for more than fifteen seconds, couldn't finish a sentence without changing the subject, and couldn't find something he had in his hands three minutes earlier if his life depended on it. Finally, the oldest son, Scott, was just an angry kid. He weighed in at 105 pounds already, and his expressions and words were typically tinged with anger. Fortunately for Jack, Scott seemed to find comfort in taking his angst out upon his mother. Served her right, Jack often thought. But that was his brood, the happy Horton family of Syosset, Long Island.

Jack was a commercial insurance executive in Manhattan, a career he entered into by accident when a company called Avistar recruited him out of college. He hadn't done his research and just assumed they were an aviation concern and he'd be selling aircrafts. He showed up for the interview and discovered otherwise; Avistar was an insurance company. But, he was offered a job and he took it because he feared nothing else would come along. That was thousands of policies, hundreds of clients, and a multitude of years ago. He had survived burn out at one point, but eventually evolved to suffer a chronic state of boredom.

But now he was enjoying a rare moment of happiness. He was sprawled atop a beach towel, with no one to bother him, and he could feel the sun infusing warmth into his soul, or what might be left of it. Occasionally he raised an insulated flask of cool white rum to his lips and felt the burning relief of the fluid as it ran down his throat and into his gut. His straw hat rested atop his balding head and his aviator shades shielded his eyes. He didn't seem to mind that the rest of his body, save that which was covered with his multi-colored swim trunks, was being glazed by the sun.

Jack was immersed in fantastical daydreams filled with visions of young girls, like those running around half-naked, back at the resort. He also saw himself possessing immense wealth pulling up to the island aboard his 100-foot private yacht, accompanied by more young girls, half-naked of course.

Between the rum and the hypnotic pulse of the waves, the sun, and the daydreams, he began to slowly drift in and out of a light snooze. His perpetually stressed body was finally relaxing. He began to dream, unfortunately not of young girls, but of getting lost in a museum and was just at the point where he was being struck by a large bone-wielding homeless person, when suddenly Jack's peaceful solitude was shattered. He immediately realized he had in fact been struck in the head. Not by an artifact but by an oversized, hot-pink Frisbee. If this weren't enough, he realized he was also hearing the shrieking laughter of his lunatic middle son, Tim, who was being charged by the angry older brother, all 105 pounds, ready to pounce.

Jack Horton was back in hell.

• • •

Fifteen hundred miles north, the mid-day temperature in New York City had risen to all of eighteen degrees. A front from Canada had meandered through the northeast the night before and dumped over ten inches of snow, dropped temperatures twenty-five degrees from the March average, and left the city in that momentary chaos that weather sometimes endows. Schools were closed and many work-ers couldn't make it to their jobs because most streets were impassable at sunrise. But when the citizenry absorbed the dilemma and declared a "snow day," people felt as though they had been handed a gift.

The skies had cleared by mid-morning and by noon Manhattan looked like a fairy tale. The snow was still fresh and white and most of the streets had been plowed and sanded where necessary. The absence of the usual volume of traffic had not yet turned the streets into the slush and mud-filled strips they would soon become. The people, who had braved the frigid arctic air early that morning, seemed to step a little lighter than usual. Perhaps it was the absence of the bustle combined with the rare natural beauty of a concrete city braced by steel, and graced by the soft cover of snow.

But to Phil Cassavetti, this natural splendor was only a pain in the ass.

He alighted from the steps of his hi-rise condo entrance to the sidewalk only to slip on the icy surface, barely maintaining his balance. Cassavetti recovered with nothing more than a quick adrenalin rush and a smudge on his $400 loafers.

"Whoa, Phil, watch out there. It's slippery," his waiting driver, Jules, offered. "Fuckin' weather. You're sure all the flights are runnin'?"

"Yeah. Called them myself," Jules responded with pride, as though the act was quite an accomplishment.

"The 2:30 to Miami on Delta?" Cassavetti appreciated the long-time employee's effort but didn't trust his competence for a minute.

"Yeah boss, I even tried to confirm your reservation."

"And ..."

"Well they said that I had to be you." Jules looked down at the sidewalk as he opened the rear door to the Town Car for Cassavetti.

"Don't you worry about it, Jules. Just get us to La Guardia without smackin' into a fuckin' wall." Cassavetti slid into the back seat of the Lincoln and was greeted by warmth and the smell of rich leather. He smiled and shook his head watching the fifty-year-old man outside scrambling around the car, his hand atop the hood to avoid falling on his ass. Poor guy couldn't think his way home half the time; but he was loyal and dependable, at least as far as a driver went. Airline reservations, however, were a little out of his league.

Cassavetti was leaving town. He needed to establish a presence somewhere beyond the confines of Manhattan for the next few days to ensure an alibi. Within the next eight hours, a particular man would die. It was necessary; the code that exists amongst his underworld clan had been violated, and the guilty man would receive his due. A thief within their ranks who was stealing from the family had no right to live; the matter was pure and simple. And it was Cassavetti's job to ensure his demise. Cassavetti was responsible for his family's finances and therefore, when this act of treachery had been quietly discovered, it was Cassavetti's additional responsibility to invoke justice.

But it wasn't all that simple to Cassavetti anymore, and if for no other reason, he was getting too old for this stuff. He wished the violent side of his chosen life could have died with Gotti, but inescapably, from time to time, it still reared its frightening head. As they made their way to La Guardia he was conscious of the gnawing in his stomach and anxiousness seemed to pulse through his body. While he wouldn't be doing the wet work himself, he might as well be pulling the trigger, bagging the body, and sinking it into the bottom of the East River. This act was on his watch as the underboss responsible for the prosperity of his "family" and ultimately, it was Cassavetti who gave the command. Even if the accused had been a twenty-year friend with a family of his own.

Cassavetti hoped that the further away from New York he got, the faster the guilt would subside. He hoped the sickening feeling of remorse would wash away with the tides of the Caribbean and a few stiff vodkas. At least this is what he hoped for as he and his less than brilliant driver made their way, faster than expected on this wintry morning, to the airport and the friendly skies beyond. He was bound for the island paradise of St. Martens where a complimentary suite awaited him at the Sand Dollar Resort and Casino. Cassavetti's penchant for gambling was no secret to most casino operators in the western hemisphere. Whether it was the Caribbean or Vegas, he was always welcomed with smiling faces and open arms.

Jack Horton trudged along the sun-drenched beach with his three dysfunctional boys in tow. In the quarter mile between his momentary refuge and the Sand Dollar Resort, there had been an argument. Then one child cut his toe on an object in the sand and put on an act that a stranger, unfamiliar with the boy's propensity for drama, would have considered calling in an emergency airlift. And as always, in that quarter mile, six-year-old Harry, the quiet one, didn't even open his mouth. It was just another day on the beach for Harry.

Arriving back at their two adjoining rooms, they were greeted by Alice Horton who was wrapped in a towel, in fact a large beach towel, and it was quickly apparent that she was agitated over something. "Where have you boys been?" she barked, seemingly including Jack in the category of "boys."

"Are you hungry?" Jack responded, completely ignoring her question.

"I don't know, ask the boys?" she replied, not even looking at any of them as she walked into the bathroom and closed the door behind her.

The boys now stood staring up at their father as if the answer was obvious. "Well, why don't you go in your room and change and we'll get something to eat," he said to them. As he quietly gave the instruction he opened the door that separated the two adjoining rooms, stood aside and the three boys quietly paraded into their room. He closed the door, leaving the three to their own devices and stared out the large window at the incredible view of the Caribbean. But he wasn't really seeing the scene, for he only thought of what it would take to extract himself from the moment.

In the bathroom, Alice was staring, too. She surveyed her naked self in the mirror, all 150 pounds, the same hairstyle she had worn for five years running, the stretch marks on her lower abdomen and her ample sagging breasts. For a moment she pretended to assume that a week's vacation would make some sort of difference. But she knew better. It was always the same.

Alice had grown up as an only child in Manhattan on the Upper East Side with her upper middle-class parents. Her academic performance was never up to par with her real intellect, and because of that she never aspired to do very much with her education. She knew her destiny would be to meet some average guy, settle down with an average family, and lead a rather mundane life. The two had met in their last year at Queens College, where Jack was a business major and Alice was finishing up a teaching degree. Jack was certainly that average guy and their life had been rather mundane until the kids came along. Their first few years had a little spark to them. The newness was rather fun, their sex life seemed adequate, they laughed with each other, and they rarely ever fought.

But then the first boy came and then the second and then the third. That's when everything seemed to spin out of control. They weren't the least bit prepared for what lay ahead. Sleep deprivation, little babies that were like aliens, and unexpectedly hectic work schedules totally disrupted their lives. The fun quickly vanished. So, the last ten years were spent just trying to hang on. Pleasure was found in a stolen moment of solitude driving to the grocery store alone, or in an hour with a decent book in the middle of the night, unscathed by a sick child or a husband seeking sexual release. She hated herself for accepting it all as fate. But, as she looked at her frumpy thirty-four-year old body, what could she do.

And so, another annual Horton vacation was off to a running start. Harry would have a good time.

CHAPTER 2

The Delta Airlines Boeing 767 drifted onto the runway as softly as possible for a 180,000-pound hulk of steel at 150 mph. The buoyant load of vacationers applauded the captain's finesse and Phil Cassavetti rolled his eyes and stared out at the familiar site of the St. Martens landscape surrounding the tiny airport. It took him a moment or two to get his bearings as he had been able to grab a nap, lulled by the drone of the engines, and a couple of stiff drinks shortly after takeoff. But now the plane erupted in activity as the pilot pulled up to the jetway and everyone began to lunge for carry-on bags. They did so as though their vacations were depending on the speed in which they readied themselves to deplane. Ultimately, there was no point in hurrying, as they would only be forced to stand and wait for the line to move at its typical agonizingly slow pace. Cassavetti, accordingly, sat in his first-class seat and waited.

Once he had disembarked, collected his bags, and cleared customs, he immediately caught the smile of a waiting driver, one of the veterans from the hotel who was waiting with a ridiculously long stretch limo. Cassavetti was a regular on this tropical paradise, having discovered it well before the resort was built, long before the cruise ships invaded but no so long ago that he had become bored with it. There was always something going on, behind the veneer of the gorgeous beach and the seemingly hospitable native ranks. But perhaps a greater attraction to the forty-five-year-old bachelor and mob boss was the anonymity. Many of the management staff at the resort knew him, some even knew who he was back in New York, but regardless, they simply treated him like the next high-roller at the casino, or a partygoer at the disco, or just another beachcomber strolling on a secluded beach. This kind of unfettered living was something he savored every day of his stay.

Phil Cassavetti was born and raised in Brooklyn and it seemed, despite an attempt in college to study business with the hopes of becoming an accountant, that he had been a crook since adolescence. Maybe that evolution began even earlier, as a child, when he scammed his ten-year-old friends in baseball card trades. His father had worked at the shipyards all of his life and worked like a slave to keep his family in food and clothing. There was nothing easy about his father's life and nothing appealing either. Not the long hours and lack of reward for a life of labor, nor the monotony of a family. Nothing about it appealed to the young Cassavetti. So as a young man, the allure of the mob was too much to resist and twenty years later, his father dead and gone, he hadn't looked back.

He wasn't born into it, he hadn't whacked someone to earn his button, nor had he groveled to earn entrance; he had brains and he was connected by default. His best friend through high school was Ricky Tutoni, son of the infamous

Al Tutoni. Tutoni was an underboss in New York's Gallo family through the 80's, but in 1989 he was sentenced to the death penalty for ordering the hit on a Chinese drug dealer, his wife, and their ten-year-old son. Back in the 80's these scenarios still happened and Tutoni would eventually pay the ultimate price. For now he resided on death row at Attica awaiting the outcome of his fourth and final appeal to the New York State Supreme Court. Soon, it would be over for the sixty-eight-year-old legend; it was inevitable.

Growing up, the boys would do odd jobs for Ricky's dad. They ran bags of cash from numbers joints, or as teenagers, they took the occasional collection job for one of Tutoni's loan sharks. It was a rush back then and it paid a whole lot better than working on the docks or in a fast food joint. It was hard sometimes to explain his financial windfalls to his parents, but he kept his nose clean otherwise and for a good-looking tough guy in Brooklyn, he always did remarkably well in school.

His aptitude for numbers caught the attention of Tutoni and several of his associates early on. By the time he graduated from high school he was already taking care of the books for a couple of Tutoni's operations. The numbers flew right past his friend Ricky, who preferred theft and assault to finance any day. Ricky's entrance into the mob was a given by birth. But he was a loose cannon and his periodic indiscretions got the best of him fifteen years ago when he seduced the wife of a rival family's lieutenant. Three weeks later he was found crushed to death in a 1978 Buick Skylark at a wrecking yard in Yonkers.

After moving through the ranks and becoming an underboss himself by making money for the mob instead of exerting muscle, Cassavetti was now forced to end the life of another man. And it was one of his own, a fellow gangster who had been caught with his hand in the till to the tune of one and a half million. For something of that magnitude, the old code still applied. To steal from one's own family was unforgivable and Cassavetti had no choice but to give the order. The first time, Cassavetti had done the deed himself in self-defense. A sale of guns had gone badly and Cassavetti took out the other guy while catching a bullet in the shoulder in the mayhem that erupted. It was a night he would never forget.

This time, two Irish brothers were the hired guns performing the hit. He didn't even know their names. He had given the go-ahead to one of his lieutenants several weeks ago and tonight the life of Tony Dimaglio would come to a screeching halt. The greedy bastard would get what he deserved and Cassavetti was working on making peace with the decision. This was the code. He made the choice to live this life of gray silhouettes and obscurity, accepting a zone of underworld morality for his life and his culture. For his dedication to this life, he had become a rich man.

He exited the obscene white limo at the posh Sand Dollar Resort and Casino and inhaled a deep breath of Caribbean air. The ever-present scented breeze that wafted about the island was far removed from the stench of the beloved city he had left behind. This was escape. Sure there was gambling, but it was legal gambling. And yes there were women, but the vast majority were not crack heads or hookers. They were lonely single women and sometimes, lonely married ones as well. But whatever their circumstances, they were consenting and usually cost no more than a few drinks and a few laughs. They were here for the same reasons as Cassavetti, which was to have a good time, get laid and maybe, just maybe, and possibly meet someone you might want to know back in the real world. But Cassavetti doubted that would ever happen.

He handed the smiling driver a ten dollar bill as the native in a suit handed Cassavetti's bag to yet another smiling native in a suit. As he watched the porter lead the way to the front desk for check in, his mind began to find its ease.

In his mind he thought, *let the games begin*.

CHAPTER 3

Whether the Hortons were at home, in a tropical paradise, Disney World or wherever, it didn't matter. Getting the two hellions and their silent brother ready for an outing, even in this case for a simple dinner, was cruel and unusual punishment. And, on top of these wining little misfits, Jack Horton had to contend with his wife. In the previous fifteen minutes, Alice had changed clothes at least three times. Then, with that matter apparently settled, she suggested one of the Sand Dollar's three different restaurants, and when Jack agreed, she changed her mind again and ultimately said no to each. After ruling out all options in the outer world, Alice suggested that they just have room service. Jack finally held his ground. They were in paradise, he told her, and they needed to get out and enjoy themselves. Sitting in a hotel room eating burgers and watching TV may work for her and the boys, but not for him.

In the background, in the adjoining room, the two older boys were arguing over the television remote control. Perfect, Jack thought to himself, she's screaming because she can't deal with a minor decision and these offspring of mine are willing to tear each other limb-from-limb over cartoons versus a reality show featuring anatomically enhanced ex-strippers eating large worms for a $50,000 grand prize.

Finally, out of desperation he tried to turn things around. "Look Alice, you look fine, we're here to enjoy ourselves, why don't we just try to get a grip and go downstairs and have dinner. Maybe the buffet place would be the best."

Jack heard her slap her brush down on the bathroom counter and she quickly emerged. "Get a grip," she snapped. "Why don't you just take your rear end downstairs to paradise and leave us ingrates to ourselves. Maybe we could use a break from you for a little while." She finished her ranting and disappeared into the bathroom again, slamming the door. "Get a grip!" he heard her mimic scornfully from behind the closed door.

Jack was in disbelief that this exchange happened. He stood in the middle of the $600 a night room, closed his eyes, and raised his head to the ceiling. As if on cue from the next room he heard a slap, a crash and a scream of agony. He dashed around the bed toward the kids' room and noticed Alice pop her head out of the bathroom with disgust on her face, then quickly retreat. Her son's cry didn't even seem to faze the woman. But by the time he entered the boys' adjoining room, he couldn't immediately determine which one fell victim of the assault. The two misfits were already engaged in an obvious counterattack and were entangled in a brawl.

Jack grabbed an arm and in a moderate rage hollered, "Get off each other, *now!*" He yanked one child off the other. "If you guys don't quit ..." "He won't give me the remote!"

"He tried to stick his finger in my nose." "You scratched me first."

It was all Jack could handle.

He practically flung eight-year-old Timmy onto the bed and glared at them both. Meanwhile, Harry, the quiet six-year-old, sat cross-legged on the floor in a corner by the sliding glass door and stared out the window at the beach. Jack noted the boy would have looked so peaceful if it weren't for the fact that he was gently slapping the floor with one hand, then alternately slapping his face with the other. And he did so rhythmically, and repeatedly. There was really something wrong with that child, he thought to himself in the middle of all the chaos.

Jack stood at the door leading back to his room and looked up from his possessed younger boy to the other two and said, "Look, do you two want to just stay in tonight?"

"Can we watch a movie?" they chirped in unison.

Jack didn't even answer, he resigned himself to defeat, and steeled himself for what had to follow if he was to get some relief from this lunacy. He closed the boys' door and went back over to the bathroom. He finally had enough of all this and knew that he had to extract himself. For a millisecond the words *for good* flashed through his mind, but for now, he would deal with the evening at hand. So, in a very rare gesture of self-preservation, he stood up for himself, but in his own manipulative way.

"Alice, I don't know what to do. The boys want to stay in and you're pissed off; maybe I should just go downstairs on my own for awhile." He stood in front of the closed door and awaited her response—which never came.

"Alice?"

"What?" she said in a monotone response behind the closed door.

This was a recurring game that seemed to go on and on. All he wanted to do was relax and have fun, maybe even enjoy some "quality" family time. Unfortunately, he knew that notion was a cliché that did not apply to him. "Quality" family time just didn't exist in his world. But nobody was interested in his plans, and now he would be punished for not wanting to stick around and participate with the inmates of the nut house.

"Did you hear me? The boys would like …"

"I heard you," she interrupted. "Go do what you want. At this point, I really don't care."

"This point?" he replied, feeling his pulse quicken. Of course he knew that he shouldn't engage her further, and he sensed he should just walk away. "What exactly is 'this point'?" He asked, unable to help himself.

"The point at which I don't give a shit," she said as she opened the door quite obviously ready to rumble.

"Alice, I'm done fighting. Look where we are for God's sake, this whole argument is ridiculous."

"Whatever, Jack, just leave and give us a break." And with that, the bathroom door shut, once again.

This time Jack was smart enough to shut up. He turned to the clothes closet, eyed his assortment of vividly flowered shirts, and grabbed the loudest one he saw. He yanked off his swimsuit and pulled on some underwear and a pair of khaki shorts. Grabbing a brush off the dresser, he peered into the mirror on the wall, quickly organized what little hair he had, and finished with a slow, deep breath. It was time, and he was out the door.

CHAPTER 4

The city had lulled well into the evening and the air was as remarkably fresh as it was crisp and cold. The winter storm had come and gone. The "snow day" was over and all that remained was the blanket of white that covered the parks and the precious fenced rectangles that were scattered about most of the better parts of Manhattan. These cordoned gardens were all some New Yorkers knew of shrubs and trees, but tonight they were covered with snow. The city workers had cleared the streets as well as they could, but there were still snow banks along the sides of almost every building and mounds running along the curb of almost every street. Remarkably, in the dogged unstoppable manner that New York trudges through any form of adversity, the traffic was moving about, the busses and trains were all back on schedule and life buzzed along in the Big Apple.

Many New Yorkers had welcomed this quick and unexpected turn in the weather and there were those who, quite naturally, weren't all that pleased. Small shop and restaurant owners lost most of a day's business because of the snow, and many had to run stores and cafes without any of their employees, or at best, an extremely reduced staff, as stranded workers remained in the boroughs. But while those few soured individuals lamented over mother-nature's interruption, there were thousands of school kids who got the day off and as many adults and older kids who were stranded or just stayed home. For those folks, the day had been a good one.

•   •   •

Elliot Murphy slugged back what was probably his ninth bourbon on the rocks and decided it had, in fact, been a good day. One might not think that a "snow day" would affect the pursuit of criminals—the work of the law—but for this twenty-year veteran of the Federal Bureau of Investigation, it was reason enough to cut out a little early and get tanked.

Murphy was perched upon his regular stool at O'Reilly's Pub at the corner of Thirty-eighth and Eighth Avenue in a relatively obscure part of Manhattan. It was close to Madison Square Garden and The Port Authority, but not a part of town known for much else. It was a vestige of the city that allowed one to remain anonymous, and reduced the likelihood of being seen. It was also a perfect little drinking neighborhood for pros who took the preoccupation a little more seriously. The area was littered with bars and pubs, some of which had been around for decades, but they were quiet little establishments that weren't associated with anything resembling the hip bar circuit.

Murphy lived further uptown, on a sleepy block in the Upper West Side, in a small one-bedroom apartment he had been renting for the past year and a half. His soon to be ex-wife would keep their modest suburban home in Cedar Grove, New Jersey, along with everything in it including her car, the dog and all the memories of twenty-one years of their life together. She could have it all. At this phase in a drinking spree, the swirl of thought that drifted through his intoxicated brain didn't look favorably on the life he had left behind. And it was also typically at this point that there was nothing else he thought of; although he knew it was a subject to avoid.

He concluded it was a pretty typical deal involving a marriage of two people too young to know any better. They met, they were both young and naïve, they had some fun, and it was easy. He was fresh out of Vietnam where he had served as an officer for two rotations. He had been in intelligence with a degree in criminal justice from Princeton, thinking all the while that he would go back to school and obtain a law degree. But shortly after his return, two things happened and his life seemed to naturally follow a path he could only assume was correct. First he met Sally and second, the FBI came knocking at his door to recruit him. Very quickly his courtship with Sally ended up in marriage and eventually he even obtained the law degree, which was a big plus in accelerating his career with the bureau. Everything seemed to be coming together and for quite some time, it was together.

There were children, two boys who were in their junior and senior years of university life at Cornell. So there were some memorable years as the boys were growing up and his job allowed some time with his family. He especially enjoyed the vacations and holidays in the earlier years when he felt more strongly connected. But over the last five or six years he had decided that Sally was no longer the woman he thought he had married, that his present needs were more important than all those memories embracing a marriage and a home for the boys. He had to make a break. But during this period of decline, he had also started to drink. Despite what Sally would say, he drank to relax and enjoy himself, until he passed out that is.

Tonight, Murphy drank to celebrate the snow day and the developments in a case that he was working. Like most other senior agents with the Manhattan office of the bureau, he was working domestic terrorism. The date 9/11 would resonate in him for years to come and his unit was tracking yet another 'charity' group that claimed to fund pre-school education for Arab immigrants. In fact the money was being funneled back out of the country to an Al Qaeda cell in Germany. He had worked with Treasury to obtain paper trails of contributors and tracked the money out of the country. In the past forty-eight hours the patterns had been so firmly established that he was confident the U.S. Attorney would authorize a raid and several arrests would result.

This was currently the top duty in the Bureau's stratosphere. Terrorism was a highly urgent matter throughout law enforcement and a popular cause in the eyes of the taxpayer. Therefore, it was politically correct and fully funded, unlike the departments focusing on organized crime or drug interdiction, which had taken funding hits since 9/11 changed the landscape of public sentiment and the government's pocket book.

But Murphy didn't care so much about the worthiness of his mission lately. He just did his job, enjoyed the security, and so long as he broke one open every once in awhile, his superiors overlooked some of his behaviors that developed over the last several years. The divorce had taken a lot of time, and on more than one occasion, a night of self-pity and a bottle had rendered him incapable of working the next day. Sometimes two.

But tonight was a Friday and he was actually off for the weekend. No matter where the evening led him and his friend Jack Daniels, he would have a day or two to recover. No questions asked. Not by his boss, his co-workers, his soon-to-be ex-wife, Sally, or their boys, and he certainly didn't have to worry about friends.

He didn't have any left.

CHAPTER 5

Jack Horton now stood in the hallway in front of the door to his hotel room and he contemplated his options. He knew that to follow through with this exit strategy would have serious implications. His wife would probably not recover quickly and odds were good that she would punish him for days. On the other hand, *to hell with it*, he thought to himself. She had given him the green light and told him to leave. But he also knew that this was all part of the game. He rarely abandoned them, but when he did it was to avoid conflicted circumstances like this. In him, there was a growing need to escape the dysfunction and hostility that clouded his existence. But when he did leave, he knew there would be a price to pay.

This was the moment, and for him it was like jumping off a cliff. So, he willed himself to turn and face the elevators. Jack took a slow step forward, moving away from the door, when he heard a child scream something unrecognizable and paused as a conditioned reflex. That was all it took. His pace picked up and he was on his way. Jack Horton was emboldened and in full stride headed down the hall towards a few hours of sanity. He knew exactly what he would do and where he would go. He had been eyeing the bars and the casino and was ready to be a part of humanity with people who at least appeared to be enjoying themselves and not trying to kick the living shit out of one another—even the husbands and wives.

As he waited for the elevator, three women bopped around the corner, laughing and chatting. They were obviously a few drinks removed from sobriety and were dressed in the standard evening attire for the resort; next to nothing, yet colorful. A sheepish smile appeared on Jack's face as he nodded an acknowledgment of their arrival.

As Jack held the door for the women to board the elevator, he had a flash of regret. He knew he could go back upstairs at anytime and beg for mercy and perhaps this time, Alice would actually forgive. But this time really was different, and he knew he had to stick to his guns and stay away for a while. He had been right; it was ridiculous to spend any more time battling over trivia on their vacation. The boys were uncontrollable, and of course, that was a given. But Alice needed to put a little effort into rising above her self-pity and enjoy herself. As the elevator descended, Jack thought to himself, *Alice just needs to pull it together, or go away.*

For his age and lack of hair, Jack wasn't the worst looking guy in a lineup. He actually had a handsome, friendly face and he was in decent shape. He didn't get much in the way of exercise, yet he was blessed with a rather muscular physique. He'd never had much reason to worry about his looks anyway, at least not in many years. Suddenly though, he felt a little self-conscious as he caught one of the women on the elevator giving him the once over. After they got off, he found himself smiling. *This is going to be okay*, he thought to himself.

The lobby was bustling with activity when he spilled out of the elevator. It was a large open expanse, floored in marble with gothic stone columns forming an inner quadrant where seating areas were positioned. As he walked away from the elevators to his left, Jack observed the check-in counters staffed by formally attired personnel and beyond this area was the concierge desk. Ahead and to the right were the entrances to two bars and the casino. There was a walkway to the pool area with its cabana bar and Horton knew it would be hopping at this time of the evening. The beach side of the hotel faced almost due west and the sunset, which was already in progress, was usually spectacular. He didn't hesitate and headed outside towards the bar.

As he rounded the corner and approached the massive cabana bar, a lengthy stretch of varnished wood covered by a weather-beaten thatched roof, he noticed a couple pulling up from their seats. He moved steadily toward the two open stools and a small free space at the bar as a reggae band grinded out an island version of *Knocking on Heaven's Door*. Lured by the music, the sunset and most likely a special on fruity drinks, the bar was packed. But Horton was lucky and smiled as he saddled up to his newly acquired space and eyed the wall of liquor bottles. He saw stuffed tropical birds and island memorabilia, like coconut heads and carved sentimental plaques that contained profound island adages. One read: Relax, just do it on The Island!

As he pulled a stool underneath his rear, a bartender was quick to notice him and said, "What'll it be?"

"How 'bout a Michelob," Horton responded to the friendly native behind the bar. "And, uh, a shot of Schnapps, please," The words were barely out of his mouth when Jack noticed an abundance of scantily clad women at the bar.

The bartender had already twisted the cap off the beer and was pouring out Horton's shot. He leaned forward and asked the bartender, "What's with all the women here tonight?"

The dark-skinned man was clad in the standard garb for employees that worked around the pool—a brilliant flowered shirt and navy Bermuda shorts. He replied with a smile, "It's ladies night, mon; they get their drinks for a dollar!"

Before Horton had a chance to comment, someone nudged him from the side. He turned to face one of the women who had been on the elevator with him. *The one who had smiled!* She was kind of exotic looking, but approachable and young. Jack guessed her to be in her late twenties. She was a brunette with a bright smile and a killer body. She was wearing a soft blue halter top and tight little white Capri pants, very hot, Horton thought to himself. He smiled broadly.

"Hi," she said, with a broader smile than before.

"Hey," Horton responded. Then he instinctively took a deep breath and sucked in his gut.

"You using this chair?"

"Uhh, no. Go ahead."

She slid around to the front of the stool and placed a small, sequined hot-pink pocket book on the bar. She stared at the busy bartender and tried to get his attention while Horton slugged back his shot of Schnapps.

"Pretty busy here tonight," he blurted in his most confident voice, the heat of the schnapps quickly moving from his throat to his head.

"Yeah," she smiled.

Horton awkwardly leaned forward and waved to get the bartender's attention, the same one that had served him earlier. She smiled a little brighter, acknowledging his assistance.

Jack's head was already swirling and it even felt as though his heart was racing. This wasn't the first time he had ever interacted with a woman aside from his wife and co-workers, but something felt significantly different and it had nothing to do with this cute little brunette sitting beside him. Somehow he felt a barrier, or protective wall had been lifted. Apparently, the altercation earlier in the hotel room was more profound to him than just another fight. At that moment he realized that he was in a hopeless situation, and was perhaps on the verge of doing something about it. If Alice was incapable of enjoying his presence on a tropical island paradise, then what did that say for the marriage? Not much. And as Jack ordered another shot, he watched the girl finish her frozen daiquiri and decided he needed to formulate a home-exit plan.

In the meantime, he realized he wouldn't mind a little female company and here she was, inches away and smiling.

Nothing he would regret later, maybe just a little conversation and a few laughs.

A few laughs, he thought. *Wouldn't that be different?*

CHAPTER 6

Phil Cassavetti sat in his suite, dressed for an evening in the casino, staring out the sliding doors that led to his private balcony on the resort's top floor. While his view was of the incredible setting sun, a spectacular sight from this vantage point, his mind and thoughts were somewhere entirely different. He was waiting.

He could see the sequence of events unfold as if he were there. It is a run-down section of the outer borough that was home to dilapidated warehouses and a few light manufacturing companies that would be closed and empty by now. Tony Dimaglia, the man who had stolen over a million dollars from the Gallo family, leaves the Uptown Social Club in Queens right about now, seven PM. He drives through a part of the neighborhood that's usually deserted at this time of the evening. The man is unaware that he has been found out and is completely unsuspecting that he is in danger.

The shooters will time it perfectly. When Dimaglia comes to a stop sign just a few short blocks from the expressway entrance, a car will screech to a halt in front of him, cutting him off and ensuring that it's too late for any defensive measure. The killer in the passenger seat of the other car discharges a powerful shotgun blast that takes out the windshield of Dimaglia's brand new Cadillac, along with a sizeable chunk of his head, and mortally wounds the wiry little traitor. The driver of the hit car leaps out and over the top of Dimaglia's roof and unloads half a magazine from an Uzi automatic machine gun into the front seat of the Caddy. After this, the second hit man emerges and they both cautiously approach the target vehicle to inspect their work. Dimaglia is dead or dying and his body is oozing blood from multiple wounds. One of the hit men pulls out a handgun and puts two in his brain.

Assuming at that point there are no vehicles approaching the scene, the two men quickly extract Dimaglia, the fifty-year-old father of six, from the Cadillac. His lifeless body is quickly transferred to the trunk of the hitter's car and they drive off. The body is taken to an automotive repair shop in Brooklyn and the two men methodically dismember the corpse, and his remains are placed in weighted plastic bags near the massive induction pipes leading to a water treatment plant along the East River.

Cassavetti knew that Dimaglia would never be found and his family would never recover any physical remains to bury. They too would pay a steep price for his misdeeds, whether they were aware of them or not.

Ironically, his widow would be taken care of. She would receive a small monthly stipend, her house would be paid off, and she might even receive a new car someday. This was a tradition, to provide for the family they had just attacked. The philosophy behind the practice, oddly enough, came from the belief that the victim's loved ones should not suffer more than they already had. They would never be told what had actually happened, but in most cases, they knew. Their husband, their father, the strength and the head of their home, was gone.

Killings like this didn't happen with great frequency any longer, and even hitting an outsider who threatened the mob, or for any other reason, was a rarity. But Cassavetti experienced the phenomenon of inflicting death years ago and it was a feeling he never forgot. Regardless of the justification, Dimaglia's violation of their code of justice, Cassavetti still had a conscience and at this moment, the guilt poured over him. This victim had been a friend and a "brother" in the Gallo crime family. Even though he was removed from the scene of the crime by hundreds of miles, it was the words from *his* lips that ordered the end of the man's life. For a moment, it didn't matter that Dimaglia had signed his own death warrant by violating a tenet of the code. In those quietly, sublimely painful moments, as he waited, the burdensome weight of the act rested entirely upon his shoulders. Without getting on his knees, without shutting his eyes, in a rare moment for an underboss, Cassavetti asked God for forgiveness. But he knew redemption wasn't possible. He also knew he would live with this for the rest of his life.

At that moment a cell phone on the glass coffee table chirped. It almost seemed merciful; as it brought the otherwise rock solid Cassavetti out of his introspective trance.

He grabbed the phone up, answered it, and a deep Irish accent said, "Sorry, guess I have the wrong number." Then the caller hung up. It meant the deed was that Dimaglia was dead, and they would be taking him to be butchered, as planned. If anything had gone wrong, a different cryptic code would have been used, or worse, the phone might never have rung.

Cassavetti slowly placed the phone back on the table and stared for the first time, at the incredibly beautiful setting sun. It almost seemed poetic. As he shook off the thoughts of the killing and brought himself back into the moment, the sun silently exploded on the horizon, casting reddish flickers that simultaneously rose into the sky and sank into the Caribbean.

The night had begun for him, and Tony Dimaglia was a thing of the past.

CHAPTER 7

Elliott Murphy wrapped up his ninth drink and decided it was time for a change of scene. He left O'Reilly's Pub on Thirty-Eighth Street and walked a couple of blocks uptown to another bar, that was even less conspicuous and all the better for it. He realized he was getting hammered and he instinctively wanted to be as discreet as possible. After all, a senior special agent of the FBI wasn't supposed to be seen stumbling around a mid-town Manhattan bar, drunk. Snow day or not.

Ironically, he stumbled into a dive joint called *Sally's* that catered mostly to bus drivers and building maintenance workers. His ex-wife, Sally, would be honored. With this much alcohol in his system, and his senses beginning to numb, he could still see. Well enough to notice the neon "A" was not working in the red flashing sign above the entrance. He perched on a stool at the far end of the bar and kept an eye on the door should any wanted-terrorists walk in while he was silently trying to pronounce "Sally" without the "A". Elliott decided it couldn't be done.

He was raised in a strict home, attended a private Catholic boys' school and then went straight off to college where he was focused on his education and sports. He had been a wrestler through high school and most of college before he dislocated his shoulder and had to sit out most of the season his senior year. He remembered a few beer blasts during that period, when he was a little down over the disappointment of not wrapping up what was a NCAA level three career. He was one of the top wrestlers at Princeton, and ironically, his hardest fall came when he fell out of favor. But he refocused his efforts on his studies and finished up his last year with honors.

He graduated in pre-law and while most people, including his parents, would have expected him to immediately go on to law school; he surprised everyone by enlisting as an officer in the Army. After intelligence training stateside, he shipped off for two tours in Vietnam. Then, upon return to the states, he was almost immediately recruited by the FBI and he never looked back. He took his job seriously and drinking was never anything that he enjoyed very much or did more than occasionally and it was always purely social. At least, that's the way it used to be.

But somewhere around four years ago, things began to unravel at home. A year or two before the first of his sons left home for college, the fighting began. Sally decided that without children in her nest, she had nothing. He had his career. But she was left with a big, empty home to take care of, the grind of daytime television, and the worries of being married to an FBI agent who preferred working on the street versus a desk job, which he could have had years ago. In Washington no less!

To Sally, at that point, it wasn't much of a life. She decided it wasn't fair, something would have to change, and it was his responsibility to change it. She decided to look into real estate school for herself, but he was going to have to explore getting off the street and into a desk. He needed to learn how to play bridge and take her to a movie once a week. They needed to plan a few trips together, to Europe or England, places she had always dreamed of going. They had to start over and build a new relationship that would carry them into their old age. That was Sally's plan.

This was all ridiculous, according to Elliott Murphy. Absurd. Why should he be forced to change just because she was bored? She could go to real estate school and get a job to stay busy all day long. In fact, the extra money would be great considering he had dual tuition bills to pay every six months. But the rest of Sally's plan, in fact any of it that applied to him changing, was crap.

And so the beginning of the end began.

When he looked back over the last three or four years in a moment of clarity and honesty, he realized they represented the point where things seemed to spin out of control. But if he was to get totally honest, gut-wrenchingly honest, he would also see the correlation between the booze, the bitter fights, the vicious words, and ultimately, the resulting abandonment. But he wasn't ready for that last step yet.

Elliott was currently engaged in a conversation with a city bus driver although "conversation" implies some modicum of intelligent communication between two conscious beings, and even a trained observer would have a difficult time establishing those components. Elliott wasn't sure if he was listening to another sad tale of a life gone sour, a wife who left, another promotion robbed, the damned President or whatever. Lately, he had listened to quite a few of these sad tales. Miraculously, after maybe fifteen or more drinks since five o'clock, he knew that it was time to go home.

It was around ten as he staggered out of the seedy bar, *S_lly's*. The street was now abandoned and the wind had kicked up and was whipping wisps of snow through the frigid night air. The few cars that trudged along Tenth Avenue seemed to crackle along the frozen road. He paused for a moment and attempted to get his bearings and think about how he was going to get home. He rarely took cabs, he usually took the subway or bus as he no longer had a Bureau vehicle as he did when he lived in New Jersey. His seniority had earned it but it was impractical now that he was living in the city so while he had a car available to him while he was on duty, he made his own way to and from work. Besides, he probably couldn't start a lawnmower on a night like this so it was just as well.

He began to walk uptown and planned to cross tenth at Fortieth Street and head inward to the Eighth Avenue subway line. At Thirty-Ninth Street, the corner seemed dark and foreboding and Elliott felt as though he was all alone in the city. It was rare at any time or any place not to see a moving car in New York, but this was suddenly one of those moments. The wind was out of the north and continued to bear down on him, as he walked directly into it. He wore a thick wool overcoat and galoshes, but he was still cold. He slid here and there on patchy ice, for which his anesthetized motor skills couldn't compensate. Without the ridiculous level of alcohol in his body he was a pretty formidable guy at fifty-one, and was powerful and quick on his feet. But as it was, the booze had slowed his reflexes, dulled his senses, and rendered him almost defenseless.

He remembered feeling the bulk of his holstered nine-millimeter, a standard issue SIG-Sauer P228, underneath his suit jacket as he had donned his coat back at S_lly's. This was the thought that shot through his mind as he approached the curb to cross Thirty-ninth and Tenth Avenue and glimpsed a blur of movement that struck out at him from the left side. Elliott quickly extracted his gloved hands from deep inside his coat pockets, where they were enjoying the warmth, and he attempted to do something in his defense, anything. He felt a surge of adrenalin rush through his body.

Aaron Jackson, age twenty-two, crack addict and convicted felon, had been waiting. He was surprised to see a fairly well-dressed dude in this part of town, at this time of night, but that was perhaps his good fortune for the day. Hopefully it meant the difference between one lousy high, and a decent score that could carry him for a while. Who could tell what the dude might have. A couple hundred bucks, credit cards, maybe even a Rolex.

Jackson carefully watched the guy approach and tensed. He could see that he was fucked up as he swayed and meandered his way down the sidewalk. This was perfect. In Aaron's gloved right hand he wielded an eight-inch serrated kitchen knife he had burned from an unsuccessful robbery a few nights ago. The guy he had robbed didn't have shit in his swank little efficiency apartment on the Upper West

Side. But this time Jackson could smell it. This one would be a sweet score.

Jackson waited until he could attack the man from behind, and he lunged. As he came within a foot or two of his prey, he thrust the knife with all his might so as to penetrate the heavy clothing, including that thick coat he planned to steal. His worn army jacket wasn't doing shit to keep him warm in this lousy weather.

The first attempt didn't work. As Jackson thrust the knife into the man's left side, he hit something that was rock solid. It stunned Jackson for a moment and he wondered what could possibly have stopped the knife.

The man spun to face Jackson and the young hood could easily see the man's eyes were glazed and he was confused by the assault. Nonetheless, the man attempted a surprising dive towards Jackson, apparently to subdue him. The move seemed smooth enough that Jackson thought the dude might be trouble. But as the man lunged forward, his feet flew out from underneath him and he fell flat on his ass onto the sidewalk. Now it was Jackson's turn again, and he attacked with the resolve of a hungry predator. He leaped on top of his prey and again thrust the knife—this time into his shoulder—as he directed his body weight to flow through his forearm and landed a severe blow to the man's throat. Both actions were successful. The knife sunk deep into the man's flesh and the weight of Jackson's body seemed to crush his throat. Aaron sprung off him and from his knees; he thrust the knife into his victim again, this time into his gut. And again. But even after this, the man was still flailing around and Jackson wanted him unconscious, if not dead, in order for him to search him and grab his wallet, his jewelry and anything else that would buy him some crack. He wound up with his bare fist and blasted a punch to the left side of the man's face that was powerful and perfectly placed. Years of street fighting, muggings, and defending himself from other losers had molded Aaron Jackson into a rather pathetic, albeit lethal weapon.

Finally, the dude was out cold. Jackson quickly went about the business of undoing the man's overcoat, searching all of his pockets, and within thirty seconds, knowing he had everything there was to be had. He also knew he had made a huge mistake, but it was too late now.

Aaron Jackson held in his hands the wallet of a senior special agent of the FBI. It contained a little over $110 along with an American Express card and two Visas. It also contained pictures of two teenage boys and a woman. He had an inexpensive watch, but it could be pawned for twenty bucks. He also had a gun. A big one.

Suddenly, the weight of Aaron's surprising discoveries hit him like a bitter cold wind in the face, or cold steel in the gut. He needed to get the hell out of there.

CHAPTER 8

Cassavetti made his way down from his room as quickly as he could after receiving his ominous call from the Irish caller. He had taken the cell phone and crushed it with his foot on the concrete balcony, broke it into pieces, and deposited the remains in a trash receptacle by the elevator. It was a throw away cell phone, the kind you can buy over the internet or in a convenience store. The phone came with one hundred pre-paid minutes, there would be no record of ownership, and his end of the call was completely untraceable. The call from the assassin of Tony Dimaglia was the only one he had ever received on the phone, the only one he ever would. Destroying the phone symbolically put the matter to bed in Cassavetti's mind. At least he told himself it did.

He had dressed in his usual gaming attire. He didn't go in for the wild and colorful garb that most of the resort guests donned in the evening. He wore expensive linen slacks, $500 loafers, and a silk short sleeve shirt. He never was much for jewelry, although he always had on one of his many eye-catching watches. Tonight he wore a top of the line gold Chaumet that matched his tan slacks and taupe shirt to a tee. With his handsome attire and his carved good looks, perfectly groomed salt and pepper hair, and a credit of $150,000 waiting in the casino, which was money he had wired from one of his offshore accounts prior to his arrival. Cassavetti was ready to play.

The elevator ride down seemed to take forever. He was still feeling tense and remorseful but as the doors opened and he heard the clanging of the slot machines and the buzz of the players chattering across the lobby, his spirits lifted immediately. He knew the night ahead was just what he needed. He smiled and strutted across the lobby to the casino entrance, paused for a moment, and was recognized by one of the many casino bosses who were obviously stationed there for just this reason. To recognize and greet high rollers as they made their way in for an evening of gaming.

"Good to see you, Mr. Cassavetti!" said the young man enthusiastically, as he reached out his hand. Despite the tropical setting, the casino boss was wearing the universal attire of casino management world wide—a high quality, good-looking, dark suit.

Cassavetti recognized the thirty-something guy but not from the Sand Dollar. "Hey," he said as he firmly shook the young man's hand. "I thought you were working at Caesar's in AC."

"Thanks for remembering, sir," the young man responded, politely. Despite the nature of their business, widely regard as highly corrupt and immoral, casino workers, from the waitresses to the pit bosses and directors, were the most well-mannered, professional business people he knew. This anomaly seemed to add a touch of class to an otherwise morally bankrupt trade. "I moved down here six months ago," the man explained.

Cassavetti exchanged a few more pleasantries but was ready to get going and warm up with a few games of craps. This was going to be a long night and he was bound to be a winner, he just knew it. He had to win. It would clear away the thoughts of taking a man's life tonight. A man with children, a wife, hopes for the future for himself and his family. So, he ordered a drink at one of the tables and patiently waited to be allowed into the game.

The young man who had greeted him at the door slid in beside him for a moment and placed a tray in front of him that contained $50,000 in chips. Just a third of what Cassavetti was prepared to lose over the course of the next few days, it was still enough to give him a momentary rush, as it always did, and he was ready.

He placed $2,000 on red to win.

Jack Horton was engaged in a meaningless conversation with the girl carrying a pink sequined purse and answering to the name of Rachel. She was also from New York, as so many of the guests who frequented the island, and was an administrative assistant at an investment bank. They were chatting about a movie, and Rachel apparently had a thing for Kevin Costner. Somehow she had decided there was something redeeming about Waterworld and was trying to convince Horton that she was right. It wasn't working.

"I'd give him some credit for *Tin Cup*, or the wolf movie, ah, *JFK* I guess, but *Waterworld*?" Horton was ready to move on. He had chugged two more shots and three beers in the last hour and he was feeling a little buzzed.

He was ready to mingle around the casino, except he was a little worried about having his new best friend tagging along. He was uncomfortable being seen with a woman. After all, his wife and boys were just ten stories away having the time of their lives.

"Well, I enjoyed it Rachel, but I'm going to head back upstairs. The old ball and chain is probably wondering where I am," he said, lying on both counts.

"That's too bad," Rachel said with a mock pout. "I was really having fun. Why not at least pull a few slots with me in the casino."

Horton thought for a split second, *what could it hurt?* There was no one at the hotel that he knew, so there was really nothing to risk. Besides, it's not like he was doing anything wrong. This was a man who was becoming a master at rationalization.

"All right, but what about your girlfriends?" asked Horton, recalling the two other women that rode down with them in the elevator.

"I know it's a little weird, but they're a couple." She smirked.

Horton's eyebrows rose. It was a knee-jerk reaction to the thought of a lesbian couple down the hall. All he could manage was, "Wow!"

She was off her stool and pushing her way through the partiers surrounding the bar and he followed her back inside the hotel atrium and toward the casino.

Three hours into the night Cassavetti was on a roll. He was up $32,000 and had decided earlier at about $20,000, that his winning was vindication for his part in the murder of Tony Dimaglia. It was amazing how his mind worked, especially in the rush of gambling and several vodkas, straight up. And on top of his winnings, he was being followed around by two scantily clad, yet heavily painted women that no doubt were on somebody's payroll and assigned to take care of him as a high roller. The casino itself wouldn't employ these women, but a pit boss could report the expense as "customer development" and management wouldn't think twice about it. In fact, they would wink.

He was seated at one of the blackjack tables. Both girls had on very tight, very short skirts and skimpy, colorful halter-tops. One was a light-skinned black woman who had short hair and deep brown eyes. The other was taller, with an olive-hued complexion that showed no effects of the sun. It set off a tantalizing contrast to her vivid red hair. They were captivating sitting next to one another, and between the girls and the streak the Cassavetti was riding, he was garnering quite a bit of attention. That always made him a little nervous, so he decided it might be time to usher these two upstairs to his suite and take a break for an hour or so.

Horton and his new friend were seated on stools next to one another playing the slots. Jack had made a run to the ATM machine in the lobby to extract a couple hundred bucks because he only had thirty-five dollars in his wallet. Guests at the all-inclusive resort only needed cash when they gambled.

Rachel was working a Lucky Seven machine and Horton was feeding the Diamonds are Wild. Rachel had already won a forty-dollar pull but Jack wasn't having much luck at all. It was getting close to 10 o'clock and Jack had been gone from his room for over three hours. He had continued drinking at the slots due to the waitresses plying everyone they could. He was starting to get bored and a headache was looming from the beers Jack knew it was about time for this little escape to end. Hopefully the boys were asleep, although he doubted it, and hopefully they hadn't given Alice a hard time upstairs. If they had, Jack would surely pay. Besides, he had gone through the $200 he withdrew earlier, except for a little change, and that was remarkable for such a miser.

"It's really time now, Rachel. I gotta get upstairs." Jack now feigned a sad look, but actually he was really starting to enjoy her. Her upbeat demeanor and her bright smile were incredibly refreshing to Jack, who was accustomed to a woman who functioned in a manner that was barely this side of morose.

"Ohhhh, come on. Just a little while longer?" she cried, once again adding the pout for dramatic effect. Jack thought it was kind of cute.

"Come on," he said firmly. "Walk me out of here and maybe we can try it again tomorrow night."

Jack knew that wasn't going to happen. "Okay," she frowned.

They hopped off the stools and made their way down one of the many aisles, all lined with money sucking slot machines manned by mostly inebriated operators more than willing to give up their cash in hopes of a big win. As they passed the end of the aisle, Rachel grabbed Jack's hand and pulled him over to a large dollar slot called the Sand Dollar Dynamo. It was lit up in a hundred colors, and its front was decorated with pictures of near naked beauties and bronze Adonises frolicking on the beach. At the top of the machine an LED ticker streamed across in red flashing letters stating that the jackpot was now $147,850.

"Do you think anyone ever wins this thing?" she asked.

"Yeah, right," Jack replied cynically. He just wanted to get out of there and face the music upstairs.

"Come on, let's try it," Rachel pleaded. "We only need four dollars to win the jackpot, and I've got two."

Horton figured what the hell. Grant her this last wish and then he would be gone.

"Okay, I barely have two bucks but here," he said as he fished in his pocket for the last of his quarters. He had exactly eight and he inserted them into the machine.

She added her two dollars worth and said, "Come on, let's pull it together!" Horton raised his brow in acknowledgement, and with his hand on top of hers and they pulled the lever of the massive slot machine.

Four sand dollars across were required to win the jackpot. The first spinner stopped on a sand dollar.

The second stopped on another. The third sand dollar appeared.

"Oh my god," Rachel said under her breath. "Holy shit!" yelled Horton.

The fourth wheel had finally stopped and it was the most beautiful sand dollar Jack Horton had ever seen.

As if orchestrated, they both screamed, "WE WON!" At the same time a siren blared on top of the machine signifying a winner. People started to rush up and marvel at the event.

As Cassavetti and his playmates walked out of the casino, above all the other casino noise, a siren went off and people started screaming. He turned quickly because he knew that one of the high stakes slots had just been won. The girls turned and instinctively walked back in to see who and what had been won. Cassavetti assumed they were simply monitoring winners who might be interested in their company later on. He admired that, it was good business. He followed them back to the slot machine where everyone was crowding around.

When they approached the source of all the commotion, it appeared that someone had won almost a hundred and fifty grand on one pull of the Sand Dollar Dynamo. Fools luck, the mobster thought. He caught a glimpse of the two winners. They were jumping up and down hugging each other.

Looked like a couple from Jersey or something, maybe on their honeymoon.

Good for them, he thought to himself, *they could probably use it.*

CHAPTER 9

It was shortly before midnight when Sally Murphy's phone rang. Although her husband had not been living at home for over a year and a half, her reaction to a late night call was always the same. *Something has happened to Elliott!* was her first thought after twenty years of marriage to an FBI agent and expecting the phone to ring with bad news. This time it was true.

Elliott had been spotted by a cab driver and his lifeless body was sprawled out in the frigid night like a casualty of war, his torso resting on a bloody snow-bank, and his legs extending onto the veneer of the icy sidewalk. The cabby radioed it in, his dispatcher called the police, and a patrol car arrived fifteen minutes later. When the cops received the call they assumed it was just another street person passed out drunk and if it hadn't been for the fact the temperature was now close to zero, the police wouldn't have bothered with the call. The typical bum would normally move themselves before sun-up to catch a free meal at a shelter or begin their day of scavenging and panhandling.

When the uniformed officers hopped out of their vehicle and took a closer look, they could see two things immediately. The man appeared to be alive, though closer to half-dead, and he was no bum. They immediately called for an ambulance and back-up officers. He had a weak pulse but was breathing slowly on his own, so while they watched him and waited, they tried to figure out who he was. One of the officers frisked through his pockets and eventually found a holster—an empty holster. At that point, the man's life was probably saved. The cops went into overdrive. They assumed the man was in law enforcement and immediately picked him up, carried him to their car, and slid him into the back seat. To hell with the ambulance, they decided, this guy needed to get to a hospital immediately.

Eventually it was determined that the frigid temperature had probably saved his life. The cold had slowed his cardiovascular system down, which in turn slowed blood flow and minimized the blood loss. He was suffering from hypothermia on top of two stab wounds, a concussion, and a broken wrist. But when the police cruiser pulled into Lenox Hill Hospital, there was barely a pulse.

Sally Murphy was being driven into Manhattan by one of Elliott's work partners, Sam Taub. Taub was a friend that lived within a few miles of their home in Cedar Grove, New Jersey, where he received the call about Elliott's assault. One of their own was down and it was time for the FBI to jump in and take care of their downed agent, and his family. Taub was asked to bring Sally Murphy in from New Jersey and serve as a liaison with NYPD to determine what happened to their senior special agent.

"So, that's all I know at this point," Taub said to Sally as they slowly made their way along the Garden State Parkway approaching the Lincoln Tunnel exit. He was driving a black Ford Expedition that was a bureau vehicle. It was equipped with four-wheel drive, grill and tail light emergency flashers, and a siren. Taub had the flashing lights operating but didn't bother with the siren because the road conditions precluded him from driving any more than about forty miles per hour. It made for an excruciatingly slow trip for both of them.

Taub had less seniority than Murphy and was several years younger in age. But while Taub honored Murphy's tenure and still respected the man, he had witnessed Murphy's decline over the last few years. And he knew he wasn't the only one at the Bureau who had seen the same. Most career agents displayed an edge that was the mark of a high level law enforcement officer. Murphy seemed to be showing signs of losing that edge. It wasn't anything blatant, but showed up in more subtle things like his focus, his pace, and even the hours he worked. Murphy rarely put in any overtime these days despite the fact he lived alone in the city since his separation from Sally, which had almost been two years.

As they entered the tunnel, Sally Murphy was overwhelmed by how peculiar it all seemed. She sat silently staring out the window as the emergency strobe lights on the vehicle shot bolts of white and red light that glazed the tired walls of the aging tunnel. She thought to herself, as she had a million times since their marriage began to falter—*how could this be happening?* It seemed to color this nightmare, Elliott having been critically injured, with an additional layer of tragedy.

Despite the fact they hadn't lived together for some time, there hadn't been any hesitation. She knew she needed to be by his side. They emerged from the three-and-a-half-mile concrete tube that passed below the Hudson River and ascended into the winter night. Finally on the New York side of the river, she just prayed for his survival.

When they arrived at the hospital's emergency entrance Taub let Sally out of the massive SUV and parked. By the time he joined her in the waiting room, an ER physician had just walked up to Sally and he overheard her say, "I'm his wife."

Taub instinctively removed his wallet from his jeans and displayed his golden special agent's badge and photo ID. "I'm Sam Taub with the FBI and a friend of the family as well."

The physician reached out his hand and firmly shook Taub's. "I'm Ben Slater. I'm the supervising internist tonight. Why don't we go in here," said Slater, pointing to a door across the hallway. He opened the door to a tiny room with a small table that had four chairs crowded around it. Taub and Sally followed him into the room with anxious looks on their faces as they greatly feared what they were about to be told. As they seated themselves at the table, the doctor began his report.

"He's in critical condition and to get right to the point, there's a chance he won't make it until morning." Sally's eyes opened wide and a glistening sheath of moisture quickly glazed over her pupils. Taub covered her hand with his.

The doctor went on, "He has lost a great deal of blood and we're replacing it as quickly as we can, but he has just gone in for emergency surgery to fix the internal damage caused by the knife wounds. One in particular has caused quite a bit trouble in his gut. I just need to be frank, Mrs. Murphy, it's going to be tough to put it all back together." Now the tears were streaming down both of Sally Murphy's cheeks. Taub swallowed and squeezed her hand more firmly. Slater continued, "Now, on the other hand, your husband is a strong guy and between the cold and the alcohol in his body, his system had slowed, but didn't shut down. The combination of those two factors, in an unusual way, may have saved his life."

Taub nodded slightly to acknowledge what Slater said but silently noted the comment about the alcohol. It didn't matter right now; the guy might not even be alive in the morning. But obviously, Murphy had been drinking.

"Aside from the critical stab wounds, he has a broken wrist and a concussion, which he probably received when he fell or was pushed onto the sidewalk. None of these injuries is life-threatening. "So," he said as he stood up, "Unless you have any questions, and that's really all I know at this point, we just need to wait it out. I'll be around until eight in the morning, he'll be out of surgery well before then, and I'll let you know the minute they finish. The surgeon will fill you in from there. One of the nurses is going to have some questions for you Mrs. Murphy, so I'll send her in."

Taub stood up and shook the physician's hand, "Thanks Doc."

Sally Murphy sat bathed in a strange numbness, quietly sobbing and wondering how this could be happening. It was approaching two in the morning and as she followed

Sam Taub out to the waiting area, the ER was still bustling. A young black nurse approached them and said, "Mrs. Murphy, why don't you both follow me. I'm sure you'd be more comfortable in the surgery lounge." Sally and Taub obediently followed her down a maze of halls to another waiting area. This one was unoccupied and clearly more comfortable. It was adorned with several couches, cushioned chairs, and tables with lamps, which was in stark contrast to the open coldness of the ER.

They sat down and the nurse began, "My name is Alicia and I need to ask a few questions."

Taub half-listened to the exchange. The nurse asked about the basics of age, previous health problems, and allergies, but Taub's mind was somewhere else. How did this thing happen? What the hell was Murphy doing drunk, in that part of town, on a bitter winter night?

Two men approached Taub and he immediately pegged them as cops. The nurse stopped her question and answer session at their interruption, and one of the men said, "Excuse us, but are you Mrs. Murphy?"

Before Sally had a chance to respond, Taub was on his feet and said, "She is, and I'm Special Agent Taub, FBI. Are you guys NYPD?"

The three law enforcement officers flashed their badges at one another while the nurse watched in silence.

Sally sat with her face in her hands, staring down at the floor, and listened to the official exchange. It reminded her of Elliott and how seriously he used to take his job. He had been part of the inner sanctum in the Bureau and he stayed there because he was so good at his job, and because he loved it so much. On this dreadful night, the only issues involved whether he would live or die, whether he would be disabled or permanently affected by his injuries, and if he would ever work again.

"Sally, you two finish up," said Taub. "I'm going to talk things over with these two. Thanks Alicia." Taub smiled at the nurse, whom despite her young appearance was handling herself very professionally and he could tell she was providing comfort to Sally. Sally nodded and feigned a brief, weary smile.

Taub turned and led the two detectives around the corner and down the hall a few steps.

"So, what do you guys have?" he asked them. They were both rather burly guys; one had a shaved head with a goatee, and the other had short curly hair and moustache.

"Not much, sir," the bald guy answered, pulling a small note pad out of the pocket of his parka. "Looks like the guy had been out boozin' and ended up at the wrong place at the wrong time. One of the nurses told us his blood alcohol was point zero eight." He looked up for a reaction, knowing this compounded the matter.

"OK," Taub said thoughtfully. As all of this sunk in, he felt a wave of sadness. This wasn't going to work out well for Murphy. Assuming he survived and wouldn't be seriously disabled, there were definitely going to be repercussions with the Bureau.

The other cop chimed in, "You gotta understand, this happened around mid-night in a pretty desolate part of town. There were no witnesses, we've canvassed several of the buildings near the attack, and there are really just a couple of apartments within a reasonable distance. No one heard or saw a thing and none of the area businesses were open."

"We do know he was at a bar called *Sally's*," added the bald cop, "a couple of blocks from where he got knifed. The bartender identified a Polaroid. But he didn't have anything to give us. Your guy came in, sat down for a few drinks, and left. The barkeep said he probably had a few before he arrived, because he remembered him stumbling a little going to the john at one point. No big deal, though. He reportedly talked to another patron for a half hour or so, and then left."

The two men had nothing more to add, and just looked at Taub who couldn't help shaking his head.

"What the hell was he doing? He's a good guy fellas; he's been going through a divorce and I guess maybe he just needed to blow off some steam. Anything at the crime scene?"

"Nothing but his own blood, no one else's, and a holster with no weapon. Nothing else," answered the man with the mustache.

"All right," he said as he reached in his jacket pocket for his wallet. "Here's my card. Please let me know if anything develops. We'll do some homework on his current cases, see if anyone we know might have had anything to do with this, but I think you're right. On the surface, it sounds like the poor guy stumbled into a mugging, a random deal."

The three men exchanged cards.

"One other thing guys, do your best to keep a lid on the alcohol thing with the press. You know they're going to be onto this one in the morning. Let's just spin it for what it was. A random mugging."

"We hear ya," the bald cop said. "And we're real sorry about this. It sucks no matter how it happens, when one of the good guys go down."

They shook hands and Taub turned to join Sally Murphy again. Since 9/11, losing anyone in law enforcement had taken on a special meaning. He felt as though Murphy would probably survive, but the underlying question was had he already been lost? Taub felt a twinge of guilt mixed with his sadness. Had they let this guy slip through the cracks? There was definitely a sense of machismo in any law enforcement agency and most certainly at the Bureau. Murphy would have felt, like the rest of his colleagues, that whatever he was going through had to be kept out of the office. But still, there had been signs. And no one had bothered to ask why.

Sally and Taub waited. They sat silently in comfortable armchairs, and Taub would nod off occasionally but Sally would close her eyes from time to time but never slept. Her mind reeled through the tapes of memories; her marriage through the good years, the admiration her sons held for their father, and even the passionate moments between them, which had become few and far between over the years. It was a selective, euphoric recall, but it is what people do in times like these. As she thought of those times, mixed with the flashes of the slow burn of the marriage in the few years before Elliott left, a feeling of disgust crept up on her, a thought she had tried to repress over and over during the past year and a half of their separation. How had she let this happen?

How had she allowed what was good and right between two people that had loved one another just slip away into the abyss? She rationalized that she had been frightened. Frightened that as the boys left for college and full adulthood, there would be nothing left for her. Her thoughts had danced around this before, during the many sleepless nights and lonely days that followed Elliott's departure. But she never put it together so clearly in her mind, as on this night, with her husband lying on a surgery slab, and doctors fighting to save his life. Had she perhaps not really given him a chance, due largely to the fact that she was so obsessively concerned about her own next move, that she had forgotten about the "us" in their marriage?

Sally began to realize that her preoccupation with her predicament prevented her from seeing the deep dark place where Elliott had drifted. He turned inward more severely than she had ever seen him do, staying absolutely silent through many of her tirades until he'd finally explode. This was followed by more silence for days. This was so uncharacteristic of Elliott. Of course, the drinking that followed was completely self-destructive, and she knew it, but was so wrapped up in her own discontent that she never bothered to notice, much less help him.

The intensity of these thoughts seemed to persist through the excruciating hours of waiting. She checked herself from time to time; reminding herself that guilt was naturally pouring all over her remorse for what had happened to her estranged husband. But there was truth as well. Maybe this horrible event could turn out to be more than just a tragedy; maybe this crisis could prove to be the catalyst for change that they desperately needed. In her exhaustion, Sally consoled herself with that thread of possibility.

At exactly 4:15 in the morning, two weary looking men dressed in light green scrubs, wearing surgical masks hanging around their necks and paper slippers on their feet, came out of the surgery entrance.

"Mrs. Murphy?" one of the doctors asked.

Sally's eyes opened wide, she nodded and Sam Taub instinctively stood up and introduced himself. This time he didn't bother with the gold shield.

The surgeons introduced themselves and the older of the two began, "He's made it through the surgery but it was pretty tough going. He was losing blood internally at an incredible rate, but we managed to get his wounds under control. We had to remove a section of his intestine because it was so severely lacerated and his stomach was essentially cut open. The wounds are all repaired now, but the next hurdle is the distinct possibility of infection. So, he will remain in intensive care for a few days, and if he doesn't have any set backs over the next forty-eight hours, the prognosis is good to excellent that he'll live."

The doctor paused for a moment to give Sally a moment to absorb what he was telling her. "To be honest, it's a miracle he's still with us. I've seen plenty of gut wounds and this one would have certainly been fatal for a weaker person. He's a very tough guy."

"Yeah, he is," Taub chimed in.

"When will I be able to see him?" Sally asked.

"We'll send a nurse down in a few minutes," the other doctor said, "to take you up to ICU. You can look in on him, but he won't be conscious for a few hours. Between the trauma, the anesthesia, and the postoperative drugs, he's going to be out for awhile."

Sally and Taub thanked the two physicians as they turned and left in quick stride to their next emergency. Through the numbing fog of shock, Sally Murphy relaxed the slightest little bit, sighed, and became aware of tears that were streaming down her cheeks. Taub stood next to where she was seated and placed an encouraging hand on her shoulder.

He was silent.

CHAPTER 10

It was almost 2:30 in the morning and "Jumpin' Jack" Horton, as he had become known during his stint in the Sand Dollar Casino, was just rolling back up to his room. His arm was around Rachel, who was now his new best friend, and co-winner of the $147,000 jackpot.

And what an evening it had been.

After defying the one-in-a-million odds of winning the grand master of all the slot machines in the casino, the night turned even more unbelievable, as if winning hadn't been enough. The casino general manager had personally dealt with payment. The machine didn't pay anything directly over $300. Drinks were already free but on top of that, Rachel and Jack were served up a late-night lobster dinner in the finest restaurant in the hotel. An offer was made available for them to enter the high-stakes poker room and all night long people came up to them offering their congratulations. They felt like celebrities.

Standing on the tenth floor, in front of the elevators, there was an awkward moment between them. There had been plenty of hugs and other affectionate gestures throughout the evening but Jack had written it off to the euphoria of the situation coupled with plenty of liquor. Now, after a brief hug, Rachel's head was tilted back, her eyes closed, for she was warmly aroused and expectant of a kiss.

Through the evening Jack had become more and more attracted to the young woman. She knew he was married, albeit unhappily, because he had made that disclosure while they were in the bar. It didn't seem to bother her, but why would it? He hadn't made any moves toward her. But she was full of fun, she seemed to enjoy his company, and somehow they had spent over six hours together without any arguing or nit-picking. It was in complete contrast to his life with Alice.

Jack hadn't thought about what was happening between them all that much, but as they stood there, in that moment of intimate pause, his heart quickened. Not out of fear, or anything negative, but out of desire for this woman. It shocked him, primarily because desire was not an emotion he had felt much of, if at all, in over a decade. In fact, he thought that entire emotional arena had been lost to the years and a lousy marriage.

He leaned down and as rusty as he might have been, closed his eyes, and managed a kiss on her pouty lips. He held it longer than he would have had it been anything but friendly. He felt a rush go through his body, from his head directly to his groin. But as he opened his eyes he looked down and discovered that her eyes were open. Rachel was looking up at him with a look of apprehension which was immediately followed by a sexy half-smile that crept onto her pretty face.

"Hmmm, that was interesting, Jumpin' Jack," she said softly.

"Yeah, well, it was quite a night."

"Let's do it again sometime."

He slowly pulled away and admired Rachel's easy demeanor.

"Sure. Maybe I can get out again tomorrow night," he said with a smile and a wink. "If Alice thinks I might come home with another $75,000, she might just let me out again."

They exchanged a farewell wave, and went their separate ways.

As Jack approached the door to his room a short burst of panic overcame him. He looked behind him and Rachel was out of view, having already turned a corner at her end of the hallway. In front of him, the hall spooled out as a long ribbon of pastels and patterned wallpaper with uniform distances between doors and light fixtures. It was like a dormitory for people escaping from the 'real world.' But there was a certain emptiness to the image that compounded his sudden angst.

The night had been surreal starting with the fact he had the guts to walk out the door in the first place. Then he met Rachel, followed that with the lucky pull of the slot machine, and enjoyed drinks along with a little attention; it was not a 'Jack Horton' kind of evening by any stretch of the imagination. Everything about his existence had become so mundane and predictable that everything that had happened that evening was way out of the box.

Now he had to face his wife and the thought literally twisted his gut into a ball. In fact, with each step closer to the hotel room door, he knew that in one sense, it was a different person returning from the man who had left earlier that evening. He had a taste of excitement tonight, he had laughed with another woman, and in the last few moments, he had even felt long-lost desire. But rather than a pure physiological response, he was actually attracted to more than the prospects of having sex with Rachel. It was also the possibility of breaking out that seemed so alluring to him.

His head had cleared from the alcohol as he had stopped drinking several hours earlier, so he knew his experience wasn't a simple case of "attraction in a bottle." Although there were times he wished that he was a hard drinker to escape from his life, it was never really his thing. No, there was a complicated equation playing out here, and this was all happening for a reason.

Jack hadn't bothered to call up to the room all night long as he knew Alice would figure out some way to bring him down. Odds were good that she would be asleep but he also knew she was a light sleeper and would wake when he came into the room. He decided that he would show her the money and maybe he might even get lucky. With all the excitement and the effect that being in Rachel's company had on him, he was definitely aroused. Despite all of his revelations and his usual disdain for his wife, he still wouldn't mind getting laid.

As he opened the door slowly he saw that a light was still on in their room. He crept in to find his wife asleep, snoring, with a Danielle Steele novel open and her reading glasses still in place on her face. As quietly as he could, he lifted up the book and began to remove her glasses when she woke.

She was startled until she realized it was Jack, and appeared somewhat disoriented as she immediately looked to the bedside table to see the time, which was now 2:37.

"Where the hell have you been?"

"Okay, you're not going to believe this," he said and he sat by her on the bedside, which was very uncharacteristic for him.

"You reek of alcohol and perfume," she said and was obviously becoming more alert. "Tell me Jack. I can't wait. You've been out drinking while I've been stuck up here with these brats. Do you realize the older two dragon slayers just went to sleep about an hour ago? It's been hell." She sat up suddenly and pulled the sheet up over her ample bosom which was already covered by a large t-shirt that said, "Question Everything."

"Well, I met this girl," he said, as he paused for effect. Alice raised her eyebrows momentarily, but was silent. "Anyway, we had a few drinks at the bar and then we went into the casino and just partied and gambled all night."

"Well, that's just great Jack. You should be proud of yourself. That's what family vacations are for—to leave your wife and children, go find some girl, get drunk, and gamble away our money." She shook her head in disgust.

Jack felt a moment of sympathy for the woman. She really was so predictable, though, as he found most angry people to be. He believed her anger wasn't surging because of what he had been doing that night. She was bothered by the fact that he hadn't been around to share in her misery. That he had managed to escape for a few hours and actually had some fun. He decided that he didn't want to play her anymore.

"Actually, I would have been back up hours ago, but Rachel and I …"

"Rachel, is it?" she snapped.

He went on, "Yes, we were almost out of money. I blew all of two hundred dollars."

She shook her head, "Two hundred dollars is two hundred dollars!"

"Let me finish the story. We put our last quarters together for one last pull of the huge slot machine at the entrance to the casino, and we won!"

"Great, did you get the two hundred back?" she responded with a tone of sarcasm and disinterest. She placed her book on the night table and began to remove her harsh, dark framed glasses that made her look even more severe.

Jack reached in his pocket and first pulled out a wad of one hundred dollar bills. He had a little over a thousand less than his original take that was around $74,000. He had taken a voucher from the casino for $70,000 and the rest in cash. He started peeling off the bills one at a time, and dropped them like falling leaves onto her chest. At first she appeared annoyed, but then she perked up.

"How much did you win?" she asked excitedly.

"Oh, a little more than $200. What's it worth to you?" he said with a slight cockiness.

She ignored the obvious intent of the question. "Come on, Jack. How much?"

He continued to peel off bills, he counted, "Twenty-four, twenty-five ..."

"Oh my God!"

He had counted out all the bills, all forty, and he made his move. His heartbeat picked up. Not in the way it had earlier with Rachel, but as it did anyone in anticipation of rejection. Even though they hadn't had sex in a couple of weeks or so, it had been years since he thought she really wanted it. Therefore, he still had to put on a full-tilt campaign.

He leaned down and kissed her on the neck. It had been ages since they kissed on the lips during sex.

"There's more where that came from," he said softly.

She pushed him away, but he noticed it was more of a knee-jerk response as opposed to a solid intentional rebuff.

"I'm sure there is Jack, but it's really late and the boys just took it out of me," she said, almost apologetically. He knew the door was still open ever so slightly. He leaned down again, and when she didn't stop him, he resumed kissing her neck. At one point in what seemed a lifetime ago, this had been an erogenous zone for her.

"I was talkin' about the money. There's more money, Alice," he cooed.

Now she pushed him back from her even harder, but it was in obvious response to his claim of more cash.

"What! More than all this! How much more?"

He gave her a snide look, "How much will it take?"

"Come on, Jack. There's really more?"

"I'll tell you if you close your eyes, hold out your hand, and promise me that if the number works for you, you'll let me have my way with you."

"Okay fine," she said quickly. He knew he had her. "Close your eyes," he commanded and she obeyed.

He placed the check for $70,000 in her hand and she opened her eyes immediately. At first she was silent, and just stared at the hotel's official voucher. "Oh my God," she said in a whisper. "How did you do this?"

"I told you, we won the grand slam of slot machines."

"This is unbelievable."

He stood and dropped his khakis and removed his shirt, displaying his more burnt than tanned coloring, which contrasted the paleness of his midsection. He slid under the sheet, moved in, and quickly it began.

And quickly it ended.

Afterward, Alice lay on the bed still wearing her tee shirt, although it was all she had on. Jack pulled the sheet over both of them and rolled over to face away. She rattled on about all the things she thought she might spend the money on. He, on the other hand, thought of Rachel and the excitement of feeling apart from Alice and the boys, and all that went on earlier in the night.

As he drifted off, Alice chattered in the background, and Jack actually had some anticipation of a new day.

CHAPTER 11

The Caribbean sun rose softly in the eastern sky, and was slowly painting the water with dancing flashes of light. By 7:30, the sky was awake and the sun was slowly lifting high above the shimmering water line. Phil Cassavetti watched every bit of this unfold as he was out on the beach with the faintest trace of dawn's light, somewhere around 6:45, taking a peaceful stroll—as was his habit almost every morning he spent on the island of St. Martens.

His mind had been back in New York and it was more than the sharp contrast in the weather that differentiated the city from his current locale. Back home represented a dark place to Cassavetti right now, where his underground life was centered. The night before he had used gambling, and a few hours with two call girls, and a little bit of booze—all of which served to put the guilt and misgivings away for awhile. But this morning, in the serenity of daybreak, it wasn't so easy.

His underground life was all he had ever known as an adult, but from time to time, he dared to question. Self-doubt involving the family business was an unsettling train of thought for him to endure. But at moments like these, on the heels of "evil-doing" such as the murder of Tony Dimaglia, it was a train of thought that was powerful and unavoidable.

There wasn't anything Cassavetti could do about it; he was in the mob for life. He had risen to an important level, and along with the obvious benefits such as the money and the power, came a blood oath, which was an eternal commitment; it stood above God, above family and blood ties, above *all* else. But nonetheless, at soul-stirring moments like this, he fantasized of escaping. He dreamt of leaving his crime family, leaving New York, and packing off to a tropical island with the shirt on his back and a satchel of cash. But surviving a leap from a tall building would be more certain than burning men with the resources and tenacity of the mob. He would be found and he would suffer a slow painful death. In that case, his death wouldn't be the clean assassination of Dimaglia, which would be considered merciful by comparison.

Eventually, though, he did have a reasonable dream. He hoped to eventually step down from his position as his family's financial officer and his involvement would lessen to that of a consigliore, or advisor. This was years away, probably ten or fifteen to be more exact, but it held promise and was the only consolation Cassavetti could find. Moving forward with that logic, he had to work at icing up, as always, and maximize profits both for himself and his employers. He would continue to conceive new ways of using their significant capital to make money in the legitimate world, and concoct new schemes to defraud and steal in the underworld. This was, of course, a field of landmines. But it was Cassavetti's field.

The morning walk had been therapeutic. In fact, he had come full circle with these thoughts of remorse and doubt. The hotel came back into view on the return leg of a journey that had taken him several miles down the beach. He was feeling better about things to the point of fond anticipation of the few days that lay ahead. It was Saturday and he would return to New York on Tuesday. He wanted to relax, get some exercise, party some more, and gamble. It also occurred to him that he wouldn't mind hooking up with the two girls again, sweet Monica and Nicole.

They had, after all, put on quite a show.

• • •

Jack Horton woke up to the sound of pounding. His first reaction was utter confusion as remembrances of the prior night shot through his brain and he was totally disoriented. Did all of those things really happen to him? But the pounding persisted and as he rolled over he could see that Alice wasn't in a position to do a thing about it. She lay asleep, breathing loudly through an open mouth, and her arm rested on her chest with a piece of paper loosely clutched in her hand. It was the $70,000 check, which he realized she hadn't released since he gave it to her—just before their sexual encounter.

He suddenly heard laughter followed by the pattering of little feet from the room next to theirs and remembered the three boys. He pulled on a pair of shorts, navigated around the bed, and after a quick stop in the bathroom, unlocked the door that separated the two rooms and gazed upon what looked more like the aftermath of a bombing than a hotel room. Furniture had been moved, remnants of last night's dinner were on the dresser, as well as on the floor, and more suspiciously, the sheets had been removed from the beds and didn't seem to be anywhere in view. A continuous trail of toilet paper ran out the bathroom door, meandered about the room, and then out the open sliding glass door to the balcony. A small banner of toilet paper gently wafted about their balcony, suspended by the gentle winds for anyone who might look up to see.

The two older boys froze. Scott, the ten-year-old, was clad only in his underwear, which was strained by his belly hanging over the elastic top. Tim was naked and had what appeared to be ketchup or something rubbed across his chest and face.

"Where's Harry?" Jack asked in a tone that projected his dismay with the scene in front of him.

"Ah," Tim said as he looked at Scott with a mischievous smile, which also conveyed an accusation. He started giggling.

"Shut up," snapped Scott. "We were just playin' around, dad."

It was apparent that Harry wasn't in the visible main area of the hotel room so Jack opened the bathroom door. Harry lay in the bathtub, sound asleep, was covered with sheets, and appeared to be lying on a blanket, his head resting on a pillow. Well, Horton thought, at least the little shits had the decency to make him comfortable.

ANTHONY EDDOLLS

Day four of the Horton family vacation was off and running!

CHAPTER 12

The weekend passed and Elliott Murphy survived. He made it through the critical stages that followed his surgery to repair his wounds from the savage attack two nights earlier. The doctors were encouraged with the lack of complications and it seemed apparent that Murphy was a tough, resilient guy. The nurses were glad to care for him since he regained consciousness mid-morning Saturday. He had been totally amicable and never demanding.

It was now Monday morning and Murphy lay in bed, alone in his room at Lenox Hill Hospital. Saturday had essentially been a blur, but by Sunday he was more alert and that improvement was highlighted by a visit from his two sons, Elliott junior and Stan. They had made a quick trip into the city from their respective colleges and spent a couple of hours with their dad. Sally was in his room most of the day as well. His good spirits contrasted the pain he had to be feeling, but the pain was effectively masked with an intravenous morphine drip that flowed into his veins on a timer; a new dose was administered every couple of hours, automatically.

Murphy stared at the ceiling and he tried to gather his thoughts. He had been sleeping on and off since the previous night, waking as the narcotics began to wear off, and going back under as a new dose spilled into his body. He looked up at the mechanism attached to the IV stand, and at the top, the bag of fluid that contained the powerful drug hung at the ready. An LED counter ticked down the minutes before the next dosing would begin, and as the fourteen minute mark passed, his anticipation for the next dose began to tingle more like anxiety.

For the first time since he remembered waking after the surgery, he began to think about what had actually happened to him. The truth was, he barely had any recollection at all. He knew he had been drinking, alone, and for no specific reason. But those conditions had become the norm for some time. He also recalled the moment he had instinctively felt that something was wrong before the attack. A split second where his senses tried to alert him, the same senses that guided him in Vietnam and that had led him away from danger over the years in law enforcement. Those once-keen senses flashed danger at him on the night of the attack. Obviously though, if he paid attention to the alarm at all, it was too little too late. He took a beating from a doper, was robbed, and almost stabbed to death for a wallet that had less than $120 and a few credit cards.

But what about my gun? No one had really given him any details yet and he hadn't thought to ask. What happened to his weapon? Have they caught whoever did this? It began to dawn on him that he might be in trouble with the Bureau, perhaps serious trouble. Management, the senior agents in the FBI, wouldn't take to the details of his case very well, especially if he lost his gun. It wasn't as if he tripped and fell, or was hit by a car. He was mugged and robbed after a drinking spree. This was not the kind of situation the Bureau liked to see attached to their own. Especially a senior special agent who happened to be heading a team investigating matters of national security. He had to find out about his weapon.

The door to his room opened and his friend and co-worker, Sam Taub, walked in. He was dressed in a well-fitting but plain blue suit, white shirt, and non-descript tie; standard garb for the Feds. Over his arm was draped a dark wool trench coat and in the other hand were several golf magazines.

"Hey buddy, how ya doin'?" Taub asked quietly. There was a hint of sympathy in his voice and a hue of pathos in his face as he spoke.

Murphy feigned a smile and reached out with his right arm, the arm that had the IV in it, and shook Taub's hand. The left arm had a cast on it from his hand to his mid-forearm where he had broken his wrist.

"Thanks Sam. Sally told me you were the one that got the call and drove her in to the hospital. I appreciate it," replied Murphy, clearing a throat that was dry from sleep and drugs. "Would you mind getting me a glass of water?"

"So how does your gut feel?" Taub asked, as he put his coat and magazines down, grabbed Murphy's cup off the bed tray, and filled it from a pitcher of water. "That's gotta hurt."

"Only hurts when I breathe," Murphy smiled.

"You're being brave. Whoever did this to you really cut you up inside. The docs were pretty concerned on Friday night," Taub said, and immediately paused and before correcting himself. "Well, Saturday morning I guess."

"So, does NYPD have anything going on this?" asked Murphy.

"Haven't heard anything new, so I doubt it. They would have called me. I met the two detectives handling the case and they've got very little to go on." Taub paused for a moment as he framed his next question. "What were you doing Murph? Were you just out on a bender or something?"

Murphy slowly turned his head away in shame and looked out at the cloudy sky that peered between buildings from his twelfth-story view. His emotions were in high gear between the trauma and the narcotics. It seemed as though he could start bawling at any moment, which was something he hadn't done since 9/11. He shook it off, figuring it had to be the morphine.

"I guess so, Sam. I was just killin' time, I suppose, on a Friday night." Murphy looked back up at his friend with a sheepish grin. "Guess I was just in the wrong place at the wrong time."

He glanced up again at the numbers on the LED indicator. Eight more minutes remained.

"I understand," Taub lied. "Skinner wants me to fill him in when I get back to the office. We haven't spoken yet, but obviously the whole division knows what's happened. A lot of people asked me to send you their best."

Cal Skinner was the Deputy Director for the New York district of the FBI. Both Taub and Murphy reported directly to him and he reported directly to Washington. Skinner was a good man and Murphy had known him for over a decade. He was one of the management team who had some time in the trenches under his belt. He wasn't someone who did all of his crime fighting in courtrooms and textbooks, like many of the jurisprudent appointees that were scattered at the top of the FBI food chain.

"What about my thirty-eight?" asked Murphy, somewhat reluctantly. He had to know.

"When they finally got to you," Taub replied, "they only found your holster and your clothes. Nothing else. So, the gun is a problem."

There was no shortage of legal and illegal hand guns in the city of New York, but it was rare they reached the wrong hands because the FBI lost them to junkies. Losing a weapon to a bad guy was not a good thing, even under these circumstances. Murphy, even in his painful and drug-hazed state, knew that losing his weapon would cause him some grief.

"Shit," was all Murphy could say. He was really getting anxious at this point. Instinctively he looked up at the meter again.

Taub noticed his gaze and moved toward the apparatus that managed the drip. He turned the bag so he could read the label.

"So," Taub said with a smirk, "they've got you on the good stuff, huh?"

"Yeah. Thank God."

"I bet. Well, get some rest Elliott. We'll get through this. I'll get hold of NYPD and brief Skinner. I'll let him know you're in pretty rough shape and he should go easy. It was a random thing and could have happened to anyone."

Taub looked down at the pale, sunken features of his injured friend. He sensed that Murph's story wasn't all true, and he wanted to pursue that line of questioning. He wanted to ask him how bad the drinking was, or if he thought he had a problem, and so on, but it wasn't the time. The man was in legitimate pain and this incident probably scared the shit out of him. Hopefully it was a wake-up call. Taub left it at that.

"Thanks for coming by, Sam. Tell Cal that he's welcome to visit in a day or two," said Murphy.

Taub said good bye, picked up his coat and left. Just as he did so, and silence crept into the room, Murphy heard a tiny beep from the IV machine. He could see the wheel inside begin to turn and release its nectar into the long plastic tube that led the magic to the needle and the vein. He was transfixed on watching the fluid slithering along its path. He had come to like, with growing anticipation, the mellow feeling of *swoosh* he was about to experience. He shut his eyes and knew that he was within moments of relief. And as the coolness trickled into his veins, he began to feel quite relieved—and so, so groggy. The morphine drip had arrived on schedule, and was doing its much-needed job of masking pain.

Both on the pain in his body, and the burden in his mind.

CHAPTER 13

Two days after Jack Horton and Rachel won the slot jackpot, things had returned to normal for the Horton family. Alice woke up on Monday morning with a migraine and remained in bed with a damp washcloth on her forehead, popping Excedrin. Jack took the boys down to the pool where the two older ones swam in tee shirts. Their bodies were glowing pink from too much sun despite their father's constant efforts to keep them slathered in sun screen. Harry sat cross-legged by the pool playing with some type of plastic alien creature whom he had dubbed his *real* brother. He was talking to the creature in some sort of Martian dialect that he had concocted over the course of the vacation. Jack listened to him with envy; at least he had figured out a way to connect to someone in the family. Harry wasn't really burnt by the sun, but rather quite tan. Jack wondered where he really came from. Very little about the kid fit the family. Had there been a mistake at the hospital?

As the days and hours ticked on, he thought of Rachel more and more. These thoughts were quite foreign to him as it had been years since he had felt desire for someone, other than a passing fantasy over a magazine model, or an actress on TV. He had never yearned like this for Alice, she had just happened. In contrast, he had several crushes in high school and college, and that is what this new wave of feelings about Rachel felt like. It was unsettling to Jack as it made him realize that he had become quite comfortable in his discontent over the years.

He had seen Rachel earlier in the morning but he had his three boys in tow. She had smiled and winked and suggested that maybe he might try to get out tonight. Even though it was the Horton's last night on the island before they returned to New York the next day, Jack told her he was hoping he would have another chance to see her before they left. They agreed that he would try to meet her at the bar around seven and if there was a problem, he would call her. Then he had to dash off and save a potted tropical plant that was being shaken violently by Darth Vader, otherwise known as Scott Horton, the angry child.

For the moment, things were relatively under control at poolside. That meant none or the boys were bleeding or misbehaving in a manner that might risk expulsion from the resort. Jack was keeping an eye on things from a comfortable chaise lounge chair, sipping on a light beer, reading a work-related book—*Actuarial Technology*—and working on his tan.

Since his exhilarating night on Friday, Jack had taken every opportunity to catch some sun and he had even managed a couple of runs on the beach. He had taken a new found interest in his appearance and thought he might even join a health club near his office in Manhattan when he returned.

He knew that winning a jackpot had nothing to do with him, as it was pure luck. And because his lascivious thoughts towards Rachel were probably just infatuation, he tried not to get too worked up about either incident. But what was unusual about the entire process was how empowering that fateful evening had been. Somehow, he was left with the concept of possibility. Perhaps there was more to this life than the prison he placed himself in and maybe, just maybe, he could make some changes that would bring him a little more happiness.

He lay daydreaming on the chaise lounge under the full sun of late morning, but as quick as he drifted into a dream about Rachel, he kept crashing back to earth with jagged-rock thoughts of Alice. If ever there was a woman who epitomized the expression 'ball and chain,' it was her. Over the years, as the marriage became more and more miserable, he would fantasize about her just disappearing or even leaving him of her own accord. In really bad times Jack would fantasize about her dying in a fiery car accident. Yet, he had never before contemplated divorce and as he lay there feeling the sun glazing his flesh, he wondered why. The possibility of damaging three young boys might be one reason, but as he thought about it, he knew they would survive. There was something else, and it was fear. His confidence had been moderate at best ten years ago, and today it was in the tank. Beaten down as he had been, he despised his life with her, yet he hadn't mustered up the strength to do anything about it. At least that had been his dilemma in the past.

These thoughts streamed through Jack's brain with crystal clarity like they were hitting him for the first time. And maybe they were. At one level, he felt disgusted with himself, but on another, he felt exhilarated. It was time for a change, Jack Horton said to himself, and the time was now.

He ordered another beer, perhaps to celebrate this revelation.

Phil Cassavetti was deep into a novel sitting poolside on the last morning of his short vacation. He was relaxed; the guilt and remorse he had felt earlier over the execution of Tony Dimaglia had faded away to nothing more than a passing thought. Not only had time cured his worry, but the on-going company of the two girls and some serious winnings in the casino really helped as diversions. He had managed to take the house for over $90,000, which was his best take ever at the Sand Dollar. Hopefully he would manage to hold on to it.

The book he was reading was intriguing. It was a courtroom thriller, a genre that was his current reading passion. It was ironic, he knew, that someone who lived way on the other side of the law, took such an interest in the law. He could usually relate to the bad guys and he often thought he was learning something preemptive from the legal detail that most of these stories possessed. He was also addicted to *Law and Order* on television, a pastime he didn't share with his associates in the Gallo crime family back home. Nor did he share his penchant for Grisham and Patterson. Hell, he didn't even tell anyone he read.

As the thoughts of guilt faded and the countdown began for his departure from paradise, his mind started focusing on "what next". Aside from overseeing the finances of his family, Cassavetti was also charged with uncovering new business ventures, both legitimate and illegitimate. Basically, he was the 'genius' behind the scams his people perpetrated on the banking business, various corporations, insurance companies, and even the government. Some of his methods involved using the Gallo family's capital to lure a desperate business owner into an association, and ultimately take it over, or to buy real estate from a not so willing seller at a price the seller "couldn't refuse". Sometimes they used smaller banks that would look the other way as cash was laundered as discreetly as possible. They had committed arson many times to perpetrate insurance fraud, and even set up a phone center that pumped various low priced, high risk stocks in companies that were nothing more than smoke and mirrors.

But the Gallo family also owned numerous legitimate businesses as well; a limo company that was one of the largest in the metropolitan New York area, a chain of dry cleaners that was always the cheapest on the block and had put several Korean and Chinese operators out of business. There were also the more passive investments. Cassavetti had created structures that insulated and disguised the Gallo's participation in the ownership of real estate, securities, and several completely legitimate businesses that the family didn't actively manage. They included a medium sized high-tech firm that had needed fifty-five-million when the capital market had dried up for start-up software companies. Cassavetti believed in their concept—spam prevention—and the fly ball investment caught wind and became a home run. The operating principals might have their suspicions about who their majority stockholders were, but on paper it was a Dutch corporation owned by a Bahamian corporation, which was owned by yet another trust that was controlled by a Panamanian attorney; and no one could prove anything to the contrary.

Cassavetti was always on the make, always looking for someone's vulnerability or a window of opportunity that he could capitalize on. And for him, gambling was no different. Tonight was his last night at the tables, for he too would be returning tomorrow. He had been observing several players that he planned to entice into a poker game in one of the private rooms reserved for high rollers. The house would retain 10% of all the winnings and while it sometimes wasn't extremely profitable for the casino, they never lost money either.

• • •

Jack was immersed in a fantasy about Rachel. In fact, he was contemplating a sexual encounter with her tonight while currently keeping an eye on his kids. His son Scott was still in the pool watching two other kids play with a Frisbee when the disc landed in front of him. The boy instinctively lunged toward it, clumsily jumped up in the shallow end of the pool with disc in hand, spun around, and with no concern whatsoever as to where it was aimed, slung it with all his might. Jack was looking towards the pool from the comfort of his chaise lounge and Scott's sudden movements followed by the wild trajectory of the Frisbee caught his attention. It was now on a collision course with the front row of his fellow sun worshipers. He could predict the destination by its flight path, and grimaced. Horton watched helplessly as the Frisbee descended, at a considerable rate of speed toward a brawny looking Italian guy who he recognized from the casino. He was well built, good looking, and there was something about him that was rather ominous. "*Shit*," Horton said under his breath.

Phil Cassavetti had put his book down and behind the shade of his Bolle sunglasses, his eyes were shut as he lulled in the warmth of the sun. His natural olive skin soaked up the pure rays and was in the process of turning his flesh to an even darker shade of bronze. It always seemed to go this way; a day or so before it was time to leave any vacation spot, he always found himself wound down to a state of complete relaxation.

Suddenly his tranquility was shattered by a loud crash, which was accompanied by ice-cold liquid splashing all over his swim trunks and chest. In that blur of a second, something hard bounced off his forehead and sent his $275 shades flying off of his face. Cassavetti leapt up off the lounge chair, his honed reflexes not discounting anything short of an assault from a hit squad, and surprised everyone by jumping several feet in the air.

Horton knew he needed to perform damage control and was up before the Frisbee had even made contact. As he was doing so, he saw the disc bounce off the side table, send the man's cocktail flying as it bounced up and clipped the top of the man's head, knocking his sunglasses off. The man literally flew out of his chair and spun around quickly as though he was trying to figure out what had just happened.

Within seconds Horton got over to the site of the attack, "Hey, I am really sorry," he said, pointing to his guilty son who, like the other two boys were speechless and staring at the big man with frozen eyes. "Scott, you get out of the pool right now and apologize to this man!" Horton snapped.

"I didn't mean it!" the boy pleaded. He was petrified and sunk lower into the pool. His brothers turned and swam in slow retreat to the other side of the massive pool. They wanted nothing to do with this situation.

Horton faced the Frisbee victim, who still had not spoken. "Let me at least buy you another drink." The man quietly went through the process of reassembling his things, picked up his sunglasses and a towel from the end of his lounge chair, and wiped off his hairy, vodka-coated chest.

"Naaaw, don't worry about it. Kids will be kids, ya know. That's why I never had any," said the man. Then he looked up from placing the tall plastic glass on the side table and reached out his hand to the appropriately apologetic father. "Phil Cassavetti. I remember you from a couple of nights ago. You and your wife won playing that big slot."

Horton shook his powerful hand.

"Ah, yeah, that was me except she wasn't my wife." They were both silent for a moment.

"Whatever," smiled Cassavetti. "Looked like a pretty nice haul. You much of a gambler?"

"Naa. I fool around a little bit down here, or every once in awhile I get a chance at a convention in Vegas. But I'm an amateur."

"Why don't you join me for some poker tonight? Bring your girlfriend if she brings you luck. I've got a private room reserved and I'm tryin' to get a few guys together. No big deal."

Jack found there was something alluring about this guy. Something powerful, yet friendly, particularly considering his son had almost broken the guy's nose with a Frisbee. It wasn't Horton's nature in the past to step out, accept invitations from strangers, or to get roped into a card game with someone he didn't even know—but what the hell. He was into stepping out these days.

"I might just do that," replied Horton, knowing that he would.

Horton again asked if he could buy the man a drink but it was refused. Cassavetti told him where he would find the card room; Horton thanked him and apologized again for his son.

Jack left the big man to gather up his delinquent offspring. It was time to take them down to the beach where they were less likely to cause any further bodily harm or property damage. But despite his anger at his son, he was kind of glad the Frisbee incident happened. He was very intrigued with Cassavetti, and wondered if he was seeing the opening of another new door.

CHAPTER 14

As Jack and his boys made their way back into the hotel from their action packed sessions at the pool and the beach, Jack thought about his plan of escape for the evening. He mapped it all out. He would start the ball rolling by suggesting to Alice that they should clean up the kids and go out to dinner at one of the better restaurants in the hotel. This would inevitably start a chain reaction that was as predictable as the rise and fall of the sun. It would be a repeat of the fight they had the other night and at the point that it would start to get ugly, Jack would make an exit and meet up with Rachel. If that didn't work, and Alice defied the odds by being on board to go out, off they would go. Later, when they returned to the room, he would announce that he was going back downstairs at the invitation of his new acquaintance, Phil Cassavetti, to play cards for a short while. No big deal. And if that didn't go over, he was prepared to just walk. At least for the evening.

As his mind secured the plan for that night, Jack and the three boys trudged down the hall to their room. The obscene sounds of inner thighs covered with soaked and sandy bathing suits resonated down the flowery pastel hallway and were accented by the slurping and squishing of soft rubber flip-flops. They carried towels over their shoulders and various sand-coated beach items. Jack carried pool paraphernalia stashed in two canvas bags that held molds for sandcastle construction, Frisbees, empty plastic soda bottles, candy wrappers, and a few sopping wet comic books. Jack was bringing up the rear to ensure one of the boys didn't veer off and end up in a stairwell or housekeeping closet.

They entered the hotel room and Alice was sitting on top of the bed staring at the television, some talk show seemed to have her captivated. For a fleeting moment, Jack felt a pang of sympathy for the woman. There they were on this gorgeous tropical island and she couldn't find a way to extract herself from her misery. Complaints and arguments and talk shows were the order of the day, and it seemed impossible that she would bring herself to step out and leave it all behind. But when Jack heard her begin barking orders to everyone, as if in some auto-pilot trance, his sympathy quickly vanished.

"Get out of those wet suits, hang up the towels, rinse off the flip flops …"

Jack simply feigned a smile, he couldn't wait to put his plan in motion, "So, how about dinner in the nice seafood restaurant?" Jack said energetically as he shut the door to the room.

The boys were the first to react with a series of whining "ahhhhs" and "come on, dads".

"Let's not go through this again," Alice chimed in, as expected. "The buffet has been fine, and even room service is pretty good. It's our last night, let's not complicate things,"

"All the more reason for us to get a little dressed up and have a nice dinner together," Jack said as he continued to smile at his disbelieving wife.

"You're kidding, right?"

Jack feigned a look of exasperation, "No Alice, I'm not. Is it not possible to pull it together and join the rest of the living like dozens of other families are going to do tonight? Maybe if we just turn our attitude around, we might just enjoy it. It doesn't have to be a disaster," said Jack in a condescending tone. He knew how to fuel the fire and he also knew that dinner in a posh restaurant with the boys would in fact be worse than a disaster. It would be humiliating. He prayed this manipulation worked.

And it did.

"Don't give me any of that shit," Alice barked in an argumentative voice. The boys cut through their parent's room and into their own quickly and silently. They might raise hell on their own, but they weren't comfortable in the same room when their parents were arguing. Jack winced for a moment knowing that none of this was necessary, and it was only manipulation to serve his own purposes. But he was determined, so he let the argument escalate for a few more minutes, and when he knew it was past the point of no return, he closed the deal. "Enough. Forget it. You and the boys have it your way, I'm going downstairs later and I'm going to have a few drinks. I met a guy by the pool that invited me to play some cards. You can order dinner up to the room and the boys will watch TV while you read or something. I don't really care," he said quite angrily, which wasn't really his initial intention. It didn't escape her however, and she slammed the door to the bathroom.

Jack knew that the fight could go on and on if he pursued it, so he escaped to the relative safety of the boy's room. He decided he would spend a little quality time playing video games with them before he changed to go downstairs. It would give Alice a little time to be miserable on her own, and besides, it was still early and he needed to kill some time before he met up with Rachel.

After an hour or so of video games on the TV interspersed with an argument here and there over whose turn it was or how someone cheated, Jack had experienced enough fun and it was time to get ready to go. His pulse quickened in anticipation of further sparks with Alice, but as he entered their room he sighed with relief at the sight of her taking another nap. It wasn't until Jack had showered, shaved, and was getting dressed, that she woke.

"So you're really going to leave us again? I guess because you won all that money you think you've got a license to do whatever you want," she said. What stung Jack, even if only just a little, was that she didn't speak angrily. She almost sounded pathetic, which wasn't her style.

But Jack couldn't give in. Rachel was going to meet him at the Cabana bar at seven-thirty. If his plan hadn't worked he would have found a way to call her and let her know what option "B" was going to be. But he was going forward with his original plan, and just needed to steel up and keep moving toward the door.

"Winning the money's got nothing to do with it. But who knows, maybe I'll get lucky again and come back with another twenty grand. Seemed to work for you last time," he said with a snide smile.

"Fuck you Jack," said Alice, unimpressed by his innuendo. "Don't come in here at two in the morning expecting anything out of me this time. I don't care how much money you win."

Oh well, that was okay, jumping on her again was *not* part of his plan. "You don't need to worry about that," he replied, and let it lie.

He was energized with the prospects of meeting up with Rachel and interested in getting to know this Cassavetti guy. He seemed to be successful, had two drop dead gorgeous women following him around everywhere, and was seemed quite intelligent. After all, he had mentioned he was never married.

Jack felt relatively confident that his last night on the island of St. Martens would be one to remember. Now, he just needed to get out the door without any further misery from his angry, pathetic wife.

CHAPTER 15

It was early evening and Elliott Murphy was again staring at the machine by his bedside. The timer counted down the minutes before the machine would dispense what had now become Murphy's liquid mistress; Lady Morphine was her name. Forty-eight hours after regaining consciousness, Murphy was convinced that the machine went into slow motion the closer it got to the programmed release time. He drifted in and out of agony as he waited. There was physical pain, no doubt, but he also craved the wave of relief that the morphine delivered to his brain as well as his body. His thoughts would slow down when it came, and somehow the gravity of his horrific situation would be reduced to nothingness by the overwhelming sense of drug-induced peacefulness.

Elliott gazed over at his wife who sat in a comfortable armchair by the window in the stark room. Her trim reading glasses were perched at the end of her slender nose and her gentle auburn hair was pulled back in a loose bun exposing the pleasant and attractive features of her face. Age had been good to her, at forty-six, she looked ten years younger. Even the last few years—which had been the toughest—had not robbed her of her youthful appearance.

He wondered for a moment what he was doing with his marriage. He remembered without exception in the years before all the problems, Sally was at his side during times of need. He tried to string logical thoughts together, but he wasn't sure of anything at this point. Between the symptoms of trauma, the drugs, and the many unknowns, any attempt at serious thought ended up muddled. He swung from dread to euphoria, and it had not slipped past him that there was a corresponding relationship between the schedule of his morphine drip and his state of mind at any given time.

Even though he was agitated and craving that blessed relief, he was still admiring his wife. There was nothing muddled about that image, and he was glad she was there. The thought of going through something like this without her was somewhat terrifying, and for a moment, the thought of following through with the plan and finalizing the divorce seemed like a leap into the abyss. He wondered whether his mixed feelings were due to his weakened and vulnerable state or some broader cosmic wake-up call of serious proportions. Regardless, as he looked at her now, he wondered what on earth he was doing with his life. He left Sally behind, holed up on his own in the apartment, cut himself off from any kind of meaningful life for over a year, and barely paid attention to his two sons, in whom he'd invested everything just three or four years ago when he put them through school. He looked at his wife with deep fondness one moment and then felt helpless and afraid over the consequences of his 'new' life, the next.

All in all, his mind was a mess, his body was wracked with pain, and he faced an uncertain future. He tried his best to shut off the thoughts of uncertainty and regret and fear. But he couldn't. It was only as that familiar electronic beep sounded and the drugs flowed into his body, that anything made sense. His body was becoming rapidly addicted to this powerful opiate upon which his mind was so dependent. He simply loved the feeling of checking out.

Sally put the book down on the windowsill, sat back in the comfortable chair, and closed her eyes for a moment. In addition to the novel, she had been reading magazines, doing crossword puzzles, and taking the occasional cell phone call from a friend or relative inquiring about Elliott. But for her, this tragedy screamed about the depths to which Elliott had sunk. This never should have happened, and wouldn't have, had he not felt so alone that he had to be alone. Sally wondered if, perhaps, they had never split, or if he hadn't started drinking, and on and on. She couldn't help feeling an element of responsibility.

The split had been his doing but she saw it coming and let it happen. In her own discontent, she was blinded by selfishness and convinced herself that the separation made sense. She ignored the signs of his unraveling and did nothing to intervene. She saw a therapist briefly, right at the time Elliott moved out, and he told her that she wasn't responsible for the actions of her husband. She had to worry about herself, he told her, and begin exploring who she really was. Now she sat in her husband's hospital room, his aching body bandaged because he was wounded and beaten and bruised. Monitors were attached to his chest, IV's dripped fluids into his arms, and the gravity of the scene and the images and the memories made her realize what big mistakes they had made.

Elliott had always been her Rock of Gibraltar. He was hugely confident as a young man and very serious about his pursuits, and demonstrated these traits in both his career and his pursuit of her. He was relentless in their courtship. They met in Philadelphia shortly after he returned from Vietnam on a blind date set up by her cousin. Sally had recently broken up with a young man she had dated since her first year of college, and ironically, had watched him drift away from her as alcoholism slowly began to rule his existence. Elliott appeared on the scene around that time and he was polar opposite of that. He was strong and sober, intelligent, athletic, and at a time when some of the young men returning from Southeast Asia were resentful and shell shocked, Elliott was together and motivated.

Their courtship was swift, and for a brief time, she felt things were happening too quickly. But their relationship blossomed at the same time Elliott was recruited by the FBI, and from his first posting at Quantico where he attended the FBI academy, they didn't want to be apart. Three months to the day after meeting one another, Elliott asked Sally's father for his daughter's hand in marriage, and a month and a half later, they were wed.

From their early beginnings it seemed as though they were living a worthwhile, productive and meaningful existence together. First as a couple, and then as parents when their horizons broadened and the boys came along. The babies arrived one year apart and gave them intense joy and challenge, all wrapped up in two little bundles that contained more than they could ever have imagined. Sally gladly played the role of the stay-at-home mom and Elliott was good about focusing on his sons, despite long hours and the occasional assignment that took him away from home, sometimes for weeks at a time.

Through the children's high school years Elliott was very involved in their lives, helping them train for athletics and encouraging their academics. He was very much in tune with them, and as he moved along into his second decade with the Bureau, his seniority allowed him a little more vacation time, not so many ten-hour days, and his posting in the Manhattan Division didn't require as many out-of-town trips.

At that zenith, the bottom fell out. It was subtle at first, but in the span of a few months after their oldest child left for college, things began to change. Elliott's distancing behavior would have shocked Sally to the core and driven her to panic, had it not been for the fact she spun into her own malaise. Simultaneously, they both seemed to drift their separate ways.

But now, as she opened her eyes again to watch her husband breathe quietly in blessed sleep, she knew it had all been a mistake. She had ridden a roller coaster the last two years, lost with no control over the rise and fall of the moods. And it wasn't all Elliott's doing. Despite Sally's stepping out into the world and proving her ability to master independence, and even after making quite a decent living as a teacher and then in the real estate business, there was always a wee underlying voice of conscience that told her it wasn't right.

She used to watch other couples and compare the ways in which people drift apart. Usually there was some dramatic event, like an affair, or in one case where a neighbor's husband had been arrested soliciting a prostitute in Manhattan. The woman filed for divorce two days later. But with Sally and Elliott there was none of that. In fact, she hadn't started seeing anyone since the separation and was confident it was the same for Elliott.

A doctor walked into Elliott's room, and she welcomed the interruption to her soul searching. He was a rather adolescent-looking resident who had been appointed by the hospital to be Elliott's attending physician. The surgeons were phasing out of the picture over the last couple of days as Elliott's recovery was reasonably assured. So, Dr. Tannenbaum, a rather hyper thirty-something bald man that looked as if he was fifteen, was calling the shots, so to speak.

"Hi folks," he said loud enough that Murphy stirred and awoke to the heavenly glaze of his freshly administered load of narcotics.

Sally stood up. "Hi doctor. Any word on his tests from earlier today?" she asked.

"He's doing extremely well. Still no infection," he said in short spurts as he began to pull the sheets down to inspect the bandages on Murphy's stomach and shoulder. He looked up at Sally for a moment. "We'll keep him on IV antibiotics for another day or two, same with his pain management. By Wednesday he can begin taking oral medications, and we'll probably try to introduce soft foods tomorrow."

Given the fact his wounds were to the stomach and intestine, Murphy hadn't swallowed anything but water since he had regained consciousness. He was receiving his nutrition through his plastic pipelines.

"How much longer will his pain last?" Sally asked. This question prompted Elliott's eyes to slowly move in his direction.

"It should begin to subside quickly over the next day or two. Internal injuries like these can be severe and dangerous, but if we stitch them up correctly and there are no infections, the patients usually heal up pretty quick. Movement will be our next challenge. Maybe tomorrow we'll try to get him out of bed."

Elliott listened while his wife, or soon to be ex-wife, maybe, and his doctor— who appeared to be younger than his son—discuss the state of his body. At the present moment, Elliott was more interested in the state of his mind. In the ebb and flow of his relationship with Lady Morphine, he was riding the wave of whoosh and really didn't give a shit about much. But from what he could make out, it sounded like he was doing okay. He was ready to take another nap and let them figure it out.

CHAPTER 16

Several hours of the evening had flown by in a flurry of laughter, a couple of dances, and plenty of booze. Jack and Rachel were acting as though they were on their first date—the kind of date that actually works, and the magic of mutual attraction lights up the night.

Jack felt electric. Something had clearly enabled him to take this leap of defiance and pursuit of his own pleasure, having left his family ten stories above. He made sure that he had reinforced himself early in the evening with several shots of tequila and three or four beers. The buzz was a boost to his confidence and helped him decide that whatever might happen tonight was destiny.

Jack and Rachel had a place at the Cabana Bar and the same bartender who served them Friday night was taking care of them again. Rachel was dressed in a colorful bikini top and a white cotton skirt that flowed down below her knees but was slit up the side, way up the side. Her bikini top was skimpy, didn't leave much to the imagination, her breasts were a highlight of her shapely five-foot two figure. As the night drove on, Jack became more and more entranced with her body.

Hell, he was entranced by the entire package. She was intelligent and witty and maybe those were her most appealing attributes. She had a keen sense of humor and Jack was able to be funny with her, which was a nice change from his cynical day to day. Around Alice, a good lambasting seemed common, but kidding around rarely took place. The laughter with Rachel was definitely a turn on. "So where to next, Jumpin' Jack?" she asked as the music quieted, the band took a break, and the speakers reverted to low volume calypso music.

"Well, this guy I met by the pool invited me to play some cards. You can come too, of course. I wouldn't mind playing a couple of hands," he said and paused to look at his watch for effect. "But that's not until ten or so." It was only 8:45. "You want to grab a couple of beers and take a walk on the beach?"

"Hmmmm, sounds romantic," she leaned up and purred into his ear.

Jack didn't waste a moment. He called to the bartender for a couple of light beers and off they went. As Jack passed one of the outbuildings by the pool, he grabbed a couple of towels. She raised her eyebrows suspiciously, but then grinned.

"Always be prepared! This is the new motto of Jumpin' Jack Horton," he said proudly and they both laughed.

They left their shoes under a table before taking one of the walkways that led down from the pool area to the beach. The night was spectacular; accented by a three-quarter moon that lit up the Caribbean Ocean under a canopy of stars that were ablaze, and glimmering in every quadrant of the winter sky. It had cooled to around seventy degrees and occasionally a gentle breeze wafted in off the water.

They were both a little buzzed from the Cabana cocktails and they laughed and walked along the water's edge. The gentle waves rolled up and slid above their ankles and the night couldn't have been more perfect—until Rachel finally broached the inevitable.

"Jack, I really am having a good time with you, but tomorrow you leave and we can't forget you're taking your wife and kids with you. What's the deal? If you're so unhappy, why don't you do something about it?"

Jack took her hand.

"Maybe I'm ready to do just that. You know somehow we get into a rut and feel like there's no way out of something, and maybe we feel so lousy about ourselves that we don't think we're worthy of anything else," he said, and gazed out over the water. "This trip has really been something though. It's been a cross between the worst of my marriage, and a taste of a very different life beyond. And it's not just the money we won, or me lucking into a couple of nights with a beautiful woman."

Jack gently squeezed her hand and she responded by resting her head on his shoulder for a moment. Their pace slowed measurably.

"But what about when we get back. I mean I'd like to see you but I'm not so sure I'm interested in an affair. I tried that once," she said with an odd tilt to her head. "Well, maybe twice. But they end up painful and empty and I think I like you a lot. I don't want to go through that again."

He stopped and placed his hands on her shoulders.

"In all these years of misery, I haven't so much as been attracted to anyone else. I really don't know why, but I'm definitely interested in you. So much so that I've broken plenty of my own rules just to be here with you tonight. Let's just enjoy the time we have, and we'll see what happens down the road."

Before she had a chance to say anything he drew her close, leaned down, and kissed her softly and with as much finesse as he could muster. Aside from their brief kiss the other night, it had literally been ages since he kissed anyone with true passion instead of simple animal lust. Both of which he was experiencing at the moment.

She responded and soon their mouths opened and tongues mingled softly. Jack's heart was racing, his head felt light, and not only was he intensely attracted to this woman, but for the first time in over ten years he was actually with someone else. It was as though he had crossed over some mystical divide and been emboldened to keep going.

He slowly pulled her away from the water line up onto the beach and they giggled softly as they tried to remain kissing as they moved. Jack finally pulled away for a quick moment to lay down the towels.

They were at least a half-mile away from the hotel now and no one was in sight. Quickly, the few clothes they wore came off in fits and Jack felt arousal pulsate through his entire body. Not just in his groin, but also in his hands, his chest. He was lit up everywhere, and Rachel seemed turned on, too. Unlike his wife, who could lay flaccid and receive him, and usually with obvious disinterest, Rachel moved and touched and moaned and sought him out with great intensity.

They progressed in their lovemaking, under a moonlit sky, swiftly and with great hunger. They both needed what their efforts, and their bodies, would yield.

And then it was over. Not too soon, but long enough that their hunger had been fed.

Jack was staring up at the sky, lying exposed, and feeling spent. Rachel had draped her skirt over her mid-section and joined him in watching the stars. It was Jack who spoke first.

"Well, that was incredible. I felt like there was somebody else inside of me that had been hiding out for years and just appeared for the first time in, well, forever!"

"I felt it," she acknowledged enthusiastically. "Whadda ya say we jump in the ocean."

Rachel didn't answer but sat up quickly, flung her skirt back onto the sandy beach, and raced towards the inviting water, naked and proud. Jack watched her for a moment, admiring her rear end, and thought how impossible all of this would have sounded four or five days ago. He always thought that cheating on his wife would be filled with guilt and remorse, but he realized at least for this moment, only minutes after a climax with another woman, he felt neither. He believed this wasn't about cheating on his wife, but was more about breaking free. It was only the beginning.

Jack hopped up and followed his nubile little playmate. She was already in the surf and gracefully stroking through the shallow rolls of the in-coming tide. Jack swam up to her and they embraced, Jack feeling electric everywhere and the feel of her in the warm water was more erotic than anything he'd ever known. Their embrace led to even more passionate kissing and fondling and he rather quickly brought Rachel to another climax while they wallowed in the ocean.

Jack felt as if he had died and gone to heaven.

Suddenly their solitude was broken as they realized someone was calling to them from the shore. The light of the moon still lit the sand like a distant spotlight, and Rachel could see that it was her lesbian roommates.

"Oh my god, it's Laura and Maureen," she said quietly to Jack. "How did they find us?"

Before she could answer, one of the women shouted out, "What are you two doing out there?"

"Ahh, well, if you really want to know ..." replied Rachel sarcastically, but with a smile on her face.

Jack wondered if he had ever known anyone to smile as much.

The two women faced each other and spoke quietly and Jack couldn't hear what they were saying from thirty or forty feet out in the rolling water, but obviously they decided to jump in, and Jack watched in disbelief as the two women quickly tossed off their minimal clothing and ran towards the water.

Jack and Rachel looked at each other, tentatively, but Jack said, "I guess anything goes tonight."

"Okay, but I'm not into the girl-girl thing. At least not tonight, so don't get your hopes up."

"Right now I'm not hoping for anything more than what we've just had. You're wonderful," he said and he kissed her again. He felt a little embarrassed with himself, for he wasn't used to sounding like a Hallmark card.

The other two women swam out into the surf, but respectably kept their distance. They obviously had a plan of their own.

Rachel slowly pulled away from Jack and said, "Why don't we give them their moment in the surf. Let's head back to the casino, see if we can win a few more slots, and I'll even watch you play in that card game for awhile. How did you meet this guy, anyway?"

"My kid hit him in the head with a Frisbee and he ended up inviting me to play poker. He looks like a high roller. Kind of gangster looking."

"Hmmm, sounds intriguing."

They shouted over to the other two naked swimmers and let them know of their departure from the ocean. An arm rose above the surf, and waved a silent response in the soft moonlight and shimmering swells.

CHAPTER 17

Rachel and Jack entered the casino around nine-thirty, so they still had a little time to kill before Jack was to meet up with Phil Cassavetti.

The casino was clanging with the usual evening bustle. The slots were dinging away; guests were laughing and shouting out their victories over the one-armed bandits. Most of the patrons were on their way to getting drunk, if they weren't there already, and the ever-dominant calypso music bumped along softly in the background. As usual, the casino floor was populated with scantily dressed women and slicked-down, ready-to-party guys.

The booze flowed very freely and Jack Horton was ready for another belt himself. He was done with tequila and beers so he decided to shift to vodka on the rocks. Rachel ordered white wine. The waitress delivered their cocktails to them as they sat at a row of dollar slot machines.

Out of his winnings from the other night, Jack had given Alice about five hundred dollars cash and kept the rest himself, about $2,300. He had also taken the $70,000 casino voucher and deposited it with the cashier the morning after he won it. It would be accessible if he needed it for the poker game, but Jack had instructed the cashier to make sure he was the only one that could withdraw anything against it. He didn't want Alice to get her hands on it.

He watched Rachel as she pulled the slot in her cute little skirt, and he enjoyed watching her breasts heave about in her flowery bikini top as she energetically pulled the handle. For a moment, he imagined a life that included her. Sure, he had thought of life without Alice a thousand times over but now he began to introduce Rachel as an ongoing figure to this train of thought. It was a pleasant fantasy but he was a realist; a girl like this probably wouldn't be interested in him back home. But who knows, the way his life had been turning this last week, perhaps anything *was* possible.

But what if he could keep this up? He knew that he had been a different person around Rachel and perhaps this was the real Jack finally being set free. It may have been timing, it may have been the moon; it really didn't matter to Jack. The bottom line was that he felt liberated and happy and it tightened his gut to think of it ending.

They moved around and tried a few other machines, but with no great success. A few minutes before ten o'clock, they decided it was time to find the poker game. As they left the bandits, Rachel had actually won a few hundred dollars, and Jack had blown seventy-five. They made their way to the back of the casino, past all the rows of clanging slots, to the card tables. Most of the blackjack tables were filled, a crap table had a crowd around it as someone was obviously on a roll, and finally they came to a couple of rooms that weren't closed in completely, because fully-private games weren't permitted in the casino. These two rooms had signs in front, on metal stands no less, which read "High Stakes Poker—Invitation Only."

Jack looked in the first room and didn't recognize anyone, and when he peered into the second game room, he saw Cassavetti. Flanking him were the two girls Jack remembered being with him with the night he hit the jackpot. It was the night that began his personal catharsis. In addition to the three of them, there was another couple and two single guys at the table. There was something about this crowd that was a little edgy. Jack found it exhilarating and was more than a little surprised that he was intrigued by this, rather than intimidated. These guys were pretty serious about their gaming, and Jack knew that right away. But he was ready to give it a shot and attempt to extract some of their money.

Or hand over some of his, whatever.

Jack was emboldened with his new attitude, and he got off on this new experience. He wasn't normally shy, but he wasn't outgoing either. He had been so ambivalent about everything in his life he never really tried to step out of his envelope. But tonight, it had begun with Rachel, and now it was time for this crowd and the next evolution.

He went directly up to Cassavetti, as the game had obviously not begun, and the players were having some light conversation and sipping on drinks.

"Hey Phil, Jack Horton," he extended his hand. Horton was impressed with the clamp of Cassavetti's handshake.

"Jack Horton," Cassavetti paused for effect, and gave Horton a grimacing look. "You're the guy whose kid almost cut my head open. That little mother fucker!"

There was a sinking silence for a moment.

Then Cassavetti burst out and laughed, "Hey, kids will be kids, right?!"

Jack gazed down at Rachel for a second with a wide eyed look that inferred relief.

"That would be me—father of the little motherfucker!" he said and threw his hands up in an admission of guilt, to everyone's enjoyment.

"Well, I'm glad you're here, Jack. Who's your friend?"

"This is Rachel Stern," Jack said proudly.

Phil introduced the others. There was a guy named Steve who was from Miami and spoke with a thick Brooklyn accent. Harold appeared to be the oldest at the table, and he was from Chicago. And the couple was from Buffalo, and called themselves Terri and Al. Cassavetti also introduced the two women accompanying him as his 'friends,' Monique and Cheri. Neither spoke when introduced. Monique nodded and Cheri just smiled. But they looked incredibly exotic and Jack could only fantasize what went on between the three of them.

Although he figured that he had a pretty good idea.

They sat down and Phil announced that they would be playing five-card-stud poker with a minimum buy-in at a thousand dollars.

Rachel took a seat behind Jack and he noticed that Terri from Buffalo also sat behind her husband. The two speechless "friends" of Cassavetti's, Monique and Cheri, remained standing by a side table on which sat several bottles of liquor and ice. Jack felt a bit of a rush as he could tell that this was serious business to the other men sitting around the table. For a moment a flutter of hesitation spilled over the question of what the hell he was doing, but it was certain that this game would be a thrill, and he had recently become quite the thrill-seeker.

On the other hand, Jack was no stranger to cards. He had grown up with parents that loved to play and they taught him well. They would periodically keep him up until the early morning hours playing poker with some of his friends when he was a teenager. He remembered that his parents would drink and smoke and laugh till the sun came up, and even now, on the verge of such excitement, Jack still savored those times and clung to the memories. Jack chuckled under his breath. Outside those selective memories, there wasn't exactly a lot of laughter around the Horton house in those days, as his parents had been pretty distant and self-absorbed. Though in some ways he was just another mouth at the table, there were times when his parents demonstrated interest in him.

Even though Jack had developed a knack for cards, it was something he never pursued outside the games with his parents and a handful of times in college. Still, he could track the deck using natural ability, intuitively sense the odds at different stages, he knew how to hedge bets, and open the throttle when the time was right. Typically, he went home from those college poker games with everything he came with, and a few bucks more.

Just as the first hand of five card stud was being dealt, a young man in a suit who was obviously one of the floor managers, popped into the room and walked over to Cassavetti.

"Anything we can get you, Mr. Cassavetti?"

Cassavetti had silver reading glasses on and was examining his hand. He didn't look up.

"Just make sure I win tonight, Ron."

Phil Cassavetti was obviously no stranger to the casino.

There was a tentative chuckle around the table as the game began with the players dealing from the anxious side of the deck. Jack could feel the adrenalin in the room silently pumping, and felt his chest tighten with the same process.

With a silent nod, Jack asked the floor manager for a discreet word to arrange for more chips than his cash on hand would provide. He felt himself role playing. *The big hitter.*

Young Ron, dressed sharply in a suit, came around the table and leaned down to Horton.

"I've got a credit with the cashier," Jack whispered, "would you mind getting me, uh; let's say five thousand in chips? My name's Jack Horton, room 1005."

Ron nodded that he understood, and was off.

"You'll need to take a marker from me for a minute," Jack said to the group, trying to appear nonchalant as the game was on the launching pad.

No one spoke, but Cassavetti nodded.

Jack assumed they would consider this fumble was due to a lack of experience. This could work, he suddenly thought, to his advantage.

The first round of cards were dealt, the first bets made, and Jack's little high-stakes adventure was underway. But watching poker is a lot like watching a staring contest. If you don't love it, it gets old in a hurry. An hour later, Rachel told Jack she was ready to go. After chump-change losses through a couple of hands, Jack had hit a nice pot with a third king on the last card, and was up over seven thousand dollars. Jumpin' Jack Horton wasn't about to leave. Rachel said she understood and indicated she would track down her friends and maybe go to the disco. Jack said sure. He was on a roll.

By one in the morning, two of the other players had left the game after losing a huge pot to Cassavetti. They left because they bet the farm on strong boats and neither of them could beat Cassavetti's incredible ace-high straight flush. It was down to Harold from Chicago, Cassavetti, and Jack.

Horton was up over $25,000, Cassavetti appeared to have even more than that, and Al from Buffalo was still in the game but trailing in chips. After a short bathroom and refreshment break of a few minutes, another game was started, and three more hands were dealt. Jack's hole card was an ace of spades. A good start. When his first face card was dealt, the ace of hearts popped up and he almost wet himself. Not a bad start for a hand of five card stud. His ace was the high card showing so he opened the betting with the maximum to test the resolve of the other two players. It's what's known in some poker circles as sitting in the cat-bird seat.

As they got to the last card of the hand, the pot was huge, Jack held a winning hand, he knew it, and he decided this would be it. He forced a look of concern over his cards, but it was thin bravado as he had been betting the moon on his pair of aces anyway, because it had matched up with his pair of tens. They had to figure he already had a strong hand, probably three-of-a kind, and didn't need the last card. Jack simply maintained his perfect poker face. He also knew that Cassavetti was staring him down, sizing him up as he had been most of the night. He didn't care and he didn't flinch. Cassavetti was showing a low pair and the fact that he'd stayed probably meant he had three of them. Nobody could figure out why Harold was still in, as he didn't look like he had much. There were no other aces showing, which gave Jack hope.

Jack's raise was matched by both of the other players and the tension over the last, critical card began to rise. The dealer's hands moved in a flash of professional coordination and out flew the last three cards to the table, face down. Jack's ace showing coupled with his pair of tens was still the high hand showing as the three men carefully looked at their secret last card. Cassavetti's face didn't twitch. Al's lip curled and cigarette smoke slowly exited his nostrils and wafted over the table, much like his chances of winning were also going up in smoke. Jack looked at his card, and to his great and wondrous surprise he'd amazingly hit a third ace. Full-boat, aces over tens. In a five card stud hand, aces over tens don't lose very often.

"I'm going to make it ..." Jack said, as he opened the betting with yet another maximum stack of chips, "or break it on this one, boys."

Cassavetti smiled, shook his head, and called the bet.

"Shit, I'm out," Al said in disgust. "I couldn't buy a decent hand with a blowjob."

Cassavetti stared at Horton for an uncomfortable moment and then slowly grinned.

"Well, I guess that does it then," Cassavetti said. "It's show time." Jack laid down his cards and exposed the incredible hand he'd been dealt. Cassavetti shook his head again, tipped his head as a show of honor to the winner, and laid his cards face down over the three cards he had showing. He was beaten.

Jack could've taken a hit on that last hand, and been left with a measly two pair. And if his glamorous host had hit on the last card, he would've lost with his precious aces.

But he didn't.

In fact, that pot alone was worth another fifty-five grand, so Jack walked away with a total approaching $80,000. Including the $73,000 he won the night before, his total haul would be over a hundred and fifty grand, which was more money than he had in his savings and investment accounts. And this windfall had been accumulated in less than a week. *This was the life*, Jack thought. Just maybe he'd found his niche.

The odd thing was that under normal circumstances he would have felt guilty. But he didn't. He felt like was he was in the twilight zone and needed a drink. He also wanted to find Rachel. Despite this incredible run of luck, he hadn't forgotten about her and wanted to see her before the night was over.

"Phil I gotta thank you for letting me play. I obviously had a good night, and now I need to try to find Rachel."

Through the night, there had been a little bit of small talk. It seemed that camaraderie had developed through the evening.

"Hey, no problem. Come on up to my suite if you track her down and we'll have a few drinks," Cassavetti suggested. "The room number is fifteen hundred."

"Let me see if I can find her first. She may be with a couple friends." "The more the merrier," Cassavetti winked.

Jack shook hands with Cassavetti, and then with Harold from Chicago. He nodded to the speechless Monique and Cheri who had spent most of the evening sitting in a corner, having quiet conversation, and doing their nails.

Jack first took his chips to the cashier and had them added to his account. He had the clerk issue a check for the entire amount, including what he had left from the jackpot. It was in the amount of $153,000. He shook his head as he stared at the check before putting it in his wallet. *Incredible*, he thought to himself.

The time was now after two in the morning and he was going strong. He was pumped up over yet another big score and focused on two things—finding Rachel and getting a drink. Once he reached the disco both goals were accomplished with ease. He spotted the girls, Rachel and her two girlfriends, walking off the dance floor having just danced with one another. A waitress walked up to their table just as they all converged. He ordered a bottle of Krystal champagne and, as a first order of business, told the three of his big win. Then he invited them up to Cassavetti's suite.

"There's something about him that's sinister, don't ya think?" Rachel giggled. She obviously hadn't stopped with the cocktails.

"I dunno. He's a little mysterious I guess. What do you think of those two women who were tailing him around everywhere?"

"What two women?" asked Maureen, one of Rachel's lesbian friends.

As soon as the champagne was finished, they headed up to Cassavetti's suite. When they reached the right floor, Jack immediately noticed there were far fewer rooms on this level. It was the VIP section and each room had a name like the Sundown Suite, or The Cabana, and when they reached fifteen hundred, the name on the door read *The Presidential Suite*.

"Wow," Rachel said with her patented smile.

They stood in front of the ornately-carved wooden doors and Jack rang the doorbell. His paltry room, Jack observed, didn't have a doorbell.

Cassavetti opened the door and inside were the two women along with Harold from Chicago and yet another pretty face, another girl who didn't have much to say but giggled a lot. She didn't look more than twenty in contrast to Harold. He must have been sixty. Al and Terri from Buffalo had also rejoined the group. Apparently they had won on the craps table after losing at cards and were feeling a little more festive than before.

Music drifted though the huge, opulent suite and an assortment of liquor and food adorned the bar. What a spread, Jack thought. This was right out of the *Rich and Famous*.

Everyone drank and laughed and, in general, had a good time. Cassavetti gave Jack a hard time over taking his money; Rachel's gay friends seemed intrigued with Monique and Cheri, and Rachel discovered that she and Terri had worked for the same investment bank, and even more coincidentally, as administrative assistants.

Several cocktails and an hour or so later into the wee hours, Jack and Cassavetti ended up on the balcony overlooking the Caribbean. The view, with the moon still casting a pale light on the surf, was incredible. With drinks in hand, the two men chatted easily.

"So, ya said you're in the insurance business?" Cassavetti asked.

"Yeah, since college. Going on fifteen years now."

"You specialize in anything?"

"Commercial real estate," Jack said almost apologetically. "Nothing exciting."

"Well, it's a living?"

"I dunno. It supports my family, we got a house on the island," Jack said, referring to their home on Long Island. "And we can afford a vacation and drive two cars. I guess it's a living."

"You know, we have a few buildings. Maybe you might be able to get us a better deal on our insurance?"

"Who's we? If you don't mind me asking," Jack said, but as he spoke the words he instinctively felt he might be going where he shouldn't.

"No problem. I manage an investment portfolio for some associates," Cassavetti responded. "No big deal. We have some real estate and a couple of companies."

Jack reached for his wallet and pulled out a business card.

"Well," Jack said as he handed Cassavetti the card, "if you decide to call me, I'd be happy to take a look at your properties."

Cassavetti took the card and nodded. He placed it in his pocket without looking at it.

They were both silent for a moment, idly looking out at the water. No new topic surfaced and they stood there in silence just soaking up the scene.

"What time is your wife expecting you back?"

As Jack answered the question, he knew it was time to go.

Jack rounded up Rachel and the lesbians and they said their good-byes. Once they arrived back at the tenth floor, he gave quick hugs to Maureen and Laura, and once again, he and Rachel were standing in front of the elevator bank.

He pulled another card out of his wallet and handed it to Rachel.

"I know this is awkward and maybe now isn't the time to talk about it, but I want you to know I want to see you again."

Rachel wasn't leaving for a few more days, whereas the Horton brood was leaving the following afternoon.

"I've had a lot of fun with you, Jumpin' Jack. But I'm not so sure it would be a good idea."

Jack's heart skipped a beat.

ANTHONY EDDOLLS

Rachel continued, looking up at him with glassy eyes. It was now almost two-thirty in the morning and she had consumed plenty to drink through the course of a long night.

"But I will call you. Maybe we can have lunch," she said as she put her arms around Jack and kissed him. Despite their exhaustion, and level of inebriation, the kiss was deep and passionate.

The embrace, at least for Jack, sparked hope again.

But the kiss broke off eventually, and they said good-bye.

Jack once again stood before the door of doors. Behind it loomed the reality of his life, forgotten briefly for another night, but now before him. It didn't take very long for him to be brought crashing back to earth from his high-flying adventures.

He quietly opened the door and from the darkness, in a voice that was more hiss-like than human, he heard, "Where the fuck have you been?"

Jack felt his skin crawl at her anger. Perhaps he deserved some sort of a rebuff, but it seemed his disdain for the woman was building by the minute.

It was time to go home.

CHAPTER 18

On Tuesday morning, although he could hear plenty of commotion out in the hallway, Elliot Murphy was alone in his hospital room. He was wide awake and staring at the stark ceiling. It was a bright day outside and the light bathed the room that was small and crowded with his bed, a few chairs, and the medical equipment that remained. Noticeably missing was the morphine drip.

His doctor had been in earlier and explained that he had been on the powerful narcotic long enough, and in fact, indicated Murphy was probably mildly hooked. He had recovered sufficiently to switch to an oral painkiller, and the doctor had started him on something called Oxycontin. He had just been given his first dose and he sure as hell hoped it would kick in soon.

In the meantime, it was just him with his thoughts and an anxious feeling that he figured was the beginning of withdrawal from the morphine. And of course, there was still plenty of physical pain, but he knew he was healing quickly and was scheduled to be out by the end of the week. Sally had offered to take him home for a week or two, or until he was completely recovered. Elliot accepted.

But there was another reason for his anxiety. He was afraid, and it was only the last 24 hours that he started to recognize the fear, and figure out what it was all about.

It finally became clear to him that this mess had a lot to do with his drinking, if not everything. No question about it. The attack would never would have happened to him had he not been out drinking, hanging out in a neighborhood in which he didn't belong, blind drunk, and with no way to defend himself. And it wasn't just this incident. He recalled many other times over the last few years where he drank himself to sleep, drank to forget, and drank himself into oblivion, over and over again.

He had told himself on other occasions that he needed to slow down or set some limits. He was able to live up to some commitments, but others waned fairly quickly. Before the attack, there hadn't been any major problems which caused grief at work or social embarrassment.

But was that assessment even true?

What about Sally? What about the boys and a life of over twenty years, left on the New Jersey side of the tunnel, like his home life could simply be forgotten in work and drinking. Was this the life he wanted while giving up his family?

Eventually, the new pain medicine started to take effect and Elliot began to relax and he told himself he would give this matter some thought later. There had to be more to his life than that. He wouldn't have just given everything up, or traded it in so cheaply. Or had he?

He slowly started to drift off as the medication prompted a pretty swift kick of drowsiness. He heard a faint knocking at the door but couldn't manage to get his head off the pillow to see who was there; it was as though he was paralyzed. He managed to glance over and see that as the door slowly edged open, the cast of a young black man was imposed in the light streaming through the door. He was unable to speak, unable to move and he felt terror sweep over his body. To his horror, he recognized the man as his assailant, he couldn't remember his face or much else about him, but he knew it was the man who had inflicted these painful wounds upon him just a few short days ago.

Murphy focused everything he had at willing his body to move, to raise his arms or just open his mouth to scream out, but it was futile. Then the man raised his arm and clutched in his hand was the SIG, Murphy's stolen pistol. Murphy's gaze moved back up to the man's face and although the features were unrecognizable, he could see a broad smile on the man's face. Then he saw the trigger finger clench inward and heard a loud, thunderous bang. For a millisecond, he knew it was over. It almost seemed to make sense, but then no sense at all.

And then he woke to a completely different image, that of Cal Skinner, his boss.

"Murph, you okay?" Skinner asked. "I didn't mean to startle you."

Murphy shook it off, as quickly as he could in his drug-dazed state. It had been a dream, a nightmare, one that unsettled him to the core.

"Ah, yeah. I'm fine. Guess I was having a dream or something," Murphy managed, feeling disoriented and grasping to get his wits about him.

The tall, fit man with a head that was adorned with distinguished gray hair, came over to the bed, and donned a sympathetic grin.

"Elliott, how the hell are ya?" Murphy cleared his throat.

"I'm doing okay, Cal," answered Murphy. He and Skinner went way back and were on a first name basis, other than the occasional formal situations.

"Taub has kept me posted throughout this thing. I hope he told you I've been concerned. One thing to take it in the line of duty but even worse that it was just some random punk. Sounds like you're gonna make it though. I guess this was a bad stroke of luck," he said as he gently shook Murphy's left hand, which wasn't bandaged in a cast like his right.

"Guess I was just at the wrong place at the wrong time."

"I'll say," Skinner said convincingly, which allowed Murphy to feel instantly relieved. "These things happen, old buddy. We can talk about it in detail later. In the meantime, I understand Sally has been here quite a bit. I'm sure she's been taking good care of you."

"Yeah, I think I'll be going home with her for a week or so. They don't think I'll be able to go back to work for at least that long."

"You bet. Take your time recovering. We've got things covered."

The two visited for ten or fifteen minutes, talking comfortably about kids and sports but avoiding work and the incident, especially the missing gun. Murphy was relieved to keep it light.

"Anything new," Murphy asked, unable to resist a little bit of banter that was work related, "with the Al Hamid situation?" Al Hamid was a charity Murph had investigated and discovered that they were a front for an Al Quaeda cell.

"It's moving forward," was all Skinner gave up. "I gotta run Murph, give us a shout if you need anything, and I'll stop in again before you get kicked out of here."

"Thanks Cal, I appreciate it."

Skinner left and Murphy was again concerned. He was a senior agent and Skinner loved to talk shop. Why had he been so brief on the Al Hamid question? Maybe he had just been in a hurry, he rationalized, but it struck Murphy as strange.

· · ·

Chaos reigned between the two rooms that had been occupied by the Horton family for the last week at the Sand Dollar Resort & Casino. The boys were finally told to just sit in front of their TV and stay out of the way, as their father packed for them.

Alice was silently doing her packing, still furious over the previous night when Jack didn't come back to the room until almost three in the morning. Her anger seethed through every pore of her body and it was obvious. Jack decided to steer clear, so he pulled his bag together while she was in the shower and remained in the boys' room, slowly packing their stuff to avoid contact with hostile troops.

Normally, Jack would break the silence with some groveling. That typically involved an apology, a reasonable explanation, or in extreme cases, a plea for mercy. Usually, these scenarios took place over the most ridiculous infractions. On one level, Jack could see why she would be angry. But Jack didn't care any more; in fact, he almost enjoyed it.

The astounding thing was that in the short span of this trip, he had come to realize that he could escape this miserable life with Alice and more importantly, that he had the resolve to take action. He could leave, he could start over, and he would prosper. If he felt any remorse on this beautiful Caribbean morning, it was that he had wasted years of his life with this angry troll of a woman.

It was time to move on.

• • •

Phil Cassavetti sat out on his fifteenth story balcony and was reading Sunday's New York Times and smoking an expensive cigar because there were no restrictions against them on the island. He was already packed and ready to go, and the limo was scheduled to take him to the airport in about an hour. He wasn't apprehensive about returning to New York, despite the killing of Tony Dimaglio. He was ready to get back and make some money. Phil was looking on both sides of the law, considering a couple of legitimate deals, in addition of course, to a couple of new scams as well.

He was relaxed, tanned, and sexually spent. Monique and Cheri had nearly killed him over the past four days, and he was leaving with sixty-two thousand more dollars than he brought with him, despite his loss to this insurance guy, Jack Horton.

But on the positive end of that night, he had made a contact in the legitimate world. Horton would be good for a few more card games once they got back to the city, and who knew how useful he'd be in the future. He kind of liked the guy. He was somewhat quiet, but certainly had some balls, as evidenced by his playing at Cassavetti's poker table, winning, and screwing around with some babe while his wife and kids were upstairs in their hotel room. He admired the guy's moxie.

Cassavetti had already decided he would invite Horton to join a small group of men who enjoyed a standing poker game every couple of weeks. The others were legitimate guys, too, which made it all the better for Cassavetti. There was a lawyer, a banker, and a doctor in the group. Hell, there was even a judge in the circle at one point. Horton would be invited to sit in, and like the others, legitimate or not, he would be drawn to the game with the hopes of winning more and winning big. It was always a high stakes game.

Considering his sharp insights into human nature, Cassavetti was confident the mouse would go for the cheese, and he would get his money back.

He always did.

CHAPTER 19

It had only been a week since Phil Cassavetti returned from his short vacation. In that short time frame, his world had rapidly become very complicated. It was amazing how life was like that, Cassavetti thought to himself, as he sat in his high back leather chair, feet up on his polished cherry desk, smoking a freshly lit Epicure #2 from a box that one of his admiring underlings had given him. Once a month the associate would give him a box of the illegal Cuban cigars along with his cut of the man's prostitution ring. Cassavetti's end was typically thirty to forty grand.

Behind Cassavetti, the bustle of the last remnants of morning rush hour crawled up and down Park Avenue. The view was facing uptown from the fifty-eighth story window of his office suite in the Metropolitan Building, above Grand Central Station. Outside of his spacious office there was a small reception area that was occupied by his assistant, Maria. A leather couch, a chrome and glass coffee table along with her secretarial desk filled the space. The metal sign in the outer hallway next to the entrance to the suite read, "Mid-America Trading Group, Inc." although the name had absolutely no relevance to the business that was actually conducted behind the door. The door itself had wood veneer but was actually made of reinforced, bullet-proof steel. Access was controlled by electronically controlled double deadbolts that essentially made the suite impenetrable. A security camera flashed a view of the entrance to a monitor on the credenza of Cassavetti's desk.

Although building security was very tight, it was the good guys that Cassavetti was worried about. In the event of a raid by the Feds, or the local cops, for that matter, he would need time to shred whatever incriminating documents that might be lying around at the time—but he didn't leave himself vulnerable to that situation unless he absolutely had to. A paper shredder sat next to his desk.

The problems began early that morning when he received a call from an associate in Queens, a captain in his family. This guy had a pal whose brother-in-law worked at the medical examiner's office. Apparently, over the weekend they were called out on a matter that involved the discovery of a human head. It was floating along the shore of the East River, about a half-mile from a water treatment plant. A convict on a work detail from Rikers Island saw it bobbing merrily in the murky shallows just a few feet from shore contained in a plastic bag that buoyed the head in the water. The con and the rest of his crew had been cleaning up trash on a small stretch along a waterfront park. The prisoner took his spiked pole, used for picking refuse off the ground, and stabbed it into the floating head, carefully picked it out of the water and hauled it on to the ground.

Realizing what he had fished out of the river, he proceeded to vomit directly onto the human remains.

Between the stab gash and the vomit and the decomposition, the evidence was fairly compromised. But nonetheless, the forensic cops had already made the identification and Tony Dimaglia's wife had been called in to undertake the gruesome task of a positive ID. The head belonged to Anthony Dimaglia, Jr., the same thief and traitor the Gallo family had paid outside contractors to dispose of by inconspicuous means.

Those fucking Irish hit men, fumed Cassavetti. *This was not supposed to happen.* And they would soon regret the mistake that had been made.

Regardless of this development, Cassavetti dropped his feet down from his desk, and switched on his computer. He had two monitors mounted on the corner of his desk, one that constantly displayed stock and bond quotes along with other financial indexes. The other monitor displayed whatever he might be working on at the time. He checked his email to look at his latest messages.

Along with some junk and a message from his sister, he had a cryptic message from a banker in the Caymans that confirmed a transfer he made to a Swiss account for three million dollars. He also had a reply to an email he sent to Jack Horton, the insurance guy. 'Yes,' it read, 'I would love to join you. Let me know where and I'll be there. JH.' Cassavetti had invited him to a private card game to be held on the upcoming Friday night.

Cassavetti smiled. Mice and cheese. Even though the share of Horton's winnings from St. Martens he had paid amounted to less than six grand, Cassavetti never liked to lose. Especially to a chump who was on a lucky streak. He would win his money back and then some.

He also had a message from primo@xray.com. This note was from Al Carino, the consigliore to the Gallo family crime boss Salvatore Ruggiero, known to all as the Don. As he read the message, Cassavetti's blood began to boil. Word had already reached the top. The message simply read, "Understand an old acquaintance has turned up. Let's discuss. Soon."

Cassavetti stared at the message.

He knew what would have to happen. For starters, he would contact Andy Vassallo and put a contract out for the Irish hit men. It would have to be done immediately. Today. If they heard of the discovery of Dimaglia's remains, they would know they were in danger and disappear. He would also tell Vassallo to get word to Dimaglia's widow. She would be told in no uncertain terms that if she uttered one word related to the Gallo family, her future would be in serious jeopardy. She would obey. She would be told that the hit happened because her husband was a thief. Long ago, she would have accepted the consequences of marriage to a mobster. It was part of the deal. If she wanted to see the light of another day, let alone receive the financial support she knew would follow from the family, she would have to keep her mouth shut.

So, despite the perfect winter morning that was unfolding out of his 58th story window, the day was becoming very dark. It was a day, just like the other when Dimaglia was hit, that he would not soon forget. For the second time in just over a week, Phil Cassavetti would bring an end to life.

But this time, it was a little easier decision. He had never met these idiots, but they obviously deserved it, and finally, they were Irish. Cassavetti had no choice because if they were arrested and faced the death penalty for an execution style murder, they would sing like jay birds. No doubt about it. Besides, their agreement was to completely dispose of the body. Whatever they had done hadn't worked. The next thing he could expect was to find out that the cops had found a leg or a couple of feet bagged up and floating around in the river. Tony Dimaglia's remains were to be weighted down in heavy plastic bags, never to be seen again. Obviously, someone had fucked up.

He typed out a brief response to Carino that simply replied, "On my way."

He picked up the phone and called his driver, Jules, and told him to be at the entrance to the building in thirty minutes. He knew he had woken the man and figured that after he dropped Cassavetti off, as usual, he found a parking spot close by and dozed off to sleep.

Regardless of the urgency this matter held, Cassavetti still had several items of business to take care of. He had two positions in high tech stocks that he thought might be ready to sell. Earnings reports were coming in on several of the major players in the tech sector this morning, and he felt certain that the smaller companies he owned shares in would get a boost. He began to work the internet to obtain information, view the reports, and watch the market move.

Within ten minutes he had a handle on it. The earnings for Dell Computers came out higher than expected and Cysco was right on the money. The surge began and the two stocks he held, both suppliers to the big manufacturers, took a leap. He placed his sell orders on-line and would find out later if he hit his mark.

Next, he needed to make a call. He had placed an offer to buy three, five-story apartment buildings in Queens. They were perfect for demolition and redevelopment into condos. They were in the Chinese neighborhood where prices for condominium apartments had been skyrocketing. The seller was asking an arm and a leg for each building. Cassavetti hoped that his broker would convince the elderly oriental of the fact that Cassavetti would purchase all three buildings simultaneously, pay cash and close within two weeks. The broker was apparently in a meeting, so he left a message.

He grabbed his black leather trench coat and told his secretary Maria he would back later in the afternoon.

Jules picked him up in the Town Car and they drove to Brooklyn. Carino and Ruggierio kept an office behind a coffee shop in a middle-class neighborhood. It was very unpretentious, a throwback to the days of social clubs and mob joints in complete contrast to Cassavetti's office suite on the fifty-eighth story of a very prestigious Park Avenue address.

As they arrived in the blue-collar neighborhood and approached the restaurant, Jules pulled the car off the street into an alley behind the row of small store-front businesses where the Sardinia Café was located. The coffee shop had previously belonged to a relative of a predecessor of Ruggie-rio, and eventually the entire building was bought by one of the cloaked corporations the family controlled. The coffee shop itself was leased to a couple of first-generation Italian immigrants. They gratefully accepted the opportunity to have their own business in exchange for their discretion and silence when it came to the activities and comings and goings of the individuals who frequented the back.

The Gallo family had held court in this small back-office for over forty years. Decisions had been made that cost men their status, their fortunes, and their lives. Strategies were decided upon that would steer the way to the empire they now controlled. Today Cassavetti knew that he would meet with Carino only. As an underboss, Cassavetti would not be subject to a rebuke and therefore it would not be appropriate for anyone else to be in attendance. Hired killers had screwed up, and Cassavetti was obviously not at fault. But it would be his responsibility to cover tracks and to ensure the situation didn't get any worse.

Cassavetti hopped out of the Lincoln and knocked on the metal door. It opened immediately and Al Carino greeted him. Carino was tall but wiry; he had the pallor of an undertaker and on this day, seemed to have dressed like one. We wore a dark blue suit with a blasé striped maroon tie and black oxford shoes. Al's style was in stark contrast to Cassavetti, who wore a very dapper hound's tooth jacket over a black turtleneck with black, pleated wool slacks and, of course, finished it off with his black leather trench coat. Together they epitomized the old and the new; they were two generations of mobsters, but with only one code to live by.

"Phil, good to see you son," said Carino with a broad, sincere smile. "Salvatore sends his regards and as always, wonders when you are going to settle down and take a wife?" The consigliore, or advisor, raised his hands in the air as if to say, "I'm just the messenger!"

"Some things never change Al," replied Cassavetti and they embraced as was their tradition.

Carino sat behind a large oak desk that was as old as the building it occupied, which was at least sixty or seventy years. Cassavetti took a comfortable leather side chair.

"We're sorry to bring you in on this Phil, we know you're busy and by the way, you continue to make Salvatore proud. Your earnings are almost what we're pulling off the street," Carino said, referring to the family's income from drugs, theft, loan sharking, and prostitution. "But the fewer people involved in this mess the better and considering Dimaglia's hit was your order, we need you to clean this one up for us."

"I understand, and expected that. And please convey my apologies to Sal," Cassavetti responded. "I will contact Andy Vassallo, take out the Irish fucks that screwed this up, and let the wife know to keep her mouth shut. Then we will just have to see where it goes. But, I bet not far."

"We have been so effective at keeping a low profile for some time now, it would be a shame to allow ourselves to come under scrutiny again," Carino said, shaking his head with dismay. "We can't afford this Dimaglia thing to get blown out of proportion. Obviously the cops know that it was a hit, but they don't know who called it. I'm sure they're assuming it was a rival family, or maybe even the Russians. Dimaglia was flirting with them, too. But it's imperative they don't find out it was us."

"I understand."

"You take care of it, Phil. I know you will do what's right."

"You can count on it."

"So tell me, what are you looking at these days?"

"Ah, a little more real estate. We have an offer in on a few apartments. I'm moving a little money around in the market. I'm also working a new banking relationship in the Caymans. Might save us a few points."

"You with the modern world of finance! It was so much simpler thirty years ago. We made it, we spent it, we put the rest in a vault, and the Feds were none the wiser."

"Not so anymore, everything has a trail. Everything."

"Well then, tell me what you're buying personally," the older man asked. Carino never hesitated to glean a stock tip or investment suggestion from the family's money wizard, Phil Cassavetti. The matter of Tony Dimaglia, deceased, was now concluded, although Cassavetti stuck around for ten or fifteen more minutes and jabbered away with the aging consigliore. Cassavetti was held in high esteem by the older regime and they were fascinated by his grasp of finance and the new global economy. Carino enjoyed every chance to talk about this brave new world with their moneyman.

Cassavetti kept up while the small talk continued, but in the pit of his gut he felt a gnawing sensation, just as he had the night of Dimaglia's execution. As he chatted away with Al Carino, after they had decided that two Irish lives would need to be ended, it was as though they had decided to walk the dog. It was just that matter-of-fact.

But it wasn't.

CHAPTER 20

For the first time since Elliott Murphy had left the hospital he was alone and awake. He was at the home he now considered Sally's, and the very one he had left eighteen months earlier in Cedar Grove, New Jersey. Sally had insisted that he stay with her for a week or so to recuperate. She was being very attentive and helpful and seemed to always be around when he was up. But for the moment, Sally was gone for a few hours to show several houses to a young couple from out of town and he was wide awake and feeling very uncomfortable.

He had not allowed her to give up the master bedroom and they certainly weren't going to share a bed, although they both privately wondered why not. He was in Elliott junior's bedroom and his emotions and senses were running high. He was in pain, the pills just didn't seem to get the job done so well versus the morphine, and on top of that, he ran the gamut of emotions from nostalgic euphoria to feeling covered in a cloak of dread.

He thought of the boys growing up. It couldn't be helped as he gazed around the room and viewed all the memorabilia of a young man's wonder years. He saw sports awards and trophies, pictures of famous athletes, class photos, and even a few posters of female rock stars. All very touching but, at the moment, more torturous than anything else.

On top of that, just being in the house was inconceivable. One moment it would feel like he never left, and the next, as though he had to escape. And just as his mood had swung around in the hospital, synched with the injection of narcotics, it seemed the same thing was happening now with the pills.

So with his wife gone and the realization that the drugs not only relieved the pain but also lightened the load in his head, he decided to double the dosage. He reached over to the nightstand and popped another one, which was on top of his last pill taken an hour earlier than prescribed.

Then he took another. Why not, he decided, he knew he could handle it considering his size and all the morphine he had consumed without a problem.

As the Oxycontin ramped up, so did his euphoric recall. He thought of the better times and didn't dwell on his dilemma nearly as much. It didn't take any time whatsoever before he decided this was all meant to be. Divine intervention had brought this terrible tragedy upon him in order for him to recoup what he had lost. And he'd lost a lot, if you consider his family, his home, his dignity, and even the love of their dog, Sam, a lot.

He couldn't wait for Sally to return home and tell her what he had decided. He had made a mistake. A terrible mistake. And they were meant to be together and happy and married and all that stuff. It was meant to be, and he just had to tell her.

By the time Sally Murphy returned home she found her husband sound asleep. After twenty years of observation she knew how the man slept and there was something odd about the way he was breathing. She instinctively attempted to rouse him. He eventually roused, but only after she violently shook him awake. His eyes attempted to focus, but his look was glazed and he appeared to be completely disoriented. Sally was panicked with a sudden fear that something was terribly wrong.

"Elliott, it's me. Are you okay?"

She was sitting on the side of their son's twin bed, holding her husband around his large shoulders after having sat him up in bed.

He mumbled something she couldn't understand and it was driving her crazy trying to figure out what was wrong with him—when it dawned on her that he was having a bad reaction to something.

"Elliott, try to focus. What is wrong with you, sweetheart?" The "sweetheart" just slipped out.

He seemed to focus in on her with eyes that were red and glassy.

"Sally, I never should have left," he said in a slur, almost sounding drunk. "I love you."

The words struck her hard. She hadn't heard him utter those words in many years. The last week and a half had been incredibly difficult on her. It wasn't just seeing someone she still loved near death, but the situation had also rekindled so much in her that she thought she'd put away. She had begun to wonder about the possibilities, or perhaps she never reconciled the split in the first place. She'd been living in denial so the impact of the words, never having been spoken since their troubles began, resonated uncontrollably.

She shut her eyes for a brief moment and got hold of herself.

When she opened them, she saw that his head was lilted over, his eyes had shut again, and she was holding his limp body.

"Elliott!"

Again, his eyes slowly opened to half-staff.

"Please try and wake up, what is the matter?"

"I'm okay," he mumbled again. "Maybe just a little bit nauseous."

She laid him back down, quickly scurried into the adjoining bathroom, and grabbed a small, circular wastebasket. This was a routine she had completed many times through the years as a mother, and the flashbacks of this same drill for the benefit of one of her boys came back to her.

When she dashed back into the bedroom, Elliott was attempting to get himself out of the bed. She helped him as best she could, but he was six foot two and one hundred ninety-five pounds, and her slender one hundred fifteen pounds was not much use.

"I think I'm going to be sick," he said with obvious discomfort.

And with Sally walking behind him, hands under his arms to help guide him along, her patient made it into the bathroom and immediately threw up.

She didn't flinch, and while he was bent over the commode, she dampened a washcloth and filled a small water glass. She hadn't forgotten a mother's way of bringing comfort. Who knows how many times she had dealt with nausea, but this was different for some reason. What was making him sick? It hadn't been a problem before. Should she call the doctor? One thing was for sure—she had never had to convalesce anyone through a stab wound and the accompanying internal injuries, so maybe there was something going on here that required medical attention.

She managed to get him back into bed, and almost immediately he seemed more alert.

"What is wrong with you, do you have any idea?" she asked.

"I think it's the medicine," he groaned. "I may have taken too much."

"What do you mean, too much?" she was confused. "You took more than the prescription called for?"

"It didn't seem to be working."

"Is the pain that bad? You seemed to be doing so much better."

Suddenly, he seemed agitated. It almost frightened her, especially in contrast to his earlier mutterings of love.

"Look, I'm the one with the pain, Sally. Please. Just let me be. Christ, you never change."

The words stung. But something was going on with him. Even through the separation and subsequent encounters, he was never rude to her. Unless of course he was drinking, then Mr. Hyde would rear his ugly head.

As the words passed his lips when Elliott issued the rebuff to his wife, while she stood there with a cool washcloth in her hand, having just escorted him to the john to vomit, he instantly wished he could take it back. He felt totally out of control. Helpless against his own mind. A swell of emotion, of remorse, came over him and he felt a vaguely familiar physical response flow over him from a hidden place. It was something he hadn't felt since God knows when.

He began to cry. And after those gates were opened, he sobbed uncontrollably.

• • •

At first, Sally Murphy was dumbfounded. She couldn't comprehend what was happening to the man. But then, instinctively, she again sat by his side. She held him, patted his head, and with great wisdom, said nothing. She just held her husband as her own tears made tracks down her cheeks. Elliott had broken. As sure as she knew the scent of his body, the touch of his hands, or the chiseled sculpt of his face, she knew he was in grave trouble.

And she knew he needed help.

"It's going to be okay, Elliott," she said finally. "We're going to find someone to help you."

They both sat on the bed for some time, in a silent embrace where two people appear almost as one. Two people who had spent a lifetime together, and perhaps in the process, both had lost their way. And just maybe, they were both on the verge of finding a common direction again.

CHAPTER 21

As the work day ended, Jack Horton began to feel a sense of dread similar to that which he had felt virtually every night since he and his family returned from vacation. It was brought on by the simple fact that he had to go home.

He wanted to meet Rachel for a drink, or coffee, or anything at all after five, but she said she had to work late. He thought she seemed a little cool on the phone when he spoke with her, however. He didn't have any recent experience with this, and certainly none in the last fifteen years, but he instinctively knew he should slow things down a little. After all, they had just spent the entire weekend together.

Jack had gone home Friday night and announced he was going to have to work the following day. This was met with ambivalence on behalf of his three boys and annoyance on Alice's part. She usually insisted on Jack taking care of the boys for the better part of each Saturday so she could have some time on her own. But for the Saturday in question, Jack could have cared less. He had a plan, and nothing was going to stop him.

He woke up at the crack of dawn Saturday, drove his car to the train station, and was in the city by nine. He went directly from Grand Central to Rachel's apartment and they didn't come out until dinner. Even then, it was Jack who left for a few minutes and returned with Chinese food. Jack felt like a teenager and was amazed at his stamina and virility. The entire experience with Rachel had provided a truck load of new sensations and feelings, most he'd lost touch with long ago.

After dinner, Jack called Alice from his cell phone. He told her that the project he was working on wasn't complete yet, that he was tired, and that he'd decided to grab a hotel room in the city. And that was that. Alice said a quick goodbye before she could unload, but Jack knew she was pissed. He didn't care.

Sunday was glorious. Despite the fact it was still late winter, the temperature zoomed up to the low fifties, the sky was a sharp blue, and there was nothing more than an occasional breeze. They walked the streets of the upper west side, where Rachel lived, and eventually strolled into Central Park. Jack couldn't think of anything that would make him feel better than he felt that day.

He finally made it home Sunday evening, and he was right; Alice was pissed to the point of fuming. It had nothing to do with where he was, for she would never dream he was capable of having an affair. It was all about being solely responsible for the boys all weekend. It didn't seem to matter that she didn't work and had six hours of her own time each and every day, and rarely did anything with it. Or that Jack usually managed the boys on his own much of the time when they were all together. Jack knew this was just a prime excuse for her to be pissed. He just fell back on the one solid beam of support he had which was his unflagging indifference to anything she had to say.

But now it was Monday. He had absent mindedly muddled through the workday, and it was time to go home. He was exhausted from the weekend, worried about the tone of his conversation with Rachel, and dreaded going home to his wife.

He left his office on Forty-sixth at Third Avenue, walked to Grand Central, and boarded the 5:45 to Syosset, Long Island where his empty suburban life awaited.

He sat by the window of the train and stared at the ancient walls and struts and beams that flashed by as the commuter hustled through the tunnel beneath the East River. The scenes zoomed past in a blur, and he registered nothing. How could all of this have happened so quickly? His life had been turned upside down in the matter of a week; it felt completely bizarre He had won a ton of money gambling and had cheated on his wife. But more importantly, he had stoked fires within that he didn't even know could be lit. He was crazy about Rachel, and at the same time the disdain for his wife and his life had become so real that it was something he could no longer continue. In a few short days he had become passionate about escaping his world with Alice, but it was building to that point for over a decade.

He knew what he had to do. Leave.

So why did it take an affair to bring all this to the surface? Why had he settled for this misery for so long and even played into it? Even his boys were a pain in the ass, his job was completely monotonous, he knew he had no true friends; hell, he didn't even like the family dog much. The thought of attempting to change within the marriage, for the two of them to seek counseling and do the things married people do when they are in trouble, wasn't even an option. He was obsessed with Rachel, miserable with Alice, and all he wanted was out.

The train continued to jostle along, the bridge and tunnel crowd slowly thinned out as the train made several stops along the way, before finally reaching Jack's stop. He made his way out to the Park and Ride, hopped into his car, a Jeep Cherokee, and headed home.

Instead of listening to WNEW, the all news channel, as he had a thousand times before, he found something different. Classic rock.

The rebellion had begun.

• • •

Alice could not believe what she was hearing.

She knew that something was up because her standard game wasn't working. Instead of groveling for forgiveness, Jack was uncharacteristically standing his ground. He returned late Sunday from wherever he had been all weekend, and they hadn't spoken. Tonight, she decided, he would pay.

But nothing she dished out seemed to affect him. In fact, he was being downright belligerent. This was through the course of the evening as they ate leftover spaghetti, practically held the boys down to get their homework done, and finally threatened them with life imprisonment to get them into bed. Eventually the boys caught on as well, and realized that their father wasn't taking their shit. And once the boys were down for the night, it was just the two of them.

She looked up at him as he had come into the television room, stood where he would block her view of American Idol, and glared down upon her. He grabbed the remote and turned down the volume on the show he thought was trash and entirely ridiculous, and a typical waste of her time.

"Listen, I am done with all of this," Jack said firmly.

"What do you mean?" was all she could say.

"You, our marriage, this house, all of it!" She was stunned into numbness.

In three seconds, it all flashed in front of her. She too was miserable. For years now there had been a part of her that was waiting for this shoe to drop. She knew it, yet she had been helpless to do anything about it. Or she hadn't wanted to. And now that she was faced with it, it felt inevitable. Inescapable. She instantly knew it was over for her and Jack, the image of her alone with the boys raced in front of her mind's eye, and she couldn't register anything but anger.

But she wasn't furious because she didn't want the breakup to happen; she saw red because that was who she was.

"I see. So you have a little fun on vacation, our family vacation I might add, doing who knows what with who knows who, and you decide to continue the party. I don't know what's happened to you, but don't think you're going to leave with one damned thing."

She stood up and got in his face. She was certain she could break him, but was surprised to see he didn't flinch.

"Alice, I really don't give a damn anymore. You can have it all. I'd rather start all over with nothing in my pockets, than go on like this. Take it. Take the house, the boys, take it all."

He turned away from her but it was obvious from his look that he backed down not out of fear, but out of disgust.

He was serious. This was really going to happen. He had crossed the line and there was no going back. Suddenly she felt panic course through her entire body as she felt herself slipping into a deep abyss. Yes, she was miserable, but she was also very dependent, or perhaps co-dependent to use contemporary vernacular. How could she manage everything alone? The weight of it all was too much, it overwhelmed her, she turned up the volume to the television, and watched as some American Idol fool with no talent decimate a Barry Manilow tune bringing the tears to her eyes that flowed down her weary face. It was time to face the reality of her miserable existence, head on.

CHAPTER 22

From the living room of Phil Cassavetti's thirty-second story condo, the city lights flickered in the frigid winter night. The temperature had dropped again after a warm weekend, and visible from a generating plant across the east river plumes of heavy steam billowed up into the night sky, crystallizing in the sub-zero air.

His view was to the southeast from a corner apartment that featured expanses of glass to ensure virtually every room had a spectacular view. From this high vantage point, after he was alerted to the first of the 9/11 attacks, he had witnessed the second American Airlines jet plow into the side of Tower Two of the World Trade Center. Then, over the course of the next few hours, standing fixated in a spot with a perfect view to the south, he watched through binoculars as both towers eventually collapsed into rubble. As the dust and debris shot up into the air, the horrific nature of the attack sank in. His cousin's son and daughter worked in the Trade Center. One of his stockbrokers, an investment banking firm the Gallo Family used, and a law firm that Cassavetti utilized for several real estate deals had offices in the massive structures, all were there, right om front of his eyes. The impact was overwhelming.

But in time, he discovered that all had survived except his cousin's son. Nonetheless, that was tragic enough. The young man was recently married with a four-month-old baby, was fresh out of Princeton, and had completed two months on the job with an accounting firm that was based in the tower. The following Monday, after completing his orientation, the young man would have been transferred to the firm's mid-town office. These ironies abounded in the face of the people of New York for the months and years that would follow the horrible tragedy.

There wasn't a day that Cassavetti scanned the southern skyline of this majestic city and failed to notice the void in the cityscape where once the Twin Towers had stood. It was odd, he would sometimes think, that a man could be that sentimental, and still have the heart to rob, steal, defraud, and murder on a moments notice, as a way of life.

This was one of those evenings where the irony was not lost upon him.

He sat smoking a cigar between sips of cognac while Winton Marsalis played softly in the background on his $30,000 sound system. He was surrounded by the finest of things. The ten-year-old condo had been completely updated two years ago to include new hardwood floors, granite counters in the kitchen and bathrooms, new appliances, and fixtures. The furniture was also the finest. It was a combination of antique and traditional, but each piece was one-of-a-kind and provided him with great comfort and prestige.

His home was a safe place, the building had excellent security, and his entrance was installed by the same company that put in his doorway and security devices at his office. While the facade of the doorway might appear to look the same as the other three apartments on his floor, most certainly the others weren't bullet proof and monitored by video surveillance. Here, he was able to relax.

Except perhaps, on a night like this.

Tonight, just as he had on his first night on St. Martens, he waited for the phone to ring. This time it would be Andy Vassallo. He would call from a throw away cell phone, just like Cassavetti had used, but Vassallo would call the Underboss's private home number. There was no fear of a wiretap as the phone was constantly monitored for any such intrusion. Today, Cassavetti frequently marveled, his work was as much a challenge on technological battlefields as it was waging strategies and wars on the street. There was very little the Feds could try in their efforts to entrap, to obtain evidence, or to snare, if one had the resources to be on the defensive. And the Gallo family had the resources.

But despite all the countermeasures and twenty first century innovation, human error was still a factor. He supposed the Irishmen had just screwed up and it was about to cost them their lives. They probably hadn't weighed down the bag containing Dimaglia's head sufficiently. They should have just carved him up and buried the remains. Or used concrete like in the good ole' days.

But now the evidence chain had to be cut off.

The brothers were members of a loose-knit gang of thugs known as the Westies. They were a group of fifty or sixty Irish guys that pulled off petty heists and a low-level drug deals, but mostly they were hired guns and muscle. If you needed something done and you didn't want to get your hands dirty, they were usually the one's to call. Typically, they could be trusted; their survival depended on a certain "loyalty amongst thieves." But when the cops tagged these guys to Dimaglia, perhaps with some evidence forensically removed from the skull or the bag such as DNA or even a fingerprint, their 'loyalty' most likely would vanish. When faced with a crime that carried a mandatory capital sentence, probably death, trust would go out the window. They would have started talking immediately. Andy Vassallo had hired them and Andy Vassallo was known by the Feds to be a soldier within the Gallo organization. They had to be eliminated, without question, to protect the family.

Tonight Vassallo would right the wrong, and bring the number of deaths at the order of Cassavetti up to three in less than ten days.

Despite the fact that Cassavetti had ordered the hit on Dimaglia to be outsourced, because Dimaglia was one of their own, the Gallos were also hired guns. In addition to prostitution, loan sharking, and drug dealing, all of Cassavetti's business ventures, both legitimate and crooked, the Gallos also would provide discreet elimination services for the right price and for the right client. But murder for hire was something that Cassavetti had very little to do with, other than to invest the fees into real estate, stocks such as Microsoft and General Motors, construction projects, and hell, even a small chain of daycare centers! This could be done after the money had been sufficiently laundered.

So, he was complicit, no question about it. In a way, the bosses and Cassavetti were as one, collectively culpable for everything that happened, and Phil Cassavetti knew it.

At a moment like this he was beginning to think he needed a reality check. He was living in his five-million-dollar condo, working from his prestigious Park Avenue address, making money for the mob on Wall Street versus the mean streets, and just maybe he had become jaded. Given a moment's reflection, he suspected that line of thought was all bullshit, and deep down he knew it.

Because the truth be known, he was nothing but a crook.

All the veneer in the world couldn't hide the fact, especially when he looked in the mirror, that he earned his living from the spoils of crime. Even if it were profits from legitimate dealings, in the beginning the money came from theft, and murder, and a variety of other crimes against society.

He got up and poured himself another drink. The phone rang.

It was Andy Vassallo.

The Irishmen were no longer a problem.

Cassavetti could have felt remorse, or he could have felt guilty. He assumed somewhere these young men had a mother who would soon find out that her sons had been executed. But Cassavetti couldn't afford to think about a grieving mother or some dumb ass Irish fucks who had screwed up a simple hit.

What he did feel was anger.

It came from the realization that his life was out of his hands. There was no turning around or changing lanes in terms of who he was. This was it for him.

And as he slugged back his drink, his fourth in a little over an hour, he resolved himself to accept his lot. He had worked his way into a very cushy position, but he was all mobster, from head to toe. He was an underboss in the Gallo family controlling over $450 million of assets, businesses, and property. He needed to be bigger than the emotional crap that was swirling around in his soul.

Hell, maybe it was time he took someone out himself; he thought and smiled to himself.

That would steel him up.

CHAPTER 23

It was now just twelve days since Elliott Murphy had been mugged and stabbed, and he was ready to get the hell out of bed and stay out, get back to work, and probably go home to his apartment in Manhattan. He hesitated on that point, as he hadn't exactly minded being home in New Jersey. Well, technically it was about to be Sally's home, but nonetheless, she had made it his home again, and when they were together it was as if they hadn't missed a day of living together. Those indicators were very encouraging.

He had recently been trying to back off the pain medication after his near-fatal overdose reaction a few days earlier. Weaning off the medication had been difficult, not to mention irritating, and there had been a corresponding increase in his anxiety levels, not to mention other symptoms of trauma and withdrawal. But the toughest part was now behind him, and his mind was clearing.

He was finally getting an accurate read on his level of physical pain, and was pleased to discover he was farther along than he thought he might be at this juncture. He could walk around within the house, and he was managing to do some minor stretching while in bed. He had a little experience with this routine, as he had been wounded in Vietnam and the resulting injuries had required rehabilitation. He was grazed by a bullet and fell down into a riverbed and fractured his leg. He remembered that it wasn't until after he willed himself to get moving that he finally believed he would survive. Back then, if he hadn't taken the initiative himself, they would have left him stationary for weeks.

Sally had been more than simply a big help. She had always been there for him so this came as no surprise. It was really something to watch her tirelessly cook and clean and manage the house, not to mention her powers of making him comfortable in her own unique ways. She would adjust his pillows and cook his favorite foods, although everything had to be soft for time being. She would do all of this and then run out from time to time and conduct her real estate business. It amazed Elliott in light of what he put her through over the last few years. She put her heart into his care despite the fact he had broken it, which was an observation he never acknowledged to her, but he knew it was true.

Something else came to light as he felt himself turning the corner in his physical recovery. He hadn't had a drink in almost two weeks, which was a good thing, he supposed. On this issue however, he was a little confused. A part of him knew that the drinking had been getting out of control and that he should stop, then he typically would modify that approach and would tell himself he just needed to cut back. He spent quite a bit of time thinking about it, but a decision had never truly been made.

In these moments of denial, he didn't blame his drinking for the mugging incident, he just wrote it off as being at the wrong place at the wrong time. Never mind he had no business being out that night anyway if it hadn't been for the pursuit of a drunk. He didn't consciously correlate his leaving the marriage with alcohol, either. Of course, there were legitimate problems, but they were probably not unique to what any relationship suffers as life changes around two people. Their boys were leaving, Sally needed a sense of purpose, and it was all nerve racking to Elliott. But not reason enough to walk out. And normally, through his entire adult life, walking out was not something typically did.

But the booze became a private preoccupation, and it was one he couldn't safely pursue within the confines of the marriage. Elliott never consciously acknowledged this, continued to stay away from home to drink, and, for the most part, kept the drinking from Sally, so she never confronted him with it head on. Of course, periodically she made a few comments that were understandable, considering he had been a teetotaler for the previous eighteen years. Work had been affected as well. Fortunately, not in any significant way, but who was to say where Elliott would be on a career track if it weren't for his drinking and the loss of zeal that goes with it. He had been keeping up, usually, but he was no longer the crusader at the Bureau he had always been before. He hoped that this whole business didn't cause him too much grief, especially losing his gun. He knew it was only a matter of time before he would have to answer to someone, and that would probably be Cal Skinner, his superior. He was relieved when Cal seemed cordial at the hospital when he came for a short visit.

He was deep in thought as he heard Sally come up the stairs. She knocked softly at the door to his son's bedroom, which he occupied, and he told her to come in.

"How are you doing?" she asked and flashed that classic smile of hers. She could light up a room.

"Better every hour."

"Well, I just sold a house," she beamed. "And a big one at that. You know that big Tudor at the end of Sleigh Bell Lane? Well, they accepted my client's offer for four hundred and seventy five thousand." She threw her arms up in the air in a victory gesture.

"Good," said Elliott. "Good for you!"

Elliott hadn't paid much attention to Sally's career in real estate. She was just beginning when he moved out a year and a half ago. He never thought of her as a business person of any sort, but apparently she knew what she was doing. He knew that she had made $75,000 in her first year, which was exceptional for anyone new to real estate. He also knew that it was almost as much as he made after twenty years on the job. As a senior special agent with his level of tenure, he made slightly under $110,000.

She leaned down to him and kissed his forehead. The gesture caught him off guard. He looked back up at her and smiled and deep down somewhere he felt a bit of pain. What had he done, leaving her, this home, and their life together? He grimaced at the thought it was all about to slip away. In less than two weeks, the divorce would be final.

The truth be known, he felt quite a bit of shame over what he had done. This was a good woman. They had a good life, and he ran out on her when perhaps all they needed was to band together and deal with their stuff. It never occurred to Elliott to question whether he was any good at relationships, or not. He only had this one, not counting his boys and those few agents he worked with. Friends had come and gone, and both of his parents were deceased when he had met Sally. They had died in an auto accident while he was stationed in Vietnam.

So, Sally was the one and only. He decided he had to test the waters and see if she might consider stalling the legal proceedings, and perhaps attend some counseling and work toward reconciling. He just knew it was the right thing to do.

His heart raced, he felt himself flush, but he lowered his head and forced the words past his lips.

"Sally, I've had a lot of time to think about things, and I wonder if perhaps I made a terrible mistake," he said, and paused. "I don't know what you think, but maybe we should put the brakes on this time apart."

Sally Murphy heard the words and on one level it was exactly what she wanted to hear, but it was also like getting hit by a truck; she couldn't stand the notion of going through that private hell all over again.

She had to sit down on the side of the bed because both extremes overwhelmed her.

She looked into his eyes and could see there was in pain. She could see he was lost and probably afraid, not unlike herself. There seemed to be a common feeling that everything between them had simply spun out of control.

But still, she tried to appear reserved.

"Well," Sally finally said in a soft voice, "I don't know what to say. I mean with everything that has happened, do you think it's possible you're just feeling like the wounded soldier who falls for his nurse?" It was a sincere question on her part. She wanted this new twist to be real, to be true, but, perhaps more than anything else, she needed Elliott to be honest.

He didn't respond right away, but chose instead to stare out the window above his bed which ran the length of the wall. The barren trees outside stood perfectly still and the sky was a stark shade of blue; there wasn't a cloud to be seen. It was peaceful, and a familiar view he had relished for years from the bedroom right down the hall.

Following his silent pause, he faced her again, and looked unflinchingly into her deep green eyes.

"I am confused, Sally. I don't know exactly what I've done. Maybe I need to talk to someone myself first. But despite the fact I was stabbed and beaten and needed you to help me, I don't think my misgivings about the separation are out of guilt, or some sympathetic reaction to my nurse. Maybe I've just come to my senses."

Sally couldn't help herself. A tear rolled down her cheek. She felt the back of his hand slowly stroke her face, wiping the trail of the tear with his finger, and lighting a long-forgotten path between them. She slowly leaned down and kissed her husband.

She lay down on the bed next to him and for some time they held each other, caressing each other and gently kissing each other's face. Passion began to develop between them, a strong emotion that had been put away for much too long and finally, Sally was the one to take things to a place they hadn't been in over eighteen months.

She stood for a moment and quickly removed her clothes, leaving her bra and panties and returned to bed. Not a word was spoken but it was a desperate moment for each of them. Neither had been with anyone else in all this time, neither had wished to cross that line.

Like they were made for each other, as it had always felt, they made love. Sally was fit and agile and she made sure that Elliott was satisfied without causing any embarrassing injury. For her, just the massage of his fingers was enough. She shook as she climaxed and then minutes later, again.

Then they lay next to one another, spent.

Sally knew that he had meant what he had said. There was deep hunger for her in his lovemaking, despite the few remaining bandages and a cast on one of his arms, he was tender and deliberate, like he used to be years ago. Perhaps they could turn this around. Perhaps both of them had come to their senses; he realizing that this had been some kind of mid-life crisis, and her realizing she could have done more to stop the worst from happening. He had always been the Rock of Gibraltar. But maybe he was entitled to a little imperfection.

CHAPTER 24

By Friday, Jack was functioning on a level that could only be described as full-blown mania. He had just hung up the phone with one of his largest clients, who had purchased insurance on a shopping center they had just bought in Atlanta for a premium of over half a million. This would earn Jack close to about $50,000, and even considering that he made over two hundred grand a year, this was a big hit.

"I'm on fire!" he whooped from his tiny interior office at Avistar, the insurance company where he had worked for almost fourteen years.

He jumped into the hallway to find someone to tell the good news. A large bespectacled black woman was walking by, and Jack had to move out of the way to let her pass. He smiled at her, recognizing her from another department, though he didn't know her name. She looked up at him as if he were nuts. There was absolutely nobody around with whom he could share the good news.

Screw it, he thought, he would call Rachel instead.

He had told his wife on Monday night that it was over. On Wednesday night he told the boys. That didn't go over as badly as Jack had feared, primarily because Scott, the oldest and meanest, had a friend whose parents had split up and both parents spoiled him rotten. Scott explained that this friend's dad was always buying him stuff and his mom had taken him to Disney World. He told his two brothers the divorce would be cool and briefly reflected a rare jubilant moment for an otherwise angry, deviant child.

Harry, the quiet one, reacted for a moment. In a very uncharacteristic move, he came over to his father as Jack was talking and latched onto his father's leg. He looked up at Jack and looked as though he was about to cry. Then his face went blank, he released Jack's leg, and returned to his perch on the couch, where he stared at the blank television screen, waiting for the "talk" to be over. It unnerved Jack for a moment, but only just a moment.

Meanwhile, as Jack was making peace with the boys, Alice sat at a kitchen chair, flipping angrily through a magazine, not saying a word.

He took off from work on Thursday, packed up his clothes and a few other essentials, and moved into a furnished corporate apartment in the city. It was located on the west side, at Amsterdam and 76th, and in the span of three or four days the transition was complete and the nightmare was over, or so he thought.

He spent his first night as a newly liberated man at his girlfriend's and she appeared to be pleased with the new developments. They didn't talk about it much, other than Jack assuring her this change was a long time in the making, and that the marriage had been a nightmare long before Rachel had come along. Once that was resolved, the two enjoyed a celebratory evening in which the pinnacle was something Jack regarded as some pretty kinky sex. Rachel handcuffed Jack to her four-poster bed and when Rachel had finished her tricks, Jack was sure he had died and gone to heaven.

Rachel already had plans of her own for this particular Friday evening, with a girlfriend who was in town from California, and Jack had plans of his own. He was invited to a card game that Phil Cassavetti was hosting. Unbeknownst to Alice, Jack had cashed the check for over $80,000 in casino winnings from the Sand Dollar and kept the money in a small safe that was provided in his apartment, not unlike the better hotels provide in their rooms. He decided to take twenty grand with him tonight, mostly because he just knew that his lucky streak was still in motion with everything going his way.

He had already met with a lawyer, who specialized in family law and his firm also did some work for Jack's company. During this first meeting the attorney assured Jack everything would be okay—after Jack told him he didn't want anything. Including the boys. Maybe a weekend or two every month, but he didn't want to rush that demand. He had anticipated that fighting for his rights would be fruitless in this deal; after all, he was leaving a pathetic woman who didn't work and was responsible for three young boys. No court in the land would be sympathetic. Jack kept it simple and asked that the attorney concentrate on negotiating a fair figure for child support. The lawyer said he'd do his best, but didn't look him in the eye. Jack wasn't encouraged but sloughed it off.

He left Alice with enough money in their joint account to last a week or so and he would continue to pay the bills. He told the boys he couldn't come by this weekend but would try to stop in some time next week. Jack knew that he was being selfish, but he also felt it was the first time as an adult that he stood up for himself. At least where Alice was concerned. He had been completely whipped for way too long, and it still surprised him that he had so much resolve. He had truly crossed the point of no return.

The day ticked on and when he began to submit the paperwork on his big sale, one of the partners came to his door. Jack heard a knock and saw a man with a big grin on his face. It was Ted Duboski, one of the top people in the firm, and was someone who had nudged Jack a thousand times, telling him he could do better. Ted was probably close to sixty, short and stout with a few wisps of white hair that were all that remained on each side of his perfectly round head.

"Jack, my boy, I heard you landed a big one!" he said as he gave Jack the old thumbs up. "Maybe after all this time you're about to get into your stride."

"Thanks Ted," Jack tried to be nonchalant. "I've written a few small policies for these guys but they're finally getting into the big leagues. They just bought a shopping center in Atlanta and it sounds like they might pick up a few more over the next couple of months."

"Great news, kid," Duboski said. He had a penchant for calling every male in the firm under fifty years of age, by the name of kid or son or boy, although he finally caught on that 'boy' wasn't PC and dropped that one.

"Did you hear that Alice and I split up?" Jack said because he couldn't help himself. He hadn't shared his news with anyone at the office yet, and Duboski had been a bit of a surrogate to him.

"What?" exclaimed the forty-year veteran of the company and devout Catholic. He stepped inside Jack's tiny office and shut the door behind him.

"Yeah," Jack continued. "I left earlier this week."

"Christ, boy, are you sure it's the right thing?"

"I've never been surer about anything, Ted."

"But your boys, son," Duboski said, as he shook his head from side to side. Jack should have known he'd have to defend his actions sooner or later.

"Ted, we've all been unhappy. This will all work out for the best, trust me," Jack said as earnestly as he could speak.

"Well, where are you living?" Duboski asked.

Jack went on to explain everything, except the Rachel part, of course, and soon they were back to business as usual.

"Well, keep this up Jack, you're gonna need every penny you can get your hands on!"

Jack nodded, "You got it. I have a feeling my numbers are going to shoot up. I know it's unfortunate, but I feel like a new man, I really do."

Ted left and Jack made a few more calls and before too long the workday was wrapped up. He left the building and decided to splurge and take a cab home to his new apartment, and within minutes he was headed uptown.

He was ready for a night of poker, where he could have a few drinks, see Phil again, and get to know a few new faces. Cassavetti apparently rented a suite at the Four Seasons one

Friday a month to host these card games, and it sounded like a very exciting night. Cassavetti sure had a lot of class, Jack thought idly as the cab crawled its way uptown in the middle of Friday rush hour. He thought of Monique and Cheri. Now they were classy, for hookers anyway. He was curious to know more about Cassavetti, the type of man he was, and how he made his money. Jack had sensed a strong networking contact when he first met Phil, and he was encouraged by the fact he that he had mentioned he was buying some real estate real soon.

Maybe they could do a little business together. What could it hurt?

CHAPTER 25

"Your suite is ready, Mr. Cassavetti, and we have the bar fully stocked and I will send room service up immediately with fresh hors d'oeuvres," said Francis, the concierge at The Four Seasons Hotel at Forty-Eighth and Park in Manhattan. The little man behind the teak and marble "Guest Services" desk was expecting Cassavetti and had his room key in an envelope, thereby avoiding the normal check-in procedure at the front desk. There would be no registration, no credit cards. Phil Cassavetti had an account with the five-star hotel and would simply pay the tab in cash when he left. He always did.

Cassavetti made his way up to the fifteenth floor and entered the posh suite. He had been running this game once a month for years and had previously hosted lawyers, doctors, executives, and at times, even politicians and judges. They all had two things in common—their passion for gambling and their intrigue with Cassavetti. A few of the players knew how the dashing bachelor made his living but never spoke about it openly. After all, Cassavetti had a legitimate front. He traded stocks, bought and sold real estate, and invested in worthwhile businesses. Where the money came from was never discussed. So these upstanding citizens didn't feel tarnished by their association with the gangster, in fact, quite the contrary. Cassavetti was regarded as someone to know.

Somehow, he had managed to stay under the radar, had never been charged with anything more serious than a traffic ticket, and had never been given any mention in the press. The "money man" of the Gallo family was all but unknown to the law, and therefore not a risk by association to some who might not otherwise be comfortable in the company of a mobster. Once he had attended a fund raiser for Rudy Giuliani during his first campaign for mayor. At the time, Giuliani was a crusading federal prosecutor, having made his mark putting guys like Cassavetti behind bars. Cassavetti made sure to grab the colorful mayoral candidate aside for a few minutes and spoke to him about zoning restrictions that Cassavetti wanted lifted in an area where the family owned several rows of tenements. One year later, they were free to tear the old buildings down and up went a residential and retail project that Cassavetti eventually sold for a huge profit to a Korean investment group. He anonymously sent Rudy a bottle of Dom Perignon and a box of Cuban cigars on the day the deal closed. Cassavetti was all class.

The circle of card sharks around the table usually consisted of a half-dozen high society players, but this week there were two cancellations. So Cassavetti had called upon Jack Horton, the insurance broker he had met in the Caribbean. He knew only what he had learned during their last evening together, when Horton more or less held his own and took the table for over fifty grand. There was something about the guy that caught Cassavetti's interest. How many guys would pick up a broad at a resort while his wife was a few floors upstairs? Cassavetti smiled to himself. Horton clearly had a gift for the cards. He would throw an interesting twist into the game tonight, thought Cassavetti, and in some mysterious way, he just knew it.

Jack showed up at the Four Seasons wearing a navy blazer, tan pants, a white oxford button-down over a white tee-shirt, and black loafers. It was his country club look. He took off his overcoat in the lobby and strutted across the marble floor, with his head erect and sporting a grin on his face; he was on top of the world.

While getting dressed for the evening, Jack tried to recall, aside from a wedding a couple of years back, he couldn't remember getting dressed for a Friday night. He couldn't even remember going out on a Friday night. Alice preferred to watch TV and park her caboose on her corner of the couch. She would ignore the boys completely, which resulted in Jack being forced to manage the little menaces. But not tonight, thought Jack. Bet Alice is having a blast, he laughed to himself.

Jack Horton made his way to the fifteenth floor of The Four Seasons, and walked down the hall to suite number 1500. He knocked on the impressively carved wooden door and a very debonair Phil Cassavetti answered, greeted him with his powerful handshake, and offered a smile.

"Come on in, Jack," he bellowed. "Meet the rest of the crew." He motioned to an older-looking gentleman who was seated in one of the leather chairs at the large oak card table. "This is Judge William Heller. Judge, Jack Horton."

Jack moved quickly over to the Judge, extended his hand and said, "Pleased to meet you, your honor."

"Likewise. Please, call me Bill. Phil thinks that as a judge I am owed a little more respect. Then he turns around and takes all my money at the poker table," said the Judge with a warm grin and a soft, elderly handshake. Everyone in earshot laughed.

Jack noticed that the suite was huge as he was led across the room to two other guests who were chatting by the balcony doors. There were several plush couches, glass and chrome coffee tables, and the carpet underfoot was patterned in several vivid colors. The entire place was exquisite.

He met Art Hanson, a plastic surgeon, Syl Divinius, a patent attorney, and Mark Feinberg, who owned a software company. They were all smiling and friendly on the surface, but Jack was smart enough to know they were all there to rob him blind. But Jack was going to surprise them, for he was confident and once again had the feeling he was going to win.

Following the introductions and superficial chit-chat, the men were seated at the table, jackets came off, cigars were lit, drinks were poured, and the first game began.

The game ran in ebb and flow, covered in smoke and sweat and money, and the night lasted until practically sunrise. The big surprise of the evening for Phil Cassavetti had been his new, and very lucky, friend—Jack. As he grabbed little bits and pieces of this man's life story, he realized he had come upon this guy at a breakthrough' point in his journey. Some good things were happening to Jack Horton and it was clear that he was feeling rather invincible. Not the least of which was the fact that during the past several hours he had stacked up winnings of close to $30,000.

The judge folded around midnight and the others had hung in until it was over. The good Doctor, Art Hanson, had to give Cassavetti a marker for over five grand. He kept thinking he could turn his luck around, but it never happened and he lost over $20,000. Cassavetti broke even, and seemed pleased with the amusement of watching the newcomer take everyone else to the cleaners when it didn't cost him anything.

Horton stuck around for a few minutes after everyone else left and helped Cassavetti close up the suite.

"So Jack, what's your secret?" Cassavetti asked as the two men were donning their overcoats to leave. "Looks like you're still on a roll since the Caribbean."

"It's funny," offered Jack. "About the only thing I can think of lately is making the decision to leave my wife. Even that crazy slot machine! That never would have happened if I hadn't walked out on Alice that night. I didn't think at the time it would go this far. I've even continued to see Rachel, that girl I introduced you to on the island." He hadn't mentioned anything about his girlfriend in front of the others. He assumed no one would be interested and didn't want to appear like a schoolboy.

"She seemed okay," Cassavetti said indifferently. "So listen Jack, I need a little help with something and I think it might help you some, too. Maybe you can consider your help as a thank you for your inclusion in the game here tonight."

"Sure," Jack answered quickly, anxious to hear what Phil could possibly want of him.

"I just bought these buildings and I need some insurance. Only thing is, this particular company of mine is pretty new and this is the first piece of business I've run through it."

"Well that's okay," Jack said. He was quietly relieved that Phil just wanted some insurance. "Usually with a new entity we can just have you sign personally for the company."

"Well that's the thing, Jack. I really don't want to do that."

There was an awkward silence as they waited for the elevator. The hallway was empty at four in the morning and Jack felt a twinge of something wrong, but he blew it off. It was late, he was exhausted, and it wasn't an unusual request. A lot of guys he knew who had made it big didn't want to sign anything personally, as opposed to through their business. Maybe that had something to do with how they got to be big wigs. And on top of never wanting any personal liability, they were also usually cheap as hell. But that didn't seem to be Cassavetti's M.O., as his trademark up to this point seemed to be more in the vein of extravagance.

"Why don't we talk on Monday? I'm sure we can work something out."

"Yeah, that would be good," Cassavetti said with a smile. "You know, if you take care of me on this Jack, I bet your luck keeps on running."

They boarded the elevator and rode down in silence. There had been a lot of talking and laughing and more than a few drinks, and it was increasingly obvious that the two of them were in a bit of a daze at this late hour.

But inside Phil Cassavetti's head, the wheels were in motion. He slept very little and was used to these hours. He was physically tired, but he was always exhilarated mentally after a game and when a good idea struck, especially one that he could profit from, he never ran out of steam.

Horton, on the other hand, was beat. He did have a grin on his face, however. How could his life be changing so dramatically? And all for the better. That had never happened before, but now he had close to $50,000 in his pocket, the $20,000 he brought to the table, and his winnings on top of it. His new girlfriend was coming over to his new apartment around noon, and he knew in his loins what they would be up to for the afternoon. Best of all, he was in the process of getting rid of his wife.

How long could this hot streak last?

Just roll with it, he told himself. Maybe his time had come.

Downstairs, Phil had two Town Cars waiting for them. He had mentioned earlier that he had given Jules the night off because he knew it would be a long game, and because of that, Horton was surprised to see the limos waiting but didn't say anything.

"I'm going to the East Side; you're going to the west. You deserve your own ride after a night like tonight, huh Jack?"

"Guess so, thanks Phil!"

They shook hands and Jack's driver opened the door to Horton's sleek black limousine. The interior smelled rich as he slid onto the soft leather seat. The chauffer closed the door and Jack thought of Alice for some reason. He knew that tomorrow morning she would be loading those three little brats into her minivan. Her car was perpetually filthy and stunk of milkshakes spilled under seats, French Fries greasing the floorboards, ketchup dried on the seats, and apparently somewhere, there had to be a dead rodent.

Those images were in sharp contrast to the Lincoln in which he currently floated up Madison Avenue in silence, the streets looking eerily empty. This was a time in the city he had never recalled seeing. A time when the only occupants of the sidewalks were the homeless scattered here and there, and the only vehicles moving along the pavement were a few empty cabs, a garbage truck, and every once in a while, a cop. For a moment, he actually felt lonely. But even in his state of exhaustion, he realized he had been lonely for years.

He shut his eyes for a moment and diverted his thoughts to Rachel. Soon she would be with him again, they would have another wild time, and he had decided to take her out for a big night on the town.

As he departed the limo he handed the driver a twenty, for it was only other people's money after all, and Jack asked him for his card. He considered hiring the limo to impress Rachel.

He could get used to this new lifestyle.

CHAPTER 26

Despite the fact that on and off, over the last several weeks, Elliott Murphy had his moments of clarity and recognized that his drinking had been out of control, had almost cost him his family and had had a great deal to do with putting him in harms way and almost getting himself killed, he was ready for a drink! It was insane, and a part of him knew it, but he was suddenly preoccupied with thirst for booze. It was Sunday afternoon, a little over two weeks since he had been mugged and the irony was that he woke up feeling better than he had in a long, long time. He hadn't taken any pain medication in several days, his wounds were healing rapidly, and he was starting to get a little exercise. And he *needed* a drink.

He woke up thinking about drinking. He took a walk and began to plot a way to sneak a couple of belts without Sally finding out. But he realized that that was too risky, and if she caught him, he couldn't bear letting her down again. He decided to tell her that it might be time for him to return to his apartment. He thought he would say that while they were talking about reconciling, a short break might be a good idea to think things through, so as not to rush things. Besides, he was thinking about going to work briefly on Monday, and it would be more convenient if he were already in the city.

However, the reality was that this scheme was solely for the purpose of having a few drinks in the privacy of his place, without the risk of getting caught. And if "a few" drinks turned into many drinks, that development would be okay too.

As he sat in his old easy chair, staring at the blank screen of a TV that wasn't turned on, Sally entered the room. Something inside snapped him back to earth and told him in a loud, sobering voice that his thinking was ludicrous. Apparently, he hadn't figured it out yet, even after being close to death, struggling back from surgery, and trudging through withdrawals from narcotics he liked far more than he should. He had a problem with the booze and perhaps anything that took him out of the here and now, such as other drugs. And he also knew the ultimate solution was to *just stop. But could he?*

He stared at Sally blankly for a moment as all these thoughts came together and then he reacted to the genuine, vivacious smile she beamed in his direction. Her eyes seemed to sparkle more than he remembered, and what little makeup she wore was just perfect. Her hair was swept back and she wore a tight green turtle neck over jeans, which completed the gorgeous picture of the woman, with a beautiful face that was the centerpiece.

He couldn't risk losing her again, he thought. He just had to quit the booze and keep himself together. He needed to hit it hard at work, make things up to Sally, get back into the boys life, and maybe even start going to church. He had been a good guy for a lot of years, and he knew the drill. What scared him was that the drill he had known existed before he developed a relationship with Jack Daniels.

"What's on your mind, handsome?" she toyed.

"Just thinking about you," he replied and he meant it. It was amazing, he thought, how quickly his love for her had all come back.

"Well, how'd you like to go look at a couple of homes with me? I have to preview three properties for another out-of-town client."

Elliott sprung right up, because he knew he should, and they were off. Sally drove her three-year-old Buick Century and they headed through town on their way to an area called Lazy Hills. It was almost an upper end sub-division with homes ranging in the $600,000 to $800,000 categories.

Their conversation was light as they meandered along, and Elliott attempted to stay focused. But there was an edge that he felt as he observed people milling about on the sidewalks of the bedroom community of New York City. They seemed so normal, and he realized that he was feeling out of place, awkward. Then they passed a business he had frequented quite often in the months before he left Cedar Grove—Patches Liquor. He lost his train of thought in mid-sentence as he was answering a question Sally had asked. She noticed his preoccupation.

"You okay?" she asked.

It took everything he had to shake the distraction off.

"Yeah, sorry, I just thought of something I need to follow up on at work," he lied. "Funny, I guess I've been so out of it lately, I'm still a little disoriented."

They drove on to Lazy Hills and as the distance between him and the liquor store grew, however, he felt like he'd left behind an old friend. An old friend he was not so sure he could abandon forever. Perhaps there would be a time, he thought, when they might be reunited—and it would be different this time.

Perhaps.

CHAPTER 27

Jack Horton's weekend in the city had been spectacular, at least until late Sunday afternoon. He had won close to twenty grand Friday night and had an entirely bizarre afternoon of sex with Rachel on Saturday afternoon, although he thought the girl was a little twisted, he loved it. Saturday night they went out on the town and spent over two grand for a limo, dinner at Le Cirque, clubbing in the meatpacking district, and plenty of expensive champagne along the way. These were things he had only read about. These activities were as likely to occur in his old life with Alice, as the possibility of him flying a 747 in his underwear. Yes sir. It had been a big night, living the good life.

However, Sunday afternoon brought him back down to earth. In fact, one could argue, crashing back down to earth. Rachel put the wheels into motion by dropping a bomb on him. *This has been fun*, she told him, but she was getting a little freaked about it all. She wasn't sure if she wanted to be in the middle of his divorce and breaking up a family. Suddenly the girl had developed a conscience. Jack pleaded with her to understand, "*it was going to happen no matter what.*" He lied.

"And there's someone else, Jack," she said. "He's an old boyfriend who's interested in giving it another try. Maybe."

She didn't know for sure. But no matter what, she made it clear that the situation was a little much for her.

"It has been fun," she told him, "but maybe we need a break."

He tried to convince her that if she wanted to slow down a little, he could understand. He argued that she would eventually see that the split with his wife wasn't about her. Although he really wanted that to be true, deep inside Jack knew if she hadn't come along, he might have gone on in misery forever!

They parted with the understanding they wouldn't talk for a few days in order to give her time to think about it. Jack, of course, was devastated.

Then the downward spiral continued.

It was now Wednesday afternoon and he was on his way to meet Phil Cassavetti for the first time since Friday night. Phil had called and wanted to discuss the insurance on the buildings he was buying, so Jack had agreed to come up to his new friend's office. But first, Jack had a meeting with the divorce lawyer.

That was a disaster.

Alice had also hired a lawyer and apparently the guy was a pit bull. They had made an aggressive move and had beaten Jack and his lawyer to the punch by filing for the divorce first. She was suing him for alimony and child support, she was after almost seventy-five percent of his income, and on top of that she wanted custody of the boys, the house and everything in it, as well as half of Jack's re-

ANTHONY EDDOLLS

tirement plan. Jack could have his Jeep, on which he owed more than it was worth, and he was certainly entitled to his clothing. She was claiming mental cruelty, emotional abuse, and parental neglect of the children.

"This guy is good," his attorney said as though it was no big deal. "But hopefully we'll get a reasonable judge and negotiate something that works."

"Works for whom?" Jack said in disgust.

Jack almost threw up in the lawyer's office. Alice accused him of stealing the casino winnings from their joint account and was suing him for every bit of it. She also established a restraining order and requested that Jack have a psychological evaluation before visitation with the boys would be allowed. It was ludicrous. Would a judge actually let this happen, he wondered?

A hearing was scheduled for the next week and the attorney told Jack not to worry about it. He suggested he move whatever money around he could and begin deferring as much of his income as possible. The attorney's advice didn't sound good at all and despite the man's assurances, Jack thought he was going to have a heart attack.

The aftermath of that meeting left Jack dazed and he finally began to gather himself in the elevator on his way to Cassavetti's office in the Metropolitan Building. The building was pristine and elegant, and was a New York City landmark. It was the dividing line along Park Avenue between uptown and downtown, sitting square in the middle of the prestigious avenue and 42nd street above Grand Central Station. Jack had often marveled at it, but today he barely noticed where he was.

When he walked up to the entrance to Cassavetti's suite he noticed the name-plate, Mid-America Trading Group, Inc. Jack had never heard of it, but assumed it was just a holding company. He turned the doorknob and in his state of distraction he kept moving forward, smacking his head into the door which he discovered was made of rock solid steel. The door was locked.

While he stood there in no small amount of dullish pain, having dropped his briefcase on the floor in order to clutch his head, he heard the distinct *thunk* of a deadbolt as it was electronically released. He quickly picked up his briefcase, opened the door and entered, his free hand still clutching his forehead.

"You okay, sir?" asked the dark-haired, retro-looking secretary seated at her desk in the small reception area.

Jack pulled himself together and gave her a feigned smile, even though he was actually still in a state of shock, not from the door, but the Pearl Harbor meeting where his wife took the first steps to ruin his life.

"I'm okay," he said vacantly, "I just wasn't thinking."

"I'm Maria and you must be Jack Horton," she said with a thick Brooklyn accent. "Phil is waitin' on ya'."

"Thanks."

She walked to the door that led to Phil Cassavetti's office, knocked, and waited a bit awkwardly for another *thunk*. Jack suddenly lifted the fog of his preoccupation and wondered why there was such imposing security. But he entered trying to put best foot forward.

"Jack!" Cassavetti exclaimed from behind his desk.

"Hey, Phil," Jack replied and he managed a smile as the two shook hands over Phil's desk.

Horton was immediately struck by the view up Park Avenue. It was a classic New York panorama of the east side of uptown Manhattan. The day was clear, the sun was shining, and for a moment, despite his worries, he was awestruck.

"Good to see you, Jack," Cassavetti said as he motioned to one of the two leather chairs that sat in front of his massive, cluttered desk.

Jack sat down, quickly surveyed the office, and was impressed. Cassavetti worked from a two-monitor computer system that had one flat screen sitting on the corner and the other on a return that extended off the right side of the oak desk. Jack noticed that some of the papers cluttering Phil's desk were prospectuses of mutual funds and partnerships, as well as research reports from several of the top investment banking firms. On the walls to either side, he noticed what appeared to be original art, and though Jack didn't know a thing about paintings although he could tell they were expensive.

"So how are ya?" Phil asked.

"To tell you the truth, I'm lousy," he said, angrily. "I just left my divorce attorney's office and my wife is trying to fuck me over."

"Yeah, these things are never easy. I've never been married but I've watched plenty of guys stay miserable to avoid this divorce crap. You sure this was your best move? I've never met your wife, but I know you got kids," Cassavetti said as he lit a large cigar.

"There's no question in my mind. I've been unhappy for years; I guess I just haven't had the balls to do anything about it."

"What changed?" Cassavetti asked with the faint smile of someone who already knew the answer. He drew on the Hoyo de Monterrey Double Corona, and a look of pure contentment washed across his face.

"Well, Rachel obviously was a little incentive, but now she's flaking out on me too. She says she's uncomfortable being in the middle of a divorce."

"Hmmph. So she's already getting tired of ya?" Cassavetti asked as he released a rather large plume of distinctly scented smoke.

"I don't know. I guess women haven't been my strong suit. But I'll tell ya', this bitch wife of mine could disappear and the world would be a better place. That's how bad it is."

"You really think that? I mean, after all, she's the mother of your children."

"They're so fucked up and I really believe that she's the reason. She's awful with them."

Cassavetti just raised his eyebrows.

"Sorry, I guess I just needed to vent for a minute. I literally just came from this lawyer's office and had this crap dropped on me."

"What exactly is she after?" Cassavetti asked as he leaned forward and began to type stock symbols into his computer for quotes.

Jack knew Phil was getting a little impatient and probably wanted to move on to business.

"Not much, just the house, the cars, the boys, the money, and almost all of my income. Plus, she's going for a restraining order even though I've never laid a hand on her. But I'll find a way to deal with it," Jack said quickly as he reached down and removed a file from his briefcase. "Anyway, enough about me. Let's go over this proposal for you."

Cassavetti left the computer screen, took off his metal reading glasses, and turned to Jack with a serious look.

"Look Jack, you keep me posted on this thing. Maybe she needs to have someone talk some sense into her."

Jack was caught off guard by the sudden shift. There was something ominous about what Cassavetti had just said. Jack realized the man was serious.

"You can get that done?" Jack responded hesitantly. He didn't know what else to say.

"No, but I might know someone. Look Jack, I do a lot of things. I'm in the construction business, for example, and you can't help but know a few bad guys when you're in the construction business in New York City. Just keep it in mind."

"Well, why not just make her disappear?" Jack said spontaneously and then couldn't believe he said it.

"That's the kind of thing you want to give a lot of thought to," Cassavetti said as though he were counseling someone on buying a new car.

"Okay," Jack said. "I will." He decided to move on to another topic, as this one was getting a little too weird. It wasn't so unnerving that the conversation was taking place, but it was the fact that it instantly got his attention. Could he actually do something to her, he wondered? Could he?

He presented the insurance quotes for the three buildings Cassavetti was buying. Cassavetti had requested maximum coverage and he estimated the replacement value considerably higher than what he was paying for the apartments. The deal was closing next week and Jack agreed to forego the rigorous inspections and underwriting that would normally take place. The premium for all three buildings was over $80,000 annually, and although Jack showed Cassavetti a monthly payment schedule, Cassavetti wrote a check for the full amount. On the spot. Cassavetti handed him the business card of his attorney and instructed Jack to stop by the lawyer's office to get the necessary signatures on behalf of the corporation that owned the buildings.

For this particular sale, Jack would make around $12,000. Maybe things were looking up again, he thought to himself. Phil stood and walked Jack to the door of his office, but cut Jack off before he left.

"Listen Jack, I can do a lot for you and you can do a few things for me. I don't know why, but I like you," Cassavetti said with a smile as he put his hand on Jack's shoulder. "So if you need a little help with this situation with your wife, just let me know. We can't let her take you down. I mean, I just let you into my poker circle."

Jack laughed and replied, "Thanks Phil. I've just never been in a situation like this before. Never thought I would be."

"Well, it's gonna be okay. Trust me."

Jack left the office trailed by the resounding *thunks* of two security doors and descended down to the main lobby where he exited though Grand Central Station onto 42nd street. As he pushed his way through the ever-present mob scene that milled purposefully in all directions about the busiest commuter intersection in the world, he went over and over in his mind what had transpired during the day.

His wife had launched a legal action that could have him in a vise for years to come, and his newfound friend, the mysterious Phil Cassavetti, had offered to "deal" with her in a way that could only be interpreted as threatening at best, or more accurately, violently. And somewhere within himself, perhaps in a deep dark compartment that he had never called upon, it seemed to be sitting, waiting for him, the very thought that a violent solution might be okay. She deserved whatever he could dish out in response to what she wanted to do to him. He wasn't about to let her ruin his life, this *new* life he was working to piece together, to make up for all the lost years he had wasted with her.

He managed to grab a cab, a miracle at this time of day, and he took a breath after he gave the driver his destination and leaned back into the seat.

"Are you having a troubled day, sir?" asked the Indian cab driver as he gazed back at Jack, wearing a big, goofy grin in the rearview mirror, which made him look suspiciously like a cab-driving therapist.

"You could say that," Jack answered.

CHAPTER 28

The ride to One Federal Plaza in Manhattan seemed bizarre to Elliott Murphy. It had been three weeks since he last worked, three weeks since was stabbed and beaten, and three weeks since he had taken a drink.

But when he finally reached the building and looked up at the modern forty-two story structure, he felt comfort in the familiarity. This had been his home. In this building and the others where he had been assigned during his twenty-one years with the bureau, he performed a job that he deemed meaningful and important. He was an FBI agent before this building was even constructed. And today, like every day since 9/11, it had more meaning than the day it first opened its doors. The building was a symbol of American law enforcement; today it represented the front line in the fight against terrorists, those who would think nothing of murdering innocent civilians in their anti-American campaign of extremism. Elliott was proud of his efforts to prevent anything like that fateful day from occurring again. He was one man in a huge collective effort, but he knew he had given it everything he had, or at least almost everything. The last year or so had been a little more difficult, perhaps he hadn't been focused as well as he should have been given the rise in his boozing.

Sally had offered to drive him into the city but Elliott preferred to get in on his own, partially because he didn't want to inconvenience her, but also because he wanted to make this trek by himself. Once he arrived he sailed through security in the main lobby, because his photo ID designated him as a senior special agent. He boarded an elevator and was on his way to the top floor. He was supposed to report directly to Deputy Director Cal Skinner, Director of the New York City Division.e security desk for the executive level, clearance went a little slower. His ID was verified in the computer and Skinner's assistant was called.

"She'll be right out to take you back, sir," the uniformed guard said in a monotone as he handed Murphy his brand new ID wallet back. The old one, of course, was stolen with his gun. Elliott had considered it a good sign a couple of days earlier, when Sam Taub had dropped his new ID off.

A few moments later a tall black woman bounded out of the security door, with graying hair and a smart looking red business suit; she was Emma Carson, the assistant to the director and an old friend.

"Elliott Murphy—returned from the dead!"

"Hey Emma," replied Murphy and they gave each other a quick hug. This wasn't standard Bureau protocol, but acceptable given the fact they had known each other for over a decade and been through plenty together as friends and comrades.

"You doin' okay, young man?" she asked.

"Guess so. The doctor cleared me back to work and I'm actually feeling fine. So what's going on?" he asked as she led him back though the security door and down a hallway to Skinner's office. "I feel like I've been gone for months."

"I heard that you and Sally are getting back together," she said, apparently avoiding his question.

"I guess Sam Taub has been spreading the news. Hopefully, we're going to be able to work things out. Emma, tell me, am I in more hot water than I think?"

"I wouldn't know, Elliott. I'm just glad you're okay," she said quickly and motioned for him to take a seat in Skinner's office. "I've got to get back to a meeting. Cal is actually in the meeting as well but he said he'd be out in just a few minutes."

She left him alone.

Something was definitely wrong. Emma Carson knew everything that was going on when it came to internal politics and controversy within the division. She had obviously ducked the issue of current Bureau activities along with Elliott's status. But, he figured, he would find out soon enough.

In the few moments that passed while he waited for Skinner, he tried to think of what might happen and how he would deal with it. They wouldn't be doing anything as rash as suspending or terminating him, because he would have heard from Skinner already. He was probably going to be 'written up.' After all, he had lost his gun to a thug and it never would have happened if he hadn't been drunk. What an embarrassment, he thought to himself, for about the one-hundredth time in the last two weeks.

He heard footsteps behind him and he turned around in the chair to see Cal Skinner purposefully coming through the door. Elliott stood up quickly to greet his boss.

"Elliott, good to see you back," Skinner said with a warm smile. Murphy took this as a good sign and reached for Skinner's hand.

"It's good to be back, Cal," Murphy replied. They had been on a first name basis for a number of years.

Skinner stepped back to the door and closed it. That was *not* a good sign, Elliott knew.

"I wanted to wait until you were ready to come back to work; we need to talk about this whole situation, Elliott."

Murphy felt his face flush, and steeled himself for what was about to come. "You and I know each other well enough and you know that I'm not one to bullshit around. Do you think you have a problem, Elliott?" Skinner didn't waste any time. He had moved around to a large, high-backed leather chair behind his desk. He unbuttoned his grey, double-breasted suit jacket and sat down.

Murphy couldn't help it, he swallowed hard. While he had contemplated this moment over and over, he found himself dumbfounded. It was as though he was witnessing this conversation between Skinner and someone else, *how could this be happening to him*? He had always been the guy who walked the straight and narrow. But it *was* him in the room and it *was* him who had been found in a snowbank, drunk and beaten and robbed of his weapon.

But despite all the contemplation of this discussion, he didn't know what to say.

"What do you mean?" he said softly.

"With alcohol, Elliott. You know what I mean," Skinner shook his head as if he was ashamed to say it himself. This was an uncomfortable conversation for both of them. "Look, we both know that you were blind drunk when you were found. You put yourself in a defenseless position. You were walking around loaded in a seedy neighborhood, and on top of that, your edge seems to have all but disappeared over the last year or so. Come on, Elliott, give me a break. I want to help. As difficult as it is, I have to consider this matter as your superior, but also as your friend."

Elliott lowered his head, took a breath, and then pulled it together. A silent pause wafted between them as Elliott rubbed his hands, and his options, together. "I suppose you're right, Cal. I guess it's just gotten away from me during the split with Sally. I can't believe this happened, but I really think I'm okay now. Sally and I are talking about getting back together and this break, while I've been on sick leave, it's given me a chance to pull myself together. I haven't had a drink since the night it happened, and I don't plan on it. I'm ready to go."

"Well, you know we have referral services, and our insurance covers counseling, and you know Harry Elson is in AA. He's been at it for over five years and swears by it. I just want to make sure you're okay. But I also have to do my job," Skinner said and then he looked out his window for a moment. "I'm afraid I have to take you off the Terrorism Task Force, Elliott. I'm going to put you back in OCU."

Murphy had spent five years in the Organized Crime Unit and had been pulled off to run a terrorism team almost immediately after 9/11. This was not a good thing. It was a demotion and would be a blemish on his record, even without an official disciplinary action being sited.

Murphy instinctively felt compelled to defend himself.

"Come on Cal, I've got a lot of momentum going in several different situations, not the least of which is the Al Fayed laundering thing. I don't really think it's fair to say my performance has been off. It certainly didn't come up before this mess, and really, it could have happened to me stone cold sober."

"Those situations are all under control, Elliott, and you can't look me in the eye and tell me that you, of all guys, you, would just get taken down on the street by some crack head, not be able to put up a fight, and lose your weapon. Look, I'm not going to argue about this. We both know I should be writing you up. I'll just note your file that we pulled you off terrorism to give you a chance to get back to one hundred percent. I'll handle it so it won't look so bad."

Murphy was staring at his shoes. He felt as though his blood was boiling, and he couldn't look Skinner in the eye, and more than anything, he wanted to get up and walk out. But he knew at some level that Skinner was essentially right and was probably being extremely lenient. But in twenty-one years, this was the first sit down with a superior that even resembled a disciplinary action. The ordeal was tough to swallow.

"Who am I going to be working with?" he managed.

"I've got a young guy, an Italian guy actually, Chris Marciotti, who has some leads working on the Gallo Family, and don't worry; you'll be the senior agent. We've been finding bodies here and there; we think they're in the middle of it. Tony Dimaglia's head was found in the river and earlier this week NYPD got a lead from a hooker on two brothers that apparently had been offed, cut up, and buried.

"Anyway," Skinner continued. "There's plenty going on and I know it's not the level of assignment that you knew in terrorism, but we can keep an eye on you and take things slow."

Murphy nodded. He had hardly heard one word. He was silently furious and on the verge of trembling. Mad at Skinner, mad at the Bureau, mad at the bastard that did this to him—and yes, to some degree, even mad at himself.

"When do you want me to start?"

"Why don't you take tomorrow seeing it's Friday anyway and we'll see you on Monday," Skinner said and smiled for the first time since he greeted Murphy at the door. "Are you going to be moving back to New Jersey?"

"We'll see. I'd like to pop in on the guys and see if there's anything I can do for them," Murphy said, referring to the guys on his old team.

"It's under control, Elliott. Taub has picked up your group and they're just fine."

"I see."

The phone beeped and Emma Carson's voice sprang from the intercom. "Sorry to bother you sir, but it's Washington."

"Thanks Emma," Skinner responded, then stood and took Murphy's hand. "I have to take this, old buddy. But you look good. Take care."

"Thanks Cal. I'll see you first thing Monday. Tell this kid to have a briefing ready for me and to get some rest over the weekend. We're gonna hit it running," Elliott said and managed a bit of a smile.

"There you go. That's the Elliott I remember," Skinner said and picked up the phone.

It was a little before noon by the time Elliott made it out of the building. He stopped by his office on the ninth floor, a small inner space that he had worked from for six months or so. It was a bit of a status symbol, though. Most field agents had nothing more than a cubicle. He checked his mail and said hello to a few of the guys. He was either paranoid or the word was out, and everyone seemed to treat him a little strangely. To Murphy, it felt like sympathy, and he hated it.

As he stood out on the sidewalk in front of the massive black office tower, he contemplated his next move. Suddenly it swept over him and he knew relief was not far away.

He needed a drink.

With this thought as a trigger, the battle within ensued.

He knew he shouldn't, but it had been over two weeks. It was still early, and if he just had a couple now, Sally wouldn't notice by the time he got home. He was still healing inside from his injuries, but he felt as good as new. Better. If he got started, he might not stop. Of course he would stop. He was, after all, the master of control. He had just been given a secondary assignment at work because his boss was worried about his drinking. Then again, what he didn't know wouldn't hurt him.

Ultimately, Elliott chose to have a couple of beers with lunch and head home. He took a cab to the other side of town, back to the same neighborhood in which he had been stabbed, beaten and robbed, and Murphy popped into O'Reilly's pub for a sandwich and a beer. This was, of course, the site of his last binge.

He never had a sandwich. He never had a beer.

He drank bourbon. In fact, he drank six bourbons at O'Reilly's pub. Then he made his way up *to S_lly's* for a couple more. When he finally staggered out, it was late afternoon and he grabbed a cab to Upper West Side. He thought he would check his mail and his apartment. But Murphy got sidetracked and ended up in yet another bar, and this time he drank light beer. But after two, he was ready for a little more whiskey, so he ordered a shot.

And another.

And that was it.

That was the last thing he remembered.

As Sally Murphy drove home from her last appointment and made a quick stop at the grocery store, she actually beamed. It had probably been self-preservation, but she hadn't outwardly admitted how unhappy she had been the last eighteen months of separation. She had been lonely, for sure, but she had also felt very uncertain about her future. Being married, having a family, and planning a life together with someone was all she had ever known. It was what she had always wanted. When that disappeared, she did the best she could to build a new life for herself but it hadn't been the same, not for a minute. And now that she was on the verge of getting her husband back, she had quickly realized how unhappy she had been. He was her soul mate.

It was with these hopeful thoughts that she pulled into the driveway, unloaded the groceries, and entered their modest four bedroom home from the garage.

"Elliott, I'm home, honey," she hollered as she put down the bags on the kitchen counter. There was no response.

She had been a little longer than she planned, it was a few minutes after six, and he was expected home before five. She checked the answering machine. First a message from one of her boys—they were both coming home for the weekend.

Elliott and Sally thought it was time to tell the boys they were going to reconcile. Then she listened to two messages that were work related. Then finally, she heard a voice, and an eerily familiar message that made her flush to lightheadedness, while her heart practically beat out of her chest. It couldn't be him.

"Sally,' ith me. Goin to stay—city. Jus' don' worry—okay? I non't feel too good. It's Elliott."

Elliott was extremely drunk. She had never heard him so drunk and she was horrified. Her first reaction was to figure out how to find him and get him some help. She also knew their wonderful new beginning would come to a screeching halt if this were to continue. The man was killing himself.

How could he do this to himself after everything he has been through?

She dialed his number in the city and of course got no answer. She tried his cell phone and it wasn't even turned on, which sent her call right to voice mail. She left a message for him to call her but knew that wasn't good enough.

She had to find him. In a rush that was close to panic, she hopped back in her car and headed toward the Lincoln Tunnel.

An hour later, when she arrived at his address, it took her a few minutes to find parking. She had actually never been inside the little four-story building, although she had driven past shortly after he first moved out. She had been on a trip into the city to see a Broadway play with a friend. It didn't seem real then, and it didn't seem real now.

She walked into the tiny entrance where two rows of mailboxes and an intercom were located. The second door, which led into the building, was locked. She buzzed his apartment and there was no answer. She stepped back to the sidewalk and tried his phone from her cell again. Still no answer. Then she saw someone coming out of the elevator through the glass doors and she tried to make it to the door to rush in behind the man, but before she could grab the door, it shut.

"Shit!" she exclaimed.

The man had noticed her attempt to gain entrance and he stuck his head back in the door.

"Can I help you with something, lady?"

She explained that she thought her husband was sick, and he must have believed her because he let her in. She thanked him and quickly climbed the stairs to the second floor and found apartment 2B.

She knocked on his door and nothing happened. She heard no voice, or noise of any kind. Her heart began to race again. She was alone in the city, a place she enjoyed from time to time but wasn't all that comfortable with, and she had no idea where her husband was. What would happen to him this time, she wondered.

The thought crossed her mind that maybe he was in the apartment and had fallen asleep or passed out. Before she looked anywhere else, she had to rule that out, but had no way to get in. She returned to the entrance and while holding the inner door open with her foot, she looked at the names on the intercom board and buzzed the one marked "superintendent."

Fortunately for Sally, she was believable and the super let her in, despite the fact the super made her show an ID to prove she was Murphy's wife. He had heard about Elliott's earlier misfortune, the mugging, and seemed eager to help.

She entered the apartment and felt a chill shoot down her spine. The super stood at the doorway to the tiny studio apartment, and there on the floor, laid her husband.

Elliott had removed his coat, suit jacket, shirt and tie and the items had been tossed on a couch that was obviously a hide-a-bed. He appeared to be out cold, on the floor, in his pants and an undershirt. There was a sharp odor of vomit in the musty apartment and as Sally approached her husband she covered her mouth and nose. There was a pool of vomit next to his head, and close to his mouth on the floor there appeared to be fresh blood. These were not good signs.

He was breathing, but in a shallow, tenuous way. She knelt next to him and spoke his name, and when she didn't get a response, she tried a second time, even louder. Nothing. The reek of alcohol wafted like a stale beer joint around his face. It was distinct and pungent, and sadly, a brutal reminder of her plight. And his.

"Jeez, lady, what's wrong with him," asked the elderly man who continued to stand at the door.

She didn't answer the question, but started to direct the action. "We need to call 911."

"We pumped his stomach and have him on an IV medication that will stop the internal bleeding," said Dr. Gordon of Lenox Hill Hospital ER. The same Dr. Gordon who had admitted Elliott several weeks ago. "I don't think he did any damage other than aggravating a stomach wound that wasn't one hundred percent healed. What on earth was he thinking? I looked at his chart from his last stay with us, and he's lucky to be alive."

Sally Murphy was relieved, but embarrassed and afraid. She was glad her husband was going to be okay, but she couldn't believe she was back at Lenox Hill Hospital again, talking with the same ER physician who admitted Elliott on the night of the stabbing.

"I don't know what he was thinking either. I'm really at a loss."

"Hang on," said Dr. Gordon, and he went behind the nurses' station and returned with a card. "This is a guy I know that specializes in addiction and alcoholism. I think you need to give him a call. Quickly. It would seem that your husband's drinking has become self-destructive, and he can't stop."

Sally just stared at the card. This was uncharted water to her. She had never known anyone that had a drinking problem and she never would have dreamed that this could be her husband. An alcoholic.

She stared at the card and absently thanked the doctor, for the second time in less than three weeks, and proceeded to sit alone in the chaotic waiting room, once again, and attempted to get her thoughts together.

She would give him one more chance. She would call this guy and have Elliott speak with him. If he resisted, he would have to sink or swim on his own. She was angry, now that she knew he was okay. What could have happened to push him to a place where he practically killed himself? She stared into the room full of long-faced, worried people, all waiting on the details of their own little nightmares, and Sally saw nothing that brought her any comfort. Her mind was reeling through the unknown, and her chest tightened under the strain of sadness, concern, anger, and fear. This was going to be a gut-wrenching test.

She just knew it.

And right when everything seemed to be looking up.

CHAPTER 29

Jack Horton and his attorney left the courtroom and walked away as fast as Jack could move without breaking into a full gallop. His roll of good fortune seemed to turn for the worse the previous week, when his wife filed for divorce and was going for his jugular, not to mention his balls. As Jack scurried along the hallways in a blur, he looked like a man who had just watched his life take a screaming nose dive into hell.

His attorney tried to keep up but was hard-pressed, carrying his heavy leather satchel that contained the document, just signed by a judge, which dramatically changed the course of Jack's existence.

"Slow down, Jack. Let's talk about this," the lawyer beckoned to Horton, who was now several strides ahead, and aiming at the exit.

"I'll tell you what," Jack said over his shoulder, "let's just get the hell out of here."

Once they were outside, Jack waited a few moments on the courthouse steps for the lawyer to emerge. Horton took a deep breath, put his hands in the pockets of his trench coat, and stared down at the steps below him. If he thought it would do any good, he would have flung himself down and tumbled to a harrowing death. But he knew, with his luck, he'd end up with a fractured skull and a broken limb or two and worse off than he was before he took the leap. On the other hand if he was presented with a chance to throw Alice off the long stone staircase, he would have done so in a heartbeat. Jack's eyes leered quickly from side to side, as he scanned the busy steps.

The lawyer caught up and attempted to console his client as he calmed himself.

"Look, this sort of thing happens. You left her, there are three kids involved, and she doesn't work. The judge just wants to make sure she's taken care of during this next phase of the process."

"Taken care of! She's going to live like a fuckin' queen, while I end up on the street. How could this happen?"

"I admit, it's a little excessive. She's got a pretty aggressive attorney. They went for broke and they got a ruling in their favor. It's just the beginning. I'm not usually that aggressive, for I believe a judge usually respects a little moderation."

"Yeah, well, this time you made a mistake," Jack said, although he hadn't looked at the lawyer once. He was so angry that he was worried he might slug the guy.

Alice's attorney had been successful in obtaining temporary orders that required Jack to pay Alice $7,000 a month, plus make the house payment, as well as allow her to have exclusive use of the house, custody of the boys, what little there was in their bank accounts, plus Jack was required to pay her all of the winnings from the casino, which were over $140,000.

"Can you afford the support for a few months? I'm sure we'll be able to get it lowered," the little man said while looking at his watch. "Once final proceedings begin."

"I see you need to go," Jack snapped. "What difference does it make if I can afford it or not? I have to pay it. I would have thought that the time to prove I can or can't afford it has come and gone. I know for a fact that if I'm making the house payment, she can do fine on two grand a month. Seven thousand is absolutely insane. I'll just talk to you later," Jack said, finally looking the man squarely in the eye. He was pissed and his lawyer knew it. Jack wheeled around and hustled down the stairs to the street below.

He knew right where he needed to go.

He had called ahead to Phil Cassavetti's office and fortunately his new friend was in at the time and had some time to see him.

After arriving in a huff, Horton sat across the desk from the man and after five minutes of ranting and raving, Cassavetti raised his hand.

"Ho, Jack, stop. You're making me angry for Christ sake. So whadda ya want me to do about it? You tell me. I mean, I can help you, but how far do you want to go?"

"I want to get rid of her."

For a moment, the room was filled with silence. A chilling silence. Then Cassavetti opened one of his desk drawers and pulled something out. It was a long metal device, something like the wands that security personnel use in the airports. He got up and walked around the desk to Jack.

"Get up," he commanded. Horton obeyed.

"What are you doing?" Jack asked.

"Just making sure you're not wired."

"Wired? What the hell do you mean? Of course I'm not wired. I'm the one talking about getting rid of my wife."

Cassavetti moved the wand up one side and down the other and within seconds he was noticeably relieved.

"Exactly. It's not every day that a suburban dweller insurance guy walks in here and asks me something like this. I mean I know you're goin' a little crazy, but this is something extreme, Jack. There's no going back on something like this," Cassavetti said as he returned to his desk and put the device back in the drawer. "Once you put something like this in motion, it won't stop and when it's over, your kids will never see their mother again."

"I understand and I've given it a lot of thought," he responded. "She's miserable. She's not going to stop pressing me until I'm ruined. My girlfriend is barely interested in seeing me so long as there's this entanglement. And as for my boys, they'd be better off without her. She's evil, Phil. The woman's fucking evil!"

Jack was telling the truth. He had been giving this option plenty of thought. It seemed incredible to him one moment, and the next it seemed essential for survival, as if something switched on inside him; and into that acidic swirl came a loathing, and a hatred, like he had never experienced before. This business over the money was just the beginning. This woman would ruin his life, several times over, if he let her.

Cassavetti was silent for a moment, but then he spoke in a somber tone. "Fifty grand," said Cassavetti. "Have the cash with you tonight and my driver will pick you up. Have it in an envelope. Get in the car, hand him the envelope, and I don't want you to say a word to him. He's going to drive you to a certain location and drop you off. Bring cab fare."

"Who's going to do this?"

Cassavetti looked unflinchingly straight into Horton's eyes, "Don't ask those kinds of questions, Jack. I told you before, I have friends. Let's just leave it at that."

"I got it."

"Make sure you do. And you and I, we're never going to talk about this thing again," Cassavetti said as he slid a post-it pad across his desk. "Write down your wife's address."

As Jack wrote out the address in Syosset, Long Island, he realized the magnitude of what he was doing. He willfully iced himself inside as his hand wrote the last numbers. There was no turning back now, he thought to himself, and he knew it was true.

Aside from helping his situation, perhaps he was sparing his wife from more anger and misery when she was already the most angry, miserable woman he'd ever known. As for the boys, they could go live with their grandparents for a while.

It was time for *him* to live a little.

CHAPTER 30

As he prepared to speak the words, he couldn't believe they were forming in his mouth. Most of what had occurred during the last week seemed completely unfathomable. But on another, more profound level, he knew it was happening, he knew the moment was necessary, and he knew the statement was true.

"My name is Elliott and I'm an alcoholic."

He paused for a moment before he continued, as a swell of emotion hit him so intensely that it made him feel lightheaded, and surged through his entire being. He looked over the circle of others. Some faces were drawn, some faces were smiling, and a few faces looked down at the floor—but every countenance seemed to be listening. These were the people to whom, over the last week, he had given his faith and his truth. They too were alcoholics, trudging through their lives without booze, but soberly, and without the incumbent chaos of that liquid haze. He was at an eight o'clock meeting of Alcoholics Anonymous in the basement of a Presbyterian church a few miles from his home in Cedar Grove.

He had spent only one night in the hospital after practically killing himself, again. The incident had luckily proven to be only a minor setback in his internal healing from the surgery to repair his gut after the stabbing. But this little slip could have been fatal. He had been told not to drink alcohol, not to even eat spicy food, for at least six weeks after his release from Lenox Hill. He woke up in the hospital feeling worse than he had ever felt in his life; physically, emotionally, you name it. He knew he was in deep, deep trouble and he was finally reduced to being open to anything that would help. He remembered that Cal Skinner had mentioned that Harry Elson, a fellow agent, was in AA and he asked Sally to give him a call. It was a Saturday morning, the agent dropped everything he was doing and drove from his home in Peekskill, north of the city, to New Jersey, and traded the rest of the day to be with a beaten, fearful, and very remorseful, Elliott Murphy.

The good news was that Elliott had asked for help and had received it. When Elson showed up, he was like a frontline trooper rolling in to help. Harry had been through much worse than Murphy had experienced. He lost his family, almost lost his job with the Bureau after a driving while intoxicated charge; and worst of all, near the end of his drinking career, survived three years of solitude as a reclusive drunk. That was over eight years ago but it was certainly something to which Elliott could relate. He talked with Elson for hours and attended an AA meeting every day. He began to see his own truth through hearing the truths of others and after having chosen booze over his family, he finally realized that he was losing his soul in the process.

Tonight was the first time he had the courage to speak to the group. But once he started to talk, the words just came to him. He was one of them, an alcoholic. And while he didn't have stories to tell of his own arrests, wife beatings, or living on the street, neither did most of the other men who sat in the room. He described the dependence that had come out of nowhere, the destruction of his marriage, the failing job performance, and ultimately, the stabbing, which he finally attributed to his drinking. If he hadn't been out boozing it up, alone, in a deserted part of town, it simply wouldn't have happened. But the real insanity was his last spree. How could anyone pull what he had, while risking humiliation like he had never experienced in his life, and literally risking death with a healing stomach? Not to mention the embarrassment it had caused his wife, who had just a few days before, agreed to reconcile. She had every reason to run.

But Sally had stood by him. They managed to keep the incident quiet. The only people who knew were the people he had met in AA, Elson and the hospital. However, Sally made it clear; he either sought help and quit drinking for good, or he was back out the door. On Elson's advice, Sally had attended a couple of Al Anon meetings where those affected by alcoholism gathered to support one another and learn how to set boundaries. She learned a few things at each meeting, but she didn't particularly care to rant and rave about her husband like some of the women present.

After all, Elliott was really a pretty good guy, aside from the niggling fact that he had essentially up and left her.

In the span of less than a week, life had once again taken a drastic change within the Murphy family. Elliott returned to the home in Cedar Grove and planned to stay there. He gave notice to his landlord in the city to vacate the apartment. He returned to work, and despite his reassignment to the OCU, he was glad to be back and was easing himself into the work without resentment.

Before 9/11 he had enjoyed working in Organized Crime and he spent the first week getting up to speed with the primary cases they were working. Some of the faces had changed, but most of the games were still the same; drugs, prostitution, money laundering, and murder were still part of the 'thing.'

After he was done talking, spilling his guts in front of these men and women who were strangers to him only a week earlier, he felt an immense sense of relief. It was like a thousand-pound gorilla had been lifted off his shoulders. The open admission of such insanity had actually been very empowering. After sticking around drinking coffee with several of the others, he left the meeting feeling as though a new day had dawned. He sensed he had another chance, one that a short time ago he didn't even know he needed. Denial had been more pervasive in his thinking than he had ever thought possible.

And the veil was lifted for Elliott Murphy.

CHAPTER 31

As Alice Horton made her way home from the short drive to the school bus stop, she had no idea she was being followed. She wore a bulky blue parka and beneath it she was still in her long flannel robe, a baggy sweat-suit and on her feet she wore white socks and tennis shoes. This routine of dropping the boys off was something she reluctantly performed every school day morning. Today she planned to crawl back in the bed, watch the morning shows, eat Krispy Cream donuts and drink coffee for at least another hour or two. She had nothing else to do today. Her parents had agreed to pick up the boys from school and take them for the weekend. She had nothing what-so-ever to do all weekend, in fact.

The Horton home was located on a quiet street and faced a small greenbelt park. The property was on a bend so that no one had a view of the house unless they were directly in front of it. It was therefore deemed a safe place by the two contractors dispatched by Andy Vassallo to grab the woman. They had been keeping an eye on her for a few days and noticed that this was the only routine that they could count on. She didn't go to work, she didn't leave for the grocery store at any certain time, and she didn't attend exercise classes or anything else reliable. This was the time to snatch her.

There were two of them. Paul Visante and Jimmy Corelli. Visante was in charge, and had been given the assignment by Andy Vassallo, one of Cassavetti's henchmen. Corelli was just along to drive. Visante had served a five year sentence for armed robbery and had been "made" or anointed for life as a member of the Gallo family with all the designation's rights and privileges right after he had returned from prison. At no point did he ever open his mouth and barter for a lighter sentence in exchange for damaging information or testimony that invariably every member of the mob stashed in their heads. His loyalty was repaid shortly after being released by being 'made.' But he wasn't too bright and wasn't that big of an earner, he was assigned the simple stuff such as loan sharking, theft and muscle.

He was a lonely man, his only female companionship was typically the occasional hooker, or one night stands with drunken loners like him. Not because he was ugly or unpleasant, but because he was painfully shy with women, afraid of rejection perhaps, and solidly convinced over the years that he would never have any true companionship. But perhaps, he thought, he might be able to change that dilemma with the opportunity in front of him.

The two men watched as the car pulled in the drive. Then the plan sprung into action. Before the car had even stopped inside the open garage, Visante was out of his vehicle and quickly walking up the short drive and into the garage. The woman opened the door and by the time she realized what was happening, a large, ominous figure was rapidly approaching her inside her own garage. She let out a scream and flung herself back in the car and attempted to close the door. The man sprung at the closing door with amazing speed and agility for his size and grabbed the door before it closed. He quickly pulled it from her grasp and opened it. In a flash, he reached in with one hand, grabbed her by the hair, and with the other jammed a wet rag over her mouth and nose.

The last thing she would remember was the sharp, smell of the ether-like fluid. That and the disbelief of what was happening to her, although, if she remembered anything about what had happened, she also might recall a brief millisecond of anger over missing out on the Krispy Creams.

Visante pushed her off the driver's seat and managed, with some difficulty, to get her limp body situated across the rear bench. She was a little heavier than he had expected but he was strong, and eventually accomplished the task.

He paused for a moment; he looked down at her flailed out across the rear seat. Visante pushed the hair off her face and for the first time he actually took the time to notice her appearance. She was a little plump and there were bags beneath her eyes, but he thought to himself, *she will do*.

The keys were still in the ignition so he started the minivan and pulled out of the driveway, looking carefully to ensure there were no people walking dogs or jogging down the empty street. It was clear. He pulled away with Corelli following close behind and navigated out of the subdivision taking a previously selected route. Once he made his way to the expressway, he finally relaxed.

Their two-car caravan made its way down the Long Island Expressway through Queens, crossed the East River on the Tri-Borough Bridge to Interstate 95, and traveled up the Hudson on Route Nine in the direction of the Catskills. They stopped at the first rest-stop, which was uninhabited, and the two men managed to discreetly carry the woman out of her own car, which they abandoned, and moved her into their van. With an electric screwdriver, Corelli removed the plates from the mini-van, which was intended to delay the identification of the vehicle, if it didn't end up in a chop shop first.

When they came to the Monticello exit they turned off, and after spending another twenty minutes meandering through the majestic valleys of up-state New York, Vasselli turned the van off the road into a private entrance. Vaselli stopped in front of the gate, hopped out of the van, and quickly unlocked a chain and opened their path. They drove down a gravel drive that led into the woods to a small cabin on ten acres that Vaselli owned, totally out of view from the road.

This was his escape from the real world, a place he came to as often as he could to be alone, and be the person he never could be on the streets, in the bars and brothels, or the smokey gambling rooms that comprised the typical setting for his underworld existence. Here, he was a different person. He was known in the country stores and shops as Paul V, and was seen as just another weekender who was quiet, pleasant and not some wealthy New Yorker who looked down on the locals. No one knew who he really was back in the city, and they would've been shocked to discover he was a loan shark, a pimp, and even a murderer. Paul V. spent his time taking care of the cabin he built himself with the help of a few local tradesmen. Most of his time there was spent caring for the property itself, and hunting and fishing a small stream that ran along the back border of his land.

This was where he chose to bring Alice Horton. His orders were to get rid of her and he was in control of that process. She would never leave this place. But what he did with her in the near future had not yet been decided. He was lonely, perhaps he might just keep her alive for a short time and force her to satisfy some of his needs. He hadn't decided.

For now, he locked her in a small interior room. It was meant to be a study or a guest room and it was complete with a television, a single bed, and a half-bath. He would also place a small refrigerator inside, with a few cold-cuts and some bread, along with a couple of other things to eat. She would be fine for a few days until he could return.

And there wasn't any way for her to escape. There was one door, no windows and the door was locked with a commercial quality deadbolt. He had prepared for this possibility; he just never knew when the opportunity might avail itself, or with whom.

The opportunity had arrived.

CHAPTER 32

It had been one of those late March weekends that New Yorkers savored. A respite from winter had finally arrived as mild temperatures slid into the region and warmed the city. The sun shone brightly on Saturday and Sunday and nothing more than a gentle breeze meandered down the city blocks and across the parks of Manhattan. It was truly a glorious couple of days.

Jack Horton was one of those New Yorkers enjoying the weekend. He and Rachel strolled through Central Park, and Jack was wearing all black as he was evolving into someone who was 'cool' by night and weekend. Fortunately, he had the good sense not to bring too much of his new self to work during the week.

Despite the relaxing warmth and freshness of the day, Rachel seemed to use Sunday afternoons to make Jack crazy. This particular time she confessed to her true sexuality; she was bisexual. Her friends down in the Caribbean had actually been a little more than friends. Rachel apologized for not being completely honest. She just didn't want to freak him out since they had just met. Regardless, she was still exploring this side of her sexuality and she just couldn't commit to him in any way while she was also sleeping around with other women. But he was the only man, she explained. In fact, she went on, if he didn't mind this revelation, they could still continue having *fun* together.

The good thing about waiting until Sunday to drop these revelations, Jack thought, was that at least she had screwed his brains out for a day and a half prior. Unlike the last time, when she told him she didn't think she should see him anymore, this incident was a little different. First off, while she seemed to want to push him away a couple of weeks ago and had mentioned an old boyfriend whom Jack had suspected was fictitious right from the start, it didn't take long before they were seeing each other all the time again. If she was truly concerned about breaking up a family, she perhaps figured out that the split was the best thing that ever happened to him. Or maybe she really didn't care that much after all. Secondly, this latest proclamation was kind of interesting. As Jack thought about it and gently rolled it over in his mind, he decided there might be a little opportunity in it for *him*.

"Well, okay. I mean, I can kind of understand," Jack responded after Rachel revealed her latest twist. "I mean, it's nothing I would ever want to explore with a *guy*, but I can understand it better between two women. It's not like intrusive or anything."

Rachel agreed. "So, it's not something that freaks you out?" she asked as she smiled up at him.

She was dressed in hip hugger sweat pants that barely covered her rear end and a sports bra with a jean jacket. It may have been unseasonably warm but it was still just in the high fifties, and jackets were still essential. Anyway, Rachel looked very hot, wearing only the spandex bra, which exposed the sculpted shape of her breasts to the world.

"No, it might take a little getting used to, but it doesn't freak me out. I'd kind of like to meet one of these girls you're seeing," Jack suggested as they strolled past the infamous statue of Alice in Wonderland. "Maybe the *three* of us could get together?"

She looked up at him, at first suspiciously, but then a devilish little smile appeared. "Hmmm, we'll have to see about that. I guess it might be kind of cool."

Jack tried to restrain his enthusiasm. His relationship with Rachel had been on such a roller coaster, he had to admit, he was more than a little confused. He didn't know if he could honestly say he was obsessed with her, and he couldn't calculate if his attraction was centered in the concept of her, the sex with her or something else entirely? He was at a loss, having been stuck with Alice for over a decade, who for all practical purposes was a miserable woman who hadn't even talked about kinky sex that Jack could recall. The old man was in another universe now. Just hours earlier Rachel had tied him to a chair, blindfolded him, attached nipple clamps while going down on him, and filmed the whole thing. Jack was still a little shaky from that little number.

So, if Jack was completely honest, he wasn't clear on the focal point of his fixation. He knew he liked her and he knew he wanted to keep seeing her. So long as it didn't involve other guys, he was in. And hopefully, he was in the circle!

His cell phone chirped just as he grabbed her hand and pulled her close. "Shit," he said under his breath. He pulled the cell out of his black jean jacket and stared down at the screen. He quickly recognized the incoming number and stopped in his tracks. He wasn't quite sure if he should answer the phone or not.

Rachel could tell Jack was concerned. "Who is it?" she asked.

"Uhhh, I think it's Alice's parents," he said as he continued to stare at the phone as it chirped for a response. Finally, he took a deep breath and pushed the button. "Hello."

"Jack, it's Harvey Schmidt," Alice's father announced. Over ten years and he still found it necessary to include his last name as though Jack wouldn't recognize his monotone, fat-assed voice. Jack loathed Alice's parents, almost as much as her.

"What's up, Harv?" he asked as he stopped walking and pulled off to the side of the path so as to not hold up the procession of citizenry enjoying the day.

"Alice was supposed to pick up the boys at noon and she hasn't shown up. We can't reach her anywhere."

Jack froze. He knew what this meant; Alice was gone. But he also knew that he had to keep his wits about him. He had prepared himself as best he could. He was ready to act this out.

"You're kidding," he replied with what sounded like genuine concern.

"No, I'm not. This isn't like her. I take it she's not with you?"

Jack glanced at Rachel who was staring at him with curiosity.

"No, Harv, she's not with me," Jack said, shaking his head. "I assume you've tried her cell phone?"

"Yes," he said distantly, and fell silent.

Jack had rehearsed this call a hundred times since he met with Cassavetti. He didn't know how it would come, or when, or who would call him. He didn't know if he would be told she had disappeared, or had been found bludgeoned on the side of the road. Cassavetti had told him the less he knew, the better. So, there was an element of surprise to this news, although Horton was ready with his reaction.

"Well, I can come out and pick up the boys if that will help. Have you been over to check the house?" Jack asked, being careful not to sound too panicked. But he also knew that Harvey Schmidt and his wife, Ellie, would be at a loss as to what to do next. Making decisions was next to impossible for them, and that fact had even bothered Alice. So he knew he would have to step in and go through the motions. He would have to do what any other concerned family member would do; he had to check with friends, call the hospitals and ultimately, call the police.

"The boys are fine with us," Harvey said in a monotone. "Why don't you come out though and check her house. I assume you still have a key."

"Of course. I'll be out in an hour or so, as soon as I can get there. My car is in the garage at the house, so I will have to take the train. I'll call you when I get there."

"Okay."

Jack just hung up and looked at Rachel.

"Apparently Alice didn't show to pick up the boys from her parents. I'm going to have to go out there," Jack said apologetically.

"Huh," replied Rachel with a girlish pout on her face. "I was just going to suggest that you meet one of my friends this evening."

What timing, Jack thought. This would be just like Alice—to ruin his first chance at a life-changing event, a threesome—even in her demise. Jack turned to lead them back out of the park.

"How about later on?"

"We'll see. You know, this is the kind of thing that I was afraid of. These entanglements with your wife and kids, I just don't know if it's what I want to be involved with," Rachel decried, as the two walked toward the exit near the Metropolitan Museum on the east side.

Jack took this new information in and considered it for a moment. He didn't want to say anything he would regret later like, *don't worry, I've handled that problem*, or, *the bitch won't be around to bother us anymore.* And fortunately, he thought better of it.

"Look, this is a one in a million situation. I'll be back in the city later tonight, and maybe we can still get together."

"We'll see. We all have to work tomorrow. Call me. I'm going to take a cab uptown, I take it you're going to Grand Central," Rachel said, already looking for a free taxi on Fifth Avenue.

Jack arrived at the house in Syosset about an hour and a half later, he had been lucky to grab the three-fifteen train that left minutes after he arrived at Grand Central. He took a cab to his old address and came to find the house open. The front door was unlocked, but nothing looked broken. Jack wondered whether he should be touching anything but then he thought to himself, *think like you've got nothing to do with this.* He realized that he would come bounding into the house, check everywhere to be sure she wasn't laying dead on the floor somewhere, and then get on the phone and call the few friends she had to determine where she was under such strange circumstances.

So, he began to act it all out, although he wasn't entirely acting. He was a little nervous he might find a gruesome scene as he supposed whoever Cassavetti had hired might have blown her head off in her own house. He even checked in all the closets, under the beds, the tubs, virtually everywhere someone could be found. He looked and found nothing. He then checked the garage, entering from the door in the kitchen, and came up empty again.

Next, he went to the tattered phone directory that Alice kept on the kitchen counter and began dialing the numbers of her friends. There were only four numbers to call that made any sense, *if this were really happening.* He was able to reach three of the four and invariably, each of the women were completely obnoxious to him. Jack didn't let it bother him for a minute. They obviously had heard only one side of the split and certainly Alice would have portrayed herself as the pathetic victim. Alice was a bitch, her friends were just like her and totally bought into her side of the story—what did he expect? He simply asked each one if they had seen or heard from her over the weekend, and they each said no, and he got off the line.

Now Jack contemplated what to do next. The two area hospitals should be called, and of course, the police. His heart and mind began to race as he tried to envision how that would go. Surprisingly, he was discovering that he was pretty good at this. He calmed down and told himself, *you've done nothing wrong.* He knew that he was at the bottom of all this, but now he understood why Cassavetti had spared him the details. He knew nothing of Alice's whereabouts. He knew he just had to play dumb, innocent, and appropriately concerned, and this would all blow over. Alice would be gone from his life forever; he could live out all his sexual fantasies with Rachel. He could actually see that he would be happy. And maybe visit the boys every once in awhile at their grandparents. Life would be good!

He called Alice's father to let him know he was at the house, reported that Alice was nowhere to be found, and for good measure he began the conversation by asking if she had shown up yet. He told Schmidt that he was about to call the hospitals and the police. He even asked if the boys were okay. They were fine, the old man said, and were playing video games and fighting. *Status quo*, Jack thought.

After two more calls, Jack Horton was on the record with both area hospitals as inquiring about his missing wife. There was no indication of her being admitted to either facility, nor had she been treated at any time over the weekend in either ER.

Now it was time for 9-1-1.

"Police emergency, what is the nature of your call?" a young man's voice stated in a very matter-of-fact voice.

"My wife is missing. She was supposed to pick up our children several hours ago and she can't be reached on her cell phone, none of her friends have heard from her, I've even checked with the hospitals. She's disappeared!" Jack said in the most troubled voice he could muster. He knew he was being recorded and he wanted to sound just a little bit frantic.

"How long has it been since anyone spoke with her?" the young man asked.

"I'm not sure, I know that she dropped our boys off at school on Friday, and that's it. We're separated. I live in the city and her parents picked up the boys from school Friday afternoon for the weekend. But her parents didn't hear from her all weekend, and none of her friends have seen her, and I didn't know what to do next but call the police."

"Sir, we'll send a car over and the officer will determine if we can take a missing person report. Normally we wait twenty-four hours, but I'll let the patrol officers figure that out with you." The young man sounded sympathetic. "I need your name and let me confirm the address we have for this phone number …"

Jack gave him all the information and hung up. He knew he wouldn't have long before the patrol car arrived, but he was ready. He was really getting into character.

The Suffolk County police car arrived within ten minutes. He opened the front door before they had a chance to get to it and he was surprised to see two women approach him.

Oh boy, Jack thought to himself. *Hopefully not a couple of man haters!*

They introduced themselves as Officers Harvey and Baducci. Officer Harvey was a tall black woman who looked as though she weighed two hundred pounds but there was nothing soft about her rock solid frame. Officer Baducci was dark haired and almost a little attractive, with what appeared to be a large chest hidden behind the unflattering garb of her uniform.

"You called in a missing person, sir?" Officer Harvey snapped. She held a note pad on a metal clipboard and it was clear she was the one in charge. Baducci quietly surveyed the scene.

Jack invited them in and told them everything he knew about his wife gone missing excepting the part about paying Phil Cassavetti fifty-thousand-dollars to have some streetpunk Neanderthal get rid of her. They took the report and Officer Harvey explained this would open the case. Alice's license plate and vehicle description would be sent out, all the hospitals would be alerted, the State Highway Patrol, and other law enforcement agencies. If she didn't turn up in the next twenty-four hours, he would be contacted by the detective who would be assigned to the case.

"We see a lot of different things happen in these situations, sir. You two are separated; maybe she met someone and decided to take off for awhile. She'll turn up," said the other officer with the big boobs.

Jack had pulled it off. He had snowed these two cops anyway and now they were leaving. The black woman, Officer Harvey, had given Jack her card. Jack thanked her and had been within an inch of asking Officer Baducci for hers, but had caught himself before he made that mistake. He settled for one last look at her chest.

Oh well, Jack thought to himself. What would he want with a big-breasted cop when he had kinky Rachel waiting for him back in the city? He hopped in his car and headed back to Manhattan. He called his father-in-law from the car and filled him in on the details, and told him the cops thought she probably ran off with some guy for a few days. Of course the man was silent. Jack told him he had an important meeting in the morning, so if he wouldn't mind, the boys needed to stay on with Harv and Ellie. Harv agreed.

Jack was elated, having passed the first test in this scheme. He knew there would be more questions and more cops and more play acting, but he had survived the first episode, and in fact, could sense the two female cops actually felt sorry for him. Maybe that drama class he took his sophomore year in college had paid off after all.

Now he was headed back to his new life in Manhattan. *Who knows*, he thought to himself. *There might be time for that threesome with Rachel after all.*

CHAPTER 33

Sobriety was feeling pretty damn good to Elliott Murphy after all of a month without a drink. Despite the fact that he had only been boozing heavily for a little over two years of his adult life, as he faced the truth of the wreck he had made of things in that period, it seemed like an eternity now. He was hell-bent on making up for lost time.

Elliott was attending AA meetings frequently, sometimes twice a day. He would catch a meeting at noon in the city and another in the late evening near his home in Cedar Grove. He had completely moved out of the apartment on the Upper West Side, was back with Sally, frequently not believing that he had ever left. He had accepted the quasi-demotion off the Bureau's Terrorism Unit and was putting everything he had into his new assignment with Organized Crime. He had been one of two senior agents running the OCU prior to 9/11, so it was not unfamiliar ground and now, after a couple of weeks getting back up to speed, he was totally on top of things once again.

Doing that sober, wasn't easy. Cravings for alcohol would sometimes flow over him like a powerful wave. In a few instances he found himself taking two steps in the wrong direction towards a bar, or slowing down the car as he passed a liquor store. But the cravings passed quicker with each day. He had been given tools in his meetings and by other recovering drunks to prevent that first drink. He struggled some with the spiritual side of the program, but he began to discover that perhaps the 'Higher Power' he would ask for strength might really be legit. He never walked into those bars; he never turned off the road into the liquor store parking lots. At least not to the point of being thirty days sober.

Everyone in AA had told him to find a "sponsor." This was kind of a mentor who would guide him through the steps and be there for him on the other end of the phone at two a.m. if the need arose. Harry Elson had told him he would be there for him but didn't feel comfortable as his permanent sponsor as they worked together at the FBI. But he found a sponsor after a couple of weeks and his name was Robert M. He was a crotchety old man, probably seventy, who chain-smoked and made his living running poker games out of a back room of his house which was on the other side of the tracks from Elliott's in a town adjoining Cedar Grove. Robert M. was an odd character, but he sure seemed to know his AA and Elliott respected what he had to say. He would tell Elliott to sit down, shut up, and don't take a drink when you go home. It seemed like an elementary school primer, but it worked.

So, with the help of an old man who was apparently committing a minor ongoing felony by running an illegal gambling parlor, the senior FBI agent was staying sober. Elliott was learning that AA was about ironies and struggles and good people and bad people wanting to get better. They just didn't want to get drunk again, and neither did he.

As he was living in New Jersey and doing more field-work, Cal Skinner assigned Murphy a vehicle. It was a gesture of confidence, or at least Murphy took it as such, and the act made him feel like he was back in the game. El-liott was on his way to Queens, driving a brand new Crown Victoria with all the gadgets. It had emergency lights in the grille and the rear window, and sported a siren, radios, a cell phone, a computer terminal mounted below the dash, and even a fax machine that was mounted in the trunk. It was literally a mobile law enforcement office.

Murphy was on his own, he was on his way to the 27th Precinct where he would be meeting with two NYPD de-tectives that were on a case in which the Organized Crime Unit of the Bureau was interested. Two Irish brothers had shown up dead a couple weeks before and an informant had provided some information that promised to link the killing to the Gallo crime family. The Gallo's had been low on the priority list for quite some time, and it was their style to remain off the radar screen by conducting themselves in a low profile manner. So, several murders were a little out of character for the infamous crime family, as of late.

Murphy arrived at the precinct and parked in a reserved spot. He knew that these parking spots were not for a spe-cific person but for detectives and brass, or a visiting Fed like himself. Elliott had quickly developed a new found passion for his job, just as he had found a rekindled love for his wife, and his sons. Even the stars and the moon.

He was grateful to have survived all that he had endured, and believed he had been given several second chances.

He was escorted up to the second floor by a duty officer and introduced to Sergeant Detective Sam Rainsworth. He was an overweight slob who was in the middle of a burger at ten-thirty in the morning. He quickly brushed crumbs off his hands, and with a mouth half-full of food, greeted Senior Special Agent Elliott Murphy, FBI.

"Pleased to meet you, Detective. Elliott Murphy," he responded as he gave the man a firm handshake and immediately felt something tacky on his fingers. He ignored it. Dealing with NYPD was always a little different. But he knew what these guys faced out there on the streets and he respected the job they did, at least he respected most of them.

"Hope we can make this worth your while, my partner is on his way in with this guy—but he's a little squirrelly," Detective Rainsworth offered. "Why don't we wait in one of the interrogation rooms and I'll go over the file with you."

"Lead the way," answered Murphy.

Rainsworth grabbed a thick file off his cluttered desk and led the way to a room off a hallway that had two entrances. There was a large mirror on one wall that Murphy knew to be a one-way observation mirror and he also knew that the door on the other side of the room led to the holding cells. In the middle of the small room was a table with four chairs around it, and in the middle of the table there was an iron clasp to secure prisoner restraints. Not all the thugs that were brought into this room for questioning had very good manners.

They both took seats, Rainsworth opened the file and began, "Okay, the guy my partner's bringing in is Salvatore Gatti. Sal is a two-time loser, both charges were for felony theft, and if he gets popped again, he'll do some serious time. He's just about to wrap up probation on the second charge and we managed to get to him about six months ago," Rainsworth said and stopped for a moment to beat his upper chest briefly to loosen up a belch. "Excuse me," he said and Elliott nodded. "I should have grabbed a soda or something. Stomach isn't quite what it used to be."

"Go on," Murphy coaxed.

"Okay, well, we know this guy was running numbers for the Gallos. They run games out of the back of a pizza joint on Brushburn Street. It's never been a nuisance and it would be tough to make a case against them without some-one on the inside so we gave this guy a deal. We shortened up his probation and got Corrections to turn him over to us. He doesn't have to meet with his P.O., and there are no restrictions or nothin'."

"Okay, so what has he come up with that we'd be inter-ested in on these two brothers," Murphy asked. He wanted to cut to the chase.

"Well, apparently one night last week he was hangin' around the pizza joint and two heavies came in all fucked up. Anyway, these guys had been drinkin' and were blab-berin' away about a hit and expressed worries about reper-cussions from an Irish gang called the Westies."

"We're aware of them," Murphy chimed in.

"So he heard one of the guys referring to the victims as a couple of 'micks' and it just so happens that we have an 'unsolved' homicide that was two Irish guys, and they were brothers. We found 'em completely shot up a block or so down from a little bar where a lot of Irish frequent over in lower Queens," Rainsworth said as he opened the file. The pictures he pulled out to show Murphy were the blood-soaked, bullet-riddled bodies of two young men.

Elliott shook his head and grimaced. No matter how long you're on the job, looking at death was never easy for most cops, whether street cops or Feds.

"Does your guy know who these two guys were?" Murphy asked as Rainsworth slid the gruesome photos into the manila file. "You know, the ones he overheard in the pizza place."

"Don't know," said Rainsworth. "So far, we just got a voice mail message from him. He's a little worried because he thinks these guys might be after him. Figures they might have come to their senses after they sobered up and realized they had been a little loose lipped in front of him."

There was a knock at the door and it opened up quickly.

In contrast to the pleasant but slovenly Rainsworth, his partner was wiry and jumpy. He was probably six-foot-four and one hundred and eighty-five pounds with a lousy haircut and a big swooping moustache that was at least a decade behind the times.

"Dennis Coulter," he said quickly as he practically dragged a little man in behind him that Murphy surmised was their informant, Sal Gatti. Coulter directed Gatti to sit down and then reached over to shake Murphy's hand. Rainsworth introduced everyone.

"We don't want to keep Sal here off the streets too long, so Sal," Coulter said and faced the little dark-haired, olive-skinned man. "Tell 'em about what you heard."

"Well, I gotta tell ya, this shit is gonna get me killed."

"Just spill it, Sal," commanded Coulter.

"Okay, well just remember, you told me that if things got too hot, you'd get me out of town," the little man said through flinches and squirms. "What if someone was watching me and they saw you pick me up today?"

"Sal, *now!*"

"Okay, okay. What I heard was Stevie Bugliosi and a guy they call 'Stub' because someone shot half his foot off, anyway, these guys come into Vittorio's after I got back from pickin' up somethin,'" he said. "These guys are real juiced and talkin' loud but nobody was in there, see, but me and some kid behind the counter. So Bugliosi goes off about a hit job, something about a couple of micks somebody whacked, and they were worried they might hear something back from the Westies. I guess the dead brothers; he said they were brothers, belonged to the Westies."

"Look Mr. Gatti," Murphy interrupted, "the FBI is not interested in any low-level guys and I'm sure the men you heard weren't bosses."

"Na, but they are definitely on the inside," Gatti offered, nervously. "I don't know much about the Stub, but Bugliosi is a pretty big guy. I think he works for Andy Vassallo, which means he's into a lot of bad stuff."

Now Murphy was getting interested. As Elliott had spent much of his first week back getting reacquainted with the players in the Gallo family, Vassallo was definitely on the top rungs aside from upper management. The Feds knew that he was a captain, that he ran a crew and that his primary business was extortion. He and his guys would extract protection money out of everyone from convenience store operators to drug dealers. Tough business, but Vassallo and his boys were tough operators. They were the Gallo's muscle, and considered to be good at their work.

"Did Bugliosi mention Vassallo?" Murphy asked.

"Well, yeah. He did. But this is where I start to wonder if I'm signing my own death certificate."

"Just tell him, Sal," commanded Coulter impatiently.

Murphy didn't care much for Coulter already. Elliott's experience was that anyone who was this jumpy, usually had something to hide. He wondered what this guy's secret was.

"Just relax, Sal," Murphy offered. "We're not testifying in court here. This is just between us for now. No disrespect but bringing in a two time felon who's providing testimony in exchange for a few favors doesn't get us much mileage in court. We're interested in what you have to say and we'll use it, but we'll get our hard evidence elsewhere."

"Okay, well, if you give me your word this goes no further," the little man said reluctantly.

"You have my word," Elliott said with a nod of acknowledgement.

"Bugliosi said that "*Andy*" had offed these guys, and that '*Andy*' had put them in this position of being at odds with the Westies. Now I know there could be a lot of '*Andy's*' out there, but just as I made my way into the back 'cause I was getting real nervous listenin' to this stuff, I heard Stub say to Stevie, 'fuckin Vassallo.' That's why I know it was him they was talkin' about."

The room went silent for a moment. Murphy was jotting a few notes down on a small pad he carried with him. *This was good stuff*, Murphy thought to himself.

Then Coulter broke the silence, "All right, Sal. Let's go."

Murphy really didn't like this guy, this squirming, lanky detective. He had a few more questions and he was going to get them asked.

"Hold on," he said before Gatti had a chance to respond. "Sal, what do you know about Andy Vassallo?"

"Oh, Jesus. Don't start askin' me questions like that. Vassallo is not someone you mess with. I've never met the guy and I never will unless he comes after me over this thing! He's one mean motherfucker. He's a *hit man* for Chrissake, and he runs all the bad guys for the Gallos."

"How do you know this?" Murphy asked, probing.

"Who doesn't?"

"All right. Well if that's everything, you're free to go," Murphy said and nodded to Coulter who immediately hopped up. Gatti took the cue, and they were gone as quickly as they came.

Murphy and Rainsworth remained seated in the dingy, worn interrogation room.

"Well," Rainsworth said. "What do you think?"

"I think that we're going to need to work together on this. You guys continue to handle the homicide investigation, but I need to know where it's going, every step of the way," Murphy said thoughtfully, sliding the small, leather bound, note pad back in the pocket of his suit jacket. "So what's up with your partner? He sure seems jumpy."

"Don't know him that well," Rainsworth answered and stood up. "He's pretty tough on the streets, has a lot of collars under his belt, but my ex-partner retired last month and Coulter was transferred in from another shop just over a month ago. So, I'm still learning."

Murphy followed the portly detective out the door to the staircase leading down to the first floor and the exit from the precinct.

"I'll pull together everything we have on this and e-mail it to you before the day is out," Rainsworth said as he stood at the top of the staircase. "I'd appreciate it if you could share what you have on Vassallo."

"I'll see what we can do," Murphy said and they shook hands. "I can certainly release anything that will be helpful with the homicide."

Both men knew that wouldn't be everything the Feds had. The FBI might have become more open in exchanging terrorism intelligence, but their federal domestic crime investigations were still their domain and they weren't in the habit of turning over complete files to the locals.

Elliott Murphy fired up his Crown Vic, with its police interceptor engine and all its radios spooling up, and smiled to himself. He was back on the job and lovin' it. And, more importantly, he was sober.

For thirty days and counting.

CHAPTER 34

Other than a couple of increasingly frantic calls from Harvey Schmidt, Alice's father, nothing much happened on the Monday after Alice was determined to be missing. Jack went to work as usual, had lunch with Rachel, went home to his new pad, and watched television until he fell asleep. At lunch he tried to coax Rachel into a rain-check for the "threesome" he missed out on Sunday evening. She said she'd think about it with a wink and a devious look that Jack was now recognizing as her version of a tease.

Jack worked hard at avoiding guilt about Alice. Instead, he focused on his hate for her, the misery she infused into his life, and their resulting wrecked family. This was done in an attempt to justify what he had done to her. She was gone and he was committed to looking forward without regret. He knew that even the boys would eventually get used to life without their mother, and would be better off in the end. Jack intended to let them stay right where they were, with their grandparents. Harvey and Ellie had moved out to Long Island from the city several years ago for the sole purpose of being close to their grandchildren. Now, they could have them right under their fucking roof. Jack didn't plan on abandoning them. He just needed some time to live a little and planned to deal with them later. Much later.

A few minutes after he arrived at work on Tuesday morning, he placed a call to the Suffolk County Police Precinct that was handling Alice's case. He asked to speak with the detective assigned to the case for an update. He was put on the phone with a Detective Nguyen. Despite his Asian name, he sounded just like one might expect a New York cop to sound, complete with a noticeable Brooklyn accent. He told Horton that he just got the file and would have to give him a call-back later in the day. Detective Nguyen said he knew he would have some questions. He also asked for Jack's phone numbers, addresses, and for some reason, Jack's driver's license and social security numbers.

After Jack hung up, he stared at the phone for a moment. *What was all that about?*

Moments later, the senior partner in the firm, Ted Duboski, the man who had mentored Jack for years and Marty Schwimmer, the firm's security chief and fraud specialist, were standing at the door of his tiny office. Jack was already a little jumpy, understandably so considering he had put a contract out on his wife and now it was becoming reality. So, seeing these two looming at his doorway didn't do anything to calm him down.

"We need to talk," said an uncharacteristically stern Duboski.

"Actually, why don't you come with us to the conference room, Jack," said Schwimmer. "It's a little tight in here and we've got something to go over with you."

"What's up?" Jack asked, he couldn't think of what these two could want with him. He wondered in an irrational moment if they had found out about Alice. Of course not, he decided. Surely the cops hadn't even opened a serious file on her yet. He hadn't even told anyone at work that she was missing.

"Let's wait till we get into the conference room, Jack," Duboski said firmly. Horton followed the two men down the hallway to the conference room and as he did he noticed a few heads poking out of cubicles watching the procession. His heart began to race and he felt flushed. In his entire career he had always played it safe, he had never been in any kind of hot water. *What the hell was going on?*

They all took seats, Duboski closed the door, and Jack was already feeling claustrophobic.

Schwimmer placed a file on the table in front of him and Jack's eyes opened wide. It was the file for Tri-Coastal Investments, the offshore company Cassavetti used to purchase the apartment buildings, and the same one Jack had insured a couple of weeks before.

"What do you know about this client?"

Jack's face wrinkled with concern as he studied the material in front of him.

"I don't know if you're aware of this," Schwimmer continued, "but the three apartment buildings you insured for them burnt to the ground last night. Arson is obviously suspected, but we don't know for sure. Who are they Jack? Let's start there!"

Jack appeared as though he was going to say something finally, but simply continued to stare at Schwimmer.

"And another one," Schwimmer said, keeping Jack squirming in his seat, "what the hell were you doing issuing a policy to a first-time client without a full property inspection, appraisal and a second signature?" Schwimmer asked in a voice filled with irritation. It was his job to keep fraud at a minimum for the company, and a claim in the first thirty days of a newly issued policy was not a good thing. In fact, it was very bad!

Jack remained silent but his mind was screaming. It seemed that in a moment's time, a scenario had unfolded that shocked Jack to his core. Who the fuck had he been kidding? Who did he think Phil Cassavetti was? The answer suddenly became crystal clear and hit him like a Mack truck. Phil Cassavetti was not some smooth, debonair, man about town who just *happened* to put on private little poker games and was not the man who just *happened* to need to buy real estate in some off-shore corporation. He didn't just *happen* to know someone— who knew someone—that could get rid of his wife. *Phil Cassavetti was a front-line crook.* And in that same moment, Jack knew that he was up to his eyeballs with Cassavetti now, and he had to think fast, *really fast!*

"Guys," Jack said, in the best response he could muster at the time. "I don't know anything about this." It was pretty lame, but it was a start.

"Well, Jack, what *do* you know, son? Who is this Abe Silverman, for starters? The attorney who signed the application," Duboski added. "We're looking at a claim that is based on replacement value and you insured these buildings for over six million dollars!"

Duboski's face was turning red. Jack had never seen him so upset.

"This company was a referral. It came from this guy that I met on vacation. I really don't know much about the company, other than they apparently bought the properties for cash and needed quick coverage. I met with their attorney who is secretary of the corporation and he signed all the paperwork. I mean I didn't do anything that I haven't done before, you know Ted, it was a pretty big sale and I needed to slam it through for the client in order to get the deal," Jack responded, slowly getting his composure together.

"You mean to tell me that you willingly put us at risk for this type of coverage without a property inspection or without any history with a client?" Schwimmer barked, as he jumped in again. "From what little we know, these buildings were dumps! They were vacant and probably about to be bulldozed. Seeing as how you gave him replacement insurance, we just paid for their rehab! These guys are going to be able to build themselves a project that is probably worth ten times what they paid for it, *on us!*"

Jack knew he was right. This was a disaster.

"All right," Duboski said solemnly as he took over. He was a little calmer now. "Look, Jack, I realize that if you've done something wrong, it is completely uncharacteristic of you. I mean, Jesus, you've never had a major problem in all these years. But if you know something about these people, or this situation, that we should know, now is the time. It will be a few days, but assuming that the arson guys confirm what seems to be obvious, this thing is going to fall all over us, and you, like a ton of bricks. This is Federal, Jack, it's shaping up to be an Insurance Fraud case, and the worst one we've ever had. So, you better give this some serious thought, 'cause very shortly, it won't be us asking the questions. It'll be the Feds."

Jack was again silent. He tried to think, but he was on overload suddenly and he was frozen. He was in deep shit, and he knew it. But if he was going to survive this encounter, he had to come up with something.

But he couldn't.

"I don't know what to tell you, Ted," he said. He decided to focus on Duboski and ignore Schwimmer. The older man surely would believe him. "I really don't know anything about all this but tell me what you want me to do." It was the best he could come up with.

"I'll tell you what we want you to do," Schwimmer said, not letting up. "I want a full written statement from you. I want to know who the officers of this mystery corporation are and if this turns out to be arson, we're going to need a polygraph. You know that it is required in your contract in the event of something like this."

"No problem," Jack blurted, suddenly relieved. He knew both of those requests were going to be a problem, but he was off the hook for now. Who knows, he thought, perhaps it wasn't arson. Perhaps it would all blow over. But he strongly suspected that was nothing more than wishful thinking.

Ted Duboski stood up and Jack seized the opportunity to leap out of his chair.

"Sorry about all this, guys. I should have been more careful," Jack said as he headed towards the door. "But I didn't do anything intentionally wrong. Let's see how this plays out, maybe the fire wasn't arson."

"And maybe pigs can fly," Schwimmer responded as he followed the other two out of the conference room. Jack rarely dealt with Schwimmer, he was fairly new to the company and Jack kept his nose clean and never had reason to know the man, until now anyway.

Horton quickly made his way back to his office and shut the door behind him. He needed a minute to gather himself. He began to calm down and think the situation through. This was foreign territory to Jack Horton. He had spent a lifetime playing it safe and now he had stepped way out over the line. Just about every decision, every action he had taken in the last six weeks had been uncharacteristic. So, who was he, Jack wondered about himself. Was he the mild-mannered wimp who played by the rules and existed in a vacuum with his miserable wife, his annoying offspring, and a boring job, or was he this new risk taking, pleasure-seeking persona that had so recently emerged? He had obviously broken free of the past, but he wondered if he had broken too many rules in the process? The thought crossed his mind, or perhaps to say it came crashing down on his mind was a more accurate description.

He knew it would take a few days to confirm the cause of the fires and Jack would have time to talk with Cassavetti and find out what the hell was going on. If it had been arson and Cassavetti was behind it, was Cassavetti just going to confess to a major felony, a Federal offense in fact? Not likely, but Jack knew he had speak with him. He had no alternative.

Jack agonized through the afternoon and his mind was swimming in fear and confusion. He tried to think of all the possibilities. One of the few things he was sure of was his innocence regarding any arson plans, and the fact that he truthfully didn't know if Cassavetti had anything to do with it. But he *did* know about Alice, and that situation hanging over his head with the incoming rounds of insurance fraud landing all around, certainly clouded his thinking. It's impossible to have a rational stream of thought when one wakes from a nightmare and can't determine immediately where he is, or if the horrible images were real or not.

Horton was shuffling paper and trying to appear occupied when his intercom buzzed at about four o'clock.

"Jack, the police are here to see you," the receptionist announced.

"Oh shit!" Jack blurted. He couldn't help himself, this was too much. "Pardon me?" she said, indignantly.

"I'm sorry, I'm just in the middle of something. Tell them I'll be out in a minute," he muttered.

He could barely breathe.

His eyes were open wide, he stood up, he paced, he sat down, closed his eyes and tried to take a few deep breaths. He told himself this had to be about Alice, and that he had prepared himself for this. He believed he just had to play dumb and it would be over. *I don't know anything about her disappearance, and hope she turns up real soon.* But somehow, he never planned for this on the heels of the earlier surprise over the building fires.

He finally got himself together and decided it would make more sense if he just had the receptionist bring the police back to his office.

Jack stood at the door to his office, shell-shocked. He wondered if he was going to survive the second inquisition of the day. He straightened his tie and nervously combed back the hair that remained on his head with his hands. Then he saw them down the hallway, two men approaching with the receptionist, an Asian man whom he assumed was Detective Nguyen, and a large, foreboding black man. Both men looked grim, which was not a good sign.

"Thanks Yolanda," Jack said, feigning a smile at the receptionist. "This is just about my wife," he explained. She just shrugged her shoulders and returned to her post.

"We spoke this morning," the Asian said. "I'm Detective Nguyen and this is Sergeant Detective Brown." Neither officer offered a hand, but Jack reached out to them anyway.

Both men wore overcoats over suits and ties. They were both disheveled, wearing shirts that looked in need of ironing and ties that hung loosely around their collars. Their shoes were scuffed and Nguyen's pants didn't match his jacket. Somehow, their less than perfect appearance put Horton at ease.

"Come on in guys," he offered and they nodded and walked in to his office and they all sat down, Jack behind his desk and the two men in front. "Any news on Alice?" Jack asked, trying to take the lead.

"We need to ask you a few questions, Mr. Horton. To start with, where were you this weekend?" Detective Brown asked firmly.

So much for a friendly chat, Horton thought, but he was prepared. He knew that eventually he would have to account for his whereabouts, but what surprised him was the tone of the question. There was something scary about this guy. He was ominous in appearance, all business, and Jack wasn't accustomed to facing someone like this.

"Where was *I* this weekend? I'm happy to tell you, but why are you asking me this?" he replied with as much confidence as he could muster. "Alice probably ran off with some guy."

"Where were you, Mr. Horton?" insisted Nguyen. These guys weren't messing around.

"Okay. Well, I was in the city the entire weekend, until I got a call from Harvey Schmidt, Alice's father. Then I immediately took the train out to Syosset and the rest is history. I couldn't find her and so I called you guys."

"And you have someone who can corroborate that," said Brown. They were double-teaming him.

"I do as a matter of fact."

"Would you mind giving us names and contact info, please?" Brown asked politely, but with little improvement in his demeanor.

Jack gave him Rachel's name and number.

Then Detective Nguyen stepped in again. "Tell us about your marriage. We understand from the parents that you and your wife are separated."

"That's true. What do you want to know? We were married for over ten years, things have been lousy for years, I decided a month or so ago that I'd had enough and I moved out. She actually filed for the divorce," Jack said.

251

He was holding up. It all seemed a little Kafkaesque, but between this little chat and the one he had earlier with his boss; he was discovering he had more dramatic ability than he thought.

"Who is her divorce attorney?" Detective Brown asked.

Jack pulled a document out of his desk that contained the contact information for her attorney and gave them what they wanted.

"Mr. Horton, we don't know what has happened to your wife but with each day that passes, if something bad has happened, it's only going to get harder for us to find her," Nguyen said. "Do you have any knowledge of what might've happened to her? If you do, you need to come clean now. If you are involved, helping us at this point is going to be far more beneficial to you, than doing so later."

Jack had practiced this part.

"*No*, I don't know what has happened to her and it's ridiculous that you think I do. I want to divorce Alice, not get rid of her. She's the mother of my sons, for God's sake!"

"Have you seen your sons since this happened, Mr. Horton?" Brown asked casually, not appearing phased at all by Jack's energetic denial.

"Well, no. I haven't. They're with their grandparents and I've been working."

"Hmmph," Brown said under his breath, and then he stood.

Nguyen followed his senior partner and said, "We need you to stay close. Please don't leave the city without contacting us, and if you learn of anything that might help us out, call me immediately." With that, he placed his card on Jack's desk.

Neither said good bye and Brown was already walking down the hallway to leave.

Jack didn't say anything or bother getting up, but after they left he took a deep breath and shook his head. This was all insane, but he continued to hold onto the feeling that it would be over soon. He knew Alice would never show up, her body would never be found, and instead of fighting her in court and watching his life get ruined before his very eyes, his new life would march on and he'd even collect a little life insurance. He just had to keep it together and pay a little more attention to his moves. Of course, it did look bad that he hadn't gone to see the boys, he thought.

He would take care of that in the next few days.

CHAPTER 35

Phil Cassavetti rode the escalator down to the baggage claim area at Newark Airport's Terminal C, and spotted his driver Jules immediately. The burly guy was tough to miss. Cassavetti was returning from Las Vegas after taking some serious losses in a poker tournament at the Bellagio, where he lost over one hundred grand. As a numbers guy, he kept track of these things carefully. He even included a percentage of his winnings, or losses, on his tax returns. Thus far he was back down to break-even for the year and that didn't make him happy, at all.

He was also upset about a sequence of events that seemed to be unfolding. These events also made Al Carino, the Gallo family consigliore, very nervous and according to him, Salvatore Ruggierio, the Don of the Family, as well. A chain of deaths seemed to be following the Dimaglia hit, and it seemed like it was going to get worse before the chain came to its end. Dimaglia, the thief within their own family, was the only murder the Gallos intended in the unexpected sequence of events. The discovery of his head had resulted in the necessity of taking out Dimaglia's assassins, the Irish brothers. Subsequently, a Gallo family informant, a police detective in Queens, had identified a nobody-runner for one of their numbers joints who had overheard a conversation that would now result in the runner's death. The scumbag was working for the cops and he would have to die before he could even think about testifying.

On top of this, word on the street was that the Westies, the gang that the Irish brothers had been part of, were vowing revenge for their deaths. Someone would have to broker a peace with them, and unless they had some suicidal penchant for vengeance, a business arrangement could be offered and economics would prevail over emotionalism. Or at least Cassavetti hoped it would.

Finally, he also was going to have to deal with Jack Horton. The poor idiot had obviously just discovered he had been completely fucked in fifty ways. Cassavetti never planned to torch the apartment buildings. When he purchased them, his intentions were to tear them down and rebuild condos and a few street level shops. That is, until he saw an opportunity. Horton had taken the plunge and opened the door when he forked over fifty grand to have his wife knocked off, and Cassavetti knew at that time he had him over a barrel. Now Horton was trying desperately to reach him. Cassavetti had several messages on his cell phone upon his return from Vegas. He planned to call Jack and give him the word—he was in deep. Cassavetti would tell Jack that all he had to do was play dumb, about everything, the disappearance of his wife, as well as the fire. And the message would be that so long as he kept his mouth shut, he would be all right. Both with the authorities, and with Cassavetti. Cassavetti would deliver the message in a way that would assure Jack that he shouldn't second-guess whose shit list would be worse. For the first time since meeting the man, Phil Cassavetti would convey to Jack Horton the danger in fucking with the family.

In no uncertain terms.

On Wednesday evening, Jack took a drive out to Long Island to see his boys. It was a brief visit, as Jack was distracted with all the tension of his many dilemmas, and the boys were in their usual state of hyperactive bad behavior. Alice's parents were distraught. Ellie cried a lot and Harvey seemed to be very suspicious. Jack was worn out and figured it wasn't going to be easy being around his troubled family, but he needed to make the visit for appearance sake.

Jack returned to the city and he parked the car in a garage by his building and made his way up to his apartment. After he closed the door, he tried to reach Cassavetti on the phone again, on perhaps his tenth attempt. Finally this time, he answered.

"Phil, where have you been?" he moaned. Jack sounded like he felt, which was exhausted, sleep deprived, and rather terrified.

"Let's not talk over the phone," Cassavetti snapped. "Be on the corner of Seventy-sixth and Columbus and Jules will pick you up in thirty minutes." He didn't wait for Jack's response and hung up.

Cassavetti was coming in from the airport and had just pulled up to the curb of his East Side condominium when Jack called. He took his luggage upstairs, regrouped, and went back downstairs where Jules was waiting in the Town Car.

"All right, let's go to the West Side," Cassavetti ordered. "Listen Jules, when we pick this guy up, I want you to toss him for a wire. You're not going to find anything on him, but I want the effect."

"Just to shake him up a little, huh boss?" the big man responded.

It didn't take them long to get across town and Horton was waiting on the appointed corner. Jules got out, told Horton to wait a second before getting in the car, and the thug in a suit patted him down. A very nervous and obviously shaken Jack Horton slid into the back seat and joined Cassavetti.

"He's clean," Jules said triumphantly.

The door was shut, Jules hopped back in the driver's seat, and the car lurched forward.

"So what's up with the body search? Jack asked. "*I'm* the one who's in hot water, and I'd like to know what's going on!"

"Calm down, Jack. We both know we have a few things going on between us, and the waters have gotten pretty deep. I have to be careful, since I don't know you that well yet, and well, you never know," Cassavetti said without looking at Horton. He appeared to almost be disinterested. "So what's up?"

"What's up?" Jack repeated. "For starters, why don't you tell me what happened with your buildings in Queens?"

"They burnt down."

"I know that. Do you know how it happened?"

"Jack, the less you know the better," Cassavetti replied as he slowly turned his gaze and looked at Horton, who was pale and increasingly nervous. "Look, just take it easy, okay? You've got a lot goin' on here between your wife and this little matter of the apartments. But the truth is, no one's gonna connect you to either situation—unless you lose it. Now, you are NOT going to lose it on me, are you Jack?"

There was something about Cassavetti's tone, the way he emphasized the words. He sounded ominous. Jack realized in that instant that he had been naive, if not utterly stupid. He had been kidding himself to think Cassavetti was above board about anything. This guy was bad news and despite his handsome, well-groomed appearance, his Park Avenue office, and fancy car, Jack was suddenly very afraid of Phil Cassavetti.

"No—I'm not going to lose it," Jack muttered. Now he was the one looking out the window at the street scene moving by. They were driving along Central Park West and heading into the park. "So what actually happened to Alice?" Jack had to ask.

"Alice who?" was Cassavetti's response. "You see Jack, you need to pay attention. Forget about Alice, and you don't know anything about me and my buildings. You took a policy from an attorney who has authority to insure the buildings for a foreign corporation. Happens all the time. Just think about it. You don't know anything."

"Okay, okay. I got it," Jack said. He knew enough to shut up at that point.

"Good. Now, I, on the other hand, want to know what you've heard about he fire and what the cops are saying about your wife."

"Well, my boss called me in with our Fraud Specialist and gave me a hard time. Of course, I denied any knowledge of anything wrong because I really don't know what the hell is going on, so that was easy. They want me to cooperate with them, but I haven't heard anything more," Jack explained. "I know the arson investigation isn't complete yet."

"And your wife—" Cassavetti asked.

"Couple of cops came by the office yesterday, and I guess it was all pretty routine," Jack said quietly.

• • •

Horton was holding up, Cassavetti could tell. He was obviously still a little nervous but that seemed to be subsiding into a state of submission, or maybe defeat. It appeared that Jack had figured out he was screwed and there wasn't much he could do about it. *This was good*, Cassavetti thought to himself, *this was exactly where he wanted him*.

"Well, if they come back, I want to know about it," he said as he handed Jack a small leather-bound pad and a pen he produced from his jacket pocket. "I want you to write down the names of the cops. Also, write down this number, and from now on I don't want you calling me, this is a pager. I also want you to go to an electronics store and purchase a throw-away cell phone. Be sure and pay cash for it. Only use that phone when you page me."

Jack followed his instructions and handed the pad back to Cassavetti. Cassavetti motioned to Jules, who immediately pulled over to the curb, even though they were back on the East Side, and a twenty-minute walk back to Jack's.

"Just take a taxi home and get some rest Jack, you look pretty bad."

Jack didn't answer but looked briefly at Cassavetti as he got out of the car. His eyes were filled with fear.

Good, Cassavetti thought to himself, *that little chat had brought about the desired effect.*

Now to deal with Carino and the chain of death.

CHAPTER 36

Most Friday mornings, the Organized Crime Unit met in a conference room on the fifth floor of One Federal Plaza. This meeting was for the senior agents in the unit but didn't include all the field agents and support teams. The purpose of these meetings was for each team to brief the others, and to brainstorm and discuss strategy. This Friday was no different and Elliott Murphy was the first to arrive. He fixed himself a cup of coffee and stood gazing out the window at the street scene below.

He was doing remarkably well, attending AA meetings every day, working with his sponsor, Robert W., and working on his Twelve Steps. What kept him going was the promise of a life returning to "normal." His work was suddenly enjoyable again, his relationship with his wife was better than ever, and he was communicating with his sons more often as well. Elliott and Sally were even planning a vacation for the late spring. She had always wanted to take a cruise and so they spent a little time almost every night searching around on the internet, looking for the perfect trip.

Technically, Elliott reported directly to Cal Skinner. His partner, Chris Marciotti, was considerably his junior and it hadn't taken more than a few days for Murphy to take the lead in their working relationship. Prior to 9/11, Murphy had specialized in Organized Crime for years. But after the terrorist attack, his talents in intelligence gathering and his leadership were needed in the Homeland Security effort. A few weeks after the attack, there was a reorganization and Murphy found himself hunting Islamic Fundamentalist terrorists instead of Italian American hoods. Now though, after his dressing down with Skinner, he was back on OCU as the most senior agent. He didn't officially lead the group, but his seniority was respected and with each passing day, the rumors of this move for Murphy being a quasi-disciplinary action were slowly being forgotten. He was regaining the respect of the rest of the team, and rightfully so. He was damn good at his job.

Slowly the other agents arrived that Friday morning, and when everyone was finally in attendance, the discussion began promptly at eight-thirty. Soon there was quite a bit of discussion revolving around the Gallos. Murphy and Marciotti brought everyone up to speed on where they were in the investigation of Tony Dimaglia's murder, and subsequent killings of the Irish hit men. They also disclosed their information regarding the possibility that Andy Vassallo was behind it all, and the fact they had obtained their information from a confidential source that NYPD had provided.

Another team gave a summary of their progress infiltrating the Gallo's heroin importation business. As Murphy had remembered from years ago, the Gallo's never dealt drugs on the street, but they were big into supplying several gangs with quantities of cocaine and heroin for distribution. Rumor had it that over twenty years ago Sal Ruggeirio had developed a relationship with an Afghan importer who needed distribution in the Northeast United States. The Gallo's struck an agreement but turned the actual street dealing over to the Asians and a gang out of Harlem. The Feds were keeping an eye on both, and along with the DEA and NYPD, were working on a sting that might actually net them the primary contact within the Gallos.

There was also another group that was working the money side of the Gallo Family. Murphy was fascinated by this presentation as it was more developed than he remembered from several years ago. This part of the meeting was conducted by two young men who were forensic accountants who worked for the Bureau. They mapped out a network of companies and accounts, both legitimate and suspect. It astounded Murphy that these guys had the balls to infiltrate the Fortune 500 as well as the local construction unions. *Money*, he thought to himself, *will buy you anything*.

The two accountants listed names of lawyers and CPAs that were suspected of fronting for the mob family. They also mentioned the name Phil Cassavetti, whom they had reason to believe was the family's inside money guy. His name was unfamiliar to Murphy, so he wrote it down. The accountants, who were highly trained special agents, said they were working on turning over every leaf they could to find out more about this man. Their information indicated he was a made guy, in fact an Underboss, but it appeared the family had purposely seen to it that he kept a low profile. This gave him credibility on Wall Street and with the banks. It apparently worked, as it was estimated that the Gallo Family controlled close to a half billion dollars in market value and equities in everything from shares in public companies to apartments and nursing homes. According to these two, it was quite a diverse and intelligent portfolio that had endured the post dot-com recession and provided the Gallo's with a huge amount of income.

Finally, another Bureau team that was headed by a woman, Gina Moriarti, reported on a possible arson. Arson itself was not a federal offense, but when it involved insurance fraud, it became the domain of the Feds. In this particular case, the locals were very suspicious, but arson had not yet been established. What was interesting about this situation was the fact that the ownership of the buildings had just changed hands and the company that had bought the three run-down apartment buildings was tagged to the web of offshore corporations discovered by the forensic accounting team. It was probable, whether it was arson or not, that the Gallo's owned these buildings.

Murphy spoke up near the end of the meeting. Everyone agreed that they seemed to be opening up some promising leads on several different fronts and that for the time being, their focus needed to be on following the trail of the murders as well as the finances. Murphy was going to meet with Skinner and the Federal Prosecutor and they would seek a ramping up of surveillance, including wire taps and remote listening devices. It would be tough to get anything planted, but he would put their evidence and intentions before a Federal Judge and get the orders.

Emma Carson, Skinner's assistant, came into the conference room just as everyone was leaving.

"Elliott, Cal needs to see you for a moment," she beckoned. Murphy's heart skipped a beat, though he didn't know why.

Murphy followed Emma to the elevator and while they waited, Murphy asked, "What's up, Emma?"

"I'm really not sure. How have you been doing?" she responded.

They chatted for a moment until the elevator arrived and then they joined several others going up, which effectively ended their conversation. Elliott would have to wait until he heard it directly from the director.

Skinner was seated at his desk when Elliott entered. He quickly rose and extended his hand. He smiled, but it was reserved, and almost sympathetic. He asked Elliott to shut the door behind him, which Murphy knew, always meant something was wrong.

"It looks like your gun was used in a robbery a week ago. Your guy took out a Korean grocer and his daughter," Skinner said, his head coming up from the file as he sat back in his high-backed leather chair.

The words burned through Murphy like a flamethrower. If there was anything remaining that could go horribly wrong from his previous bad acts, this was it. His behavior had caused the loss of life of *two* human beings.

"Oh God," was all he could manage to say.

"Look, Elliott, this has been a helluva time for you. But I've been watching, and you've been handling yourself just as I knew you would. You've stepped up to the plate and done what you needed to do," Skinner said as he sat forward in his seat now, trying to console the devastated man who sat in front of him. "This is tragic, but it's not your fault. You got mugged, you were attacked out of nowhere, and there was nothing you could do about it. End of story."

"Bullshit, Cal, I was drunk and I had no business being there in the first place!" Murphy said angrily. "It *was* my fault!"

"You didn't shoot these people. This prick Aaron Jackson did," Skinner said as he looked down at the file for a second. "The guy has a sheet a mile long and he's going to get the needle for this one; it was his third violent felony. I've already spoken with the Assistant Chief at NYPD, and we're keeping that element of the story out of the press. As far as they're concerned, it doesn't matter where the gun came from, they know who pulled the trigger."

Murphy looked up from the spot where he had been staring at the floor. "I appreciate that Cal, but I know what happened. Those people probably wouldn't be dead if I hadn't screwed up."

"Well, I guess you've got one more choice to make. Are you going to let this throw you off course, or are you going to deal with it and keep doing the things that you are doing. I know you've been sober, I see you taking the lead in OCU, and it seems that you and Sally are putting it back together. You made some mistakes, Elliott, but you've overcome them now. Don't let this take you back down."

Elliott knew Skinner was right, but he felt like he had just been run over by a bulldozer anyway.

"I'll get through it," he muttered, again staring at the floor.

"Look, Murph, I can't tell you I know what you're going through, because I've never had a problem with drinking. But my uncle did, and it eventually killed him. He was in and out of AA and I learned a little bit about how it all works. Go talk to someone, talk to Elson. That's what you're supposed to do. I know that you can't let something like this haunt you. The best thing you can do for those Koreans is to keep in the game. You're one of the best we've got and you're back on top, if you don't let this get in your way."

Murphy sat silent for a moment and then he knew he had to get out of there. He was feeling claustrophobic. There was no doubt about it, two people had lost their lives as a consequence of *his* behavior, and in that moment, it was all a little too much.

"I'll be okay," he managed to say as he rose from his seat. Skinner extended his hand from his chair.

"Be careful, Elliott," Skinner said sincerely. "If you need to talk to me over the weekend, give me a call at home. I mean it."

"Thanks, Cal," he replied, and walked out of Skinner's office toward the elevator, as fast as he could. He needed some air.

And for the first time in almost six weeks, Elliott Murphy needed something else. He needed a drink.

After two weeks in captivity, Alice Horton was already beginning to lose track of the days. Despite the horror of her situation, she had begun to shift her energy and focus from fear to survival. She called upon instincts that she had never truly known—and her situation required a trait she had never shown. Courage.

She flashed back to several weeks earlier, when she awoke in darkness. It was the most disorienting experience of her life. And it didn't get any easier at day-break, as the only light came in through a skylight in the middle of the room she occupied. There were no windows on the walls, she had no idea where she was being held, or how she got there. But what terrified her most was not knowing what would happen next.

The next morning, someone arrived. At first she heard a door open in the outer areas of the cabin, then she heard rather heavy footsteps. She became frantic, ran into the bathroom, then back out again, then she contemplated hiding under the bed. Before Alice could think of any other fruitless strategy to hide, a strange man opened the door and she turned helplessly and faced her apparent captor.

He said his name was Paul and he told her that he wouldn't harm her, but her instincts told her his reassurance was a lie. She surmised this because he was far too forthcoming about who he was and what she was doing in this situation. He was in the mob, he had been contracted to kill her, but not to worry, if she behaved herself, he would release her somewhere and just tell his employer that she escaped. Alice knew that was a crock of shit, but she didn't know how long she had to come up with a plan. She asked why someone wanted to kill her and who had contracted him to do it. He didn't know, he just did what he was paid to do. One of his bosses had accepted the job, he was just the executioner.

So relatively early on for Alice, the whole thing went from horrifying to some sort of nightmarish B-Movie, and she couldn't believe she was in it. She considered the possibility that Jack had paid someone to get rid of her, but she couldn't allow herself to believe it. She was the mother of his boys, his wife of over ten years. She started feeling guilty for taking the divorce thing on a little too aggressively, but still, he wouldn't have done something like this. *Or would he?*

The mystery of why began to drive her crazy, but she made a concerted effort not to think about it. She could do that later. For now, she had to focus everything she had on escape.

Paul had left her a cooler of food and drinks along with some paper cups and plates. He even asked her what magazines she liked to read, and returned with them later in the day. Then, a few nights later when he returned, he moved a small TV and disc player into her room and allowed her to take a bath in the main bathroom in the cabin. Her room only had a half-bath with just a sink and a commode. He allowed her to take the bath privately, but he held her by the arm while moving her from her cell to the bathroom. His grasp was gentle, but she could feel his strength and knew he was a powerful man.

Despite this humane treatment, Alice knew that something terrible lay ahead for her, and though several ugly scenarios danced through her thoughts, she was sure the worst of it would be her death. And despite his seemingly decent behavior, she sensed that he wasn't keeping her around for grins, and that eventually he would want something from her. Or he would take it. She feared that he would rape or abuse her in some horrible way, or at least she had to assume that possibility. *Why else* would he be holding her captive?

Elliott Murphy returned to his cubicle after Skinner had given him the news that his gun had been used to take two lives and the weight of his guilt felt like an eight-hundred-pound gorilla on his shoulders. He had been doing a good job of putting the whole incident behind him but *now this*; it was almost unbearable.

It was noon and most of the guys usually went out to a sandwich shop a few blocks away from the building. Lunch was something that typically happened on the fly for the agents, but Fridays were different as many of the senior agents were in the building for the Friday morning briefing. The lunch was a tradition.

His young partner, Chris Marciotti, stuck his head around the corner and asked, "You ready, Murph? We're about to head over to Quizno's."

Murphy barely looked up from the stack of papers he was studying, or at least appeared to be, for in reality he wasn't seeing a single word in front of him.

"I'm going to pass today, Chris," he answered and feigned a slight smile. "I've got some things to deal with."

"Anything wrong?" the young man asked. He obviously had observed that Murphy appeared crestfallen.

"Nothin' I can't handle," Elliott said, pulling himself together. "Don't worry about it, I'll see you when you get back."

Marciotti left him alone and now the internal battle began in full force. He was fighting a tremendous, albeit insane compulsion to have a drink. He went from knowing that it was nuts and knowing that he needed to give his sponsor, Robert W., a call, to saying screw it, one drink won't hurt. He was afraid one moment and furious the next. The weight of the horrible news of the Koreans was a giant trigger and he was ready to pull off any second. He was afraid because he had no idea he was still fighting such a need, such a desire, to drink. This battle seemed to overshadow the tragedy itself, even considering the fact that *his* gun had been used to murder two innocent people.

Murphy had to get out of the building. Maybe a walk would do him some good. For the moment, he resisted calling his sponsor, which was contrary to what he had been taught in AA. He had been warned to always carry phone numbers of several other men in his group and when the craving struck, and they assured him it would, he would only have to pick up the phone. That's what they were there for. But Murphy thought better of it and decided he was going to walk this off. He just needed some air. He could handle it.

He left the building and following a short a cab ride, he was over on the West Side and walking through the door of O'Reilly's Pub. He convinced himself that he just needed familiar surroundings. Besides the drinking that went on in this dark and dingy place, he had also done plenty of thinking. *Thinking*, that was what he needed to do right now, he needed to think. He sidled up to the bar, slid on to a stool, and faced a veritable wall of alcohol. He also realized that he had willed himself to O'Reilly's and now that he had arrived, he was absolutely powerless. A flash of terror shot through him, and even though he could sense what was going to happen next, there was nothing he could do about it. It was all too much.

Murphy decided he'd have just *one* drink.

The bar-keep approached and asked for his order. He was a new guy, Elliott thought to himself, or maybe just someone Elliott couldn't remember. That was more likely, Murphy conceded.

"Jack Daniels, straight up, no ice," Murphy said. The words spilled around in his brain, almost warring with others that wanted to surface. The conflict was a battle being conducted in his head, where one side was euphoric with liquid anticipation, and the other horrified and dis-believing.

The battle was quickly lost, the order was placed, and Murphy stared at the wall of bottles. He tried not to think, although for a moment Sally sprung to mind and the boys, even Cal Skinner's face shot through his head. These were the same people who cared about him, and were giving him a second chance. But even so, he told himself it would be just one drink. He could do it, he knew he could. And if it ended up being two, or even three, he would call Sally before it got out of control and tell her he had to work a late case and would stay in the city. As for Skinner, he would never find out.

His gun had taken innocent lives. *His* gun, not anyone else's. How could anyone judge what he was suffering? And with that line of reasoning, Murph found some justification.

The bartender brought the drink to him and Murphy looked down at the glass, full of the rich bourbon. It stared back at him, seductively, and he took the glass in his hand and worked a gentle quarter turn. He felt the coolness of the fresh glass and recalled how the magic liquid would warm his insides as that first sip slid down his throat. He knew it would provide relief and familiarity, and anticipated it like a visit from an old friend. He raised it slowly to his mouth.

The glass was half-an inch from his lips when suddenly the seduction was halted. He heard something that slapped him across the face, and quickly slammed him back to a more sober consciousness. His cell phone stopped everything. He felt instant shame even though no one knew where he was or what he was doing except an anonymous bartender who could care less. But the timing shook him profoundly. The chirping of the phone brought him back to his senses; he immediately put the drink down, and stared at the glass while the little phone continued to ring.

Finally, he answered the call. It was his partner, Chris Marciotti. While the news the young man was passing along didn't register immediately, Marciotti told him that the NYPD informant, Sal Gatti, had been found dead. Under the circumstances it was too much for Murphy to digest in the same moment, so he told his young partner he would be in within the hour. As he hung up, it was clear he had been saved. He also knew he needed to get the hell out of the bar.

Murphy threw a twenty on the counter and walked out of the bar as quickly as he could, feeling as though he could barely breathe. Once he was out on the street, he sucked in a chest full of air. The day was fresh and warm, and Murph observed that it was the warmest of the early spring so far.

He stood in the middle of the sidewalk as a few people hurried past him and a smile broke out on his face. He had survived a near-miss with disaster and he looked to the sky above. He winked.

The whole incident seemed to end as quickly as it began. Now, as opposed to the intense craving to have a drink that he had been experiencing, he felt triumphant and lucky. Someone, something, some force, had been looking over his shoulder. This had been a near miss and he had survived, thanks to the bell. Or in this case, the chirp of his little cell phone.

Thankfully, it was time to get back to work.

CHAPTER 37

Jack sat quietly in his apartment. Preceded by a couple of cloudy, sullen days It was a depressing Saturday afternoon as a gentle rain drenched the streets of Manhattan and perhaps more noteworthy, he had just returned from spending the morning in Syosset with his sons at his in-laws. The boys were still okay, the visit was fairly calm as Scott, the oldest, left shortly after Jack arrived to go to a friend's. Tim and Harry were much easier to tolerate without the influence of Scott and his angry behavior. Harry, the youngest, was extremely clingy, which especially bothered Jack in light of the fact that up to now he had never given a shit about his children. He calculated they were better off at the Schmidt's and probably wouldn't miss their mother and her bitchiness. But it seemed like Harry missed his dad; that was becoming more obvious by the minute, although there wasn't much Jack could do about it. He couldn't take care of the boys in the city and he was too preoccupied with other matters to spend a lot of time in Syosset. Other matters such as Rachel and worry over the various felonies in which he had recently participated were weighing on him.

The Schmidt's seemed wary of him. Jack, already half-paranoid, recognized that it wasn't surprising given the present situation. After all, their daughter had gone missing within weeks of Jack walking out on her, and they were in the middle of an ugly divorce proceeding. But he maintained his innocence and was managing to play the role of the somewhat concerned husband, albeit soon to be ex-husband, and he felt as though he might be winning over Harvey in the process. But then he mentioned that the police thought Alice might have run off with someone, perhaps some other man. Making this claim didn't prove to be such a good idea. Ellie Schmidt broke down and asked how on earth he could even suggest her beloved daughter could leave her boys like this. Jack shrugged it off and apologized. 'We're all upset,' he told her with a trace of sincerity. Harvey Schmidt just walked out of the room.

He survived the visit, although it wasn't very uplifting, and in case the cops kept nosing around, it served as a record of another act of concern in his attempt to behave normally under the circumstances. Despite his complete inexperience with wrongdoing, Jack was amazed at how easily he had taken to the role. Regardless of the fact that he could act it all out, *he* knew what he had done, and his strong performance didn't erase his paranoia, nor did it serve to eliminate the guilt that had been slowly creeping over him. In fact, it worsened with each new lie, with each time he faced the boys, and of course, every time he laid eyes on Alice's parents.

When he left, Harry cried. Jack didn't know what to do as the boy never showed any emotion at all. His father told him not to cry, reassured him that everything would be okay, and then of course, he left. Harry was still crying.

Now he was alone and the rest of the weekend faced him. Rachel had left him a message and wanted to get together, but despite the allure of hooking up with his sex-crazed girlfriend, he couldn't get motivated to return her call as he needed a little time to sort out his thoughts.

As hard as he tried to convince himself that everything was going to be okay, he was nagged by the prospect of the sky falling in on him. *What had he done?* It was one thing to think of excuses and alibis and lies, but in reality, he placed a contract on his wife and was knee deep in an exposed insurance scam. Taking a step out of his miserable marriage and his mundane life was one thing, but as he sat alone in his expensive little apartment, he was also toying with the truth of his frailties, and the brutality of his actions. They whispered he had gone *way* too far.

Fortunately, amidst a cluttered sea of worry and guilt, there was some good news. The arson squad had come up empty so far. Apparently they had their suspicions, but nothing concrete. For now, the cause of the fire was considered unknown and Jack's insurance company would have to proceed with the claim. The amount paid to Cassavetti's company would be for total replacement and would around six-million. Jack knew that amount of instant cash would give Cassavetti a huge head start on their new construction project, which was apparently what he intended to do in the first place. The situation reeked, Jack knew the fire was set intentionally, but while he wasn't jumping for joy, he was relieved that so far there was nothing the fire department or police had come up with that could prove it. For the time being, this had taken the heat off at work.

His company, Avistar, reinsured a policy like this through a larger insurance carrier and the financial burden would be on that other company. Had the fire proved to be arson, which would establish the likelihood of insurance fraud, Jack would be completely screwed. He had taken shortcuts with the normal procedures in underwriting a first-time client, and would at best lose his job. At worst, he would be facing criminal charges.

So, overall, it was reasonable that Jack had a lot on his mind. That preoccupation made it difficult to get excited about a romp with Rachel, but that possibility for a guy like Jack, was never totally out of the question. This drizzly spring afternoon had a lazy, romantic twinge to it and he had nothing else to do besides sit and worry, so he picked up the phone.

She had the same thing on her mind. Suddenly, the thought of a couple of hours of twisted sex with Rachel cloaked all the worry in the world with anticipation and excitement. He popped open a bottle of light beer and grinned, *what the fuck*, he thought to himself.

Despite the mist and the unseasonably cool temperature, Alice Horton welcomed her first walk outdoors since she had been taken hostage or prisoner, or whatever her designation, in over several weeks. Her captor, a man she knew only as Paul, walked closely by her side. Even if she was so inclined, she knew better than to try and run away from the powerful thug. He looked to be quick on his feet, she was not fast, and he certainly had a gun beneath his jacket. She had seen it earlier in the week when he stopped by with food.

Alice surprised herself by the way she was handling this situation. It was nightmarish and horrifying, but somehow, in the span of a little over three weeks, her dominant instinct for survival had firmly emerged. Something *bad* was going to happen to her, it was just a matter of time. She didn't quite believe Paul's reason as to why it hadn't happened already, but she wasn't going to question it further. She focused instead on what to do. Alice accepted that Paul was craving her company. Once or twice, when he brought her food or stopped by to check on her, he had wanted to talk. She did her best, pretended as though she was having normal conversation and none of this insanity was happening. Perhaps, if she could befriend this man, it might buy her a few extra days, or waylay whatever it was he had in mind for her.

Now, they walked along a path through the dense woods and it felt good to Alice just to be outdoors and moving around. She had been trying to do stretches and sit-ups in the confines of her little room, just to keep herself loose and ready, and the sparse diet had caused her to lose a few pounds. She could feel it. So the walking was also welcome. She didn't know if she would be alive from one day to the next, but she was determined not to give into her demise like a helpless lamb.

Alice had not been inside a church since a friend's wedding five years earlier, but at this time in her life, she prayed. She prayed with every bit of sincerity she could muster, and focused on everything she had ever learned about faith and hope. She observed, in an oddly-timed sort of way, that what she had learned as a child and adolescent, against the current backdrop of her darkest hour, made perfect sense to her now. The fear subsided and she resigned herself to a new approach that was developing inside, one she had never experienced before. In just a few short weeks, in the midst of the most horrible nightmare she could imagine, she was changing. Alice Horton was starting to put life in general, and her life in particular, into a clearer perspective, and it seemed certain that if she made it out of her predicament alive, this visceral change would survive with her.

Alice missed the boys, and within this new framework, she even missed Jack. He had shocked her by transforming overnight and leaving her, but in retrospect from her new vantage point, she understood. Paul, her captor, had still not told her who was behind her abduction, although she couldn't believe the most obvious—that Jack was behind it. That would be too much. No, if she could manage to make her way out of this, she would confess to Jack, and own up to her role in their failed marriage. She had blamed her own misery on him for years but somehow, in the middle of the woods with a kidnapping hit man holding her for unknown reasons, Alice Horton had shed her misery. If by some miracle she lived through this horror, her life after salvation would be treasured and lived, not drenched in pain, dreaded in every way, and hopelessly taken for granted.

They walked along a path through the trees and Alice gazed about as much as she could without being blatantly obvious. She scanned the area for anything that could possibly help her, but was careful not to give Paul any reason to think she was sizing up an escape. She wanted him to be as comfortable and unsuspecting of her as possible.

The day was gorgeous; light rain showers had moved out of the area and now the morning sky was a crisp blue, the temperature was mild, and the light breeze was scented with the smells of spring. If it weren't for the fact Alice was a kidnap victim, and her entire life was turned upside-down, she would have reveled in it. Still, she felt the sun warming her through the same sweat suit she'd worn for over three weeks and it felt good. She took another shot at extracting information from Paul. He followed closely behind her as she walked along the path.

"So how much longer before I can go home?" she asked.

"Who said anything about going home? Don't ya' like it here?"

"Come on Paul," she said, sure to use his name as much as possible. She remembered from some movie that it was important to be as personal as possible with your captor. She never thought she would apply this knowledge in a million years. "You know what I mean. It's not that the place is bad, it's pretty, in fact. But I have three boys at home, a husband, and parents. I want to go back to my life, Paul!"

Paul looked down at the ground for a moment and said nothing, as if he had been struck by an arrow of compassion. Then his eyes rolled up to meet hers, and they were flat and emotionless.

"Look, lady, consider yourself lucky," he said. "You're supposed to be gone already."

Despite all of her efforts to stay on top of her emotions, she felt her eyes well up, and the muscles of her arms begin to tremble. "Damn it, Paul, you've got to tell me. What are you going to do with me?"

He looked up at her with oddly matter-of-fact eyes. "I'm supposed to kill you," he said in a monotone that had the chill of a burial vault.

"When?" she asked incredulously, as hysteria swirled inside her chest.

"I shoudda done it already," Paul answered. "I dunno. I thought maybe I would keep you around for a while."

"Why? I don't understand."

"Look, don't ask so many questions, lady. Just be glad I haven't done it yet," he said flatly and gave her a gesture to start walking again. "I jus' wanted a little company for a while. I haven't had a woman around for a long time. So, let's just pretend like we're friends and walk some more. I gotta be back in the city in a couple of hours."

Alice's mind was reeling. While she was shocked with disbelief by his disclosure, she also realized she had to formulate a plan. It came to her quickly and she didn't second guess herself. She had to put everything on the line, keep herself necessary for this freak, and attempt to get him into a vulnerable position she could exploit. It seemed clear that this strategy was her only chance for survival.

"When are you coming back this time?"

"Tomorrow or Monday," he answered quietly. "I'll leave you with plenty of food."

"I'll look forward to you coming back," she said, lying through her teeth.

They topped a small rise in the woods and the cabin was again in view. The path they had been following was apparently a large circle that began and ended at the cabin.

She would remember that.

Paul Visante drove carefully down the Henry Hudson Parkway on his way back to Manhattan from his little hideaway spot in the woods. The veteran hit man and loan shark had several warrants out for his arrest, for speeding of all things. As he drove along the scenic route that funneled commuters and travelers from upstate to the boroughs of New York, he thought about Alice Horton and his next move.

He knew he needed to complete the contract. He had been hired to kill the woman and dispose of her so that she would never be found. Instead, he kept her at his cabin like some sort of animal, not knowing what to do next, or having much of a plan. His intent was simply to have some companionship, which was something that had been missing for most of his adult life. But what was he thinking? It was ridiculous to assume that this suburban housewife was going to be his friend, or willingly have sex with him, or be anything else other than a pain in the ass! He felt like a fool.

Besides that realization, if Andy Vassallo ever found out he hadn't offed the broad, he would be in deep shit. He had already taken the money for the hit. Suddenly, a decision was made.

He would finish what he started when he went back to the cabin in a day or two. Oh, he'd have a little bit of fun with her *before he punched her ticket.* Then he would complete the contract.

CHAPTER 38

When Elliott Murphy awoke on Saturday morning he was feeling a little wobbly. Funny thing about sober alcoholics, even long after they quit drinking, the cravings still occur, drunk dreams still abound, and sometimes, as was the case with Elliott the day before, their behavior drifts close to the edge and the following day can resemble a hangover. This happens even though the alcoholic might not have had any booze in their gut for years.

In Elliott's case, approaching eight weeks of sobriety, his near miss with catastrophe had been averted by the chirping of his cell phone. Had his partner not called to tell him about Sal Gatti's killing, God only knows what would have happened. Elliott had slithered to the edge, inches away from his old friend Jack Daniels, when he was saved from his fall from the wagon.

Murphy felt as though he owed Sal a debt of gratitude and it was the reason he agreed to meet NYPD Detective Sam Rainsworth to discuss the case on a Saturday. Rainsworth wanted to talk off the record about Gatti's killing and Murphy was glad to take a drive and meet up with the city cop. Besides, Sally was busy showing houses and he welcomed the distraction. He knew it was wise to limit his idle time, given how close he had come to disaster the day before.

Murphy had a gut feeling bordering on certainty that it was no coincidence that Gatti had been in a NYPD precinct house informing on his brethren and then ended up dead a couple days later. Either the Gallo's inadvertently discovered Gatti was a police informant, or someone on the inside informed the Gallo's that Gatti was a rat. Murphy suspected the latter.

Elliott knew it was time to get as aggressive as possible with the Gallo Family. In the past several months, four bodies, technically, three bodies and one head, had been found, and the circumstances surrounding these deaths had The Gallo Crime Family written all over them. This represented a real escalation in mob killings for this outfit and regardless of the reason, Murphy wanted to take advantage of the situation and get to the highest echelon he could to bust these guys. At a time when the country, New York especially, was concerned over terrorism and war, the last thing the citizenry needed to worry about was escalating street crime. The Organized Crime Unit might not have the prestige of the Terrorism Unit, but it served an important purpose and Murphy needed a homerun. If for no other reason than to continue to regain his former standing with the Bureau, he wanted a good solid bust. One that would be read about in the papers.

He pulled up to the precinct and Rainsworth was waiting in front. As Murphy opened the door, the heavyset detective hurried towards Murphy's black Crown Victoria.

Rainsworth seemed a bit nervous and quickly said, "Let me hop in, would you mind. Let's get outta here."

Once the man was settled in the car, Murphy quickly rolled the powerful FBI Interceptor out on to the street.

Sergeant Detective Dennis Coulter, NYPD, cautiously followed the black Crown Victoria and made sure to lag far enough behind to avoid detection by the Fed. There was enough traffic milling about on a Saturday afternoon and Coulter was driving his own car, a non-descript Honda Mini-Van. If he was careful, he wouldn't be noticed.

The whole thing was a fluke. A fellow officer had over-heard Rainsworth calling the Fed about an urgent meeting. The officer had mentioned it in passing to Coulter. It was a meeting Coulter hadn't been invited to, and therefore roused his suspicions. All he could do was keep an eye on the Fed, and Rainsworth, his fat-assed partner.

Unless of course, opportunity knocked for more.

For now, Coulter patiently followed them through the streets of Queens.

"So, you think your partner is dirty?" Murphy asked after listening for five minutes or so to the speculation Detective Rainsworth had to offer. Murphy hadn't liked Coulter in the first place. In their short meeting earlier in the week when Gatti told his story about the conversation he had overheard, the guy was too jumpy and acted as though the whole exercise was nothing more than a waste of time. "You haven't been working with him that long, how well do you know him?"

"Not that well," replied Rainsworth, looking out the passenger window. Then he turned to look at Murphy as he drove. "He was assigned to me from the One-Eleven about two months ago. Look, I've never ratted another cop out and I've seen a lot of bad shit go down. Mostly money to look the other way. But if I'm right, Coulter got this guy killed and that's more than I can sit by and watch. I'm not ready to let this surface yet, and go to Internal Affairs, but you and I need to be on the same page 'cause this case needs to be busted wide open."

"I'm with you there, but I don't like operating off the radar screen when a dirty cop is involved," Murphy said while they sat at a stoplight. "Besides, the fact is, it's not my territory. Even if we just keep an eye on the guy, we're breaking important rules by not advising NYPD."

They were both silent then the light turned green and they surged forward. "Here's the problem, if we go to IAD, Coulter's gonna find out. They'll be all over him. Then we lose any chance to see where he might lead us. Isn't there any way you could put someone on him for a few days and perhaps delay the call to Central," Rainsworth said, referring to NYPD Headquarters.

Murphy thought about it for a moment. "I could do that," he said. "And I could also have my boss approach your guys with a high-level request to keep it quiet while we're in the middle of this phase. But we need phones tapped, surveillance, and forensic accounting of his bank accounts. It's serious stuff, but I had bad vibes about the guy when I met him, but at the time, I guess I just thought he was a prick. It all makes sense, though."

"In the meantime, we need to get something going on Andy Vassallo. Let's assume we're right, and he's behind all these murders, we need surveillance and some heat on the guy. We also need to get to someone in that Irish gang, the Westies. I'll bet that they're pretty pissed off about the brothers and maybe someone is willing to talk."

"Why don't you come down to our office on Monday and we'll coordinate all this," Murphy responded. "That way we're sure your partner won't have any knowledge of what we're up to. Then we'll take it from there."

• • •

Coulter had watched as the Fed dropped Rainsworth back at the station house and then Rainsworth immediately walked to the back parking lot and got in his car. Coulter fell in behind and followed his partner at a safe distance. He assumed that the man would drive himself home on a Saturday afternoon, and he was right.

Rainsworth lived in a two-story row house in a residential area not far from La Guardia airport. It was a sleepy little neighborhood that had strings of little attached homes, usually in clusters of four, with tidy little lawns, the size of his master bedroom, and a tiny little porch, the size of his wife's pantry. These homes were nothing like the three thousand square foot home he built for himself on Long Island, which no other cop had seen. It would be too obvious to anyone on the force that he lived in more home than a cop could ever afford, even with a wife that worked part-time at a bookstore.

But now he knew where his partner lived. And it looked like a cop's house. He'd probably lived there for years and would probably never be able to move. Poor schmuck, Coulter thought to himself. If he passed knowledge of this suspicious activity along to his friends in The Family, the fat son of a bitch might be hauled out in a black bag.

CHAPTER 39

The meeting had been called by Al Carino, consigliore to The Don, Salvatore Ruggierio. The location was a restaurant in Manhattan called Stemoni's, a small, authentic Northern Italian spot located in the Lower East Side. The owner was loosely connected and would ensure privacy, the best of service, and would be well compensated for his efforts.

Ruggeiro himself would be there, as would several of the other under bosses and of course, Carino. Phil Cassavetti sat in the back of his Town Car while his driver Jules was carefully navigating his way downtown, and he felt immensely on edge. A few things had gone wrong over the last couple of weeks and Cassavetti was right in the middle of it all. The heat and publicity of several mob killings were not the way of the twenty-first century. Keeping a low-profile had been essential to The Gallo's for years, and now things were definitely heating up. Those fucking Irishmen, Cassavetti thought to himself, how the fuck did they manage to leave a human head floating in the East River. Because of that little screw-up, the cops knew about Tony Dimaglia, the traitor, the two Irish brothers, and

Sal Gatti, a rat that had been terminated after a dirty cop on the Gallo payroll gave them a tip; and now, Gatti was talking to NYPD and had loosely fingered Andy Vassallo.

Vassallo was Cassavetti's "go-to" man for anything the underboss needed done on the streets. He had been a loyal soldier and a big earner. He ran a crew that profited from numbers rackets, loan sharking, protection rackets, as well as prostitution and drugs. He managed all that, and murder for hire, or at times, inflicted lesser physical punishment to send a message or aid in the collection of a debt. The man was formidable and abominable to some, but to Cassavetti and the Family, he was one of them. He was part of the equation to this "thing" of theirs.

But there were simply too many twisted elements for Cassavetti to feel comfortable about anything.

Jules pulled up to the restaurant behind another limo and quickly Cassavetti made his way out of the car and walked inside. He was ushered to a private room in the back where he was one of the last to arrive. In attendance was Carino, Eddie Gucciano, a captain in Manhattan who ran the Gallo's construction rackets and Stubs Pasquez, named for two missing fingers. Stubs' assailant was later found in pieces in a trash dumpster in Jersey. Pasquez ran collections from the various legit businesses the Family owned, like the dry cleaners and the limo service, to ensure not all the cash hit the books the IRS would ever see. He also had a highly profitable loan sharking operation based in Harlem. And finally, Cassavetti saw Duke Simone, who had to be over seventy but looked far younger, and was their union guy.

New York was one of the last bastions of union influence and that was primarily due to the mob.

Cassavetti was greeted with warmth and respect, although he suspected that everyone present probably knew he might be in the hot seat. The men remained standing, sipping on cocktails, and conducting idle banter while they waited the arrival of Ruggeiro. They all looked as though they were taken off the pages of GQ. There must have been tens of thousands of dollars in fine cloth in the room, as all the men had donned their finest attire for the occasion.

There was a slight edge to everyone's chatter, as it was rare for The Don to request a sit-down with his under bosses. Partially due to his age, but primarily to keep as low a profile as possible, Ruggeiro didn't get out much. Especially in the company of these men.

Carino took Cassavetti aside and said quietly, "How are you doing, Phil?" he asked, but he didn't wait for an answer. "Just remember to offer solutions and actions. This thing has gotten away from us and the old man wants to hear how we are going to take care of it."

"I understand," Cassavetti replied. "You know I hate this side of the business, Al. If only we could make a living without this shit. But we'll deal with it. I think we need to get Vassallo out of town for starters."

"I agree," Carino nodded.

"And I also think we need to let the Westies know that if any of them think that retribution is due, they should think twice. And if they think that leaking something to the cops is a smart idea, it will result in all-out war."

"I think they know that," replied Carino, thoughtfully.

"I just want it over and forgotten."

"As do we all," Carino answered. "Nice job with the apartments, by the way. Has the insurance money come through yet?"

"Nope. But from what I heard, the arson guys came up empty," Cassavetti touted, glad to have changed the subject. "Not a bad way to get our construction going with six-million in free money."

Everyone's attention was diverted by two men who quickly entered the room. They were The Don's bodyguards. In settings like this, it was assumed one couldn't be too careful, and consequently, everyone was subject to a quick pat-down. While perhaps several of the attendees might have been insulted, it wasn't that long ago that Paul Castellano, boss of the Genovese crime family, had been taken out by John Gotti. Nothing was impossible anymore, and a scene that resembled a secret service security check before the arrival of the President followed, and was necessary.

After the men had satisfied themselves that the room was safe, one of them said something into a walkie-talkie and the room grew quiet. They all knew The Don was about to walk through the door. Moments later another burly man in a tight fitting double-breasted suit appeared at the doorway and led Salvatore Ruggeiro into the room.

It was somewhat ceremonial and it touched Cassavetti to watch. After all the years of death and deceit, crime and corruption, there was still this great sense of honor that existed amongst these men. And despite the egos, and all the bravado that swelled about the room, the one who garnered the most respect was this frail, slow moving, seventy-eight-year old man. This was their tradition, it was intergenerational, and it was their *thing*, and meant to be revered.

As he delicately made his way across the room, each man paid their respects with a traditional bow of the head and a kiss on each cheek along with a few reassuring words. Cassavetti was at the far end of the room and the last to greet the powerful old man. Cassavetti remembered the first time he met the man. Unlike other families who had gone through several leaders over the last two or three decades, Ruggierio had been in control since 1972. Cassavetti had been introduced to the wiry Don at a wedding by his high school friend's father. The Don never forgot Cassavetti's name from that point forward, had always been cordial; and in later years, as Cassavetti was "made" and climbed the ranks to Under boss, Ruggierio seemed to show genuine affection towards the financial genius of The Family. Tonight, however, Cassavetti was nervous that there might be a bit of a chill towards him in light of the problems that had surfaced.

"I'm pleased to see you tonight, Don Ruggierio," Cassavetti said to the old man after completing his brief embrace. But The Don didn't let go of Cassavetti's arms.

"I hope all this business doesn't have you worried, Phil," Ruggierio said with a look of true concern is his deeply set eyes.

With the old man's hands still on his arms, Cassavetti replied, "I'll be okay, Don. I just want to clean it all up and not embarrass our family any further."

The Don smiled, pulled away, and nodded.

They were all seated at a long table covered with white cloth and adorned with several wine glasses at each place setting. Fine silver and china glistened in an array of plates filled with anti-pasta, olives, olive oil, and breads. It was the beginning of a feast that would go on for several hours. The conversation turned light but loud, as the men were competing for each other's attention and trying to top one another's jokes. Cassavetti mostly listened and feigned laughter at the appropriate moments. Their stories were not of murder and mayhem, but of children's baseball games, college tuitions, and even a ridiculous TV series. The irony was not lost on the underboss. They all lead double lives, but Cassavetti marveled at their ability to transcend any conflicts between their American family life, and the corruption of the very society they loved by their own dark world of illegal commerce. At least as a loner, Cassavetti didn't live with the risk of losing both.

At one point during the meal, Cassavetti noticed The Don give a gentle nod to Al Carino. As was tradition, the Don's advisor would begin the business portion of their discussion. Carino commended all of the men on their various activities, making rather vague, coded, but nevertheless obvious references to the bribes, the rackets, and even the violent felonies that provided significant revenues to The Family. Cassavetti noticed that as these accomplishments were recited, the demeanor of these men seemed to shuffle off into ambivalence. The passion they had displayed for their son's little league, or a daughter's honor roll graduation from an Ivy League college, or even a dirty joke, seemed to fade into drudgery. Thankfully, he neared the end of his portion of the program.

Carino saved the financial underboss for last. He commended Cassavetti for great profits in the markets, strong revenues from newly acquired businesses, and changes that Cassavetti had implemented that held great potential for the future. Then he dealt with the problem.

"As you all know, we also have a situation. It seems that we are experiencing a domino effect after we took care of a friend of ours," the faithful advisor said, referring to Dimaglia. "On top of being forced to remove the crew we hired to do the job, we have also had to deal with an informant we discovered through the NYPD. Phil, we'd like to hear what you think we should do to put a lid on this problem of ours?"

Cassavetti noticed The Don, who had been gazing about the room while Carino spoke, was now staring squarely at him.

"First of all, we need to get Andy Vassallo out of reach. We have a cop on the inside of this thing and the guy we took out, Sal Gatti, apparently only told them he overheard something about the hit on the Irish brothers, it was just hearsay. But we can't take any chances with this situation," Cassavetti said. "Next, would be the Westies. We need to send them a message that this conflict needs to be over. Their guys fucked up, and we had no choice, but I'm sure they're pissed about us taking out those moron brothers."

"I know that, ah, Andy was the contact with these, ah, Irish guys," Stubs Pasquez offered in a style that never played well in public. "But, ya know, seein' as we are ship-pin' him away somewheres, one of my guys knows these fucks. I could see to it the word gets through to 'em. Loud and clear."

"No more killing," the Don said quietly as everyone peered at him in total silence. "Phil, just make it go away." Cassavetti nodded and noticed a feint smile appear on Ruggerio's face that he took as a vote of confidence.

The Don began to push his chair back and immediately his two bodyguards jumped to the old man's assistance. He was leaving, and therefore the family business was concluded. Now there would be more drinking, women would arrive, and the night would go on into the early morning hours.

Cassavetti had imported Monique and Cheri up from St. Martens for the weekend at a cost of $10,000 apiece. He didn't want to waste any time with his partners in crime with a flock of strippers.

He knew how to end this unpleasant situation, and it had been sanctioned. Now he just wanted to get out of there as soon as he could, go home, and let the two women put on a show for him that the walls of his thirty-four story apartment had never seen before.

He needed to forget about all this unpleasantness. At least for a night.

CHAPTER 40

Others before him had sacrificed, as he was now about to do.

When faced with an imminent arrest or when the heat was on, sometimes the only move that made sense was to run. Anthony Geppardi of the Genovese Family had left New York for Italy several years ago and no one, including his wife and three children, had heard from him since … He faced a charge of bribing a public official and was wanted for questioning in several murders for hire. Andy Vassallo was in the same boat, except he didn't want to hide in Italy, and he sure as hell didn't plan to vanish from his family.

Andy was pissed. He was angry at the Irish brothers for fucking up and leaving a head floating in the East River. He was pissed at Sal Gatti for conveying a drunken conversation to the cops, but even more pissed at the two guys who said more than they should have, in front of the little rat. Andy Vassallo was angry with Cassavetti too— the big shot who always managed to stay away from the messy stuff, live the high life, and leave all the dirty work to him. And now Vassallo was having to pack up, make a quick exit from his home, his life, even his family, and get the hell out of the state, and move to Florida or Texas, or some other unlikely place where he wouldn't be found. Maybe even Mexico.

He threw his only suitcase in the trunk of the rented car, obtained in the name of one of his associates, George Passali, and walked back in his home to say goodbye to his wife and three children. He couldn't even tell *them* where he was going. They would also have to leave, for a short while anyway. His wife was taking the children to her sister's in upstate New York.

• • •

The developments in the case warranted a Sunday work day.

Elliott Murphy, Chris Marciotti, and another young agent, fresh out of the academy who was there to assist, and NYPD Detective Sam Rainsworth had gathered in a conference room on the fifth floor of One Federal Plaza. On a large board that hung on one of the walls, Murphy was writing out the timeline of events, the names involved, the places, the essential details of the crimes. They were trying to piece it all together, establish common links, and develop their strategy.

Earlier in the day, Murphy had obtained a Federal Arrest Warrant for Giuseppe 'Andy' Vassallo. He was wanted for questioning in the murder of Tony Dimaglia, the two Irish brothers, and Sal Gatti. Agents had raided Vassallo's home an hour ago and he was nowhere to be found. Nor was anyone else, although this was to be expected. All the metropolitan airports, bus stations, and train depots had been alerted and an All-Points Bulletin had been issued nationally.

They also had a man working surveillance on Detective Dennis Coulter. His movements had been routine so far, though the agent assigned to watching Coulter said he lived over the top. He had an expensive home on Long Island and a Hummer in the garage, and those items weren't typical possessions of a New York City cop who *wasn't* on the take. But that was a matter for Internal Affairs. The Feds were more interested in where Coulter might lead them. So far, there was nothing more than the observations about the house and the Hummer.

The only certainties were four dead bodies that led a smoky trail to The Gallo Family. For whatever reason, they hired the Irish brothers to take out one of their own, Tony Dimaglia. For now, the reason for that choice didn't matter. The Bureau team also knew, according to Sal Gatti, that the Irish sibs had been killed because they could be pinned to Dimaglia. Then, of course, it appeared that Gatti was killed, after he relayed a conversation he had overheard which, unfortunately for him, included the name Andy Vassallo.

The team also worked up a current organizational chart of known Gallo family members. Included in that family tree were Salvatore Ruggierio at the top, Al Carino as Consigliere, and several Underbosses, including a newer name, Phil Cassavetti. The mobster seemed to operate well below the radar screen, but their intelligence had placed Cassavetti in the Family as some type of financial operative. He quite possibly could be one of the more important figures in the Gallo operation. In today's world, where even the mob had adapted to corporate mindedness, the technological revolution, and advanced crime fighting techniques, most organized crime families made considerable profits in the legitimate world in addition to their criminal endeavors. The question regarding Cassavetti would be what, if anything, could they pin on him that was indeed criminal.

The Feds had never even talked with Cassavetti, let alone arrested him for anything. Murphy decided there was nothing stopping him from knocking on the man's door and asking him a few questions. At this point they didn't even know where he lived, where he conducted business, or anything else. That would be the first assignment for the young agent tasked with helping the more senior men.

They ended their meeting around three in the afternoon. Everyone had their assignments, and all went home except for the young assistant. He had plenty of research to do, none the least of which involved gathering the background on Cassavetti and fanning out to everything from newspaper articles, the FBI's own intelligence banks, and even certain internet sites.

It was time to cast a net over this organization while blood was still moist on their hands.

Vassallo had decided he wasn't going to overcomplicate this thing. He could drive to a major city along the eastern seaboard and once there, in a place like Philadelphia or Washington, he could use a fake driver's license to purchase a ticket and fly to Dallas or Los Angeles. Then maybe, he could go down to Mexico. Or, he could just drive all the way to Miami. At this point, he hadn't decided.

He was increasingly relieved as he made it cleanly out of New York, and he expelled a sigh of relief when he drove across the George Washington Bridge and headed south on I-95. The road was a blur as he drove through New Jersey and eventually rolled into Maryland. Vassallo was tiring and pulled off the throughway into a rest stop that had gas and several different fast-food selections. He was starving and the car needed fuel.

After grabbing a burger to go and filling the gas tank, he jumped into his car and hurried out of the rest stop parking lot. He found the on-ramp and made his way back onto the throughway, never noticing the stop sign he shot through as he left the parking lot.

• • •

Maryland State Trooper Alicia Phillips had just finished a late break for lunch and was seated in her cruiser. She was finishing up a call to her twelve-year-old son who was home alone on a Sunday afternoon in their suburban apartment, forty-five minutes away in Baltimore. She hated these weekends when she had to work during the day, even though it was just once a month. But, her son seemed to enjoy the time on his own, and he was a good kid. She knew that he was able to take care of himself. She just missed him.

She ended the call and put her cell phone back in the receptacle on the dash. As she looked up, she noticed a grey Ford Taurus fly right through the stop sign, not fifty feet from her position. The driver obviously didn't see her State Patrol car, any more than he saw the stop sign. Or perhaps, he just ignored it. What the heck, she thought, she needed to get back up on the southbound throughway anyway, why not add another ticket and fine in the process.

She thought it was a little over-dramatic to hit the lights and siren before leaving the rest stop area, so it took her a few moments to make her way onto I-95. Once she was on the throughway, she hit the lights and accelerator, and the powerful police interceptor quickly leapt to seventy-five miles an hour. After topping the first rise, the Taurus was nowhere in sight so she moved over to the left lane and hit it. She was quickly traveling close to ninety-five and in less than a minute she finally saw the Ford about a half-mile ahead. Trooper Phillips stayed in the left lane of the three-lane Interstate until she closed on the car, but then she slowed to a following position and pulled over to the center lane behind the Taurus.

• • •

Vassallo's heart raced inside his chest and his face flushed. This couldn't be happening. He hadn't been speeding, at least not at a rate that would get him pulled over. He looked at his speedometer and it registered seventy-two on a stretch where the limit was seventy. He tried to think fast and develop a plan. He looked closely in the rearview mirror and was encouraged to see a lone female trooper.

This had to be a traffic stop, he reasoned, and maybe there was something wrong with the turn signals or a brake light was out. He didn't know what the problem was, but he did know that if there was already a bulletin out for him, they wouldn't send a solitary female cop to take down a gangster wanted for questioning in a murder. No way. Besides, he was in a rented car, and she certainly couldn't have just spotted him driving down the throughway.

He needed to get off the throughway and then the only thing he could do was see how the situation unfolded. With any luck, the infraction was minor, and he could just go on his way with a warning. He hadn't been pulled over by a trooper for a traffic violation in years, and wondered if their procedures had changed. If she called in his fake driver's license to her dispatcher, things could get very ugly. It would probably come back clean, but the license number belonged to his son, Andrew Junior. While the birth-date had been changed on the forgery, it obviously wasn't changed in the computer. He would have to claim he couldn't find his license, and say he was Pasalli, the guy who had rented the car for him. Yeah, he thought, that might work. In fact, his driver's license number was on the rental contract. He removed his wallet from his back trouser pocket and put it under the seat, in case he had to exit the car and be patted down.

He concentrated on slowly making his way over to the right side of the road and then he saw an exit was coming up to a rural road. He made the exit, drove down the little off-ramp. He stopped at the stop sign at the end of the ramp and turned left under the over-pass and stopped under the bridge to the side of the desolate two lane country road. He wanted to keep his options open, in case things got out of control. More importantly, he didn't want Sunday afternoon drivers to witness a cop killing.

The guy didn't pull over right away but that wasn't so unusual. While she followed him off the throughway and down the exit ramp, she entered the New York state license plate into the computer terminal mounted on the right side of the dash. The results came back within a few seconds. There were no wants, and no warrants, but that didn't tell her anything about the driver as the vehicle was registered to Avis Rental Cars.

She followed procedure, picked up the radio mike, and advised her dispatcher that she was making the stop. She gave the plate number, description of the car, and reported the fact that she had run the plates and the vehicle came up clean. Trooper Phillips cradled the mike and hit the switch that turned on the digital camera mounted on the dash. The Taurus had finally come to a full stop under the overpass. Odd, she thought to herself, but there hadn't been much room on the off-ramp for him to pull over, and he wasn't acting suspicious in any other way—so she let the observation pass without another thought.

Vassallo had taken the time to prepare himself. He knew two things right now. First, he didn't want to shoot a cop, and second, he was already linked to two capital murders. One more killing wasn't going to make any difference. Getting caught would. He had positioned his thirty-eight between the seat and the center console. The cop wouldn't be able to see the gun, even if he had to get out, but he could get to it in a hurry if he needed it.

The Maryland State Patrol dispatcher finally came back on the radio and acknowledged her location; the video was rolling, and Trooper Phillips put the cruiser in park, left the engine running, and routinely put on her familiar circular brimmed hat. She grabbed her ticket clipboard from the passenger seat and stepped out of her car, and as she did so, she reached down to her holster and removed the leather clip that held the gun secure. Nothing about the situation warranted any significant concern in her mind, the subtle move was just procedure. She carefully approached the vehicle, heard the engine still running, and noticed the driver lowering his window.

"Please turn your vehicle off sir," Trooper Phillips said with the appropriate level of authority and professionalism exhibited by most highway cops. "And hand me your driver's license and rental contract."

She was standing at the window now and still she could see nothing that looked out of the ordinary. The man gave her a smile and asked the typical question.

"What did I do, Officer?" Vassallo asked, as he dug into the glove box and handed her the rental contract. She started to look it over while keeping an eye on the man as he apparently began looking for his wallet.

"Sir, you ran through a stop sign leaving the parking lot of the road-side rest area a few miles back. It's a public facility and we have to enforce normal traffic rules."

Vassallo's heart rate slowed instantly. This was only about a fucking stop sign he had never seen. Using George's identity had to work, or there was going to be another unnecessary murder over a damned stop sign. If a physical description was exchanged there would be a problem. Vassallo was six feet tall, two-hundred-and-seventy-pounds, with dark hair. Pasalli was a wiry little shit, weighed about one seventy-five, and was all grey.

"Jeez, Officer, I can't find my wallet! I guess I must have left it at the rental car place," he said charmingly, scratching his head for effect. "I can't believe I did that."

"Your name is George Pasalli?" the Trooper asked.

"Yes, ma'am," he replied.

"Okay, thanks. One moment, sir."

Trooper Phillips turned away and moved around to the back of the car. There was virtually no traffic under the bridge on this country road, but the noise of the Interstate Highway overhead could still be heard. She called in the New York State driver's license for Mr. Pasalli and waited a moment. Maryland's computers were linked with most of the northeastern states, but it always took a little bit longer. She started to fill out the ticket while she waited and walked back to the window.

• • •

"Is the information on the rental contract correct sir, the address and so on?" the Trooper asked.

"Yeah," he answered and saw that she was writing him up for the stop sign. Maybe he was going to make it out of this without creating another problem, he thought.

Suddenly he heard the crackling of the radio that was strapped to her belt. "One seventy-five," the voice said.

The cop had a microphone attached to her uniform on a flap on her shoulder. She leaned her face over and pushed the button to speak.

"This is one seventy-five," she responded, referring to her assigned officer number.

"You have a code three forty-five on subject. Misdemeanor. We're calling New York for the amount," the voice on the radio droned.

Shit, Trooper Phillips thought to herself. This meant the guy had a misdemeanor traffic warrant and he would have to follow her into the station, thirty miles away, and settle up or be held. It was a courtesy the states in the region extended to one another, but it was voluntary on the part of the officers. Most troopers didn't mess with it and she wasn't about to this afternoon. Instead, she would give the guy a scolding and encourage him to take care of it.

• • •

The previous calm evaporated into adrenalin-fueled readiness. Vassallo couldn't hear the crackling radio that well but he had made out *subject* and *warrant*. Did fuckin' George have a warrant out? He lowered his right hand to the butt of the gun discreetly.

"Sir, I'm afraid we've got a problem here. You've got an arrest warrant in New York State for a traffic violation."

That was all Vassallo needed to hear.

Before the cop uttered another word, Vassallo ripped the gun from its hiding place between the seats, and blasted a shot that probably ripped a hole right through the bitch's heart, he thought to himself. He didn't stick around to find out, all he knew was that the blast seemed to lift her into the air and all he wanted to do was get the fuck out of there, which is exactly what he did.

He turned the car around and got back onto the Interstate southbound. His heart was pounding, his mouth felt dry. It was always a rush to pull the trigger. He had only killed one woman before, and it was a long time ago and she was a loud-mouthed hooker. This one was a cop, and carried a lot more weight. He had to leave the area in a hurry. That was accomplished with ease as it was only ten minutes from the Delaware state line. He would find a town with a bus station, ditch the car, and keep heading south.

Maybe Mexico was becoming a better idea all the time.

Eight minutes later, Herbert and Louisa Lee made the same full stop at the same rural intersection they had crossed every Sunday afternoon for the last forty years. Herbert loved to take a drive on the highway after church and eat at the rest stop and watch all the folks come and go. Louisa put up with it, but her mood hadn't improved even though they were on their way back.

As they turned under the bridge, onto the road that would take them to their farm, they couldn't believe their eyes. A State Patrol car was parked under the overpass, lights still flashing, and there was a body on the pavement, right in the middle of the road. As they drove closer ever so slowly, they could see the person in the road was a State Trooper, and when they got out of their car, they could see the downed officer was a woman.

Herb was silent and began surveying the scene, but Louisa said, "Oh no! This is bad. What should we do?"

Herb got on his knees. He could tell the Trooper had been shot in the chest because her uniform was torn there, but the details were strange. The entry point was almost a circular burn mark, and there was no obvious blood. He placed his spindly, eighty-three-year-old fingers on her neck and grew very still.

"She has a pulse!" he cried out. "Go get the gall-darned cellular phone from the glove box."

"What phone?" his wife asked, looking confused. She was unaware that her husband had a cell phone.

"Just get the damn phone out of the car, Lou, before this woman dies!"

CHAPTER 41

Early Sunday evening found Jack, once again, alone in his apartment. Rachel had a cousin in from out of town and while the three of them had dinner the previous evening, Jack was left with the tab but nothing more. There had been no threesome, no twosome, nothing. Rachel had alluded to the possibility of getting together Monday night, but she said she needed to spend time with her cousin through the weekend. She offered some weak excuse about not having seen her for a year. She would call Monday morning and let him know.

Fuck that, Jack thought. He was beginning to realize this girl wielded far too much control in this "relationship" of theirs and he didn't like it one bit. He was constantly trying to please her, still she held all the cards, and the whole thing exposed the fact that he had been out of the game for a long, long time. But he instinctively knew what was going on. He was obsessed with the sexual side of it all, he needed things to work to justify everything he had done with his family, and for better or worse, he didn't want to think about anything else. Because when he did think about it, the facts haunted him. The fact that he left his boys, the fact that he had his wife killed, the fact that he was in bed with a guy, Phil Cassavetti, who had a far darker heart than his own.

Jack tried to watch a movie, as he didn't feel like going out and when he lost interest in the movie, he even tried to read. When that faded, he worked on straightening up the small apartment and as he finished, finally, the phone rang. Despite his awareness of Rachel's control over him and his acceptance of being in the palm of her hand and hopelessly obsessed, he was still desperate to hear her voice. He anxiously placed the phone to his ear.

But it wasn't her.

"Jack, it's Phil Cassavetti."

When he heard the voice, his heart raced and his mind snapped back to reality like the snap of a bungee cord. He was on the verge of a shit-storm and felt it looming on the line.

"Hey, Phil," Jack answered, sounding perhaps a little too enthusiastic. "How are you doing?"

"Listen, Jack, I need a favor," Cassavetti said and paused. Jack said nothing. "We've got another property," Cassavetti continued, "that I know you can help us with. It's owned by a completely different company, your guys will never know there's any connection with the other buildings, and I promise you, this one won't have any problems. Ever. In fact, it's a dry cleaning plant that we own and it happens to be very profitable. Nothing will ever happen to that building, trust me. And I imagine that it's going to be a pretty healthy premium, so you should make some good money on the deal. The old insurance cost us over a quarter mil."

Jack knew what he should say, but he couldn't. This was no different than Rachel, he thought to himself. She had him by the balls and this guy had him over a barrel! How could he say no to a guy that killed his wife for him? Obviously, a guy like this wouldn't take kindly to rejection.

"When did you want to get together?" he asked feebly. It was all he could manage.

"How about tomorrow, it's kind of important."

"Can we make it Tuesday? I'm tied up all day and tomorrow evening. I can get together after work on Tuesday or lunch if you like."

Cassavetti was silent for a moment. Jack didn't like that one bit. But then the mobster responded.

"If that's the earliest you can make it that will have to work. I'll call you Tuesday morning and we'll make arrangements."

"Sounds good," Jack replied, hoping the call was over.

"Hey Jack, listen, you haven't had any more trouble on that fire have you?" Cassavetti asked, his tone was serious.

"No!" Jack answered defensively. Then he backtracked. "What do you mean?"

"I mean, has anyone been asking you more questions—besides your boss?" Jack sensed, right then and there, that this guy was much worse than any bad news. He had to answer the question, and fortunately this time, he could tell the truth.

"No. Nothing," Horton answered.

"Good, let me know if that changes, Jack," Cassavetti said flatly and then hung up and left Jack with a buzzing line.

Jack stood frozen with the phone in his hand. *What had he gotten himself into?*

He finally put the phone back in the cradle and sat down, staring at the inside of his small, furnished executive apartment, and he felt like he was removed from reality. The events of the last several weeks were crashing down on him and he couldn't believe that he was in the middle of it all. Suddenly, he yearned for it all to be undone. For the first time since it all began, he longed for the boring familiarity of Alice and the boys. He had gone way too far this time, though, and the chance for any sort of middle-ground was long since gone. In this rare moment of clarity, he realized that he had allowed himself to become obsessed with a younger woman who had given him something he craved, sex, but withheld any hope of a real relationship. And he allowed himself to become enamored with a shadowy man and his money and his aura. He allowed himself to think he could possess that same aura, and that all he had to do was follow Cassavetti's lead.

And now look where it had led, he thought.

He didn't know what to do. He couldn't think of *anything* he could do. He had to meet with Cassavetti. He had to do what he asked. Yeah, that was all clear. And yet, through some insane form of denial, he also knew that if Rachel walked in the door right now, he would feel as though everything was okay and all his troubles would vanish.

Basically, *Jack Horton was fucked*.

He had a bottle of Grey Goose Vodka on the kitchen counter. He got up and filled a glass with ice, a large glass, and filled the container with vodka. Eventually he knew he would need to sleep, and the way things were buzzing around in his head, he knew he would need some help.

CHAPTER 42

It had been a long day, especially for a Sunday, and Elliott was relieved to finally be home. He had again gone into the office and worked with his partner and their assistant on the Gallo case.

The net had been cast, the strategy devised, and he could sense that their task force would begin to hone in on the crime family—it was just a matter of time. Vassallo was on the run, they would unearth something useful on Cassavetti, and as they dug deeper into the case, he knew there would be a break and busts would follow. This was what he needed—a solid case that would give him redemption. No one was asking him to prove anything, but he needed it for himself.

Sally greeted him in the kitchen; she had obviously changed out of her real estate clothes and was wearing nothing but one of their oldest son's football jerseys, and a pair of fluffy white slippers. She was in the kitchen working on dinner when Elliott walked into the house.

He took one look at her and she quite literally took his breath away. She was beautiful and sexy and she represented *home* to him. He was so grateful to have her back in his life he felt almost giddy to see her like this. She smiled, immediately came over to touch his admiring face, and she wrapped her arms around him and gave him a passionate kiss. Elliott knew this was a prelude of things to follow. The jersey, the kiss, even the look on her face, all pointed in one direction. He felt a strong sense of desire build quickly in his mind, his body, especially his loins. He purposefully picked her up and set her down on the kitchen counter.

She squealed, but certainly didn't resist. He removed his weapon clipped to his belt and returned the kiss with one of his own. He held the back of her head ith one hand and massaged her bare thigh with the other. Suddenly, for Elliott, all thoughts of the case, the world, or anything beyond their embrace, vanished.

As Elliott's hand made its way further up her thigh, their rapture was suddenly shattered. The pager on his belt went off and simultaneously the private phone line in his study rang. Something serious was going on at the Bureau, and they both knew it immediately. Sally looked into his eyes and he could see there was disappointment, but there was understanding as well. She knew what had to be a priority for him right now, and in the truest fashion of a supportive wife, her expression absolved him of any guilt.

"Go answer it, darling," she said softly. "This can wait."

He said nothing, but kissed her gently on her forehead. The phone continued to ring and he swiftly made his way to his study and answered it.

"This is Murphy," he said.

"Sorry to bother you, Elliott," said Chris Marciotti, "but we've got something working. A Maryland State Police Trooper was shot beneath an overpass along I-95. She caught one in the chest but she's gonna be okay, she had her vest on. She's been airlifted to a hospital in Baltimore. The dispatcher reported that she had pulled a car over that was rented to a guy named George Pasalli. Turns out the guy is sitting at home watching TV when the cops go to his house, they press him and he tells them he rented the car for a buddy. Get this, Andy Vassallo."

"Bingo. Have they found him?" Murphy asked. His adrenalin was pumping, both from being aroused by his wife, and increased by the news about Vassallo.

"Not yet. They found the rental car and are assuming that he stole a pick-up truck that was reported in the area at about the same time. But the car was found in Delaware, Elliott, so Vassallo's crossed state lines and we have jurisdiction now."

"I want to get down there, Chris. Is the chopper available?" Murphy asked.

"All ready to go. The crew is waiting and I'm three minutes from the heliport. We can pick you up at the Cedar Grove field," Marciotti referred to a small private airstrip near Murphy's home. He had used it over the years under similar circumstances when he needed to move in a hurry in a Bureau helicopter.

Murphy hung up, dashed upstairs to their bedroom, and grabbed an overnight bag he always had packed and at the ready. It contained a clean shirt, underwear, socks along with toiletries and a supply of ammunition and an extra pistol. The gun was in addition to the SIG Automatic that he carried with him at all times, it was the one that replaced the weapon that had been stolen from him.

Sally understood, as always, and promised a resumption of what they had started upon his return. Also, as always, she didn't ask when he would be home or where he was going. She knew he wouldn't know and couldn't say. Murphy donned his field jacket, a dark navy shell with the letters FBI emblazoned in yellow on the back, and scurried from his home.

By the time he made it out to the small airport, the Bell Jet helicopter was already waiting for him, having made the easy fifteen-minute flight from Manhattan. He hurried out to the sleek chopper and climbed into the rear. The pilot had the rotor turning before he shut the door, and within seconds, they were lifting off into a clear night sky, heading south toward the Maryland Delaware border.

"Give me an update," Murphy said as he leaned up to Marciotti to hear over the rhythmic thud of the powerful chopper's engine.

"Apparently they had a sighting of the pick-up," Marciotti said, as he turned around in the co-pilot's seat, "by a local cop in Elmsdalee, Delaware. Vassallo was going the opposite direction and the cop couldn't get turned around quick enough, and lost him. But they're getting close."

Murphy nodded and sat back. He put on headphones so that he could monitor the radio chatter.

They had a warrant to pick up Vassallo as a "person of interest" in the murders of the Irish brothers. But now, with the Maryland matter involving a cop shooting, it took precedence. It certainly painted a picture, however. Obviously if this guy was actually Vassallo, he was definitely on the run.

It took them about an hour to fly down the New Jersey coastline, inland to Maryland, and a quick crossover into Delaware. The pilot put down at a Highway Patrol station that had a small helipad and a local field agent was waiting for them in an SUV. Marciotti and Murphy hopped out of the chopper, the pilot saluted, and Murphy assumed he was ex-military and returned the gesture as he shut the door. They jumped into the waiting vehicle and a local field agent introduced himself as Brian Alexander and brought them up to speed.

"They got him!" the enthusiastic young man exclaimed. "He T-boned a Highway Patrol car at a road block, but they nailed the guy!"

"Are they bringing him here?" Murphy asked.

"I'm liaising with a buddy of mine in DBI, and he'll let me know," Alexander replied, referring to the Delaware Bureau of Investigation, the state agency that usually superseded local law enforcement in capital cases and other serious matters.

Meanwhile, Murphy was thinking of all angles. They needed time and they needed Vassallo. The cop shooting was serious but the officer was okay. The Feds on the other hand were trying to break open a significant organized crime case and they needed to get hands on their guy as quickly as possible. They also needed to keep the story out of the media. It would be tough, as it was sensational and the cop shooting element was more than newsworthy, but if they could at least manage to keep Vassallo's name out of the press for twenty-four hours or so, it would be crucial assistance to the Bureau. If Vassallo was interested in a deal, now would be the time for him to make it. And if his associates back in New York, like Cassavetti or even the boss man, Ruggierio, didn't hear about his capture, they would be less likely to try and make a run for it.

It was a window of opportunity, and it was one rare in coming. Vassallo was facing a life sentence for attempted murder of the trooper. He wouldn't have a lawyer just yet, and no one knew of his whereabouts except the law. He couldn't help but be a little shook up.

Andy Vassallo sat in the back of a Delaware State Patrol car, cuffed, his head bandaged from the only injury he suffered from plowing into the roadblock that put an end to his run from the law. On one level, he was fuming with anger; how could such a ridiculous sequence of events have unfolded to put him in the back of this car? What infuriated him even more was that he had been forced to run in the first place, all because of the screw-ups of others, and for no better reason than to protect those above him.

And now this.

He knew he was fucked. He hadn't even had a chance to toss the gun he used on the trooper, and he'd been told the bitch was alive and well. Obviously she would be able to identify him.

And there was something else. He thought twice about this before he ever left his house earlier in the day, and wished that he'd grabbed a clean gun. In retrospect, it was perhaps the dumbest thing he had ever done in his life. The gun was the same one he used in the hit on the Irish brothers. He had blown them away with a shotgun, which could never be matched in ballistic testing, but one of them had lingered after the initial blast, and he capped him in the head with his Berretta, which was used in the attempted murder of Maryland State Trooper Alicia Phillips.

He knew he was toast.

The cops, or worse, the Feds, would put two and two together and he would get the chair. He couldn't fathom why he failed to get rid of the gun. As he thought this through, a chill flowed through his core. In a strange way, it was almost calming and dreamlike, as though it was happening to someone else.

This was a moment that he and his associates anticipated but never spoke of. This was the manifestation of a possibility that would overwhelm or debilitate if much thought was ever given; it was something that the gangster machismo kept deeply buried. They were soldiers; the battlefield was everywhere, they operated on the wrong side of the law on a daily basis, and always faced capture if caught. This possibility always loomed over their heads, but Vassallo never thought he would be taken down this easily, and particularly with so much going against him. He now faced the consequences for a cop shooting, probably two other murders; it was more than a capital case and he already had a felony conviction for car theft and aggravated assault. They were ten-years-old and he had done a brief stint in Attica, but all in all, he knew when you added it all up, this was really bad.

The question floating in his thoughts now was who would he take along for the ride? He would have to think about that. Who could he give up that would keep him out of the chair? Eventually there would be an offer in exchange for information and testimony against his associates. The decision was whether or not he would become a rat and defy the standing threats from the traditions and codes he had lived by during most of his adult life. But right now, he would just shut up and let the cops have their fun. He wouldn't say a word. He would listen to them, see what they actually had against him, and wait until his lawyer showed up.

They had him in an interview room at the Delaware Trooper station and meanwhile, chaos reigned. Murphy was the ranking official with the Feds, and was accompanied by Marciotti and two other field agents on his team. Delaware had members of their State Department of Investigations along with plenty of troopers and even local police. Two carloads of Maryland troopers had arrived, including a sector chief, and of course, they wanted to get their hands on Vassallo as quickly as possible as the superior crime in their minds was the shooting of Trooper Phillips.

But Murphy had a Federal Warrant now, for suspicion of murder, and he and Marciotti would question him first. There really wasn't much the others could ask about the shooting that they didn't already know. He simply tried to blow away a Maryland State Trooper in order to avoid being identified and arrested. They had already transmitted a picture of Vassallo to the hospital in Baltimore and Trooper Phillips identified him as the shooter.

Murphy entered the room and faced Andy Vassallo. His head was bandaged to cover a gash on his forehead. He was handcuffed to a steel plate in the center of the sturdy metal table where he sat. His hair was mussed, he was unshaven and dirty, and the arm of his shirt was practically torn off, presumably from the accident.

Murphy stared at the mobster and there was a brief moment of silence as the two men sized each other up. Despite Vassallo's physical appearance and predicament, there was definitely that mob-style defiance about him. He looked Murphy in the eye and if he was afraid, he didn't show it. For Murphy, Vassallo was an abomination. He had been chasing men like this practically all of his life. He abhorred men who lived above the law, men who operated by a twisted code and moral guidepost, and scoffed at his authority and the law. It was a fascinating social study, if it weren't so violent and ruthless. He had always thought it amazing that these guys had the balls and the conviction to risk exactly what Vassallo now faced, to perpetuate their creed. Now it was Murphy's job to determine just how committed this man was. Would he roll over on the spot and look out for himself, or would he go down in flames to uphold his honor with his family of thieves?

"So, you doing okay?" Murphy began. "I understand you have been read your rights and you apparently put a call into a lawyer."

Vassallo stared straight at him and said nothing.

"Let me cut to the chase. You and I know that you screwed up with this cop, and that offense alone will send you away for a long, long time. I'm guessing twenty-five years," Murphy said calmly. Murphy had done this hundreds of times and always began by softening the subject with a little kindness, even empathy. "I'm not here about the cop, Andy. I'm here because we're working to link you up with four dead bodies back in New York. I'm here because I can keep your ass out of the chair when we pin those murders on you but you know the drill from that point. We need something from you. And in this case, it needs to be a lot, and I believe you can give it to me."

Finally, Vassallo spoke. "My lawyer is coming. I'm not sayin' a fuckin' thing until he shows up."

"That's certainly your prerogative, and I don't even have anything concrete on the murders in New York. The two brothers, Tony Dimaglia, Sal Gatti. But I will, Andy, we both know that's going to happen. With each passing day, and the deeper we get into this, the more we'll find out on our own, the less important your testimony becomes. I've already spoken with the U.S. Attorney General's office and if you're prepared to give up a layer above you, say for instance Phil Cassavetti or Ruggierio, the death penalty goes away, no matter what else turns up. If you provide something real significant, we might just consider the WitnessProtection Program. You would have blown that opportunity if the trooper had died, but aside from breaking a couple of her ribs, she's going to be okay. So, we've still got that chip to play with."

"Hey, food for thought, huh?" Vassallo replied, a smirk on his face. "I appreciate it. But I ain't sayin' a fuckin' thing till my lawyer gets here."

Murphy looked him in the eyes, and he didn't flinch. He had seen it before, and figured Vassallo was operating on his macho sense of loyalty. Perhaps the reality of his predicament hadn't even set in yet. But nonetheless, Murphy had learned to use every minute in the absence of an attorney, and tried one last time. "You know these guys are going to run when they find out we've got you. I'm telling you Andy, the time is now. We're not going to be so generous if you give those guys time to disappear."

"Can I get a soda or somethin'?"

Murphy knew it was hopeless, at least for now. He got up and left the room. He would turn the show over to the locals and let them have some fun with the creep. It was approaching midnight, and time to hop back in the chopper and head home.

It struck him, when he had a moment to evaluate his own feelings in the moment, how much he wanted a drink. He was seated comfortably in the back of the helicopter, the pilot rolled out of a turn to head north, and out of nowhere, a massive craving for booze hit him. He knew this time he would not act on it, and in fact, this wasn't the first time his thoughts had turned to booze, even since his last close encounter on the previous Friday. Somewhere along the line he felt he had actually figured this drinking deal out. He finally recognized the insanity drinking again would bring about for him and he knew that all he had to do was not take that first drink. Even so, still the cravings circled him like vultures hoping for an opportunity to feast.

As the helicopter flew stealthily through the night sky, returning him home to Cedar Grove, the comfort of his home, and the love of his wife, he sat with his eyes closed and focused on a meditation he had learned in AA. He repeated it over and over again. And when they began the short descent to the field, he reopened his eyes and realized he was okay, the craving was gone, and he was centered again. His Higher Power must have been listening.

After they landed, he discussed an early morning meeting with Marciotti, thanked the pilot, and he got into his car and drove home. Straight home. Instead of the craving for alcohol he experienced forty-five minutes earlier, he now yearned for his bed and his wife. All in all, it had actually been a very good night. It hadn't surprised him that they weren't able to get anything out of Vassallo so soon after his capture. It was just a matter of time and Vassallo needed some time to simmer. Redemption it seemed, was like a crook about to roll over. Both needed time to cook.

CHAPTER 43

The heat was up, way up.

The word had circulated fast throughout the Gallo Family. Vassallo had disappeared, the cops and the Feds were all over the murders of Dimaglia, the Irish Brothers, and Sal Gatti, and it was time to tie up loose ends and lay low. This was exactly what Paul Visante intended to do, too, but the first thing he had to take care of was the broad.

He wasn't happy about how things had developed, none of it.

First off, Visante worked for Andy Vassallo and was as friendly with the man as anyone. Now, Vassallo was off the radar. At best, Andy disappeared because he needed to get out of town, or in the worst-case scenario, something had happened to him.

Secondly, Visante had mixed feelings about getting rid of the housewife who was nicely locked up at his cabin. In addition, he wasn't feeling that well and preferred to spend this Monday in bed, as opposed to the two-hour drive upstate to his place to take care of business. He was a little nauseous and his arms and his chest were achy, which felt strange. He never got sick, and consequently didn't know exactly what to do. He assumed he had a flu bug.

It was a dreary day; a light rain fell as he drove up the New York State Throughway. He turned off at Monticello and drove along Highway 17 towards his cabin. He felt tired, so tired he had to concentrate on staying awake even though it was only eleven in the morning. He decided earlier that he was going to have his way with the woman. What the hell, he thought, if he's going to kill her, he might as well fuck her beforehand, and give her a proper sendoff. But now, in light of his illness, he didn't know if he had it in him. He really felt like he was getting very sick.

Alice Horton had been pacing, doing sit-ups and stretches, reading, and even practiced some yoga she remembered from a class she had taken several years ago. She thought it was boring and worthless at the time; but for some odd reason, perhaps the strain of her predicament, she strived to remember every position, exercise, and meditation she could call up. Alice knew that her days were numbered. She knew that one of these times this strange and scary guy would show up to kill her, and just as obviously, she had to be prepared to do something about it. The problem was she might not get a chance. Besides the fact Visante could easily overpower her, she had also seen the gun on the inside of his ever-present wind breaker. He would probably just open the door and blow her brains out.

But she was determined not to go nuts, and was trying to stay sharp. Her mind wandered over many of the various facets of her dilemma, but inevitably, she landed on the questions that she couldn't answer. *Who* wanted her dead?

That was the most pressing question on her mind. It had to be Jack, although that too was a rather unfathomable thought. Had he gone that far off the deep-end that he would commit such a heinous crime, just to save money in a divorce and never have to deal with her again over the boys? It was mind boggling, for sure, but there was little she could do about that now. Alice forced herself to focus on the problem at hand. She needed to create a one-in-a-million break that would get her out of this mess. She could thibnk about Jack later.

Another important question was why this man, Paul, had really kept her around? Was it out of some warped sense of loneliness, as he'd said, or something even more sinister? His behavior was so strange because he had been acting civil towards her right from the beginning of this ordeal, and in fact, he had actually portrayed himself to be a decent guy. He was middle-aged, not bad looking, and although he was pretty stout, he was obviously in good shape. But she sensed, even through his nice-guy veneer, that he was awkward around her, and wondered if that was because he was naturally uncomfortable around women, or simply off his best game with women he had kidnapped. Alice shook her head slightly at the absurdity of her thoughts.

She again focused on her need to be ready to seize the first opportunity, if in fact one emerged, to get away. However, every situation they had been in thus far hadn't really exposed any encouraging possibilities. He was relaxed around her, but never let his guard down. She decided her only choice was to watch for an opportunity. Maybe she could feign an accidental fall to the ground and grab a rock in her hand that she could later use to crack over his head. Or she could throw a cup of hot coffee in his face, like in a movie she saw a long time ago, and run while he was temporarily blinded. She was determined to get out of this and she focused all her energies on conjuring scenarios. But just as her mind settled on this plan of action, the old Alice reemerged and her inner voice told her the situation was horrific and hopeless. She was going to die in the middle of nowhere, her body would probably be cut up into a dozen pieces and buried in the woods to rot, and her remains, certainly, would never be found. She might as well end it herself to rob him of the pleasure. Ultimately, after a few minutes of the old negative tapes, the new Alice returned and she calmed herself down.

And she waited.

Paul Visante drove up the drive to the cabin in his maroon Cadillac, and by this time, compounding his illness, he was having a little trouble breathing. He didn't know what the hell was going on but he was beginning to worry that this was more than the onset of a bug. Frankly, the man had spent virtually all of his adult life healthy as a horse and he was very unfamiliar with the meaning or importance of most of his symptoms. He parked the car in front of the cabin, slowly got out, and his nausea added dizziness to the ongoing aches in his arms and the tightness in his chest. He stood against the car and slowly took deep breaths of the clean, fresh air. He didn't know anything whatsoever about relaxation techniques, for after all, he was a street crook and a killer.

Visante walked away from the car and made his way along the stone path he had laid himself from the gravel drive to the front door of his modest cabin. He climbed the steps and after unlocking the door, he entered the log cabin. To hell with mister nice guy, he thought to himself, he was going to give it to this bitch, literally and figuratively.

Alice heard the door open, his footsteps as he entered, and then she heard the keys jangling followed by the sound of her thick door opening. She stood in front of her bed to face her captor. There was something very different about him. Instead of his normal healthy, dark complexion, his face seemed washed in pallor. His eyes were glassy and bloodshot. She thought at first he had been drinking or doing drugs, but quickly sensed that he was ill.

"What's wrong with you?" she asked, doing her best to sound concerned.

He didn't answer; he just kept coming at her. She realized that whether there was something wrong with her or not, he was about to attack her. It caught her completely off guard, as up this point he had been more of a strange gentleman than a kidnapper. But this was the moment, and if she didn't do something quick, she knew the worst of her nightmare was about to unfold.

Visante gripped her firmly by the shoulder with his massive right hand and he awkwardly worked on undoing his belt with his left. He motioned in the direction of the single bed.

"Over there," he grunted. She could see sweat on his brow and she became convinced that something was very wrong with the man. Fear raced through Alice's veins, but her mind was racing between the horror of what lay ahead and her search for a window of opportunity.

"Paul, wait!" she exclaimed. She saw that it caught his attention as he looked at her for a second. Until now, he hadn't made any eye contact. "There's something wrong with you," she continued. "Just calm down for a moment. Let's just talk about this. Please. I don't want you to hurt me, and I won't fight you, I promise."

He pushed her down on the bed, but he stopped fooling with his pants. He gazed down at her, appearing confused and his pupils were dilated. His breathing was labored and sweat was actually dripping off his forehead. She seemed to forget all about any plans to escape, or knocking him out, and she instinctively got up from the bed, put her hands on his brawny shoulders, and guided him onto the bed.

"My chest," he gasped. Then he clutched his chest and fell back onto the bed.

The pain was so intense that Paul Visante could hardly believe he was still conscious. He had been shot twice in the past, and had his head kicked in while he was serving a five-spot in Attica. Neither experience came close to this pain and he passed out on both the earlier occasions. On top of the sharp pain in his chest, he felt as though he was suffocating.

That's when Visante realized what was happening to him. He was having a heart attack.

Of all the fucking times, he thought to himself, just when he was going to tie up his last loose ends with this bitch. He had actually been looking forward to these final acts, at least, until he got sick.

Now, instead, he felt certain he was about to die.

Suddenly, he felt fear and ironically found himself reaching out for this woman, someone he had grabbed from the sanctity of her own home, his act paid for and ordered by her own husband, and now she represented his lifeline. She had run into the tiny bathroom, she hadn't run off in escape, and returned with a damp cloth that she gently placed on his forehead. He felt disoriented. How could this woman treat him with compassion, when he had been her captor and admitted he was hired to kill her? This was insane.

· · ·

Alice couldn't help herself. While she knew she could grab the keys out of his jacket and take off out the door, take his car and be free, she also knew that this man was in *big* trouble. She recognized what was happening as a heart attack and lacking any medical training, all she could think to do was keep him comfortable. It struck her how uncharacteristic this was for her, and how completely unlike the Alice Horton she remembered before all this had begun. Two weeks ago she had been a sloth of a person who focused on nothing but her own misery, and considered her children, her husband, and most other people to be nothing but an imposition. But early on in her captivity she knew her life would take a whole new direction if she survived, and that she would do better with the other people in her world. She would try to *live!*

She was compelled to start her newly-found life now, and oddly enough it seemed essential that she did so with the very person who had kidnapped her, held her hostage in a tiny room for weeks on end, and quite possibly was about to kill her before he was struck down with what appeared to be a massive coronary. She laid the cloth over his forehead and sat next to him on the bed while he grimaced. The pain that was gripping him appeared to subside and he finally unclenched. His eyes opened and she could tell he was trying to focus on her face. "I'm dying. I can't believe it, but I'm dying. I know it," he said calmly. Quietly. It was very unsettling to Alice, who had never watched anyone die and didn't care to see him pass away, despite the fact that his death would bring her freedom.

"Is there a phone in the cabin?" she asked. "I'll call for an ambulance or a doctor," she said ignoring his fatalistic proclamation.

"No phone," he whispered. His utterances sounded raspy, as if there was something in his throat. "Just sit here with me, Alice. Please don't go."

She was surprised by the use of her first name. He had avoided using *anything* like a name over the past several weeks.

"I won't," she said with a pained smile. "I can't even believe I'm saying that, but I suppose for a hired killer, you've been nicer to me than you had to be."

"I'm sorry," he uttered. Then for a moment he grimaced again.

"Just be still," she said as her hand stroked the side of his face. "There has to be something we can do."

Somehow, he was no longer a monster. Alice sensed her escape was assured and she felt in her gut that something bigger than either one of them was behind it all. It was a profound moment for her, and it filled her heart with strength. It was as if the ship carrying her *second chance* had just appeared on the horizon. Not just in respect to her current dilemma, but in her *life!* For now, she would stay here and do what she could for the man. That's when it dawned on her that she could also gather some important information while she was at it.

"Paul, who hired you to kill me?" she asked gently.

He looked at her again, with tragically sad eyes. "Your husband."

She saw the words form on his pale lips, heard the words resonate in the intimate space between them, and although she had suspected it all along, it still seemed unbelievable. *What had happened to Jack?* How could a man be one way for years and change so fast? Emotions flowed over her, as those words continued to resonate in her consciousness. *Your husband.* A sense of betrayal washed over her initially, but within seconds that sensation metamorphosed into anger and ultimately floated into a dull, penetrating sadness.

Visante spoke again, albeit weakly.

"I guess he didn't want you around much." He closed his eyes once again and he managed a smile. "You seem like a nice lady."

"Wow," Alice said under her breath.

Visante knew it was over. His heart felt as though it was leaping around in his chest, beating out of control. He felt dizzy and ever so nauseous, and something told him that this was a storm he wouldn't weather.

Despite the intense pain, and despite his fear, he felt an odd sense of peace. It was all about to be over. He would face his maker and he knew there would be a price to pay, for his life of sin, deception, and evil doing. Oh, there were times along the way when he had wanted to be different, but Paul doubted that would matter now. The fact that his mind had always been in conflict with his heart didn't make him unique. Lots of people can claim that affliction, and the vast majority don't choose a life of heartless crime and murder. He suddenly hoped the torment would finally end, and the irony was not lost on him, that his demise would be at the hands of his failing heart.

And now, the only person on this earth willing to stand by him was a woman who ten minutes earlier he was about to murder. He was struck with the notion that he had to perform one more act, and it was something that was completely selfless. At least this way, he could go out having done a good thing in the end.

He knew it probably wouldn't be enough to change the outcome of his judgment day, but it would be the right thing to do.

"Alice?" he spoke to her again, his opening again.

She was lost in her own transformation wrapped in the insanity of the moment. It made no sense, but then again, how much of life did? Every day she read about wife killings and other heinous acts. She assumed she wasn't different than most people, and saw these things on television or online, and they all seemed extraordinary, and so very distant. But here she was, living her own moment as a victim of insanity. And very nearly a victim of her husband, Jack Horton. Knowing this didn't make her afraid of Jack, just disgusted. She may not have been a good wife, and she had let herself go over the years, but that didn't justify her murder.

But now it was this man that she needed to focus on. For as bizarre as this whole situation had become, she held a dying man in her hands.

"Alice," he said again.

"Uh huh," she finally replied.

"Something to give you. In the bathroom," he struggled with the words. Alice knew he was getting weaker by the second. "Pull up the carpet."

"Why?" she asked.

"Quickly," he said in a whisper.

She had no idea what this was all about but she complied. She left his side, took the few steps to the tiny bathroom, and grabbed a corner of the thin, green carpet and pulled it up from the rusted nails that loosely held it down. It came up easily and beneath the carpet, cut in to the hardwood floors, was a panel with a circular latch.

"I see a trap door, or whatever it is. Do you want me to open it?" she asked him.

He said nothing but as she could see him nodding affirmatively from the bed. She pulled the hidden door open and saw a small safe. Alice stared at it for a moment, and then walked back over to Visante.

"Okay, there's a safe in the hiding place. What do you want me to do now?"

"Forty-two, thirty-one, twenty," he said faintly.

They were the last words Paul Visante ever uttered.

Alice watched, standing above him, as his face suddenly contorted in pain. She immediately sat back down on the bed beside him and held him by his shoulders. She could feel the muscles of his entire body tense, as if in a massive spasm.

"Paul," was all she could manage.

Then suddenly, his eyes opened wide and they stared directly into hers. However, this time, they now seemed crystal clear and fixed. It was a stare that would stay with her the rest of her life. And then his body went limp, totally limp, and the softest sigh of his last breath escaped.

Alice sat there, on the side of the bed, her hands on the man's lifeless shoulders, and she was frozen in the moment. Against all logic, she still felt something for him. There was an aspect about him that was tragic, something that was un-reconciled and sad. She even wondered if whatever caused that in him had been the reason he hadn't already killed her and buried her in the woods. She would never know, but she would assume that he had been painfully lonely and that was how he died.

Alice finally pulled away from him and stood up quickly, she realized that she was *free!* Excitement and apprehension flowed through her, as she digested what had just happened, and despite her compassion for her captor, this was the one-in-a-million, fluke turn of events that would allow her to escape and return to her life. Her perspective had changed radically and there was so much she wanted to do differently now that she had survived her ordeal. Suddenly, and unexpectedly, it was time to figure out what to do next.

She quickly dashed out of the room and looked for a phone, even though Paul had told her there wasn't one in the house. Alice couldn't ignore the fact, even though her immediate ordeal was over, that she was still frantic. She walked about the modest cabin and she felt strangely attracted to, and haunted by her surroundings. This place, this quaint little cabin that had been her prison for over two weeks, was randomly decorated by the man that lay dead in the next room. It was his place, and home to her metamorphosis. The cabin had prints of wildlife and birds hung on the walls, a small pine breakfast table that sat in the kitchen, though there was only one chair placed in front of it. A cloth-covered ottoman was placed almost in the middle of the open front room, a chair pointed out toward the large bay windows, and Alice imagined the lone occupant would stare out from the emptiness of his life. A life unfulfilled. And he had tried to somehow fill that void with Alice, but it was not meant to be. Visante's void could never be filled, and Alice sensed this profoundly as she stared out the large windows at the splendor and serenity that lay outside. Spring was exploding upon the trees and shrubs and grasses, in a natural beauty that she knew this man, Paul, could see but never touch. Alice was overwhelmed with the sudden need for air and she burst out the front door and stood on the porch, soaking in the warmth of the day and the freshness of the scented air that warded off the chill of tragic insight.

In a strange way, she had sympathy in her heart for her captor. In a sadly perverted way, he was probably trying to change too, and she was merely a target of opportunity for his twisted plan. It was too late for him to change, but Alice saw in the contrast that it wasn't too late for her.

Her life would never be the same.

In a sudden awareness of the present, she noticed Paul's car in the gravel drive. She inexplicably became very anxious to see her boys and her parents, and as her mind drifted, Alice knew she needed to shake this off and leave.

She went back into the cabin, proceeded straight to the main bathroom, and prepared to take a shower. But Alice was not washing off days of captivity. She was cleansing her soul for a fresh start.

As she stood in the shower, the hot water refreshing her body, a body that was thinner and firmer than before due to a sparse diet and hours of sit-ups and calisthenics, and anything else she could do to keep her sanity in the confines of her tiny room. Out of the blue, she suddenly remembered the safe and Paul's final words. The combination. She recalled it began with forty-two and descended from there as her anticipation and curiosity grew. She quickly finished rinsing her hair, hopped out of the shower, and wrapped herself in a towel. Alice walked back to the tiny room where her captor's corpse lay on the bed—the same one in which she slept for weeks as a hostage.

Alice knelt at the little trap doorway to the bathroom's hiding place and began to turn the combination of the sturdy safe. It was actually quite large, and probably a foot and a half in either direction from the sealed portal. She felt her heart begin to pick up pace as she turned first to forty-two, then back to thirty-one, and finally to twenty. She paused for a moment and tried to turn the handle to the right, but it wouldn't move. She turned it to the left and heard the metallic clank of the bolt moving. She pulled the heavy door open and froze in place.

Alice was staring at an open safe that contained banded stacks of cash. The thick metal box was packed with it. Her first reaction was to turn her head and gaze across the room at this man who in his final moment, had actually thought to bequest her probably all the money he had in the world. It was ultimately too much for her, and she began to sob softly. Not out of sadness. Not out of sympathy. She wasn't even crying out of relief; after everything she had suffered, start to finish, bell to bell, the weight of the moment and this eerie turnaround was just too much for her.

Still crying, and rather frantic, Alice began to remove the cash from the safe and stack it on the floor in the room. There were bundles of twenties and fifties but the majority were hundred dollar bills. She didn't stop to count it, but a quick assessment of the bundles indicated there was more than a million dollars stacked on the floor.

Ten minutes later, Alice Horton turned Paul Visante's Cadillac around in front of his lonely country cabin and got the hell out of there. She had quickly dressed, placed all the cash in a duffel bag, grabbed the car keys, and scurried out of the cabin.

She didn't even know where she was, but she would figure it out. Once oriented, she would make her way to her parents as she knew that's where she would find her boys.

On her way, Alice figured, she would think this through. Carefully.

Her new beginning was growing in her heart and confirmed by a duffel bag on the passenger seat next to her. And the man who gave it to her had taken her from her home, held her hostage, and forced her to live in terror for two weeks of her life. It was left to her at the bequest of a dying man who was looking for redemption in his final moment, using his final breath. It was his only chance to do a good thing before he died. To her it was compensation. She didn't question the gift for a moment.

Alice just accepted it.

CHAPTER 44

Special Agent Elliott Murphy sat in his spacious cubicle after hanging up the phone and absent-mindedly shook his head in awe. It thrilled him when technology and brainpower worked together to cast a net and pull the pieces of the puzzle together. Earlier in the day, they had random components of a case, they had Vassallo in custody although he wasn't talking yet, and they had him nailed squarely for the attempted murder of a Maryland cop. Time would tell whether his loyalty was stronger than his willingness to spend the rest of his life in prison or perhaps worse, suffer death by lethal injection. They also had intelligence pinning a seemingly successful legitimate businessman, Phil Cassavetti, to Vassallo. Murphy had witnessed this over and over again. The stronger the evidence at this point in the game, the faster the walls would come down. People would begin to talk, and tight-lipped criminals would begin to cooperate when they saw their own lives in jeopardy; this was a window of opportunity for the good guys.

And now, the sweep of the net was yielding even more.

The first break had been a ballistics match. Obviously, Andy Vassallo had screwed up. The lab had matched the gun used on Trooper Phillips to a lone bullet found at the scene of the murder of the Irish brothers. So now they had two more capitol offenses on the radar and the crime against these two men solved.

The second development had just occurred. Apparently, a retesting of a possible incendiary device found at an apartment fire in Queens had proved positive. NYPD and the Fire Department had notified the FBI that insurance fraud was probable, and *that* was a federal offense. The chain of ownership for these contiguous vacant buildings seemed to lead nowhere, as one corporation was owned by another, and eventually the trail went offshore. However, the original corporation that held the title did have a legal representative—an attorney named Abe Silverman. Silverman's name came up in the Fed's intelligence files as having ties to the Gallo's and more specifically, Phil Cassavetti. Murphy marveled at the fact that they had put all of this together in a matter of hours, and recognized that those results were directly related to the cooperation of several different law enforcement agencies, the sharing of their databases, and communicating electronically. Something that even ten years ago would probably have taken days.

So now Murphy's task force had two different situations to pursue. They would hope to break Vassallo and force him into making a deal for information—testimony under the threat of an imminent death penalty, and they would follow the path led by the arson. If as many people as possible were heated up, it was likely that several would boil over.

Vassallo could wait a day or two and Murphy knew that the decision over what to offer him in exchange for betraying his brethren would be made by the U.S. Attorney's office. While their legal eagles developed their strategy, Murphy decided to work the arson and see if that would lead anywhere.

He grabbed his young partner, Chris Marciotti, and they left to make a call on Abe Silverman, the attorney that had ties to Cassavetti and represented the ghost company that owned the buildings that had been burnt to the ground. The lawyer probably wouldn't give anything up, he would cite privilege of some sort, and the next stop would be the insurance company.

They drove to the mid-town office of Abe Silverman and after waiting in the oak paneled reception area of the small law firm, they were told by an attractive young red head that Mr. Silverman was involved in a deposition for the next several hours and would not be able to speak with them. They didn't have a warrant, so there was nothing further Murphy and his partner could do other than leave a card and ask that he call to set up a time to discuss an urgent matter. He went as far as to inform her that he needed to communicate within twenty-four hours or they would come back with a warrant. The young woman seemed a little nervous, but assured the two federal agents that they would hear from her boss.

There next stop was the insurance company, Avistar.

It was a quarter past four, Monday afternoon, and Jack Horton was in a hurry. He had an appointment with a client downtown in the financial district at four-thirty and he was running late, it would take him forty or forty-five minutes to get to Wall Street at this time of day from his office. And in addition to the stress of work, his mind swayed between disbelief in everything that was happening in his life, everything he had done, and anticipation of the ménage a tois that lay before him later in the evening. His mind was reeling back and forth, through all these different compartments, never at peace for a moment. This was how it had been for weeks now.

At least before all this began, before that fateful pull of the slot machine in the Caribbean, there had been voids. He could go through a day and have very little on his mind, never burdened with the demands of a young girlfriend, never astonished by his brutality in having his wife exterminated, and no one the likes of Phil Cassavetti to be concerned about. His life had been tedious and mundane, but it had been simple. There had been a certain peace about it.

As had been his practice over the last few weeks, he implemented his best strategy to provide an escape from his worries and fears. It was to think of Rachel and the sex. And tonight he would ramp up to a whole new threshold of physical pleasure. The threesome she had been promising was finally at his doorstep.

He bolted into the elevator immediately after two tall, serious looking guys got off at his floor. He noticed that one held an official looking walkie-talkie as they walked straight toward the double glass doors of the Avistar offices. His heart picked up a beat, but he wrote it off to paranoia. They were too finely dressed to be cops, and besides, he had already met the detectives handling Alice's disappearance, and these weren't the guys.

The door to the elevator closed and Jack was on his way down to the street where he would grab a taxi and be on his way to his meeting. He hoped it wouldn't last long as Rachel had said she wanted to get started early. She and her friend had to be at work early the following morning.

That was fine with Jack. The sooner the better.

"I'm Special Agent Murphy and this is Agent Marciotti," Murphy said to the receptionist at Avistar Insurance, "We're with the FBI." After twenty years of introducing himself as an FBI agent, Murphy still got a charge out of it. They both displayed their identification, Murphy's wallet held a gold badge next to his identification card that was the mark of a special agent. "We need to speak with your senior claims person."

The receptionist didn't seem to be phased by their presence and responded, "Please have a seat, and I'll find someone to help you."

Within three minutes a stout little man walked briskly into the reception area from the hallway that led into the Avistar offices and he introduced himself as Ted Duboski. The two Feds introduced themselves and again displayed their identification.

"Gentlemen, I'm not in claims," Duboski said as he enthusiastically shook their hands. "But I'm the senior partner in the office right now, and I'm sure I can help you. Let's go back into a conference room and you can tell me what we can do for you."

The two men followed Duboski who led them into a conference room in a corner of the modest offices. They walked along a corridor with cubicles on the left, and on the right were smallish offices with typical mid-town views, of concrete, traffic, and people milling about on Third Avenue as rush hour began in the late afternoon.

Once they were seated, Murphy began. He pulled out a file from his leather attaché. It contained the full preliminary report on the arson. "Mr. Duboski, we're looking into an arson that your company had insurance coverage on. The buildings were located in Queens, on Flatbush Avenue, and are owned by Mid-America Trading. Are you familiar with this matter?"

Duboski looked confused, "Well, yes I am, but I understood that there wasn't any evidence of arson, that the cause was unknown."

"Actually until this weekend, that was true," Murphy responded and he pulled out the specific page from the report that showed the findings discovered in the lab over the weekend. He slid the page over to Duboski. "There was a re-test that proved up some incendiary material in one of the buildings and the Fire Department is going with arson. Would it be possible for you to grab the file? We're having trouble getting to the bottom of the chain of ownership for these properties and we're hoping you might be able to help us out."

Duboski's enthusiastic, pleasant demeanor seemed to dissipate rapidly and he grimaced for a moment. He rose from the conference table and left the room to obtain the file.

Murphy and Marciotti looked at one another and Murphy said, "He's not happy."

"Nope. Something tells me they might have been worried about this, despite his initial reaction," Marciotti replied, slowly nodding.

A few minutes later Duboski returned with the file.

He opened it up and stared at it for a moment and then said, "There isn't a great deal I can tell you about the insured. To be honest, the young man that wrote the policy had never done business with the client before, and while he didn't do anything wrong, he rushed issuance of the policy." Duboski paused for a moment and then said in a quieter tone, "We spoke to him about it."

"Who completed the paperwork, who signed the application for the client?" Murphy asked.

Duboski flipped through a few pages, pulled one out, and passed it over to the two Feds.

"Silverman," Murphy said as he looked the application over.

"Do you know how your broker met this guy? We're actually interested in the people Silverman represents."

Duboski sat silent at the table with clenched fists, exposing his concern over the matter. Murphy had become more than proficient at reading expressions over twenty years with the Bureau. He had been trained on forensic psychology, but his own intuition was as accurate as anything he had ever learned in the classroom. He waited for the man to respond knowing Duboski was considering his answer carefully.

"The gentleman that wrote the policy is named Jack Horton," Duboski said quietly. "He's a good guy, been with us for over ten years. When we first found out about the fire, we were a little surprised at the way the policy had been underwritten and we talked to him. He claimed he met the gentleman that owns the buildings on a vacation this past winter. Jack said the owner was in a hurry and needed the coverage and Jack expedited it because he thought the guy would bring us more business. It happens like that sometimes."

"Did he give you the name of the owner?" Marciotti asked.

"I don't remember. We have a risk management guy on staff, but unfortunately he's on vacation. Horton is out on an appointment and won't be in until tomorrow morning, but I will certainly have him call you," Duboski answered. "He's had a rough time lately, and I think he's really been pushing to make sales. He and his wife split up, they have three boys, and then something has apparently happened to his wife." Duboski again paused, and in that cautiously hushed tone, as though he was reluctant to betray his underling, said, "She disappeared."

The remark hung in silence in the conference room. It was offered, not solicited, and Murphy knew that Duboski had more to say.

"What do you mean, *disappeared?*" Murphy asked.

"Gone. What Jack told me was that she left the kids with the grandparents and disappeared one weekend," Duboski said, shaking his head and looking past the two Feds and out the window. "He said he thought she left with some guy, but I dunno. Doesn't seem right."

"Why? What do you think happened to her?" Murphy said as he continued to draw him out.

"Can't imagine," Duboski responded. "I know Jack pretty well. You might say I raised the lad in this business. You read about things like this, you know, so I guess anything is possible."

Murphy didn't need to ask anything further on that subject. They would find out more from NYPD and quickly. This was getting interesting, he thought to himself. And their next move needed to be a conversation with this Jack Horton. He asked Duboski for Horton's contact information. The older man led them to a secretary who pulled Jack's Long Island address, as well as his Manhattan address, which apparently he had only been using for a few months.

"Thank you for your time, Mr. Duboski," Murphy said as they were leaving. Both he and Marciotti shook his hand. "NYPD will speak with you further on the arson, and I suppose the good news for you is that we will open an insurance fraud case immediately. Don't be in a hurry to write any checks to these people just yet," Murphy said as he smiled, but his remark didn't get much of a reaction out of the man.

Duboski was obviously very troubled and Murphy surmised that he worried for his younger protégé. Murphy sensed that the senior partner believed Jack Horton was deep into something, and Murphy had a hunch he knew what that something was.

They returned to One Federal Plaza, did some background on Jack Horton, and eventually grabbed something to eat. He called Sally and let her know not to wait up.

They were going to pay this Jack Horton a visit at his home that evening, and Murphy expected it to be a late night.

The appointment with the client downtown had gone well; in fact, it had been very successful. He had made a sale of a new policy and the client had committed to renewing all of his existing policies with higher coverage, meaning more money for Jack. Despite the fact he walked around with haunted images looming over his head because of the things he had done to free up his life, as he thought about it, he decided he wasn't doing too badly for himself. He was able to focus at work, and his sales were doing better than he could ever remember. He had managed to stash away $80,000 in cash in the small safe in his apartment and he was having amazing sex with a girl over ten years younger than himself. In fact, he was now at his apartment preparing for Rachel and a friend to arrive and they would have wild sex for a couple of hours. *How much better does it get than that?*

His mind continued to slide back and forth between thoughts and images that brought euphoria, and those that created dread.

At a little after seven, the doorman buzzed up to Jack's apartment and announced two young ladies were at the door—a Rachel Stern and another guest. Jack told him to send them on up. He gazed around his small apartment one last time to make sure everything was tidy and quickly poured himself another vodka. It was his third since arriving home.

Couldn't be too relaxed for this experience, Jack thought to himself as he turned on some music. Even as he looked forward to their arrival, it was also absurd. He marveled that this was going to be such a far cry from his life in a suburban home, with his angry wife, and three twisted offspring.

After grabbing a bite to eat, Elliott Murphy and Chris Marciotti returned to their office and did their homework. They ran background on Jack Horton and came up completely empty. The guy hadn't even received a speeding ticket in seven years. Then they pulled the Missing Persons report off the national database for Horton's wife, Alice. They managed to obtain the cell phone number for the Suffolk County Detective who was assigned to the case, Detective Nguyen, and he didn't seem surprised to hear from the FBI. He told Murphy that Horton was the only suspect they had in the case, but they hadn't come up with any hard evidence. There was no evidence of any foul play, yet, and Horton had an alibi for the entire weekend when she went missing. He was shacked up with his young girlfriend. But still, that didn't change the fact that the Hortons had been involved in a recently filed divorce, the wife had hired a cut-throat attorney, and she was going for everything Horton had, including a hefty alimony payment. According to a few neighbors and the wife's parents, there was no love lost between the two of them. It made a solid motive for Jack Horton to get rid of his wife somehow, but they didn't have a body, or anything else tangible, so there was nothing the cops could do.

One could even make an argument that she, in fact, had been the one to take off and leave the kids. Perhaps she did run off with some other guy. But somehow, it didn't seem as likely as the other scenario.

Regardless, it would be an additional topic for discussion with Jack Horton, in addition to the arson and insurance fraud that hopefully would lead the Feds closer to Phil Cassavetti and The Gallo Crime Family. Murphy just knew, using the intuition that had seemed instinctual to the seasoned law enforcement officer, there was more to all of this than the random facts they were reading on paper.

The surface picture was that of Jack Horton, a man who had led what appeared to be the plain and simple All-American lifestyle, including a decent job, suburban home with two cars in the garage, three kids, and bang— something happens and everything changes. It was time to talk to this guy and find out just what he might know, whom he might have become involved with, and whether or not this sudden catharsis had anything to do with the Mob, or more specifically, with Phil Cassavetti.

Elliott made a call to the cell phone of the U.S. Attorney that he was working with on the case and he was given the green light. Within fifteen minutes he had a warrant faxed that authorized him to pick up Jack Horton as a person of interest in the arson of the buildings in Queens and for the kidnapping of Alice Horton as well as a search warrant for both his apartment in Manhattan and the family home on Long Island. Frankly, Murphy and the attorney knew it was a stretch, but if Murphy could rattle the guy, it was worth a shot.

Rachel was being rough. And Jack found that he liked it. The scene was right out of a porn flick and he couldn't believe that he was the male star.

Both of the girls were naked except for black cat masks. Jack was wearing nothing but a blindfold and an archaic device that was essentially a studded leather thong that allowed his member to hang free, or protrude distinctly up-right, as was the case. Rachel tied his wrists and ankles to a tall chair formerly used to sit at the small breakfast counter, and Rachel's friend was going to work on the appendage that was protruding out of Jack's new leather device.

Jack was in another world, all his worries evaporated into never-never land as his level of arousal escalated be-yond anything he had ever known. As the two women touched him and their bodies rubbed up against his, his skin felt electric, as if it were on fire. He was unable to fondle them back, but the sense of helplessness to which he had completely submitted, was incredibly erotic. Jack was on a threshold of sexual pleasure he had never before known.

The girls were cooing and tantalizing him with nasty, nasty promises of what would come next, and Jack was moaning and crying out almost uncontrollably. Suddenly, they all went completely silent and froze in place.

In a most alarming way, the intensity of the moment was lost, and Jack returned to planet earth as he realized that someone was pounding on the door.

He heard a loud and ominous voice, say, "Jack Horton, FBI."

"Open up sir, we need to speak with you!" another voice commanded.

Even as the shock of the man's voice was hitting the trio, there was the sound of a key in the door and it immediately burst open. Jack was dumbfounded, and for a split second, still unable to see anything because of his blindfold, he wondered if this was also part of the bizarre movie. But that notion faded quickly, as the girls screamed and Jack heard bedlam in the room even though his blindfold prevented him from witnessing the chaos. *What the hell was going on!*

Murphy took one look at this comical scene, and knew one thing for sure. Whoever this Horton was on the surface, or before his wife went missing, he was now someone else entirely. The background Murphy had acquired painted a picture of a middle-class working stiff who was part of the train and tunnel crowd, commuting in and out of Manhattan every day, sluggin' it out in a job he had toiled at for ten years, married to the same woman for over ten years, father to three boys, and not a blemish on him. But now, rather suddenly, he's implicated in an arson, possibly with ties to the Mob, his wife has mysteriously disappeared, and he's found tied up in his own apartment, blindfolded and wearing some sort of hideous leather crotchless thong, being *tortured* by two very attractive young women.

Murphy would remember Jack Horton in that moment as the all time epitome of the classic *one-eighty!* A man who had crossed some invisible line and would surely never be able to return.

CHAPTER 45

After pulling onto a quaint country road at the end of Paul Visante's long gravel drive and intuitively turning right, Alice Horton drove about two miles and saw a sign identifying the road as State Highway 175. It seemed vaguely familiar, perhaps from years ago when she traveled upstate with her parents for a vacation. Shortly after, she passed a sign which informed her that the town of Monticello was five miles ahead. Now she knew where she was, she knew how to get herself home, and the emotion that poured over her was profound. She had to pull the large car over and, in a moment of overwhelming mixed emotions, wept for a solid ten minutes, for the second time since in less than an hour.

She cried with relief that she had survived her ordeal, she cried over the realization that her husband had hired someone to do this to her, and she even cried over the death of her captor, who in his last breath gave her a bequest that helped balance the nightmare, and would change her life forever.

She had managed to keep herself somewhat together for the past several weeks, a survival instinct surfaced that she had never called on before. But now, an incredible sequence of events had released her from captivity and as she sat in her captor's car on the side of the road, a free woman, the tears of relief, disbelief, sadness, and the traumatic fallout from the horror of it all, flowed like a torrent in a way she had never cried before.

Finally, she pulled back on the road and began the hour and a half drive to her home on Long Island. As she carefully made her way down the throughway she began to formulate a plan. Alice knew that she couldn't simply go back to her former life, plop well over a million dollars into her bank account, and forgive and forget her husband's misdeeds. Despite her escape from what inevitably would have led to her death, she knew that it was not over. She had to think about what she wanted to do about Jack. Alice wondered if her life was still in danger and whether or not going to the police would end all that. *And what to do about the money*? She couldn't chance telling the police about it for fear it would be confiscated. What little Alice knew about crime and legalese came mostly from watching hundreds of *Law and Order* re-runs. But she was smart enough to assume that money obtained from a felon was probably not legally hers. She had even been careful to close the door to the floor safe, wipe her fingerprints from the handle and the dial and cover the safe back up with the carpet. She felt very strongly that she had earned what had been given to her, every last dime of it, in fact. No matter what a cop or a judge or anyone else might think. They weren't there for weeks of captivity and terror.

Alice caught her breath as she turned onto her block. Everything seemed different. Her street, her home, everything seemed tainted and false. It was in this home that she had lived for years with a man who apparently thought nothing of ending her life. She fought back more tears. She got out of the car, took the spare key from underneath a planter next to the front door, and quickly made her way into the house. Before she allowed herself to think about anything else, she dashed up to her bedroom and carefully stashed the duffel full of cash in a large drawer in her small walk-in closet.

Alice walked out of the closet and gazed about her room, the same bedroom she had shared with Jack since they bought the house five years ago. It seemed haunting as she looked around and saw the remnants of her husband that still remained after his quick departure to a *new life*. Her stomach knotted up as she gazed at his side of the bed, his night table, the worn out old ottoman he would often sit on to watch TV. There was even a stack of his sweaters in the same chair that he hadn't bothered to take with him to his new apartment, the apartment that she had never even seen. Knowing that her husband was a man who was capable of all that she had endured made her feel as though she obviously didn't know him at all. She felt as though she had been living with a stranger.

But she did know him, she thought to herself. *What happened to him?* How could he have changed so radically? She considered her part in all of this. Had she been somewhat at fault, had her misery flowed over him so intensely that it had driven him to such an extreme? These were questions she asked but she also gave herself solace in the fact that she knew that this experience had changed her, *profoundly*. As she looked back on her existence and her former behavior, she saw a person who lost herself in a life that ran down the tracks without her. She saw a woman who gave up on herself, and in the process she had made everyone around her pay. She cringed. It was as if she was looking back on someone else.

But now, it was her turn. She had her ticket out of this mess, sitting in a worn duffel bag that belonged to a violent criminal, and her situation was the epitome of irony, and in the tradeoff, she also found herself again. She experienced inner strength she never knew she had, and it occurred to Alice that perhaps, this new strength was the other gift that her captor had unwittingly bestowed upon her. Alice shook her head in disbelief at the turn of events. She had to stop her mental wanderings. It was time to stop looking back and take action.

She knew the boys would be with her parents, so she picked up the phone and dialed. She had really missed them. Not perhaps in the beginning of her ordeal, but as each day wore on she thought about her sons more and more. She thought of their behaviors and how she had essentially neglected each one of them in different ways. All she had ever done was react with harsh discipline, which they usually ignored, and too many situations resulted in anger. Perhaps she would be able to give more of herself to them in the aftermath of her ordeal, after she finished what lay ahead. Only then could she get them away from all of this. Her plan would give the four of them another chance.

On the second ring, a tired, familiar voice answered. It was her father and his flat-line timber never sounded so good. She could feel the emotion swelling back up from her stomach, through her throat. She couldn't speak at first.

Then finally, she said, "Daddy ...," and the tears began to flow once again. Alice then heard something she'd never heard before. She heard the whimpering of an old man, her father, as he too began to sob. "Alice, my God!" he managed. "Are you okay?"

"I'm fine Daddy," she cried.

"What happened to you?" her father asked. "Where are you?"

"I'll tell you everything when I see you. I'm at home. Can you bring the boys over right away?"

"Your mother has them at the store but they should be home any time. Have you called the police yet, do they know you're okay?"

"No," Alice answered, a wash of dread flowed over her.

She was the victim, she knew that, but she also knew that there would be questions and she was determined not to mention the money. It was against her newly-forming fiber as she knew that omission was as good as a lie, and she was fundamentally an honest person before this mess started. She was even more so now, but wasn't about to let go of the money. Not after what she had suffered.

"I have the detective's name who is handling your case. He's been nice enough under the circumstances. Your mother and I thought the worst," he said, starting to rattle on now. "We thought Jack had done something to you. I just can't believe you're home and safe. We were so fearful that we'd never find you."

"Let's just talk when you get over here," she interrupted.

Her father told Alice he would drive her mother and the boys to her house as soon as they returned from the store. Alice knew that meant she had at least forty-five minutes to take yet another shower, and change. After all, she was still wearing the same sweat suit she wore the day she was abducted, although she had spent some days wearing oversize sweaters that Visante had given her.

She walked into her bathroom, stripped off her clothes, and looked at herself in the mirror. She pulled back her hair, which hadn't been brushed in all this time, and had only been combed after three or four baths she had taken at the cabin. She paused for a moment, looking at herself, and what she saw was a different person. Everything, both physically and spiritually, had changed.

Alice grinned for a moment. In the end, she had lost weight she never seemed to be able to shed in her former life, while she was devastated over the fact her husband had done this to her and intended to have him killed, she now had him by the balls and finally, if not first and foremost, she had over a million dollars in cold hard cash sitting in her closet.

NYPD Sergeant Detective Nguyen received a page at home at around six o'clock, after just pulling into his driveway from a long day at work. After receiving the news of Alice Horton's escape, he turned around and drove an hour to the subject's home. It was a freaking miracle, he thought to himself as he slowly rolled through Long Island

Expressway rush hour traffic. He couldn't wait to hear her story.

By eight o'clock, the survivor of over four weeks of captivity and what was obviously intended to be a murder, Alice Horton had given the Detective and a uniformed officer all the details. It was, in fact, a miracle that she hadn't been killed.

Nguyen returned to his precinct and settled in to what would be several hours of computer input as the full report would be necessary in the morning. He also had to dispatch State Police to the cabin and give the FBI a call. They had an interest in the case and he knew they would appreciate an update. Nguyen had received a call from them just a few days earlier. He looked for the note he made at the time and he placed a call to the special agent he had talked to earlier.

• • •

Murphy had just sat down with a highly embarrassed and extremely nervous Jack Horton in an interrogation room at One Federal Plaza. Horton had been informed of his rights, advised that the conversation would be recorded, and Murphy was just warming the guy up when he was interrupted by his partner, Chris Marciotti, who called him out of the room. Murphy quickly joined him in the hall.

"You're not going to believe this," the younger man said. "This guy's wife just showed up and NYPD says that she claims she was kidnapped, was supposed to be killed, but instead, the whacko who grabbed her decided to hold her in some cabin in the country for all this time and he apparently had a heart attack, But before he croaked, the guy told her that her hubby took out the contract! Our man, Jack Horton!"

"Wow," Murphy exclaimed. "This is one for the books. Of course, it's not hard evidence, it's nothing more than hearsay, but if the rest of her story checks out, it's something. I'm going to see how far I get with this guy first, see what we can use him for, and then I'll drop this little bomb on him."

Murphy reentered the interrogation room. There sat Jack Horton, looking apprehensive, afraid, and humiliated, like a puppy caught wetting the rug. He had been nabbed in an extremely compromising position and now, there was no doubt about it, he was in deep, deep trouble. But Murphy didn't need this latest revelation from Horton's wife to have him thinking in that direction. Murphy saw it in the man's eyes, in his movements, and in fact, in his entire aura. After years on the job, if one didn't have this sixth sense by now, it would never come. And Murphy had it; he had it from the start. He was feeling very good about things at this moment, and knew that this case was going to yield something. And redemption was finally within his grasp.

"Let's start with an arson we're investigating due to the possibility of insurance fraud, Mr. Horton. Do you know a Phil Cassavetti?" Murphy asked.

Horton's eyes opened wide and Murphy caught it. Horton recovered quickly but deliberately, Murphy caught that as well. He cleared his throat. Also noted. This was going to be a walk in the park, Murphy thought to himself. This was a guy who had probably never done a wrong thing in his life and was faced with something that had managed to turn his life upside down to the point where the bottom was about to fall out.

"Why are you asking me about this?" was all Horton could manage.

CHAPTER 46

Cassavetti had been here before.

It happened a few years ago when Giuliani persisted in his clean up of organized crime. It happened when Gotti and Sammy "The Bull" Gravano took out Paul Costellano, the head of the Genovese crime family at the time, in front of Sparks Restaurant in mid-town Manhattan. It happened when John Gotti was brought down. The heat was on, and that meant Cassavetti had to batten down the hatches, tie up loose ends, and lay low.

Word had seeped out that Andy Vassallo had been popped and was in deep trouble. Somehow, he had managed to shoot a cop and was also being questioned for the Irish brothers' debacle. It was all expected to be in the papers tomorrow and soon the frenzy would begin. Everyone with a badge and a gun would want a piece of the mob, once again, and it was critical to Cassavetti that he maintain his low profile, probably even leave town.

However, there was one piece of business he needed to take care of in a hurry. Jack Horton. Cassavetti had received word from his attorney, Abe Silverman, who had told him the Feds were nosing around regarding the fire that destroyed the tenements in Queens. Cassavetti checked with one of The Gallo Family's moles inside the NYPD and discovered they were now labeling the cause of the profitable blaze as arson. This piece of news, on top of everything else, enraged Cassavetti. Silverman had been inches away from finalizing an insurance settlement that would have netted proceeds which would have exceeded their construction costs for the new apartments. The news also meant he had to get to Horton before the cops or the Feds got to him. Cassavetti knew the guy was likely to open his mouth. After all, he wasn't a hardened gangster—he was a lame-ass civilian insurance guy who had flipped out over some bimbo and stepped out of his normal envelope. Maybe more than a little. Cassavetti couldn't afford for Horton to bring up any aspect of their relationship, particularly Cassavetti's involvement with the tenements or the contract on Horton's wife.

But odds were, given the pressure the Feds would put on him, he would. Cassavetti knew what he had to do. Jack Horton had simply made choices that had put him in a bad spot. He was a grown man and he should have known better, or at least understood the risks.

Jack Horton had to be eliminated.

Cassavetti made the call to Al Carino, the consigliore to the Don, Salvatore Ruggierio, and the hit was quickly cleared. Cassavetti would take the unusual step of performing the execution himself. It had to be kept quiet, the less anyone knew about any of this at a time of intense scrutiny, the better. Despite Cassavetti's strong aversion to getting his hands dirty, once again he was painfully reminded that he was nothing more than a thug. Despite the veneer of Park Avenue and the company he kept of legitimate, wealthy, and powerful people, he was nothing more than a hardened criminal.

Reluctantly or not, he had killed before, and there was no doubt he could do it again.

Cassavetti sat alone in his apartment, and the bitter scent of cigar smoke hung in the living room where he gazed out into the night. The always stunning view was nothing more than a blank screen to the man who saw this moment as one of the darkest he remembered. This situation brought the brutal reality of his existence crashing down on him again, and he felt totally numb.

Jack Horton had to go. He had involved himself in all of this willingly. He was nothing more than a middle-aged loser who got greedy and was in over his head. He chose to look the other way with the insurance on the buildings. He obviously wanted the commission and probably felt it would impress Cassavetti. The mobster was used to people going out of their way to gain his favor. But Horton made the choice, and no one twisted his arm. It was the same for the contract on his wife, which was clearly his choosing.

So, the bottom line was Jack Horton had dug this hole, now he would have to lie in it. For keeps.

Horton, however, was not the issue that was immobilizing The Gallo crime family's money man. It was the darkness of it all; the raw brutality of bringing about the end of another life. It was the dichotomy of Cassavetti's existence whereby from one perspective, he was the man about town, the slick entrepreneur who had wealth and looks and freedom, and in the other, he was a simple crook who knew that with a knock at the door, the ring of the phone, or worse, the pull of a trigger, his life could be over. He wasn't like the high rollers he hosted in his card games or the legitimate investors he sometimes brought into his real estate deals. Phil Cassavetti wasn't like most of the other people in attendance at the opening of an art exhibit, or a Friday night performance at the Metropolitan Opera; events he frequently attended. Phil Cassavetti was nothing more than a career criminal and this is what criminals had to do. They covered their tracks. They used violence and sheer terror to protect their existence.

Tonight, he was nothing more than that. A hood, a crook, and a mobster.

He did his best to climb his way out of the cesspool in which he found himself and literally snapped his head back and forth as if he had to bring himself back into the here and now. He popped up from the deep leather chair and walked across the slate floor of his living room to the wet-bar. He poured himself a healthy snifter of brandy and grabbed another cigar which he then lit. He turned and faced the spectacular skyline. The expanses of the Mid-Town Bridge and the Brooklyn Bridge, which was still further down the East River, were spectacularly lit up. They connected the island of Manhattan to the rest of the world.

The view didn't change the facts. Horton would be out of the picture, and the Family would have to decide what to do about Andy Vassallo. Too many wise guys had sung to the cops or the Feds in exchange for lighter sentences, the Witness Protection Program, or sometimes just to get their misdeeds off their conscience. Not like the good old days when a *made* mobster was almost one hundred percent reliable, with very few exceptions. He could be counted on to keep his mouth shut no matter what he was facing. Even the electric chair.

It was already eleven o'clock in the evening, but Cassavetti was wired. Sleep would not come easy, although he functioned on very little of it anyway. Tomorrow would be a day he would surely try to forget, but he knew that would be impossible. Just like the time he killed a man in self-defense, he knew that what would unfold tomorrow would be etched into his soul for the remainder of his days, and in fact, would go with him to hell when he was gone.

CHAPTER 47

The room became horrifying to Jack Horton. It took on the characteristics of a prison. He was in a sparse room, with no windows, no pictures, bare walls, other than a strange looking mirror on the facing wall, and nothing else but the table and four chairs where he was seated. Special Agent Murphy sat in the other chair at the table, and two other chairs were positioned against one of the walls. The buzzing fluorescent light had begun to wash everything into a supernatural glow. It was now two-thirty in the morning and the adrenalin had been pumping consistently throughout the night, he had consumed several cups of institutional coffee and he was now experiencing an unfamiliar feeling of being wired beyond any level he had ever known.

This, Jack decided, was the physical result of psychological terror.

The man in front of him, Special Agent Elliott Murphy, had become his nemesis. He wielded an aura of authority, which terrified Jack to no end. Murphy was tall, appeared fit, and although they had been in the room for hours, he had not removed his suit jacket or even loosened his tie. He was a handsome man with friendly features and occasionally even smiled at Jack. But Horton wasn't fooled. This guy was all business and if it came to a war of wills, Jack knew he was up against a formidable adversary. What he didn't realize was that he was in way over his head.

Clipped to the breast pocket of the Fed's jacket was a gold shield that identified him as a Special Agent of The Federal Bureau of Investigation. The shiny emblem seemed to stare out at Jack and burn though his skull. It represented the law and Jack was clearly on the wrong side of it.

How had he done this to himself?

So far, Jack hadn't given up a thing. He was play-acting as best he could, taking great care with every response. He was being asked about Cassavetti and the building fires that Murphy claimed were caused by arson. He was being asked about his wife and their marriage and his girlfriend, even the gambling and card games he had played with Cassavetti. Jack could see this guy seemed to know all the elements, but didn't have anything concrete. He also wondered how long it would be before that changed, and if it did, how much would his denial hurt when they did have concrete evidence. Jack suddenly worried that his conscience wouldn't allow him to sit here and lie till the sun came up. The guilt was already pouring out of his pores like burning lava, and he knew it.

As soon as they arrived at the Federal Building, he was informed that he could have a lawyer present, but he had passed. Something else he had learned from the movies. Immediately "lawyering up" would project an image of guilt. But he didn't know how much longer he could hold out.

And then the bottom fell out.

Elliott knew he had this guy by the balls. The problem was he hadn't confessed to a thing, and had only squirmed around and muddled through hours of questioning by simply repeating the same denials.

So now it was time.

"Mr. Horton, what would you say if I told you that your wife has miraculously appeared, and is apparently unharmed?" Murphy asked as he stared intently at his subject and watched as the man instinctually reacted. Jack's eyes widened, his head snapped up, and as much as he might've wanted to maintain his cool, the poor slob couldn't help himself!

"What?!"

"Yes, that's right, Mr. Horton," Murphy continued. "I've known this since our little chat began and so far you've given me nothing but a load of crap. You've done nothing whatsoever to help us in a very serious investigation of some really bad people, *the mob*, Mr. Horton. And when the U.S. Attorney shows up in a few hours, I'm going to suggest we treat you as though you are one of them; a common criminal who hires murderers and commits insurance fraud and tax evasion, all of it. Or, you can start at the beginning and explain how an ordinary guy like you gets hooked up with the mob and does things he wouldn't normally do—and we'll see what we can do to help you out of this mess. I'm going to get up and use the john and when I come back into this room, you either tell me everything, or I would *strongly* suggest you call your lawyer."

Murphy didn't wait for a response. He knew he had him, and simply got up from the table and walked out of the room.

Jack had seen the movies and he knew there was some cop behind the mirror on the wall, looking at him. He knew it was a one-way observation mirror and assumed that he was being watched, if not taped at this very moment, but he couldn't help himself. His head was in his hands and his head was slowly shaking back and forth.

He was *fucked!*

He debated for a moment whether the news about Alice was true. There was something about Murphy's tone of voice that indicated it was, and after all, he was sure that a lie from the Fed at his point would be illegal or entrapment or some other term he had learned on *Law and Order*. It was strange that he had waited so long to break the news, but Jack assumed they had just wanted to see what he would come up with on his own. He also believed Murphy hadn't been bullshitting about bringing in the U.S. Attorney. Jack knew he was cornered and had no choice. He had to give them everything he knew.

His thoughts shifted to Alice. Where had she been? What the *hell* had happened? Was she okay? *And did she know it was him behind the failed attempt on her life?*

Suddenly, a wafting image appeared in his mind's eye. He was standing at the massive Sand Dollar slot machine. Rachel was standing by his side, coaxing him into *one more pull*. That was where it all began. That was the point in his life when everything changed. It was the thrill of easy money, the adrenalin rush, and the intoxicating scent of a woman; it was everything his former life could never be.

And now, the odds of his life going forward, in any positive way, were ruined. He was defeated. He had gone too far and now the consequences were falling squarely upon his shoulders.

It was over.

•   •   •

Murphy re-entered the room having used the restroom and splashed some cold water on his face to invigorate himself. The agent had finally removed his jacket, loosened his tie, and rolled up his sleeves. He was ready to do business and he was confident that his subject, Jack Horton, was ready as well.

He was correct in that assumption.

Horton told him everything he knew, in fact he sang like a canary on speed. He described how he met Cassavetti and how he had no idea that he was being set up in the insurance matter. He told of the fifty thousand he handed Cassavetti's driver, for the "elimination" of his wife. He even told Murphy about the card games and who had attended.

But everything he knew wasn't enough.

It was something, but in both of the situations that mattered, the insurance fraud and the contract on Horton's wife, it was clear that Cassavetti had methodically distanced himself from direct links. He hadn't accepted the payment for the contract himself, he hadn't signed any of the paperwork for the insurance; he had been on the periphery of everything but not on the front line where it mattered.

Then Murphy forwarded an idea.

"You said that Cassavetti wants to see you again tomorrow? Well, that would be later today, actually," Murphy said as he looked at his watch. "What exactly is this meeting about?"

"He said something about another property to insure. He promised me that nothing would happen to this building and said they just needed insurance," replied a very sunken Jack Horton, as he slumped in his chair, unable to cloak the sinking feeling of his demise.

"Okay," Murphy said as he maneuvered to the next obvious step. "Here's how you might just stay out of prison, Jack." Murphy called the pathetic character across from him by his first name, but it was all part of the psychology. "I'm going to speak with the US Attorney, but I think we can count on their cooperation. I want you to wear a wire to this meeting and I want you to get some specific statements out of Cassavetti. I want you to get him to acknowledge both the fire and the contract on your wife."

Murphy let his proposal sink in for a moment.

Then Horton answered, "How will this keep me out of prison?"

"We will put you in the Witness Protection Program. We relocate you, change your name, your identity and you start all over."

"This is crazy," Horton said with an indignant tone. "I mean, this is like an episode on TV. And how do you stop him if he suspects I'm wearing a wire? He'll kill me on the spot."

"We'll have half a dozen men, myself included, close by. We won't let you get anywhere that we can't be on top of him in seconds," Murphy responded. "You know, it is a little like TV, Jack. These are bad guys, really bad. And you've managed to get tangled up with them at a particularly bad time. We've got one of Cassavetti's underlings in custody in Maryland for attempted murder of a cop. See Jack, you don't really have a choice. You either do this or I'll recommend to the US Attorney that you be charged with kidnapping, attempted murder and insurance fraud."

Jack was shaking his head in disbelief.

•   •   •

This was all beyond the Twilight Zone for Jack, and he felt as though he had been ushered to the gates of Hell and was teetering on the edge of the abyss.

Jack knew he didn't have a choice. And if he was killed in the process, so be it. For Jack, even that grim possibility beat spending any time in prison.

"I'll do it," he quietly muttered.

He looked up across the table and Special Agent Murphy smiled at him and nodded.

"We've got a cot set up for you so you can lie down and get some sleep. We'll have someone take you to your apartment in a few hours to get a change of clothes and a shower," Murphy said with a much friendlier tone. "You'll leave from there to work in the morning; no one will know what has happened to you. I'll bring in a team in a few hours and we're going to figure the details out. Before you leave here, we'll have a plan completely laid out."

Murphy stood in front of a beaten man, and actually reached down and shook Jack's hand.

"You fucked up, Jack. But I feel for you. This is your second chance," the Fed said quietly. "God knows we *all* need a second chance at some time or another."

CHAPTER 48

Shortly before seven in the morning, the sun began to illuminate the city and Elliott Murphy made some coffee in the fifth story kitchen and moved into a conference room to get his thoughts together.

His team had worked until four-thirty, preparing for the operation they were going to conduct, and the senior special agent had managed only an hour's sleep. Several of the men had checked into a nearby hotel, but Murphy opted to stay in the building and had slept on a couch in a waiting area. He hadn't forgotten his training from the military. He knew he would be better off and more alert with just a quick cat-nap rather than attempting to get several hours sleep. He had changed into a clean shirt that he kept in his desk drawer, shaved with his electric razor, and was mentally preparing himself for the day. He had over a dozen agents working on the case with him, which included analysts and surveillance teams. He was also liaising with NYPD, the U.S. Attorney's office, as well as the Manhattan District Attorney's office.

Through the night, even after the interrogation of Jack Horton, much had been accomplished. It had all been mapped out and placed into the Bureau's case management system which was much like a project manager program used in any business. Ultimately, a full description and history of the case was being compiled and it would serve as the map for the purpose of a future trial, if there was one, as well as the official record.

Hours earlier, analysts had been searching law enforcement databases and gathering information to color the picture as vividly as they could. New information had been provided through the unexpected safe return of Alice Horton. They also had the confirmation of Phil Cassavetti's involvement in the Queens apartment fires through Jack Horton's statement, along with his admission that Cassavetti had arranged for the disappearance and botched murder of Alice Horton. But they needed more than just Jack Horton's testimony to nail Cassavetti. They needed the mobster on tape, and today they would attempt to obtain that. Horton would be wired and when he met with the made Capo, he would attempt to get everything he could.

Alice Horton had already directed State Troopers to the cabin in which she was held for over four weeks. They sent a forensic team out to the site and they reported that the body of Paul Visante had been found. The Bureau's analysts discovered ties between Visante and Andy Vassallo, who they already knew was a henchman for Cassavetti.

All roads led to Cassavetti, although they didn't even know where the man lived and their best physical identification was his driver's license picture, which Horton had confirmed was similar to his current appearance. The address he had listed with the Department of Motor Vehicles was a coffee house in Brooklyn. Murphy had asked NYPD Detective Rainsworth to send a couple of men over to the restaurant, but wasn't expecting much from that situation. The owners would probably say they'd never heard of him.

They had also done a search of corporate records and compiled all the corporations of which the lawyer, Abe Silverman, was the agent of record. There were close to fifty, and while Murphy knew that not all of them belonged to the Gallo Family, many of them were matching up with companies that were already in the Bureau's database as being suspect. A limo company, a chain of drycleaners, and numerous holding companies had been tagged to real estate titles all around the five boroughs of New York City.

All of this work was accomplished through the night due to the miracle of the Internet and modern technology. Murphy smiled as he stood in a conference room that overlooked the East River. He recalled years ago when what they had accomplished through the night would have taken days of work, visits to various agencies, scouring of microfiche or other archaic methods of data storage, even reading over paper records! How the world had changed in the last twenty years, he thought to himself.

He also was conscious of how *he* had changed, particularly in the last month or so. He was sober, he felt as though he could really make it now, and he was on the cusp of accomplishing something significant at work. And he would have done so in short order. It had only been seven weeks since he was assigned the Gallo case, and he was about to nab an underboss. They already had Vassallo, who would face a capital sentence unless he cut a deal, but

Vassallo was just a high-level street thug. Cassavetti, on the other hand, was a Boss and it would significantly disable the organization to lose him. At the very least, it would hurt their bottom line immensely and economics were as much a part of organized crime as they were at any major corporation.

In the process, Murphy had salvaged his marriage and his relationship with his sons. It had really been a catharsis and when he gave it thought, he felt both prideful and nervous. He had been warned about the "pink cloud" that often accompanies new sobriety, and he didn't want to screw up and lose it.

His partner, Chris Marciotti, joined him in the conference room. Marciotti had dashed home around four that morning and probably grabbed a couple hours sleep. He was single and lived in the Gramercy Park area of the lower east side of Manhattan, so he could get to and from the Federal Plaza in minutes. He looked remarkably refreshed and Murphy could tell he was also revved up and ready to get on with it.

Today they would use Jack Horton in a sting using a brief window of opportunity to target the underboss, Cassavetti. Hopefully he would make statements on a sanctioned bug, fully admissible in court, which would put him away for a long, long time. Murphy and Marciotti would run the operation and assure Horton's safety.

Jack stared at the ceiling of the small room as he lay awake on an uncomfortable cot. He hadn't slept a moment through the early hours of the morning, and in fact, he doubted his heart rate had dropped below triple digits since the Feds came bursting into his apartment and found him bound and gagged with a couple of naked sex freaks.

Through the hours of contemplation, he wondered if he would ever see Rachel again. He doubted it, even if he didn't end up in jail. He would be relocated to a city or town far, far away, and would be in the Witness Protection Program and forbidden to make contact with anyone from his previous life. Besides, he doubted she would ever want to see him again after the shock of the federal intrusion. It would have been a lot to ask.

Then Jack suddenly caught himself, realizing that Rachel was meaningless to him now, completely irrelevant. She was the least of his worries and he abruptly pushed her out of his train of thought.

His mind drifted to his predicament with Alice and the boys. His thoughts focused in on his family, and he considered what he had done as if removed from everything, like some sort of bizarre, out of body experience. he shouldered ownership of the events, but it just felt horrific. *Abominable.* How had he metamorphosed into this completely different person, who was capable of such terrible destruction? And how had it been so *easy?*

Jack knew he would simply implode if he didn't try to find redemption.

Therefore, he was stuck as the FBI's mole and forced into a dangerous attempt to entrap Cassavetti by wearing a wire, just like in the movies, and it terrified him. It was unfathomable, but it was happening. In fact, the plan would roll into motion in mere hours.

He had abandoned them all, Alice and his three boys, and had contracted Alice's demise. Ironically, it was this acceptance of guilt that gave him strength. He had fucked up. Massively. But he hoped his redemption was waiting on the other end of what he perceived to be a long, dark, foreboding tunnel.

If it didn't work, he thought very seriously to himself, he hoped he would be killed in the process. He did what he did to his wife and children in pursuit of freedom, and ironically, that very pursuit ensured that he would never again enjoy that status. No matter what happened today, no matter where he ended up.

Jack instinctively knew that his soul would be haunted by his deeds, and that haunting would be more painful than death itself. In fact, through the merging of horror and disgust, Jack Horton already felt like he was dead.

CHAPTER 49

"**A**s soon as our techs are finished with him," Murphy said to the group of agents that had assembled in the conference room, "We'll get him back over to his apartment so he can change for work and then we'll go from there." Horton wouldn't actually be wired, as with microphones, wires, and recorders, like it was years ago. Today, a listening device can be the size of a pea and transmit up to half a mile. Horton would have a small device in his belt buckle and to provide redundancy, he would have one hidden inside a special watch.

"We want him to go through the day like nothing is up," Murphy continued. "I'll contact his boss and let him know what's going on. We wouldn't have to tell him anything except that Marciotti and I spoke with him yesterday afternoon and we notified him that the Queens fire was caused by arson. Of course, you can bet his plan is to be all over Horton this morning. I'll ask him to just leave him be. Anyway, so long as no one knows he was picked up, aside from his employer, the operation won't be compromised."

"When is Horton supposed to meet with Cassavetti?" asked a young black agent who looked like a professional linebacker in a suit. His name was Theo Williams and despite his brawny appearance, he went to Harvard Law and was on the fast track to special agent status, combining an intimidating appearance with a brilliant mind for deduction and analysis.

"He'll be waiting for a call once he gets to his office," Murphy answered. "Apparently there wasn't a firm time established, but Horton thinks it would be after work. We don't want to take any chances though; we want him in the office all day and we'll be keeping eyes and ears on him. We already have his cell phone and his work extension bugged. I'm going to station one of you in his office building's lobby and two more in a vehicle out front. Marciotti and I will be on the street. We'll have one of you in a cab that we'll use to get him to his apartment, back to his office, and then to the meet with Cassavetti."

Phil Cassavetti hadn't slept. He left the safe haven of his apartment at six a.m., drove in a rented SUV to the West Side, and parked a block from Jack Horton's apartment building. Matters had become much worse overnight and he knew he had no time to waste. If Horton hadn't been taken in by the cops already, he knew it wouldn't be long. The Gallo's informant inside the NYPD, Dennis Coulter, had alerted the family to the news; Alice Horton had shown up alive and she had told all. Visante hadn't taken her out as ordered, apparently the dumb fuck had a heart attack and she managed to escape. Before he died, the inside source had reported that Visante told her it had been her husband that ordered the hit. Coulter said they were told by the FBI to leave Horton alone for now, because they were building a case, but it was clear that he could be hauled in at any moment and Cassavetti *had* to get to him first.

On top of this disastrous development, he had confirmed that Vassallo had been popped for a cop shooting and was being help in Maryland. He hadn't talked yet, but had made it clear; he wanted the best attorney money could buy and guarantees that the Family would stick by him. Or else he would have to fend for himself. Cassavetti knew what that meant. For now, though, Vassallo was on ice. He could be dealt with later. The Gallo's would be sending a top notch criminal attorney to Maryland today and they would see how that situation unfolded. But for the moment, Horton was the priority.

Cassavetti was dressed in jeans and a leather jacket. He wore a ball cap and when the sun began to rise, he donned sunglasses. Horton's building had security systems, a doorman stationed at the front entrance, and in the lobby, visitors had to check in with a security guard. Cassavetti didn't want to risk trying to get up to Horton's apartment. He had called Horton's cell phone, to no avail, and wasn't sure where he was. He decided to wait until nine or so, and if he didn't see the man leave the building, Cassavetti knew it was too late. Horton's absence would probably mean he would be in custody for ordering the attempted murder and kidnapping of his wife.

Murphy rode in the passenger seat of the huge black Suburban that served as the command vehicle while his partner, Chris Marciotti, drove. The traffic was still fairly light and they made the trip uptown from the Federal Plaza to the West Side in less than fifteen minutes. They followed a yellow NYC cab whose lone passenger was Jack Horton. The cab was driven by Agent Theo Williams.

They dropped their subject off at his apartment building, on Amsterdam and Seventy-fifth and he quickly walked through the entrance. He carried the belt with the transmitter wound up in his jacket pocket and would put it on when he changed into his suit for work. Williams illuminated his off-duty sign that sat on top of his cab, circled the block, and parked. Murphy would radio him when Horton was on his way back down and Agent Williams would pull back around and pick him up. Horton was instructed to call Murphy on his cell phone after he showered and changed, and he was to emerge from the building, just like any other day, the cab would pick him up, and take him to work.

All the precautions probably weren't necessary, but this operation would have only one chance and Murphy didn't want to blow it in any way by some freak coincidence occurring that would ruin Horton's cover. This day needed to progress like any other day in the life of Jack Horton. Although it would certainly not end like any other day. Once he had completed the task of entrapping Phil Cassavetti, Murphy and his team would swoop in on the mobster and arrest him. They would then whisk Jack Horton away to a safe house where he would be sequestered until he was needed for trial. Once his obligation to testify had either been fulfilled, or was deemed unnecessary because Cassavetti cut a deal, Horton would be placed in the Witness Protection Program and relocated to parts unknown.

Jack Horton's life as he knew it was over. Perhaps he would build a new one for himself in Iowa or Montana or wherever he was placed, but Murphy knew that he would pay for what he had done for the rest of his days. He had paid a killer to murder his wife, the mother of his children. He would be haunted by that for eternity.

Cassavetti watched Horton exit the cab and walk into his building, but he was still reluctant to enter the apartment building for fear of being seen by the doorman, and having to identify himself to the security desk. He assumed that Horton had probably been at his girlfriend's for the night and had just come home to change before work. Cassavetti planned to wait for twenty minutes or so, and if the guy didn't come back down, Cassavetti would see if he could get into the building without being noticed, perhaps through a service entrance. If Horton did come back out, and Cassavetti felt sure that he would, he would be there to grab him and it would be the last time Horton would feel the pavement below his feet. He would get him into the SUV and drive him to a remote location on the other side of the Hudson, in New Jersey. He would then put a bullet into his brain before the vehicle ever stopped and he would dump Horton deep in the woods where his body wouldn't be found for months, if ever.

As Special Agent Elliott Murphy sat in the black SUV, Marciotti was rambling on about the case. He remarked how quickly all these breakthroughs had occurred since Murphy had taken over the team assigned to the Gallo Family. Murphy declined to take much credit, except for being in the right place at the right time.

"If we get something off this wire, it'll be a home run. We'll be one step away from Ruggierio," remarked Marcioti, referring to the Don, their ultimate objective.

"If we do get Cassavetti, we'll see what he's made of, too. He's managed to keep his nose clean for a lot of years," said Murphy. "Considering we don't think he's ever operated on the street, as opposed to behind a computer terminal, the thought of spending a good bit of his life in prison just might convince the guy to make a deal. These guys sure seem to turn over these days."

Murphy's cell phone chirped and he answered it. It was Horton saying he was on his way down from his apartment. Murphy radioed Williams and advised him to roll. Murphy's team waited for the subject to get in the cab and they planned to follow the taxi back downtown to Horton's office. Murphy and Marciotti were scheduled to wait in the SUV until Horton left the office to meet with Cassavetti, which hopefully would happen early in the day. Murphy wasn't one for lengthy surveillances; he'd seen a truckload of days of waiting around for something to happen over the years. But he wasn't going to take any chances and felt very strongly that he needed to be on the front line with this one.

As Murphy waited for Horton to exit the apartment building, he thought for a moment about his own personal demise, from which he was now recovering. He thought of the harm he had brought upon himself, his wife, and his kids, and for a moment, perhaps just a split second, he sympathized with Jack Horton. He was normally indifferent to the subjects of a case; witnesses, accusers, and certainly the criminals. For a brief moment, he wondered what had come over Jack Horton that had caused him to stray so far from the path he had been on his entire life. Then he shook it off. It didn't really matter. Whatever had happened to the sorry son of a bitch, he made the choices that brought him down this path. He had crossed the line, and Murphy had seen men do that hundreds of times over the years. And once the line was crossed, there was usually no going back. Even Murphy could see that Horton would never be the same because of what he had done.

Jack rode the elevator down the eleven floors and hoped the ride would take forever. He was almost twitching he was so nervous, and felt as though he was going to come unraveled at any moment. Fear swarmed through his body and he continually had to work at catching his breath. His palms were damp and his fingers trembled. His stomach was tied in knots. In his previous life, years spent towing the line and minimizing risks, he never put himself in harms way, and never even got a ticket for speeding excessively in his Jeep, and this growing feeling of unbridled fear was completely foreign to him.

The shock of the FBI showing up at his door, the embarrassment of the situation, followed by hours of interrogation by Murphy, had all completely worn him out. But now, having showered and dressed for work, he felt somewhat rejuvenated and it only served to enhance his awareness of one thing. He had destroyed his life as he knew it.

The elevator door slid open and he walked reluctantly toward the cab. He was attempting to appear normal and knew it would be hard to do at work. After all, he'd never see any of these people again. No matter how the sting went down. His life was slipping away with every tick of the clock.

A clock that started with a pull on a slot machine.

• • •

Phil Cassavetti sat and waited. The rented SUV idled at the corner of Seventy Fourth and Amsterdam. When Horton emerged, he would simply turn onto Amsterdam and pick him up. He would come either voluntarily or at gunpoint. But one way or another, Cassavetti would grab him.

CHAPTER 50

"The subject is exiting the building. Williams, move in and pick him up," Murphy spoke into the walkie-talkie as Marciotti started the Suburban. They waited another few moments for their special cab to arrive that would take Jack Horton downtown.

As Murphy watched Horton fidget on the sidewalk from down the block, he noticed a green Ford Explorer quickly pull across Amsterdam and lurched to a stop in front of Horton's building. At first Murphy thought nothing of it, but then he saw that the driver seemed to be leaning towards the passenger window of the SUV, summoning Horton. Then, he saw, in disbelief, that Horton walked up to the vehicle to speak with the man.

"What the fuck is this?" Marciotti said and sat up, looking in his rearview mirror to check the traffic. The Suburban was hemmed in for the moment, and unfortunately, neither man had spotted Williams' cab yet, and figured the traffic had him, too.

"Williams, where are you?" Murphy barked into the radio. "Something might be going down."

"Thirty seconds away. Stuck at the light on Seventy-sixth," was the response. Murphy looked over his shoulder and saw the line of cars, most of them cabs, waiting to cross Amsterdam Avenue.

• • •

"Just get in the car, Jack," Cassavetti commanded. "We need to talk and I'm in a hurry."

Horton's heart pounded the inside of his chest. This made no sense. What on earth was Cassavetti up to? *Oh God, now what do I do?* He was on the verge of pissing himself.

Sensing Jack's waffling, Cassavetti raised an automatic pistol up and said, "Get in the fucking car right now, Horton, or I'll spray your face with bullets before you move one inch from where you're standing."

Murphy saw it and hollered, "GUN!"

Marciotti quickly raised a pair of high-powered binoculars and immediately determined who it was. The man was wearing a ball-cap and sunglasses but he could make out the profile.

"It's Cassavetti!" shouted Marciotti. He flipped on the emergency strobe lights of the huge black Suburban, but it was no good, they were jammed in their parking space for at least ten more seconds.

Both men watched in horror as they saw Horton get into the vehicle. It jumped from the curb, cutting off a honking delivery van, and quickly turned onto Seventy-

Fifth Street just as Marciotti was able to get the Suburban onto the thoroughfare.

• • •

"What the hell is wrong, Phil?" Horton pleaded as he instinctively put his seat belt on. "What did I do?"

"You play with fire, you get burnt," Cassavetti said as he slowly maneuvered the Ford through the traffic. "You happened to come along at the wrong time, Jack. You need to get out of town and I'm here to see you do just that." He lied to Horton, but he was going to take him out of town, to New Jersey where he would shoot him dead.

"What are you—going to do to me?" Jack begged.

"I'm taking you to Newark and putting you on a fucking plane. You are leaving the city, like it or not, and you're not coming back for a long, long time. Might call it a surprise vacation."

Horton felt a moment of relief. *Okay,* he thought to himself, *go with it. I can deal with that.*

Murphy absorbed the initial shock of what had just happened, ignored the frustration of having an operation go bad with him at the helm, and simply reacted to the obstacles at hand. They passed the pickup spot, saw no body, and quickly turned onto Seventy-fifth. He could see the green SUV plodding along through traffic at the other end of the block, crossing Broadway. Cassavetti was heading towards the West Side Highway.

"Dispatch, this is one-seventy-five. Request assistance from NYPD," Murphy barked into the radio. He described the dark green Ford Explorer, gave its current direction, and requested every available unit on it. They had to grab him before he got away as Murphy knew only too well, Horton would never be seen again.

As Cassavetti crossed Broadway, he noticed the black Suburban with flashing strobe lights and assumed the siren he heard came from it as well. It could be coincidence, but something told him it wasn't. His instinct told him the ominous looking vehicle was after him.

He raised the gun again from his lap and pointed it at Horton while he navigated the traffic. "Have you been talking to the Feds, Jack?" he screamed. "I need to know the truth right now."

"What are you talking about?" Horton answered, wide-eyed at the sight of the gun pointed in his direction again.

"Tell me now, motherfucker. 'Cause I got someone following me and I want to know why the fuck that's happening."

Jack glanced over his shoulder and saw the Suburban. It was stuck at the light on Broadway that had just turned red. Two cabs were ahead of it and Horton could see that that the cabs were reluctantly pulling out of the way to allow the Suburban, strobes flashing, to pass through.

Jack turned to face Cassavetti, his adrenalin pumping so vigorously that it had glazed over his fear, and he literally felt high. He had to overcome the initial surge of that high just to speak.

"Look, they arrested me last night," Horton pleaded, deciding to give up the truth. He didn't see how things could get any worse. "They're going to get us both. Why don't you just pull over and it'll all be over?"

"Jesus Christ!" Cassavetti said, in a quieter tone.

Marciotti was crossing Broadway after the way had been cleared. He paused in the middle of the street to allow a group of southbound vehicles pass. The Suburban was going against a red light and although the vehicles emergency strobes were on, they weren't visible to the traffic to the sides as the lights were mounted in the grill and the tail.

"C'mon, people," Murphy mumbled in almost a prayer. "Hurry, hurry, hurry."

Then the walkie-talkie crackled, "I've managed to make it down Seventy-seventh to West End, where are they now?" It was Agent Williams, in the cab.

"Make a left and head over to Seventy-fifth," answered Murphy.

He looked at Marciotti and said, "Where the hell is NYPD? We're going to lose this guy!"

"We'll get him, Elliott. He's never going to get out of the city."

And that was likely a valid statement, Elliott knew. The security on every bridge and tunnel was tight. If he didn't give up, and managed to evade the NYPD pursuit, there was no way he would be able to get off the island of Manhattan. The events of 9/11 had motivated law enforcement to beef up security at every tunnel entrance and every bridge. But he still could disappear into the hundreds of miles of Manhattan streets and vanish into a garage or an alley if they lost sight of him at the wrong moment.

As Cassavetti crossed West End Avenue, heading towards Riverside Drive and ultimately the West Side highway, a cab veered in front of him forcing him to swerve aggressively and he clipped a parked car with his left fender. *Stupid fucking cabbie*, Cassavetti thought to himself. But then he saw the cab that was now behind him aggressively back up on West End to turn in behind him. It had to be a cop.

Now ahead of him he saw a NYPD patrol car, lights blazing, siren screaming, come screeching to a halt on Riverside, and with that, Cassavetti was blocked in. He knew he had only one alternative. He turned to the right at a parking garage entrance and launched the Explorer onto the sidewalk.

Jack was horrified. On top of it all, now he was in a car chase with a pistol pointed at him. This couldn't be happening. They were careening down the sidewalk, which fortunately was empty, Cassavetti holding the steering wheel in one hand, a very threatening looking gun in the other, and the man had a look of fury on his face. It was all completely terrifying and Jack felt helpless.

Cassavetti made it to the end of the block and just as they were about to leap off the sidewalk, Jack could see the police car back up, attempting to block their exit onto the street. Instead of trying to stop, Cassavetti accelerated and the front end of the Jeep squeezed past the cruiser but its rear end collided with the SUV and sent the fleeing vehicle into a spin in the middle of the intersection.

When Cassavetti got the SUV under control they were pointed downtown. This was not the direction he wanted to be going, but he had no choice. He gunned the SUV and managed to make it just a few more blocks when he saw yet another challenge materialize ahead of him. Two NYPD squad cars pulled into the middle of the intersection at the next block, and formed another roadblock. He quickly gazed into the rear-view mirror and saw the cab and the Suburban were about a block away and bearing down on his position.

He had only one alternative.

Murphy watched up ahead as the Ford again leapt onto the sidewalk, this time on Riverside Drive, and skidded to a halt near a stairway entrance to Riverside Park, which sprawled below the street level. He could see Cassavetti dragging Horton at gun point out of the driver's side of the SUV and gripping his arm as they ran through the entrance, turned down the staircase, and disappeared from view. Murphy cringed at the development, and this situation gone wrong was getting really ugly.

The cops in the NYPD cruisers had also figured out what was going on and they exited their vehicles and came running to the park entrance. The Suburban came to an abrupt halt next to the abandoned Explorer and Williams had already jumped out of his cab.

Murphy radioed his dispatch to advise that they were now in foot pursuit and jumped out of the Suburban. Marciotti had already scrambled out and dashed around to the rear of the vehicle, where he opened the back door and grabbed a high-powered rifle which he tossed to Murphy who was a marksman. Marciotti, who was only a year on the street after a year at a desk doing legal research, knew the specialized weapon belonged in the hands of an expert.

Cassavetti dragged Horton along down the hundred-and-fifty year-old stone stairway that served as an entrance to the park. As he descended the steps, he gazed about to figure out what to do next. He tried to think quickly, as he knew that the cops and the Feds and anyone else with a badge would be swarming all over them within moments.

It seemed rather futile, but he couldn't give up. That had been engrained in his soul for years. He knew that he was done for, clearly the Feds had him. Whether it was Horton or Vassallo, someone had given him up and he faced a life in prison or worse. This was something that he knew he could not face. It had always been his worst fear and he knew that when this moment arrived, faced with capital charges as he knew he would be, he would not be taken alive. For in his heart, despite the longings of his mind over the years to be something, or somebody else, he was little more than a hardened criminal, and if he was going down, it would be in a blaze of glory.

Jack felt as though he had drifted off into another realm of consciousness. Whether it was the insanity of it all or the disgust he felt toward himself for bringing his life to this point through shear selfishness, he decided, in a daze of sudden calm that came over him, that he had to put an end to this nightmare.

As they descended the last few stairs, Cassavetti's hand firmly gripping his shoulder, Horton made his move. He spun around with all his might, kicking out his leg to violently trip the determined Cassavetti, and they both went crashing down the remaining stone stairs.

The two men fell to the bottom of the staircase, Horton smashing down on his knees and then the side of his head, and Cassavetti landing hard on his side, both of them momentarily dazed.

Murphy and the others arrived at the top of the long staircase just as the two men went floundering onto the ground. He saw what Horton had done, and he thought to himself, *maybe the guy has some balls after all!*

Special Agent Elliott Murphy raised the scoped rifle up to his shoulder and with Marciotti and Williams standing on either side, their handguns raised as well, Murphy shouted, "Get up Cassavetti, *NOW!* You're completely covered."

It was hard to see exactly what was going on from the distance to the bottom of the staircase. And before Murphy knew it, the two men were struggling.

"Let's move down," he said to his two underlings. "I'll take the shot if I can get one off."

As they took a few steps down, Murphy realized that his heart rate was up, the adrenalin was pumping, and he knew he had to slow down his breathing and keep his head together. This was one of those situations that probably wouldn't have a happy ending, no matter what the outcome. A guy like this was desperate and in the next few seconds, there was no telling what he would do next.

Jack was resolute as he wrestled with Cassavetti; he was determined to keep this guy down, despite the pain in his knees and his throbbing skull, he was going to fight this one to the finish, even though Jack had never been in a real fight in his life. He only wanted to keep the mobster down until the cops caught up with them, so he summoned every ounce of strength he had and flailed away on top of his nemesis.

Despite Jack's bravery, despite a level of strength and courage that had emerged in these last few moments unparalleled in his lifetime, in the flailing of arms and legs, he couldn't stop Cassavetti's arm from grabbing the gun off the cold concrete where it lay.

When Murphy saw Cassavetti gain possession of the weapon again, everything went into slow motion. He wanted to act, but was unable to get a clear shot; there was nothing they could do but move in closer for a better angle. He lost sight of the pistol in the brawl and moved toward the struggling men, helpless. He knew that Horton was in deep, deep trouble. Yet, the guy continued to pound the underboss of The Gallo Family. Jack Horton seemed possessed, but ultimately, he was no match for the powerful, gun wielding, Cassavetti.

Everything was caving in, and Cassavetti knew it was time to die. This freak sequence of events had brought his life to an end, and he knew that what he would do now would be his last act on this earth. This stupid little fuck had brought them both to this moment. He would die too.

With Jack Horton on top of him, scrambling to try to control his gun hand with one hand, and pounding Cassavetti's head and shoulders with the other fist, Cassavetti pushed the gun into Horton's gut with a sudden, powerful thrust, and for the last time in his life, the gangster pulled the trigger.

When the pop of the gun exploded beneath him, it almost sounded as if it came from a place far away. Jack could feel the barrel of the gun pressing against his stomach, and winced from the searing pain in his gut, but he didn't stop. However, just as suddenly, images flashed before him; his boys, Alice, even his dead parents. All of them were out of his reach now. He had lost them all. After the bullet ripped through his body, the resulting pain quickly drifted to numbness, as though the incident was happening to someone else and he was just observing. It almost felt comforting.

Jack looked up the stairs and saw Special Agent Murphy's lips moving, but he couldn't hear anything now. He watched the agent raise his rifle. There was just a whir in Jack's ears, now, and he tried to smile at the FBI man, as if to say, *I tried.*

Then Jack blacked out.

For him, it was over.

Simultaneously, as Horton slumped to the side, Murphy finally had a clear shot. And he took it. The shot was resonated like a cannon in the staircase. The bullet ripped through Phil Cassavetti's skull and exploded out the other side, taking with it half of the man's brains and most certainly, his life.

Phil Cassavetti was dead; his body lay beneath that of Jack Horton. One man had lived for this day, knowing that it was always looming out there, and the other never saw it coming.

Murphy and the other two agents, along with the cops who followed, rushed down the stairs to inspect the carnage. Elliott's first moves were to remove the pistol from Cassavetti's stilled hand, and grab Jack Horton's wrist.

There was a pulse.

CHAPTER 51

It was eerie for Elliott to return to Lenox Hill Hospital. It was here that he had spent days recovering from his stab wounds and although it was barely three months earlier, it felt like a lifetime ago. He tried not to think about it as he walked the familiar halls, escorting Alice Horton to see her husband.

Jack had survived the shooting, barely. The bullet had ripped through his gut and caused extensive damage. But Jack turned out to be a fighter in the end, and according to the doctors his will and determination along with several surgeries had been the difference in his recovery. He would be released in a few days into the custody of the U.S. Marshal's office as they administered the Witness Protection Program. And from there, only he and a few Marshals would ever know his whereabouts.

He was no longer needed for his testimony because Cassavetti was dead. But the Bureau and the U.S. Attorney stuck by their commitment to place him in the program because he would always be in danger from The Gallo Family. There would be no question as to who they would blame for Cassavetti's death. But Jack would be safe, tucked away in some remote town in some obscure part of the country. He would have to cut off all contact with his family and any friends he might have, but he would get to start over. Although Murphy knew that the things he had done, and certainly the way it all ended, would likely haunt him for the rest of his life.

Murphy felt a twinge of sadness, and perhaps even sympathy for the man. The irony of being in this same hospital, even the wounds to the gut as he had experienced from a knife instead of a bullet, was not lost on the seasoned agent. This could have been him, had he completely crossed the line during his time of trouble. It shook him when he thought about it.

But he hadn't crossed over; he had just stumbled onto the threshold, too close for comfort, but made it back before it was too late. It was a time he would always remember, for if he ever forgot, he would be at risk to do it all again.

Alice Horton wanted to see her husband one last time. Somehow, perhaps through her new-found attitude about life, she forgave him for what he had done; although perhaps forgiveness had come easier with the knowledge that she would never see him again after today's visit. She had brought the boys to see him a few times over the course of the last few weeks. Tim and Scott didn't have much to say and seemed more intent on demolishing the equipment in the hospital room than they did in visiting with their father. But for Harry, the quiet one, it had been different.

Harry sat by his father's bedside, holding his hand and finally, when they were about to leave he asked his father, "Why?" *Why did you do this, daddy?*

It was heart-wrenching.

But she knew they would all survive.

She and the children, as it turned out, would be moving, too. Not to some God-forsaken town in the middle of nowhere, but to Spain. Alice had taken a job teaching at an American School in Barcelona and had already transferred her money, the $1.2 million given to her by Paul Visante, to a bank account she established there. She would buy a small house, invest wisely, and she would be set for many years to come. The boys were looking forward to the adventure and would do just fine, although it would take Harry some time to get over losing his father. Overall, this was the silver lining. A new start, financial freedom, and maybe someday a dashing Spaniard would emerge in her life and she could enjoy some romance. If that happened, it would be a first.

She entered the hospital room with the FBI agent by her side. He showed identification to the uniformed officer who was stationed at the door. It astounded Alice to think Jack had screwed up so badly that he needed protection from the mob. But he had. In the span of what seemed like minutes, he broke every rule, went past the point of no return, and now, would pay the price for the rest of his life.

They had decided not to tell Jack of her plans to move overseas. Not only would she never know where he was, she felt better if he didn't know where she would be either. She had forgiven him, but that didn't mean she could ever trust him again.

Jack was asleep and she looked at his pale face and realized the whole mess had evaporated whatever feelings of love she had for him in the first place, but he was still the father of her children and she felt sorry for him lying their in this hospital bed. She glanced at Murphy, and he too was looking down at Jack, appearing deep in thought, almost sad.

He had asked to join her when he learned she was coming to the hospital for her last visit. He too would never see the man again.

Jack finally, stirred, and opened his eyes. It took him a minute to focus and then he sat up. He was no longer attached to the numerous tubes, IV's, and monitors that were his lifelines for the previous two weeks. He looked at Alice, and then Murphy, and feigned a smile. He knew this would be the last time he would see his wife.

"Well, here's an unlikely pair of visitors," he said quietly. "How are you feeling, Jack?" Murphy asked.

"Ready to get out of here."

"You'll be out in a few days," Alice said, also feigning a smile.

"Listen, I just wanted to say good-bye before they take you away to parts unknown," said Murphy. "You did some good in the end, Jack. I hope you can turn things around and make a life for yourself. Just keep your nose clean."

The two men shook hands and Horton replied, "I will. I won't say it was a pleasure meeting you, but I suppose if a man commits a federal offense, he could do a lot worse than you." They all chuckled.

"Before you leave," Alice said to Murphy. "I need you to witness some papers, if you wouldn't mind. She pulled an envelope out of her handbag and Murphy nodded.

Alice pulled out the documents and placed them on the rolling hospital table she slid in front of Jack. He seemed to be expecting them and didn't bother even reading the papers. He went right to the signature pages, signed quickly with a pen she produced, and when he was done Jack looked away, staring out the window.

Elliott could see that the papers were the couple's divorce decree. Made sense, Murphy thought to himself. But like everything else about this visit, it stirred him. For he remembered that he had been within weeks of signing his own divorce papers just a few short months ago. The images of the scene were simply too close for comfort, and Murphy decided he needed some air.

He said goodbye and left, knowing that neither he, nor Alice, nor anyone else that Jack Horton knew—would ever see him again.

EPILOGUE

An icy wind chilled the late afternoon, a wind that rolled across Lake Superior and frosted Duluth, Minnesota. It was the dead of winter, a year since it all began, and Jack Horton was oblivious to the cold air on his face. He sat bundled up in a parka, gloves, scarf, and hat, on a bench in a small park that looked out into the harbor where the ships came in to supply the isolated, sleepy town. This was how he spent most of his Saturday afternoons, and as usual, he was alone.

He thought, as he always did, of his life before, his life during and occasionally, he would think about the days ahead. But in that regard, he didn't care much. It was his past that haunted him and ruled his world.

He had succumbed to temptation and never learned how to handle it. He hadn't been able to determine right from wrong, or what the limits were. And in his quest for what he had perceived as freedom and pleasure, he had lost it all.

Now his days were spent working at the Great Lakes Insurance Company. Ironically, underwriting policies for fire insurance. His nights were filled with television that he had difficulty concentrating on, several drinks, writing letters to his boys that he knew he would never see again, and words that he could never send.

There were more than a few times that Jack wished the bullet had taken his life. Or sometimes, he wished that he had never pulled that damned slot machine with Rachel. He had never seen Rachel again after the fateful night he was arrested, and surprisingly, he had never cared about that loss. Perhaps he never really cared about her at all.

Perhaps she had been more of a concept that he desired as opposed to anything else. But it didn't matter any longer, because she was gone, they were gone, and as far as Jack could tell, everything was gone.

He watched as a slow-moving freighter made its way through the breakers and out into the frigid open water. It pushed along through the choppy whitecaps and became smaller and smaller on the horizon. Soon, all he could see was the trail of smoke coming from the ship's ancient diesels.

That column of smoke floated up to the heavens above, leaving nothing but an image of the lumbering but steady old ship that he imagined had once been his life.

Elliott was speaking at an AA meeting for the first time since he sobered up. Sure, he had talked in these gatherings over the last twelve months, but in this was a meeting at which he would stand in front of an audience, including his wife Sally, and tell his story.

He would describe a life before, when he was the model law enforcement officer, the model husband and father, and booze didn't play a role in his life. Then he would tell the audience when it all changed, and that before he realized what was happening, he crossed the invisible line and became a drunk. He didn't focus on the misery of being a practicing alcoholic, but spent most of his speech sharing how he was turning his life around through sobriety.

And turn his life around, he had.

The Gallo case had continued. The shooting of Cassavetti had been messy and not something Murphy would have chosen. But it had been necessary and there were no legal or emotional repercussions for the special agent.

Andy Vassallo sang like a bird and his information led to the arrest of over twenty other members of the Gallo Family, including the consigliere, Al Carino. They had also nabbed a dirty cop, Dennis Coulter, who they discovered had been feeding information to The Gallo's. He was stabbed in jail while awaiting arraignment, and died on the way to the hospital.

Vassallo was now parked at a medium security Federal prison in New Mexico, which was part of a deal in exchange for his testimony. Rumor had it that he was busy writing his memoirs, and once he was released, ten years from now, he would be able to sell them to the highest bidder.

The Gallo's had been hurt but not destroyed. They continued on, though perhaps more quietly and less violently. Murphy wasn't naïve; he knew that as long as there was a society left on earth, there would be organized crime.

Regardless, the Gallo's and other crime families weren't Murphy's concern anymore. For Special Agent Elliott Murphy ended up right where he started—in the Terrorism Unit of the FBI.

He had been lucky. He had stood on the precipice and managed not to fall onto the heap of lost humanity. He had almost lost everything, but as fate would have it, he was meant to get it all back, so in turn; he could give it back to others.

Elliott Murphy had more to do in his life and tonight was an opportunity to say thanks to those who pulled him out of the abyss.

In front of thirty or so recovering drunks, their wives and husbands, and the people who had supported him when nothing else seemed to work, Elliott began his speech.

"Hello," he began. "My name is Elliott and I am an alcoholic." He choked back emotion for a moment as he stared at the crowd. *He* was back from his journey to the other side.

Made in the USA
Middletown, DE
10 March 2024